Salt Magic

Regency Magic Book 1

Margaret Ball

Galway Publishing

ISBN Paperback: 978-1-947648-12-8
ISBN eBook: 978-1-947648-13-5

Printed in the United States of America
Cover art: Cedar Sanderson
Formatting: Polgarus Studio

Salt Magic

A Regency fantasy romance

CHAPTER ONE

Despite my family's concern, my marriage to the March-Lord was perfectly happy until mainlanders troubled our island, seeking to use the magic of Faarhafn and bringing death and destruction upon us.

In truth, my mother and aunts had considerable responsibility for my marriage, even if they did not realize it. Between them they did not have nearly enough children; worse, my nephews and nieces were so much younger than I that they did no chores and raised no deep concerns. As I grew to womanhood, I benefited from so much concentrated attention that I feared my beloved family would drive me mad. They could imagine no man good enough for me; they feared that I would develop an unsuitable attachment; from morning to night they kept me busy with household chores, or tried to, all in the name of loving and protecting me.

Under the circumstances, I feel that I took the only action possible.

I ran away with an older man.

Granted, I did not run very far away; only to the island of Faarhafn, my family's ancestral home and almost within sight of their present dwelling place. But he was a much older man, my dear lord Kosta Greenmark, March-Lord of Steinnland and the Isles – having seen sixty-seven winters to my seventeen – so on average, it was a more than adequate gesture.

Steinnland had been more than good to me ever since we met by chance during one of my brief escapes from the incessant demands of my family. He understood the hungers and desires that were nameless torments to me; he named and satisfied them and opened a new world to me.

In short, he taught me to read, and gave me the run of his library. And I began to understand that my mind had been starved for learning and for knowledge of the wider world – for my family keeps to the old ways of our people, and sees no call for overmuch learning beyond knowledge of the tides and the deep currents of the sea.

Steinnland offered what they call a marriage of convenience, though to give credit to his generosity, the convenience was mostly for my sake. Not only was I finding it increasingly difficult to find excuses to spend as much time as I wanted reading in his library or simply talking with him; other people were beginning to comment on our association. "That strange child Sabira" was, in the view of landfolk and seafolk alike, now a woman grown and marriage-ripe, and nothing honest could come of her spending so much time alone with Kosta Greenmark.

"They give me too much credit, and you too little," Steinnland said with a smile when he first mentioned marriage. "Lovely though you are, Sabira, I trust you will not be insulted when I say that at my age I feel no temptation to do more than enjoy your beauty with my eyes. As for you, I know, if your family and the islanders do not, that you spend time with an old man out of kindness and intellectual curiosity, and not for any other reason."

"Kindness! That is all your virtue, and none of my own," I said. "Nothing in my life means so much as the hours I have spent here with you. If you accuse me again of visiting you out of kindness, I'll leave your library and find my friends among the waves breaking on the shore, as I did when I was a child."

"But you are no longer a child, Sabira, and the time you spend here, for whatever reason, is causing unpleasant talk." Steinnland regarded me steadily, his pale blue eyes piercing like shards of ice under his shaggy white brows. "My dear, I have no desire to beget an heir, and I cannot bear to hear your name smeared over with tavern jokes. If we marry, we shall go on just as before, except that you will no longer have to lie to your family and no one will see any impropriety in our association. Otherwise...."

He paused, and I could see by the twist of his thin lips that the words he was about to speak pained him deeply.

"Otherwise, I must ask you, for your own sake, to come here no longer. I have not so many friends that I would willingly lose one such as you, Sabira."

It came to me that it was not just my name, unimportant that it was, that was stained by smutty tavern jokes about our friendship. It was the name of Kosta Greenmark, March-Lord of Steinnland and the Isles, who all his life had been a byword for integrity among both the sea folk and the subtle politicians of the land.

"Of course I'll marry you," I said on a breath, "and I am honored to do so. If you are sure that is what you really want?"

That was a foolish question; Steinnland never said anything that he did not mean.

Our marriage was a quiet affair, attended only by the cleric who came from the mainland to speak the words over us, Steinnland's factor Hendrie, and two of his tenants for witnesses. Once the agreement was made, he was urgent to see it done, and would not wait to send word for any of his friends from the city to attend. As for my family, I felt it would be easier to reconcile them to my marriage after the fact and so it proved.

Indeed, forgiveness was much easier to gain than I had ever imagined.

"So that's where you've been slipping off to all these hours!" exclaimed my aunt Maarit when I bore the news to my family. "Oh, yes, my girl, don't think I haven't noticed. You've grown sly and underhanded. I told Norin some disaster would happen if she didn't keep a closer watch on you."

"Perhaps we kept Sabira too close, so that she felt she had no way to get any privacy except by lying to us," said my aunt Eliina, the youngest and gentlest of the sisters.

"And I am not sure that I would call marriage to Kosta Greenmark a disaster," said my aunt Seija. "With his fortune, not to mention the estate of Steinnland and the Isles – including Faarhafn," she added pointedly.

"Which will pass to some distant male relative on his death," snapped Maarit. "That is the way of the great lords; they call it an entail, and it is a law made to ensure that the lands stay together and under some man. A wife has little or no rights under that law. What good does it do Sabira to marry the man who rules the Isles, if none of the power passes to her?"

"Kosta Greenmark is a strong man and healthy, for all his age," mused Seija. "He might live for many years yet, and who knows but he might be persuaded to relinquish Faarhafn to its rightful owners?"

At this my entire family perked up, even my father, whose custom was to sit quietly in a corner lined with a mosaic of iridescent shell bits and compose his poems while the seven sisters argued everything out.

It was a long-held tradition of my people that Faarhafn was rightfully ours, that it belonged to all our people together and not to one man from distant Din Eidyn. During the long winter nights when Teran churned the waters into a fury, stories were told of how Faarhafn was lost to one of Lord Steinnland's ancestors in a game of riddles and trickery where my lord's forbear cheated. During the summer evenings when the Mother of the Sea kept Teran's fury in check and the waters were calm, we would look with longing on the fair island that had once been our summer home.

"If Lord Steinnland could be persuaded to say the words that give us back the island…." Seija reflected.

"If anybody can talk him round, Sabira can," my mother said. "Look at what she's gotten away with while I thought she was tending the outlying gardens and hatcheries!" Her tone was half irritated, half proud. It had been wrong of me to lie to her and evade my chores, very wrong to marry without her permission – but if my wrongdoing won us back our island home, how could she be angry with me?

"He would not even have to know what he was doing," said Seija. "The power is in the words; Sabira could tell him anything, perhaps that they are an old charm to calm the waves. After all, his ancestor cheated to get Faarhafn. I do not see anything wrong with using a little misdirection to get it back."

"And what about this entail?" snapped Maarit.

Seija gave a graceful shrug that made her whole body undulate. "The power of all law is words – just words. If the right words are said by the one who owns it now, Faarhafn is ours – entail or no entail."

I was not so sure that the law of the sea would override the law of the land, but I was not being asked for my opinion in this discussion.

"And what about the risk to Sabira?" Aunt Raonaid asked. "We all know what marriage to one of Steinnland's sort can lead to."

"If she does not let him use her body, there is no risk," said my mother, "and she says he has promised there will be nothing of that sort. When he's said the words and the island is ours again, she can come back to us as pure as she went."

They decided, without even asking me, that I had married Steinnland solely to trick him into giving up his rights over the island, and that once this was done I would return to being the patient, obedient, and submissive daughter of the house and niece of six aunts.

It would have been rude to contradict them, and in any case they probably would not have listened to me.

I could have told them, for instance, that one small island was a only trivial part of my lord's estate, and that he would probably give us back Faarhafn for the asking. Indeed, we had already discussed the matter. There were only two small problems hindering the return of the island. Among the folk who looked to him as their lord were a number of fishers and crofters who had made their homes along the sand of the smooth southern shore, or in the western cove where the cliffs reached out from the land like cupped hands to form a natural harbor. These people would have to be settled on some other part of his estate; it could have been done by a single order from my lord's factor, but he loved persuasion better than force, and wished for time to make the transition gentle for them.

The other matter was Steinnland's own home. He had other places to live – the Greenmark manor house on the northern coast, not to mention his town house in Din Eidyn – but like his ancestors before him, he loved the island from which his family took their title. The first Greenmark to win title to the island, the one who had been given the title of March-Lord in view of his service in making Faarhafn part of Dalriada to serve as a resting place for the boats that plied between the mainland and the Isles of the North, had built himself a modest home atop the western cliffs of our island. Every generation afterwards had added a room or a gallery to this summer home, until it had become a great, strange, rambling maze overlooking the sea. There were rooms that leaned perilously out over the cliffs, all lined with panes of clear glass whose greenish swirls transmuted the air and sea beyond into one swirling mass, so that you could almost imagine yourself living beneath the waters. There were deep cellars cut into the rock to store the wines laid down by men long dead. There were rambling halls that had been built on and on, piecemeal, to display things that had caught some Greenmark's interest, from a device to track the stars to a piece of twisted and sea-polished driftwood – for all his family had a bent towards the study of natural philosophy, though perhaps none took it to such lengths as my own dear lord. And best of all, there was the library, a high round tower with a spiral stair that carried you past his shelves of books so that you could select at will and take your chosen book to the little round room at the top where windows alternated with deep, soft leather-covered divans. Stone shelves holding lamps jutted out at either side of each divan, so that day or night, you could sink into your seat and immerse yourself in your book as long as you wished.

My lord knew that his title to the island rested on a chancy transaction involving some trickery (although in his family's version of the tale, it was our people who sought to cheat his ancestor and so deserved to be cheated in their turn) and he might have given back the island willingly – but his home on the western crest? It would have pained him deeply to leave that strange, twisting, many-windowed house in which he had taken root after his retirement from public affairs in Din Eidyn, and he could hardly have continued living there after the island was ours again.

And, after our marriage, there was a third obstacle which I could hardly explain to my family. They might have convinced themselves that I married my lord in order to trick him into relinquishing the island, but as you already know, that was not even in my mind at the time. I married him because I loved him for the new worlds he had opened to me, and because I loved to come to his house and choose a new book as I mounted the spiral stairs to his reading room, and because I was tired of inventing stories to explain my absences from home. And after we were married, I loved our peaceful life together and had absolutely no wish to end it by manipulating him into giving up Faarhafn.

We met as we chose during the day, by appointment or by accident. I was free to wander the shores and watch the storm clouds driving across the sea, or to read for hours in the library, or to visit those few of the fisher folk who did not feel uncomfortable in my presence. If I did miss my family, they were close enough for me to visit whenever I felt so inclined.

Although my lord somewhat deplored my frivolous tastes, he allowed me to send for all the latest romances from Din Eidyn to lighten the serious fare of his library of scientific and historical tomes. He laughed to see me ensconced on one of his leather divans with a three-volume tale of the perils of some virtuous heroine toppling into my lap and colliding with a treatise on the movement of the stars. We dined together every evening, and our meals were spiced by incessant, lively talk, the more so as I learned enough of his world to question and even debate his assertions. Though he had long since lost interest in the social and political life of the capital, he said that he intended to take me there one day, if only to convince me that the streets were not lined with silver and that every house did not contain a poet-swordsman languishing over a fair lady or an heiress masquerading as a kitchen-maid to escape the machinations of her wicked guardian.

As I may have mentioned, he did not altogether approve all my choices of books. But how else was I to learn what life among his people was really like? I knew nothing but my family home and this isolated hold on the cliffs. And while that life pleased me well enough, I felt it was only my duty to learn something about society so that I should not disgrace him, if ever we did go to the capital, by acting like a simple country girl. Besides, the stories were compelling in their own right. Once I had fairly begun a novel, I could hardly bring myself to stop reading until the ending was achieved and the lovers united.

Not that I was in any hurry to deal with Society as evidenced in Din Eidyn. We were happy enough as we were; I felt in my smug ignorance that Society could wait.

It was an unpleasant shock to find that Society was coming to us instead.

It happened that one of my visits to my family was marred by another fight with my Aunt Maarit over this question of getting back Faarhafn for our people, a fight in which I found myself alone against all six aunts and even my mother. After returning home I lay long awake that night, and so I slept late the next morning and woke to find Steinnland breakfasting without me – and talking to someone! There was a low deep laugh that made me shiver to the backbone, a strange voice that I had never heard before, followed by both voices dropping so low that I could not make out what they were saying.

Not that I was some servant girl to listen at doors, you understand. I was Steinnland's lady, and he would never conceal anything from me that I needed to know. If I paused before opening the door to the breakfast room, it was only to make sure that my hair was smooth and my overdress and petticoat arranged as foreigners from the mainland would think proper.

Steinnland rose to greet me when I entered, smiling his welcome, and yet I had the sense of some urgent conversation broken off, of dangerous words hanging on the air. That feeling, or something else, so troubled me that I could scarcely concentrate on what he was saying; all the air seemed stirred and quivering about the person of his visitor. Unlike the stunted fisher-folk of the island, this man was tall enough to look level into my eyes, and he had about him all the town-polish that I had read about in my books but had never seen in person: black hair artfully cut and brushed about a lean, narrow face, a white stock creased into intricate folds, a coat that fit as if it had been stitched upon his body, boots as glossy as a black seal's coat all wet from the sea, and closely fitted knit breeches that left nothing to the imagination. Not, you understand, that I was unaware of how a man is built, but we simple country folk are either naked or clothed. It had not occurred to me that clothing might be used to emphasize what it pretended to cover.

Steinnland was introducing the man as his dear friend Viscount Iveroth from the mainland, come to bring in person some important papers from Steinnland's advocat in Din Eidyn, and all I could think, like some simple country girl indeed, was, "But he's young!"

Oh, he was not of an age with me, this fellow from the mainland; he might have lived thirty winters or a few more. But I had somehow assumed that all Steinnland's friends would be of his own generation, that I would be able to deal with them as I did with my own family – keeping the mask of patient, obedient, quiet Sabira, there to run errands or do small tasks or to keep herself out of the way.

There would be no quietly keeping myself out of the way of this Iveroth, not if he wished otherwise. Young and dark and dangerous, he was, with a vital force that breathed about him in a quivering aura so bright I was surprised that even his own people, blind as they were, were not disturbed by the flash of his dark eyes under slanting black brows. *I* was disturbed. The peace of my lord's house was disturbed. In that instant I knew that change was upon us and that I had been simpler than any country fool to think it was in my power to delay it.

In the next instant, of course, I made my curtsey to him – without disturbing the arrangement of my petticoat – and welcomed him as Lady Steinnland should receive any good friend of her husband's. Whatever Steinnland thought, I had not read all those novels from Din Eidyn for nothing!

"My lady." The man was all but gaping; had he assumed, then, that Steinnland had made a mésalliance with some peasant? "I – I – Rumor had not warned me," he all but stammered, making a leg with some grace at last.

Actually, to be fair, he did it far more gracefully than I had imagined possible. There are some nuances you cannot learn from studying literature. Naturally he could not achieve the full *grande révérence* as performed by my people, but then, such a gesture would have been more than I was entitled to.

Steinnland beamed as if showing off one of the treasured possessions that filled the rambling halls of his house. "Rumor told you that I was wed at last, did it, Iveroth? But no tales could prepare you for the beauty and grace of my Sabira."

"Indeed," Iveroth agreed, and it seemed to me he stared at my petticoat a little harder than was proper. "Lady Steinnland is indeed – beyond all expectation." He did not sound one bit pleased about it. "I can quite understand your happiness."

It hardly appeared that he shared that happiness. Perhaps he was just generally displeased with the world around him. If so, he would make a good match with my aunt Maarit. For some reason I found that thought distasteful.

"My dear," Steinnland went on, "I fear Lord Iveroth has brought news that will disturb the peace of our house for some days."

It is already disturbed, I thought wildly, it is already destroyed. Can you not see that this man is a raven of ill omen? But I had just enough sense to keep those words between my teeth. The folk of the land have only one sight; Steinnland could not have been expected to read the dangerous blaze of this Iveroth's soul-force.

CHAPTER TWO

Young, he had known Steinnland's wife would be; beautiful, he had assumed, knowing Steinnland's love of surrounding himself with treasures. Beyond that, Iveroth would have said he did not know what to expect. Certainly not the buxom country lass that tavern gossips conjured up with their smutty jokes about the midwinter marriage of Kosta Greenmark, March-Lord of Steinnland and the Isles; Iveroth thought better of his scholarly friend than to imagine him fallen for the charms of some brainless milkmaid to warm his feet in his old age. So if Sabira – Lady Steinnland, he corrected his thoughts – if Lady Steinnland were young, and lovely, and well spoken, what was to be amazed at there? But from the moment she broke in upon their conversation, he was aware of a kind of amazement of the heart that dizzied his brain and tripped up his tongue.

"We are to have unexpected visitors," Steinnland informed his young wife.

"So I see, my lord," she replied with a sweet and dulcet tone that matched ill with the cold flash of those green eyes. Doubtless she preferred to have Steinnland all to herself, rapt in her wiles until he would give her anything she asked for.

"Oh, not Iveroth!" Steinnland essayed to laugh and only betrayed how much Iveroth's news had shaken him. "Iveroth and I have been friends all his life; I had the honor to shake the drops of brandywine on his forehead when his mother named him Brandubh. I'll wager it was the first and last time you wailed at the offer of good brandywine, eh, Iveroth? He is no guest here, my love, even though you two have not met before – he is like one of my own family."

"Brandubh," repeated Lady Steinnland. "In the tongue of your people, Steinnland, the name means 'black raven,' does it not? How…. appropriate."

"Aye, the boy's hair is still black as a raven's wing," said Steinnland. "The name will sit more oddly upon him when the snows of old age fall upon his head. But that is a long time yet, and in any case it is no matter; most people call him Iveroth. I have been forced into such formality since he grew so strong and square, for fear he will plant me a facer if I treat him like the child I stood god-father to."

"Steinnland!" Iveroth protested, laughing. "As if I would —!"

"I warn you, my dear lady, the boy has a wicked black temper. It's best we all walk carefully around him."

"Oh, I shall," the girl Sabira promised. "Very carefully." And as far away as possible, her cool tone said. No, she would not be happy to have anyone here who had known Steinnland in his earlier life, would she? His presence might disturb whatever spell of beauty and seduction she had woven round him. So much the worse for her, thought Iveroth, his black brows drawing together unconsciously at the thought. He had had the run of Steinnland's house and estates all his life, and he had no intention of abandoning the man who had been better than a father to him just because this jumped-up country lass chose to look down her pretty nose at him.

"The visitors to whom I referred," Steinnland said, turning serious again, "are the Duchess of Quoy and her son, young Gairloch. It was only a fortunate accident that Tulloch mentioned these legal papers were ready and that Iveroth brought them along. He really came to warn me that the Duchess intends to visit us by Langday or even earlier. And you have no hint of her reasons for this sudden journey, Iveroth?"

"The usual gossip in Din Eidyn, my lord," Iveroth said. "She is retiring to conceal the fruits of her affair with Baron Jenneret, she hopes to replace the late Duke with you, she is taking the sea waters for her health, she wishes her heir to visit the northernmost lands of the realm before he comes of age – which will be shortly after Langday of this year. None of which, of course, is credible. Whatever her doings with Jenneret, they are unlikely to present her with an embarrassment at her time of life; everyone knows that you are – er – no longer eligible as a husband...."

"Unless she were to dispose of my lady," Steinnland said thoughtfully. "That I could believe, but not that she had so much desire to be wed to an elderly recluse who has turned his back on the politics and society of Din Eidyn. I think you may sleep safe in your bed and taste of any dish her Grace offers you without danger, my love. Perhaps, after all, it is so innocent a thing as a journey for her health and for her son's education."

"Ailsa of Quoy never yet did anything for a simple and innocent reason," said Iveroth, frowning. "It is only that we have not yet discovered her motive in this case."

"All too likely," agreed Steinnland. "How long have we before she arrives?"

"Not more than two days," said Iveroth rucfully. "I heard of her plans only as she was quitting the capital, and rode to reach you before she did. She will travel more slowly, of course, for she likes her comfort, but – it seemed that it was of some importance to her to be here before Langday."

"Two days at best," agreed Steinnland. He glanced down at his young wife, who was pleating her petticoat with two fingers while she muttered half-heard words and figures to herself, as if no one else were in the room. Well, Iveroth reflected, one could apply town polish to a fisherman's daughter, but the least rub wore the polish dangerously thin. "My dear, will you be able to manage the preparations for receiving her Grace? I must retire to the reading room, to see if I can study or scry her need to be here on the longest day of the year, and you know that I prefer not to be disturbed while using the scrying-glass. I am sure that Iveroth, here, will be pleased to help you with any little thing that wants done. It should not be so difficult, after all – we have only to put linens on the beds in two unused chambers, and let Androw know that he is to bring us all his catch for the next few days, instead of a few choice pieces. You and Iveroth should have no trouble arranging things."

The young Lady Steinnland – there, at last he had schooled his thoughts to give the girl her proper title – listened with downcast eyes to Steinnland's discussion of the necessary preparation of the house. She sat so still that she might have been a portrait walled off behind a pane of glass. But once, when Kosta invited her to refer to "my young friend Iveroth" for details of how to receive a lady of fashion, she glanced up and her eyes met his with a flash of green that seemed to touch his face from across the table – a flash like that of the setting sun over a calm sea, or the phosphorescence of a summer tide. She was both more and less than he had anticipated – less enticing, bright and merry, and yet more.... more.... Impressive? Not one to be underestimated, that was the best phrase he could find. It would not do to forget that this quiet island girl with her strange pale hair wrapped in braids about her head, with her gauzy petticoat glinting strange flashes of light under a simple overskirt, had somehow brought the March-Lord of the Isles into what Steinnland had always called "the marriage-trap" and "the best end for fools."

She showed no sign of irritation that her husband evidently intended to leave all the work of preparing for the Duchess' visit in her inexperienced hands. Perhaps that was what he had married her for – to be sociable for him. But how much occasion would a recluse on the island of Faarhafn have for social life? And if that was why he had married at last, why hadn't he picked a girl who had more to say for herself than this smooth, silken, silent creature?

Once Steinnland had left the room, she drew a long, sighing breath that seemed as if it would never end, then let it all out at once, hard, like the gust of a gale off the high western cliffs of Faarhafn. "It is only to put fresh sheets on a pair of beds," she repeated her lord's words.

"And to ask Androw to let us have a little more of his catch," Iveroth finished, beginning to laugh in spite of himself.

Lady Steinnland was infected by his laughter, and for a moment they cackled together as harmoniously as two cormorants.

"Oh, dear," she said at last, wiping those amazing green eyes, "I fear my lord has never had to deal, personally, with the reception of a noble guest. Of course in Din Eidyn there would have been servants who arranged all for him. He has no conception of the charge that he has laid upon your shoulders, Lord Iveroth. Naturally I shall not expect you to become my steward for the occasion. I am sure that I shall be able to set all to rights before her Grace arrives."

There was a betraying tremble of uncertainty in her voice on the last words, a lost look in the green eyes that reminded Iveroth of his duties as a gentleman. Whether he approved of the marriage or no, here was a lady – by marriage, if not by right of birth – in some distress, and he could not simply abandon her without making at least some attempt to relieve her cares.

"Between us," he said, "we shall surely be able to prepare Steinnland's house appropriately. There may be somewhat more to the work than he thinks, but it cannot be that bad – can it?"

Lady Steinnland bit her lower lip, disclosing two small white teeth as bright and smooth as pearls from the deep. "I do not know. Will not this great lady expect to be admitted by a train of servants in rich liveries, to spacious apartments lighted with innumerable tapers and of a sparkling and brilliant appearance?"

"So far from Din Eidyn," Iveroth said with a straight face at this echo of images from those three-volume romances that all the young ladies loved to read, "she may be content with something less."

"In *Gonzalo de Rosalba, or, The Hour of Trial*," the girl persisted, "the Duke's table was never seen without at least three removes of cooked dishes, with a collation of comfits and marchpanes and suckets to follow. In *Ermina: or, Modern Manners*, it says that every meal was sweetened by an invisible band wafting sprightly strains of sweet music all the while. And," she added in a despairing voice, "the Duchess will expect me to be able to converse on Lutécian fashions and the Borghesan opera!"

At this farrago of extravagances drawn from popular novels, Iveroth could scarce forbear to laugh and to say, "I see what Kosta means about your taste in reading matter."

Lady Steinnland bridled at this, and began to look annoyed rather than defeated – a great improvement.

"All the same," she said, "you cannot convince me that my lord's house on Faarhafn is at all suitable for receiving a great lady. In *The Mysteries of Udolpho* Count Montoni's residence in Venezia had a stair-case of marble, which led to a saloon whose walls and ceilings were adorned with historical and allegorical paintings, in fresco; silver tripods, depending from chains of the same metal, illumined the apartment, the floor of which was covered with Indian mats painted in a variety of colours and devices; the couches and drapery of the lattices were of pale green silk, embroidered and fringed with green. How can I ever achieve such an effect – and in two days at the most!"

"But as you said yourself," Iveroth pointed out, "this was a description of the Count's residence in Venezia. Here at the very northern edge of the inhabited world, the Duchess is more like to expect something like Montoni's castle of Udolpho, with its 'mouldering walls of dark grey stone.' Perhaps we should arrange a tower like that of Udolpho, 'crowned by overhanging turrets, embattled, where, instead of banners, now wave long grass and wild plants, that have taken root among the mouldering stones, and which seem to sigh, as the breeze rolls past, over the desolation around them.'"

Young Lady Steinnland gave a reluctant smile. "I fear my lord's house has already too close a resemblance to that long-neglected castle. And I am glad to see that you do not disdain all novels, Lord Iveroth, since you can quote so readily from *Udolpho*."

Iveroth laughed and threw up a hand, the gesture of a fencer acknowledging a hit. "Oh, one cannot live in society without knowing something of that particular book! It is an even more popular subject of discussion than the fashions in Lutéce and the latest opera from Borghese. But truly, you concern yourself overmuch. Even in Din Eidyn no one lives amidst luxuries such as you imagine; ours is a cold northern capital, not a southern city-state like Venezia, where the soft breeze and the bright blue waters of the southern seas encourage every extravagance."

Lady Steinnland sighed. "I am sure, nonetheless, that her Grace and her son are used to more luxury than we can offer her here. And that reminds me of another confusion which perhaps you can explain to me, Lord Iveroth. My lord spoke of her Grace's son as Gairloch, not as Quoy. If his father is dead, should he not be the Duke of Quoy?"

"For any other title, yes," said Iveroth, "but the duchy of Quoy incorporates such extensive lands, and has for centuries been so essential to our defences against Anglia, that it is our custom that no heir can assume the title until he reaches the age of eighteen and can be expected to personally oversee the military service Quoy owes to Din Eidyn. In a few weeks young Erlend will become Duke of Quoy, but until that time he has only the courtesy title accorded him as son of the late Duke, so he will be introduced as Marquis of Gairloch. It is an outmoded practice dating from a more violent age than ours, but we Dalriadans never give up our customs."

"Thank you, Lord Iveroth. You have probably saved me from innumerable solecisms upon the arrival of our guests." But the girl still looked worried.

"Young Gairloch will hardly expect formality and luxury," Iveroth said to reassure her, "and as for her Grace, when she foists herself upon you at such short notice, for reasons that cannot be good, she can hardly be expected to be received like royalty."

"Why are you and my lord so certain that her reasons for visiting are of the worst?" Lady Steinnland demanded. "Especially as neither of you seems to have a clue what they are."

Iveroth made a dismissive gesture. "As I said before, her Grace never yet did anything for a simple and innocent reason. Her *petits soupers* in the capital are nothing but devices to lure society into the deep play which supports her household in extravagant style; her presence at balls and masques is a signal for political maneuvering which more than once has all but brought down the government and left us open to being taken over either by Lutéce or by some southern alliance of Borghese or Venezia with the Anglians; and I suspect, though I cannot prove, she uses unholy means to cast a fascination over whichever young man is her *cavalier servente* of the moment. Be sure that she would not put herself to the trouble of a three-day journey by coach and the crossing of the De'il's Strait unless she expected some extraordinary gain from the trip."

This summary appeared to cast young Lady Steinnland into gloom again. "I have read of such ladies of fashion," she said. "I suppose that these *petits soupers* of which you speak offer her guests all the delicacies of the four quarters of the world, all the wit and the lighter efforts of genius, all the graces of conversation—the smiles of beauty, and the charm of music."

"You omitted to mention the delight of losing a fortune at her gaming tables," said Iveroth drily. "And even if she does put on such airs now, her

Grace should be able to survive a few days of simple living without undue hardship. She lived far more simply than this when she was a goosegirl in Quoy, before she caught the old Duke's eye and trapped him into…."

Lady Steinnland's fair plaits appeared to crackle with light as loose strands stirred about her head, and the eyes he had thought green were cold and grey as a fog-enshrouded winter morning. Iveroth thanked his lucky stars that he had at least had the sense to stop before finishing his speech with the disastrous words, "an unsuitable marriage."

"I see." With each cold word, Iveroth had the fancy that frozen shapes of air broke loose from the girl's stiff lips and shattered in icy shards about him. "You can think no good of the Duchess of Quoy because, like me, she married above her station. Very well – think what you like, but I will see for my lord's honor that she is received as best we may manage on such short notice. If you respect my lord's desire that you help in this undertaking, I suggest that you betake yourself to the village and hire as many of the fishers' wives and daughters as you can find to come and help me with the cleaning."

"I?" Iveroth was startled into yet more tactlessness. "Surely you would be better able to choose suitable helpers?"

"I," said Lady Steinnland, "have experienced some difficulty in persuading the villagers to work here. You will doubtless assume this is because, like you, they think only ill of girls who marry above their station in life. Now, if you will be so kind as to excuse me, Lord Iveroth, I must inspect the linen cupboard. There is certainly nobody else about the house who is qualified to do so." And she was gone, with a whisper of skirts and petticoats like the rustling of the sea along the sandy beach, leaving only a sense of something green and cold and very much displeased in the room where Iveroth and Steinnland had breakfasted.

CHAPTER THREE

Despite Lord Iveroth's dismissive comments, I felt that the honor of my lord required that we receive the Duchess of Quoy in a manner appropriate to her high station in life, and I determined that whatever was possible I would do. A host of liveried servants and a group of musicians could hardly be arranged on such short notice, but if Androw's catch went well I should be able to set out a lobster pie, a bisque of crab, and a dish of carps stewed in brown sauce for her delectation, as well as opening a pot of pickled crawfish and another of preserved quince. What to serve the meals on was another problem. Doubtless, had we had time to send to Din Eidyn, my lord's town house there would have provided all that was required; but he had packed without the assistance of any females when he shut up the town house and retired to Faarhafn, and the result was as higgledy-piggledy as one might expect; there were pots for cooking and the Steinnland silver to eat our meals with, but the dishes were served up in wooden platters and bowls carved by an island craftsman. Well, once Iveroth sent up some women I could set one of them to polishing the silver, and as far as plates and bowls, my own family might be of some help.

At least I could see that the linen for her chamber was freshly washed and aired. I was haunted by images of Edmund's chamber in *The Old English Baron*: "the furniture, by long neglect, decayed and dropping to pieces; the bed devoured by the moths, and occupied by the rats, who had built their nests there with impunity for many generations; the bedding very damp, for the rain had forced its way through the ceiling." It was entirely possible that Lord Iveroth's chamber was equally bad, since he had arrived while I was away and I had no idea of how my lord had accommodated him – nor had I any intention of visiting his bedchamber to investigate the matter.

While waiting for women to help me with the heavy work of scrubbing and laundering, I emptied the linen closet (thereby arousing the indignation of a family of mice who had nested there for so long, they doubtless thought of it as their ancestral home.)

The mice and other small intruders had made sad depredations upon the stock of linens, so that there was scarcely a whole sheet to be found. Carrying the crumpled pile out into the courtyard, I found that Lord Iveroth had already brought as many helpers as I could well use, all of whom I knew by their names and their husbands' occupations, though most were shy of calling me by name. Those who had come provided with buckets and scrubbing brushes I set to cleaning the great hall, the passages leading from it, and the least dilapidated of the bedchambers. Two old wives with the rheumatics were happy to take on the task of cleaning the silver. I requested the remaining women to wash the linens and hang them out to dry before the house; when the sheets were clean and uncreased I would inspect them and pick out the best of a bad lot to clothe the Duchess' bed and that of her heir.

As the women helped me to shake out the sheets preparatory to washing, I felt shame for myself and my lord that I had been such a careless mistress of his house. True, I had never cared for the work of the house; I loved the sea and the shore and long silences and even longer hours of reading. That was who I was, who I had been when the March-Lord of Steinnland and the Isles offered the marriage that freed me from the well-meaning but irksome care of my mother and aunts, and he had never asked that I be anything else.

But I should have thought more of who he was and what his station in life required. A great man should not live in a house where mice are allowed the run of the linen cupboard and spiders build cities of webs in the rafters, even if he himself never thinks of these things. Men do not see what's needed to keep a house in good repair; a good wife sees it and does it whether or not he requires it of her. That much, at least, I had learned from my mother, who saw to it that my dear, dreamy, absent-minded father was well fed and clothed and dwelt in comfort even though he would hardly have noticed had he lived half-naked and supped his broth from a rough shell.

Some of the women murmured among themselves at the condition of the linens, but most were careful not to let me hear their words. They need not have troubled; I knew well enough what they were thinking, and my cheeks burned with shame, even when Jonat Farchar shyly offered to mend whatever holes might remain in the sheets I chose to use.

"Indeed, an Jonat willna say it o' herself, she's as deft with a needle as any woman of the Isles!" another woman said in her praise, and the others took up the chorus to convince me that Jonat was well qualified to darn sheets for a duchess. Nearly all of them were more friendly towards me than I had found them before; there must be something in working together to set a house to rights that makes women feel a sense of kinship. Only Bessie Clipagarthe was unpleasantly outspoken.

"Aye, Jonat will do well enough to mend sheets, though she isna' the only needlewoman on Faarhafn!" Bessie said with a toss of her head. "But it's a shame to the March-Lord that his house should have fallen into this condition. If all had been kept as should be, there'd be no holes for Jonat or anybody else to mend."

"Hush there, thou fool," said Effie Scrabster, whose man had rights to the kelp coming to shore between Ronas Hill and Mid Yell Voe. This was a good share of beach, and Scrabster's profits from the kelp burning made him a man of stature among the fisher folk. She lowered her voice, probably thinking I would not hear her. "You know who she is?" She jerked her chin towards me. "And what she can do? Would you make an enemy of such a one?"

After the brief spell of cameraderie while we shook out the linen together, to be so set apart hurt more than I was willing to show.

"I am the enemy of no one here," I said, as steadily as I could, "and I hope I have earned no one's enmity. You are all competent to wash the linen and hang it out; I shall leave you to the task in peace. When it is done, Iveroth will see you paid for your work; and Jonat shall be given a penny for each hole she mends."

With that I left them to their work. The cove of Hamarrvoe where I had returned from my family's house the previous night was sheltered by spits of rocky cliff on either side. It was one of the places where I loved best to sit when troubled in my mind; and today I had, as well, a particular reason for wishing to be allowed to sit by the seaside unobserved. The steps cut down from my lord's house to the cove were rocky and difficult enough that few people would attempt them, and those who did would soon regret the damage to their shoes.

Before relaxing in the cove, I visited my family's home for a few moments, both to retrieve a small bag of my personal belongings and to beg the loan of my mother's best platters. Fortunately Aunt Maarit was away from home, so I did not have to suffer her opinions on the kind of wife who waited for an emergency before seeing that her home was adequately supplied with bowls and plates and serving dishes. Those used by my family were light in weight, of course, compared to the shining silver dishes that should have matched Steinnland's own knives and forks; but as the one who would have to carry them, I had no great objection to this particular feature. And in appearance, at least, they would look as well as anything seen in Din Eidyn or even in Lutéce; of that I felt secure.

Once returned to my cove, I carefully bestowed the packages of dishes inside a water-carved niche in the cliffs, high enough to keep them safe from the waves. I sat for a few moments at the edge of the niche, watching the green water marbled with streaks of foam as it drove up against the sand and fell back again. As always, the ceaseless patterning of the waves and the soft music of their fall against the shore conspired to sooth my agitated soul into a tender and pleasing melancholy; and, as one of my favorite writers put it, the contemplation of Nature served also to "awaken those lively and vivid trains of fancy, that by degrees abstract the mind from sensible objects, and bewilder it amid distant and visionary pursuits."

At length, remembering my errand, I made my way down the tumbled rocks until I stood upon the sand, at the very edge of the frothy white surf. Here I knelt and first unbound my braids, that no knot or tangle should confuse the charm. When my hair fell loose and free about me, I took two smooth sea-urchin spines from the small bag I had fetched from home. I reached into the foam and drew it upon the spines as upon knitting-needles, humming as I did so:

"Round, round, a thousand turns and more
From foam to lace I bid thee go,
Till, lying on the sandy shore,
The sea gives beauty to its foe.
For sea and land forever lie
Locked in their lasting enmity,
Save Faarhafn, the magic isle,
Where both were wont as one to be."

With the first pair of spines fairly begun in their work, I drew out a second pair and set them to knitting a little way distant along the water line; and so on until the short length of the crescent beach was all but filled with pairs of spines at work, turning sea-foam into lace finer and whiter and more brilliant than even a fine lady from Din Eidyn could ever have seen. If the linens for the Duchess' bed were worn in spots, and darned by the hands of a peasant wife, at least they should be edged with lace of a quality to suit my lord's high estate.

I remained kneeling by the water at the very edge of the cove, the last pair of sea-urchin spines in my hands, that by my example the rest might remember their task and keep steadily at work. Once the words of the charm had set all to work, it was only necessary to keep the music going; I sang on, borrowing a poem from Udolpho that happened to fit the tune and that reminded me of that life which I had left behind when I married Steinnland. It was remarkable how clearly Mrs. Radcliffe had envisioned a world that in the natural way of things she could never have seen. Was it possible that she had once been a finwife and not a landwoman? I wondered if her marriage to a mortal had had the disastrous results my people predicted from such a union.

"Down, down a thousand fathom deep,
Among the sounding seas I go;
Play round the foot of ev'ry steep
Whose cliffs above the ocean grow.
And with my sister-nymphs I sport,
Till the broad sun looks o'er the floods;
Then, swift we seek our crystal court,
Deep in the wave, 'mid Neptune's woods."

The cliffs surrounding the cove echoed and sent back my voice as I drew out the last words: "Neptune's woods."

A little longer, and I should begin to roll up the yards of lace, cutting them free with the sharp edge of a mussel shell lest they yield to their innate desire to return to shapeless foam. If Jonat had mended the sheets as she promised, then this evening I could stitch on the lace by firelight and make a bed truly fit for a duchess to sleep in.

"In cool arcades and glassy halls," I sang as a new line of scallop shapes emerged from the foam,

"We pass the sultry hours of noon,
Beyond wherever sun-beam falls,
Weaving sea-flowers in gay festoon.
The while we chant our ditties sweet
To some soft shell that warbles near;
Join'd by the murmuring currents fleet,
That glide along our halls so clear.
There, the pale pearl and sapphire blue,
And ruby red, and em'rald green,
Dart from the domes a changing hue,
And starry columns deck the scene."

The work was all but done; if I repeated the initial verses of the charm while cutting off the lace, I should have a great foamy armload with which to disguise the flaws of the Duchess' sheets. I drew out the last line with flourishes and grace notes just for the pleasure of hearing the sweet, chiming echo from the cliffs.

"Deck the scene!" repeated a voice that had none of the elfin, otherworldly quality of the echo I was expecting to hear; a nasty, sneering, masculine voice. Lord Iveroth! What was he doing here? Could the man not leave me alone for one little hour?

With faltering voice I essayed to take up the chant again:

"Round, round a thousand turns and more,

From foam to lace I bid thee go…."

It was useless. Surprise and shyness dried my throat until I could manage only a whispery croak like an old fishwife. The sea and the spines would not respond to such music. With sinking heart I saw the busily working pairs of sea urchin spines collapse, splayed out upon the sand, while the billows of lace they had knitted unraveled against the pressure of the waves and became bubbles, became air and water, became light and shadow, and were gone.

CHAPTER FOUR

Iveroth had not been best pleased, when he returned from talking with the fishermen about the quantity and quality of the catch which he expected to see delivered to Kosta's kitchens, to find the women he had hired at Lady Steinnland's behest languidly swishing linen sheets around in a simmering broiler, or making half-hearted swipes at windows and floors with cloths that somehow managed to miss all the dusty corners. Where was Lady Steinnland? Why had she not stayed to supervise the women? Did she expect him to do everything?

"She'll be at Hamarrvoe, nae doubt," said one of the few women who seemed to be putting any energy at all into her task of stirring and boiling the linens. "'Tis there she goes whenever aught troubles her." Her voice was soft, with the lilting island singsong underlying her speech, but the glance she gave to one of the other washerwomen was anything but gentle.

"And a fine gentleman like you should no' be chasing after her, at all," said the other woman, a strapping lass with bold black eyes set in a high-colored face and with black curls artfully escaping the confines of her mobcap. "Why ruin your boots on the cliff path for that one?"

"Bessie Clipagarthe, the gentleman was not asking for your advice," the older woman reproved her.

"Just point out the path to me," Iveroth said with restraint. He certainly did not need his decisions made for him by some pert fishwife. If Lady Steinnland had taken the path to this Hamarrvoe, it could not be so very difficult. He had not expected that chasing down Steinnland's young wife and dragging her back to her duty would be one of the tasks required of him in preparing for the Duchess' visit... but then, so far very little about the day had met his expectations. Why should this be any different?

For the short distance that separated the foundation of Steinnland's rambling house from the edge of the cliffs, a thin covering of turf gave the land underfoot a deceptive look of smoothness and simplicity. Where the cliffs began to fall away so did this illusion, to be replaced by ledges of weathered stone that someone, some long time ago, had haphazardly chipped out into what might have been called steps. The unknown mason who cut the path must, Iveroth thought, have been an ancestor of those slatternly women who took their work of cleaning the house so casually. Where a ledge offered as much as six inches of footing, he had not bothered to cut it deeper; where a band of hard volcanic rock intersected the native granite of the island, he had not even tried to smooth the sharp edges that marred the gleaming surface of Iveroth's boots. It amazed him that Lady Steinnland, in her long skirts and gauzy petticoat, had even attempted the path; she must have been truly upset... or truly determined to reach this place called Hamarrvoe. What could be there? Her family's cottage? Had she run home to Mama? Or – He decided that he would not even try to think of what else might attract a young girl married to an elderly recluse to such an isolated spot; and so he was able to think of little else for much of the arduous descent.

At least it took his mind off the damage being wreaked on a pair of boots that Deverill of Din Eidyn had spent six months carefully fitting to the exact contours of his feet and calves.

The latter part of the descent, thankfully, was not as steep and perilous as the first part. He was able to choose where he planted his feet, to step on pockets of damp sand rather than on the volcanic rock, and to move slowly and quietly enough to get his breath and his composure back. At the last he was working his way around stacks of rock cut into pillars by wind and water, rather than climbing ever downwards. There was a continuous low wailing sound in his ears, one that made him fear he would find Steinnland's lady weeping over some fancied slight from the fishwives, until he identified it as the sound of the sea wind whistling through narrow slots in the stacks around him. Then, beyond that, he heard a high, sweet voice raised in song, and smiled grimly to himself. No, Lady Steinnland would not run away and cry over unkindness or insult, would she? She wasn't a weeper, that one. She had come to this place for some other reason.

He padded around the last stack and found himself standing upon a crescent of sandy beach trapped between two outreaching cliffs. Before him, green water foamed into white surf against the sand, and the surf was full of tiny things working and clicking away at great speed. Some kind of sea-crabs, no doubt, catching a prey that was thrown up to them by the waves.

Young Lady Steinnland leaned against one of the outreaching cliffs, so close to the pounding waves that he almost called out a warning before remembering that she was a native of these parts and probably better able to judge the dangers of the sea than he was. The silver-gilt hair that had been bound in neat braids about her head was loose now, wind-whipped about her neck and shoulders and flying in the sea spray, haloing her with a pale iridescence of fine, soft locks. Her hands held a length of some kind of fancy-work, white as the sea-foam that boiled upon the sands, and her eyes were fixed on the incoming waters as she sang a sweet, dreamy air – some folk tune of the isles, no doubt, for it resembled no music that Iveroth had ever heard at the musicales and *petits soupers* of Din Eidyn society.

There was something haunting, almost other-worldly in the scene. As he stood watching, Iveroth had the illusion that the sea itself was offering up its treasure at her feet, building up heaping billows of iridescent, frothy lace that the sea-crabs, or whatever they were, spun like snow, like starlight, like frost upon a window pane.

"In cool arcades and glassy halls," she sang,

"We pass the sultry hours of noon,

Beyond wherever sun-beam falls…."

The words were hackneyed; the images and the haunting tune were dangerously seductive. Iveroth rubbed his eyes and told his imagination to get a grip on itself. Water and foam and sand were just that and nothing more, not billows of lace. And as there was no sign of human habitation in this cove, no visible reason for young Lady Steinnland to have come here, the chances were that she had made her way to this isolated spot, and was singing seductive melodies, for exactly the kind of reasons he had determined not to think about on his way down to the shore.

"There, the pale pearl and sapphire blue,

And ruby red, and em'rald green,

Dart from the domes a changing hue,

And starry columns deck the scene," the girl sang, drawing out the last line with a wealth of flourishes and grace notes as if she fancied herself a prima donna of the Borghesan opera.

"Deck the scene, indeed!" Iveroth repeated with scarcely controlled anger. He recognized the words, now; some doggerel from that farrago of nonsense, *The Mysteries of Udolpho*.

She gasped and whirled to face him. The sea-crabs gave up their scuttling, the billows of foam upon the shore collapsed, and all was perfectly natural again, without the eerie overtones that had briefly unsettled him. There was nothing here but a young woman on an empty stretch of sand, a young woman who had unbound and combed out her hair and was singing while she waited for... oh, he could very well guess what, or rather who, she had been waiting for!

"So this is how you pass the time while the women I hired neglect their work!"

"Some of them are not over fond of being reminded that they are working for me," Lady Steinnland said. "I thought the work might go better if I absented myself."

"You thought wrong," Iveroth told her. "You will go back now and oversee them, if I have to carry you myself."

The green eyes froze, and the long loose fair hair whipping about her face seemed pale and cold as icicles. "And by what authority do you give me orders, Lord Iveroth? Do you forget that you are talking to the lady of the March-Lord?"

"I do not forget your position," said Iveroth, his patience strained beyond all bearing, "but it appears that you do! Is it seemly to run away and meet your lover while other women set your house to rights?"

"And meet…" In Lady Steinnland's momentary silence he could hear the roaring of the waves breaking upon the shore. The tide must be rising, for suddenly he was aware that he and Lady Steinnland stood upon a crescent of sand barely wide enough to hold them, while the waves broke almost over their feet. "And meet…" she repeated with disgust. A larger wave than most rolled in and broke, capriciously, over Iveroth's very feet, while Lady Steinnland stood untouched in her soft slippers and fragile, shimmering petticoat under a dark overskirt and bodice. "How dare you make such insinuations? What man do you see in this cove, beside yourself, who came upon me all uninvited and ruined my work?"

"Work!" he laughed. "Singing to the waves, and admiring the echo of your own voice – is that what you call work?"

"If you must know," she retorted, "I was knitting lace to trim the Duchess' bed linens. And I should have had almost enough, if you had not interrupted me!" She shook out the piece of fancy-work in her hands. Opened out, the snowy lace looked nothing like the famous patterned lace shawls of the Northern Isles; rather it reminded Iveroth of the cell-structures of plants, delicate networks that he had recently seen through the newly improved Majuloscope with its sequence of lenses carefully ground and arranged to make the smallest motes visible. But instead of mere connecting lines of dark on light, this was light made visible, essence of whiteness foaming out like sea bubbles, like some natural growth that had been harvested rather than made by hand.

With an effort he wrenched his thoughts from contemplation of the amazing lace and back to the reality before him. He named that reality, contemptuously, for Lady Steinnland to hear and be shamed. "A young girl, wedded to an old man, slips away to a secluded cove where there are none to see her. She does this so often that even the fishwives hired to wash the linens of the house know where she has gone. When I follow her, she is angry at being found. She claims to have been knitting, though she has neither needles nor yarn with her."

He paused. Lady Steinnland seemed insufficiently daunted by the damning facts.

"And I suppose you are disappointed to have found me alone, rather than dallying with the lover you have conjured up for me!" she gibed. "You should have remained hidden behind the stacks and spied on me a bit longer, in hopes of catching him!"

"No doubt I ought to have done so," Iveroth said. The tide still rose; the water was ankle-deep about his boots now, while the rise of sand on which Lady Steinnland stood was still, maddeningly, dry. "But I don't plan to be drowned today. And unless that made part of *your* plans, you will see the wisdom of coming with me now."

"Up the Stairs of the Vaardens?" Lady Steinnland pointed her chin at the half-carved, half natural series of ledges by which Iveroth had made his way to the cove. "You will come with me up the path?"

Iveroth had certainly no intention of leaving her there, perched on some stack above the rising tide to wait for a lover who obviously had failed to meet his paramour.

"Good," she said, surprising him. She stepped from the last bit of dry sand onto a rocky ledge and reached up into a water-carved niche in the cliffs. "You can help carry these."

If the path down had been difficult, it was nothing compared to climbing back up the Vaardens with his arms full of soup bowls.

***

The wives of the fishermen and crofters had been paid and dismissed before Steinnland came down to dinner. Iveroth had to confess himself amazed by the improvement in the place; not that he cared about such things himself – one had a housekeeper, or a wife, to direct these matters – but he could not help noticing that the hall and stairs and long rambling corridors of the house shone with an unaccustomed brightness, and that the sharp smell of soap overlaid with herbal essences filled rooms that had previously carried only the musty scent of old books. It seemed that the women had worked well enough to earn their hire, after all – or perhaps Lady Steinnland had bestirred herself to oversee them. He had no idea which it was; after he had labored up the Vaardens with his burden of dishes, and had suffered Lady Steinnland to direct him as to their placement in the tones she would have used to a servant, it had seemed the better part of valor to take himself off and out of the way of the women who were everywhere he turned, scrubbing floors and hanging sheets and – perhaps this was his imagination – secretly laughing to see him reduced to the role of a domestic servant.

If Steinnland had not been so severe about his need to work uninterrupted, Iveroth would have claimed sanctuary in the library. But the March-Lord had made it clear that such scrying as he meant to do was a dark and difficult task, and that an interruption at the wrong moment could ruin hours of careful work.

Iveroth had little belief in the ability of the arcane arts to cast any light upon the Duchess' plans; he was a man of the new generation, a man of the scientific age that was opening up and enlightening the world, and he had never met a so-called "magician" who knew any art more mysterious than that of relieving bored and stupid Society fools of their excess money. Steinnland, however, had grown up in a different age; he had been a young man when the last witch was hanged in Din Eidyn. Iveroth would not be so rude as to go against the express wish of his host for solitude, nor so impertinent as to express his belief that Lord Steinnland's work was wasted effort.

So he took himself off for a walk around the island, and – now that the finish of his boots was already beyond repair – found more of interest and enjoyment in the sights than he had expected. Most of the Northern Isles were barren, inhospitable places where men eked out a meager living and fought an eternal battle against wind and cold. Faarhafn was somehow different, though he could hardly say where that difference lay; perhaps it was just that the small harbor, where the ferry connected with the mainland and where the fishing boats from the north sold their catch, brought in more income than the more remote islands knew. But it seemed to be more than that; this place seemed gentler and softer even than the mainland coast from which he had come. The wind did not seem to blow as sharply here, the sunlight was stronger wherever it broke through the clouds, the turf that covered the hills was soft and green, sprays of pink and white flowers sprang up in every pocket of earth among the cliffs, and the crofters' tattie gardens and kailyards looked to be flourishing remarkably well for so early in the summer. Strangely, the islanders themselves were a pale and peaked race, looking as if the salt air had shrunken them, but all the sights of nature were fair to the view. He could understand why, when Steinnland retired from public affairs, he had chosen to make his home in the peace of this green isle.

He timed his return carefully, hoping to encounter Steinnland himself before he underwent another battle of words with that sharp-tongued young Lady Steinnland, and was successful in this; more successful than he had dared hope, for as he entered the house Steinnland was just coming down the great staircase that led to the upper floors, and Lady Steinnland was nowhere to be seen.

Perhaps he really ought to warn Steinnland about what his wandering wife was up to.

"I wonder where Lady Steinnland is," he said as neutrally as he could.

"What, did she not take you out to see the island? I had hoped that the two of you would entertain one another today."

"I did encounter her earlier," Iveroth said. "One of the fishwives told me to look for her at a place called Hamarrvoe – and plaguey difficult it was to reach, too!"

Steinnland laughed softly. "Aye, my Sabira's a wild young thing and must have her freedom. She ranges all about this island and beyond. Doubtless she knows easier paths to the cove than the one you or I must take – not," he added with a sad grimace and a touch of his arthritic knee, "that I would risk my old bones on the Vaardens these days."

"Perhaps that is part of its appeal to her," Iveroth said.

"That it is so hard to reach? Aye, she loves to be alone with the rocks and the sea. I knew that when I married her, and I've never grudged her the freedom to range about the island as she wished."

This would have been the perfect time to warn Steinnland. But Iveroth looked at his old friend's face, lit by the certainty that he and his young wife understood one another perfectly, and could not force the words to his lips. After all, he had no proof. If Steinnland had been a scientific man like himself, he would have seen the logic of the situation. For a lady to take herself off, unchaperoned, to an empty cove whose only appeal was that her husband could not possibly follow her – what else could that signify, but a secret meeting?

But Steinnland belonged to a different age. He believed in witches, and in scrying the future in a silver bowl, and in a young girl who was happy to marry an old man.

And that reminded Iveroth of what Steinnland would no doubt be expecting him to ask.

"Did you learn anything in your researches today?"

Steinnland's face darkened and his features seemed firmer, harder, younger somehow; the face of a man who sees a perilous task before him and does not hesitate to take it on.

"The scrying bowl at its best yields up only images, which may be interpreted in various ways. But I saw nothing good, and nothing that can be interpreted as good. I saw a woman naked upon the shore, with seven stones around and upon her body; I saw a stammering idiot; I saw green kelp and salt sea water filling up this house until I thought myself drowned, so strong was the vision."

"Did you see the woman's face, or anything that could tell you who she was?"

Steinnland shook his head. "No, but you understand these images are not to be read literally. To lie down so between the high tide and the low tide lines, with the seven stones so placed, is the beginning of an old and evil rite invoking dark magic. My vision may have meant literally that the Duchess means to perform the witch-rite and give her soul over to the demons of the sea, or it may have been a warning that she has some evil design in her mind."

Iveroth thought that if Steinnland had seen Sabira's face on the image in the scrying bowl, he would not have believed it and would have managed not to recognize it. For himself, he could more easily picture her naked upon the sand than an aging woman like Ailsa of Quoy. A tide of heat flashed over his body and he forced the image away. It was not at all the done thing to imagine the wife of one's host in such a fashion. No matter how improper her behavior had been.

And he didn't even believe in this so-called art of scrying! Must everything and all roads lead his thoughts to Lady Steinnland? "What of the idiot? Was that a face you knew?"

"I knew it, and did not know it," said Steinnland, sounding like a man startled out of a dream. "Times it seemed to be my friend long gone, Donal of Quoy. He died soon after he married Ailsa, you know. Then when I would look closer, the face changed, and all the features went slack and the mouth hung open like an idiot's, and I could no longer see Donal or anything but a jabbering fool." He shook his head. "Let us not speak more of that image; it is painful to me. As for the third, I am afraid that was created out of my own fancies and the history of this island."

All Steinnland's 'visions' had been created out of his own fancies, Iveroth thought, but this he forbore to say.

"For, you know, Faarhafn was taken from the sea, in a sense, and to the sea it shall return – not in my day, but soon after," Steinnland said in that same dreamlike tone, "and so in that I saw only a shadow of what must some day be." He brightened at the sound of petticoats swishing towards them, at the light step of his wife. "Ah, my dear lady is with us. Shall we go in to dinner, then?"

The dinner that followed, with its necessarily three-cornered dialogue, was one of the most difficult social situations Iveroth had encountered in his life as a wealthy landowner in Din Eidyn society. Lady Steinnland hardly spoke, save to recommend this or that dish as some delicacy of the isles which might be unfamiliar to a visitor.

Steinnland was lost in musing upon the visions his imagination had conjured up during the long day alone, and Iveroth mentally cursed himself for allowing his elderly friend to work himself up into such a state. On the morrow he would insist that Steinnland leave his "studies" and show him around the island; out in the fresh air and sunshine, perhaps he would stop worrying over imaginary magical troubles and turn his excellent brain to the real problem of finding out Ailsa of Quoy's plans and stopping them.

To break the silence, Iveroth remarked upon the brilliance and shimmering glow of the plates and bowls they ate from. Lightweight, strong, and seeming to shine with an iridescent inner light, the dishes were indeed worthy of admiration. What, he asked, were they made of?

"Polished shells," said Lady Steinnland. "It is a local craft."

"There could be a market for this work in Din Eidyn," Iveroth said. "Would not that give the crofters another source of income?"

Lady Steinnland's lips twitched in a brief show of amusement. "I fear not. Will you take some of this crab ragout, my lord Iveroth?"

Next Iveroth tried to introduce the subject of land improvements, a topic in which Steinnland had been passionately interested in the past, but now his old friend was too abstracted to pay attention. He simply waved his hand and said that it made no difference – at least not on Faarhafn. There would be no time to make sweeping changes to the system during his lifetime, and those who came after would have no interest in the matter.

"You know that much of your heir, then?" Iveroth asked. It was a question of some delicacy; Steinnland and the Isles were entailed, and on Steinnland's death they must pass to the next male heir, a distant cousin who had left Din Eidyn many years ago to make his way in the service of the Borghesan army. Perhaps the March-Lord was simply assuming that a military man would be ignorant of the land and how to care for the land.

"I know enough," said Steinnland with a smile for Lady Steinnland, "to plan for resettling my tenants of Faarhafn on some of my mainland farms that have been allowed to grow fallow for lack of people to work them. But it's a difficult task to persuade them to go, is it not, my love?"

"I can see why anybody who lived here would be reluctant to take up another holding, even if it were larger and more fertile," said Iveroth. "There is something in the air here, some quality of the light – I cannot describe it, but I have seldom felt such peace and contentment as I did this afternoon, strolling the grassy hills above the shore."

Steinnland laughed. "If Iveroth admits to being contented when he does not have a horse between his knees, then this island must be magical indeed! I had expected you to complain bitterly of having to leave your horse on the mainland." It was generally considered ill-advised to take temperamental bloodstock on the ferry that crossed the De'il's Strait to Faarhafn; even the calm draft horses and undersized cattle of the isles became unpredictably nervous when crossing that stretch of water.

"Indeed, and I had planned to grumble endlessly about that privation," Iveroth said, "but your island has undone me. Another two days of soft weather and soft living, and I shall be too contented even to worry about the Duchess of Quoy. I had not thought any cook but Antoine of Lutéce could produce this ragout of crab."

Steinnland smiled with gentle pride. "Nor could he. Antoine worked for me in Din Eidyn and accompanied me into my retirement here."

Iveroth's brows shot up. "Indeed? I had heard a tale that he was murdered in the street by some men who thought he had been winning more than he should in the common gaming-houses, who accused him of putting a charm upon the runestones they threw."

"So he might have been," Steinnland agreed, "had he not departed Din Eidyn with me. We thought he might live longer upon Faarhafn if he were thought dead in the capital."

After that exchange drew Steinnland from his abstraction, they managed to bridge Lady Steinnland's silences with enough light chat of this sort to pass the dinner time tolerably well. Afterwards Steinnland actually proposed that they both join him in a game of piquet. At first Iveroth had supposed that he meant that the two of them should play piquet while Lady Steinnland looked on, but it turned out that Steinnland had taught his young wife the rudiments of the game and expected her to play too.

"And how is that to be managed?" Iveroth inquired.

"Easily enough, if you care more for the game than for the final score," Steinnland replied. "My lady and I will play the first hand, so that you may become familiar with the way we play the game on Faarhafn. Thereafter the winner of each hand shall challenge the one who did not play the previous time."

Iveroth assumed this would fairly shortly turn into the same thing as he had anticipated – a duel of wits between himself and Steinnland – but it turned out that young Lady Steinnland had an excellent memory for cards and the cool intelligence to calculate the odds of success with each move.

As a further complicating factor, the Steinnland ménage had invented a multiplicity of extra rules that no one could possibly remember.

"What? A tierce containing a fair Queen is superior to any quart? I never saw that rule," Iveroth said suspiciously when Lady Steinnland quoted it and claimed the trick.

"I am not perfectly sure that I remember it myself," Steinnland said, "but not sure enough to challenge and risk losing the hand."

"What?"

"If I challenge my lady to produce the rule as written in the book, then she must do so or forfeit the hand. However, if I challenge her and she can produce the rule, it is I who pay the forfeit."

"Ah," said Iveroth happily. "I see it is no longer a game of cards and memory, but a game of guessing who is lying. Most definitely I should challenge."

"And most definitely you would pay a forfeit," said Lady Steinnland, turning the pages of the book in which she and Steinnland had inscribed the wild "rules" that caught their fancy until she could display the page explaining that the presence of a fair Queen in any tierce, quart or quint doubled the value of the series. She smiled sweetly at Iveroth. "What will it take to cure you of this assumption that everything I say is a lie?"

'A great deal more than one forfeit," said Iveroth, reaching for the book. Their fingers brushed as he took it, and he hastily drew back his hand. "Steinnland, have you…" Of course Steinnland would have quill and ink within reach of his dining table; the table would more frequently be covered with books and documents than with food. Iveroth took up the quill and went to work, scratching busily over the first blank page left in the book of rules.

"What are you doing now?"

"Evening the odds," said Iveroth. "If I must guess at the rules you and Steinnland have made, then it's only fair I should invent a few for you two to guess about." He blew on the writing to dry the ink, closed the book and handed it to his host.

CHAPTER FIVE

The next night's dinner was completely different in tone, with as many dishes upon the table as would have fed twenty people instead of five, with both Lady Steinnland and Steinnland formally dressed, and careful, general, polite conversation instead of a game of Liar's Piquet. There were even a few fishermen, dressed in their best clothes and attempting to behave as proper servants when they carried in platters and removed empty plates. Such was the civilizing influence of Ailsa, Duchess of Quoy.

The Duchess had crossed the Strait that morning but had not reached Steinnland's house until late afternoon. What Iveroth considered an easy, bracing walk across the island from the harbor to Steinnland's rambling house had been to her, or so she insisted, an insurmountable trek. Fortunately, foreseeing the hardships of travel in the north, she had brought a second coach to carry her sedan chair, had brought the thing across with her on the ferry and had been vastly discomfited to find that the fishermen at the harbor could not be persuaded by any offer of silver or gold to act as her carriers until they had brought in and disposed of the morning's catch.

She made quite a story of her difficulties in reaching the house, laughing at the fishermen for ignorant buffoons who thought a net of glistening silver fish worth more than a purse of silver coins.

"Well, you see, the ling would have been running this morning," Steinnland explained apologetically, "and they could hardly pass up such an opportunity. They get two pence on the mainland for each lingfish, but only one penny for the saithe, which are much more common. Doubtless they thought they could have the silver of the ling in the morning and your silver as payment for carrying the chair in the afternoon."

Young Lord Gairloch, the Duchess' son by the old duke, gave an appreciative chuckle. "And so they did get both! Perhaps they are not quite such fools as you think, mama?"

The Duchess did not care for this turn in the conversation and spoke instead of the clumsiness of the bearers, how they had tossed and jolted her in the chair so that she feared she had arrived at Steinnland's house looking quite as blowsy and unkempt as any island woman.

Gairloch gave Lady Steinnland a slanting look under his long lashes. He said nothing, but his eyes said what Iveroth was thinking: if she was an example of the "blowsy, unkempt" island women, his mother had some stiff competition.

Lady Steinnland did not return the glance, but paid courteous attention to the Duchess as she complained of each imagined fault in her hairdress, her gown, and her stockings – she even drew up her layers of petticoats to exhibit a neatly turned ankle and a small foot in a totally impractical red shoe built up in sections from its high heels and layered with frills of gilt leather.

Knowing from experience that this line of conversation would not cease until the Duchess had extracted what she considered her fair share of compliments, Iveroth was lavish in his praise of each part exhibited for their admiration. He even, heroically, refrained from saying what the fashionable shoe reminded him of.

Gairloch, unfortunately, was not so restrained. "I say, mama, do you know what that shoe looks like? Like a lobster trying to eat your whole foot!"

"Then her Grace must say 'Let be and let be,' as the mainlander said to the crab!" Steinnland said with a laugh, and then recounted the old story of how a man from an inland province, coming to the seashore for the first time, had had his toe pinched by a crab, upon which he jumped and cried out to the crab, "Nay, you let me be and I'll let you be!"

"And what brings you to Faarhafn, your Grace, that forced you to make so difficult and dangerous a journey?" Steinnland went on smoothly. "I am, alas, not so vain as to imagine you undertook this perilous trip only for the pleasure of my company and conversation."

"Oh… I wanted your advice," the Duchess said vaguely. "About… oh, about this kelp burning. I'm told that is a profitable venture, and as my estates extend along the west coast, I don't see why I should not profit from it as much as you or anybody else! Yet I cannot persuade my tenants to put in the work of raking and burning it for the chemical salts."

"You are better off so, Mama," Gairloch said. "Isn't it true, my lord, that the kelping takes men away from farming for most of the summer, and so much good land goes unused?"

"This is true," said Steinnland, "although it is not so great a concern upon the islands as it would be on the estates of Quoy. Many of our islands are so rough and barren that such land as there is can easily be farmed in the intervals between good kelping tides. But the lands of Quoy are fertile and benefit from the longer growing season in the south; I would advise you, madam, to let the kelping be and improve your tenants' land."

"That is exactly what I said!" Gairloch cried exultantly. "When I come of age next month…" He paused, interrupted by a dry cough that took his breath away for a moment. "Sorry – when I come of age, I mean to reorder the tenancies entirely. Far too much of the land is still divided according to the medieval practice of runrig, so that each man's holding consists of little strips far from each other, and he spends half the day walking from one strip to another. And with runrig there is no incentive to improve the land for the good of all; I can't even set in proper drains because I would destroy some man's 'rig' entirely. Don't you agree, my lord, that draining is the first consideration in improving the land?"

"Absolutely!" said Iveroth with enthusiasm, thinking of his own estates. "It has cost me something in capital to drain and enclose the land, but in future years the estate will be much more profitable. First drain, then manure, I always say."

The two young men plunged into a discussion of the new farming methods and land improvements that were being tried in Anglia to the south, ideas that they meant to put in place on their Dalriadan estates as quickly as they could without desperately offending their conservative, ignorant tenants. Steinnland joined them, suggesting modifications for the barren rocky land of the Northern Isles.

"Erlend, dear," the Duchess said, "you should not talk so fast. It makes your cough worse."

"Oh, that's of no matter, mama!" the boy exclaimed. "In any case it is much better here than in Din Eidyn. I think all I needed was to get out of the smoke of the city." And he returned to laying out a line of knives to illustrate his plan for interlocking drains.

Perhaps she had brought young Gairloch here for his health? After that interchange the Duchess sat back, looking somewhat put out at losing their attention, and showing no interest at all in the subject which had supposedly brought her to Faarhafn.

***

I could have slapped Iveroth for dragging all three men into talk of agriculture and leaving me alone to entertain the Duchess.

"If you would care to see how the folk here work at kelping," I offered to her Grace, "I could take you to see a kelp burning pit tomorrow, or we could walk over to the beach below Mid Yell Voe. That is a good gathering place, and the chances are that Effie Scrabster's man will be raking in the kelp tomorrow while his women sort it for burning."

This offer was received by silence. I thought in silent desperation of Borghesan opera and Lutécian fashions and other matters of which I was not equipped to speak. I thought with more anger of Iverroth, who was endangering the frilled front of his shirt by leaning over a dish of lobster *en casserole* to show the layout of a typical farm on his estates, and being no help whatever in maintaining fashionable conversation with the Duchess. I felt clumsy and unsure of myself, but knew not what to do save to enlarge upon the offer she had ignored.

"We might even help the women sort the kelp. If you want your tenants to make the most from the trade, they must learn the difference between ware and tangle, how to spread both on the steethes and how to klokk the tangle."

The Duchess gave a tiny, affected shriek. "Walk! In these shoes! You must be joking! No, Lady Steinnland, I have no desire to dirty my petticoats and stain my hands by involving my person in trade."

It occurred to me that if she had indeed, as Iveroth claimed, been a goose-girl before she caught the eye of the Duke, she must at one time have known not only long walks but far dirtier work than kelping. Geese are very unclean beasts. Feeling that to voice this comment would not improve the conversation, I cast about for some other entertainment to offer. The Duchess saved me the trouble. "Even the words of this trade are barbarous. 'To klokk the tangle!' Can your peasants not speak English?"

"Why, it means only to strip off the broad fronds from the stems," said I. "Ware is the soft stuff such as fronds, and the steethes are places built up with piled stones suitable for drying the kelp. You see, it is only a matter of a few words."

"Words," said the Duchess, "for which I have no use! I wish only to learn how this slimy stuff can increase my income and how to force my peasants to bestir themselves to gather and burn it. My lord Steinnland, what is it you do to make them work so hard?"

Thus directly addressed, my lord came out of the dreamy half-trance in which he had been watching Iveroth and Gairloch rearrange dishes and silverware to illustrate their ideas on proper estate management. "Why, the profit of the burning is itself reason enough for them, madam. They keep two thirds and give me one third."

"You let them keep the silver that is paid for the burnt cakes of kelp?"

"Otherwise why would they work?" Steinnland did not add what I knew to be true, that the one-third profit he accepted went into a fund to help resettle the Faarhafn tenants on some of his mainland estates. That was a private agreement between me and his lordship, and none of the Duchess' business.

"You know, mama," Gairloch broke off his conversation with Iveroth, "one must put something back into the land to keep taking crops from it. And in the same way, you must put something into the estate to keep it profitable in the long run."

"I believe you are advising me to manure my peasants well!" The Duchess's laugh was everything her pretty, petite face and figure promised; a tinkling of silver bells, true notes but cold ones. "From what I have seen – and smelt - of them, they are already well daubed. No, but really, Steinnland, it is outrageous to let them keep two-thirds. They will get ideas beyond their station. One must keep the peasants poor and hungry, so that they concentrate on getting a living and have no time to read books and communicate revolutionary ideas."

At last she had broached a subject on which I could converse as well as any fine gentleman or lady in Din Eidyn. "Do you mean books like that recently published tract, *Reflections on Natural Philosophy and the Estates of Man*? My lord and I found Mr. Douleur's views interesting and very well, if somewhat forcibly, presented."

"Yes, but he has no idea of the science of government," Steinnland put in. It was an argument we had greatly enjoyed a month or so ago, with me championing the cause of the pseudonymous Mr. Douleur. I had answered back hotly, "Never having ruled or enjoyed the company of those who rule, how should he know the 'science of government'? It would be like expecting me to know the natural geography of the land as well as I know the shoals and bays, the shallows and the high plateaus under the sea!"

The Duchess dismissed the topic with a shrug. "Oh, that sort of nonsense! A smuggled pamphlet, I believe, by some little man of no consequence. No one in Din Eidyn would read such trash. But…" she paused and smiled at Steinnland. Her smile flashed like a suddenly lighted branch of candles in a dark room, offering warmth and invitation that no one could fail to respond to. Even I felt myself warm to her, thinking that she laughed at herself as much as at us. "But, my lord, that is precisely the sort of thing I do not wish my tenants to be reading! Now do you see the problem? If I let them keep the greater part of the profits from the kelp burning, they will grow fat and lazy and read treasonous pamphlets telling them that they are our equals!"

Apparently the contents of the tract, at least, had been somewhat discussed in Din Eidyn, even if no one would admit to having read it. My hopes for a stimulating philosophical discussion were dashed when the Duchess turned the conversation back to herself, saying she vowed she knew not what she would do with herself in such a lonely place; how ever did Steinnland bear the isolation, the lack of all civilized social discourse?

Her blue eyes flickered in my direction as she asked this question with ever such an innocent air. I had to confess to feeling a little downcast. If Din Eidyn society did not permit discussion either of practical matters such as the kelp trade, or of philosophical issues such as those raised by Mr. Douleur, how would I ever manage in such a world? Reminding myself that in fact I was not required to make conversation in Din Eidyn society, only to entertain the Duchess of Quoy for a day or so, I endeavored to look more confident than I felt; apparently with little success, as Iveroth leant in my direction and whispered, "Cheer up, Lady Steinnland; you can always discuss *The Mysteries of Udolpho* or *Modern Manners*. Her Grace loves these three-volume fripperies as well as you do."

In the event I was required to attempt no more entertaining conversation that night, as the Duchess concentrated all her attention and all her charm upon my lord and Iveroth, leaving me to listen to Gairloch's plans for changing the management of Quoy as soon as he came of age. "Of course these improvements will reduce our income for a few years, but even Mama will see the wisdom of ploughing back some of our profits into the land once it becomes more productive," he told me while the Duchess fluttered her fan and her eyelashes at Iveroth and discussed her love of natural grandeur in scenery.

"Indeed, that is the other reason for my journey," she confided. "I am told that there is nothing so grand a sight as the full moon rising over the northern islands in the mellow light of midsummer, and since this year the full moon coincides with the longest day of the year—"

My lord gave a short bark of laughter. "I regret to inform you, madam, that you are out in your calculations. The moon will be full tonight; Langsday is two days hence."

For a moment briefer than the blink of an eye, I saw the Duchess' pretty, smiling face frozen into a mask of cold fury, concealed from my lord and Iveroth by the angle of her fan; then she was fluttering and smiling again, laughing at herself for being such a dunderhead and vowing that it was impossible to read the crabbed columns of the almanack.

"Lady Steinnland can read an almanack," said my lord, "and she can teach you how if you like, madam."

I quailed inside at this offer, and was thankful that the Duchess had no more interest in it than she had in the sordid business of sorting and burning kelp. "What difference, since I am already here," she cried gaily, "I shall enjoy both sights – the full moon tonight, and the long summer rays of Langsday two days from now!"

I felt that it was going to be a very long two days. It was a pity my lord was so straightforward; if the Duchess was as inept at reading an almanack as she claimed, he could well have convinced her that today was Langsday and tonight the conjunction she wished for. She and I would both have been much happier.

***

After dinner Ailsa found, somewhat to her annoyance, that she was expected to sit out on a bare, windswept terrace overlooking the cliffs that fell sharply down to the sea, only to watch the moon rise in the summer sky over the neighboring island of Skelray– and to look as if she enjoyed it! Well, she should have thought up some better excuse for visiting Faarhafn at the conjunction of the full moon and midsummer night. But who'd have expected old Steinnland, wrapped in his books as he always was, to press for the reason behind her visit? Probably he'd been put up to it by that great gawky maypole of a girl he'd wedded in his dotage. A pert young thing, the sort who thought the creamy skin and dewy eyes of youth were enough to make her a beauty – Ailsa had disliked her on sight.

And now to find that she'd been out in her reckoning, that the full moon and the longest day of the year missed one another by two full days! She might try tonight, and if it did not work, she could while away two days in this desolate place and try again. And if that failed….

Well, perhaps it would not be necessary after all. As soon as she felt she had admired the moonrise long enough to satisfy Steinnland's expectations, she escaped to her room on the plea of fatigue, made her preparations and waited until Erlend should come up to his room.

The wait was long enough to set all her nerves on edge and make her wish she had not excused herself so soon. Even pretending admiration for the view in front of Steinnland and his young wife had not been so nerve-wracking as the wait in this desolate, empty chamber. She debated to herself whether assigning such a wreched room to her had been a deliberate insult, and decided it probably had not. Doubtless patched linens laid upon a mattress she strongly suspected of damp, and a stack of mouldy old books for entertainment, consisted Steinnland's notion of luxurious hospitality. And that chit of a girl he'd married, who did not even dress her hair but simply wound it in plaits round her head, would know no better!

From the window of her chamber Ailsa could hear the voices of those who'd remained on the terrace: first the sound was that of a quartet, then after Steinnland retired for the night it was a trio lacking the bass ground. When Iveroth made his excuses she thought it would not be long before Erlend and that girl did the same, but the duet of soprano and tenor on the terrace seemed to go on forever. Mostly tenor, and the few words that came clearly to her listening ears suggested that Erlend was telling Steinnland's young wife all his notions of land reform and his plans to give away most of their income to make the peasants comfortable. What a sapless fool she had birthed! Left alone with a pretty girl, he couldn't even make love to her, but had to bore her with his endless talk of country matters.

It seemed distressingly probable that she would have to carry out her plans after all – if she could.

It would be extremely bad ton to put her head out the window and shriek at Erlend to quit boring Lady Steinnland and come to bed. Ailsa had spent too many years disciplining herself to the highest standards of Din Eidyn society to commit such an impropriety, even now.

The lingering light of midsummer began to shade into darkness; Ailsa used the single taper that had lit her to her chamber to light first one branch of candles in a gleaming silver candelabrum, then another. At least Steinnland was not stingy with his candles; there was light enough to read by, if she had been minded to waste her time and ruin her eyesight on some boring tract.

Would the boy never stop talking?

In desperate boredom she examined the books left for her entertainment. The top two books were even worse than she had anticipated; an Anglian political treatise and *Observations on the Oeconomy of the Northern Islands.* Below those she found the three volumes of *The Mysteries of Udolpho.* Ailsa considered re-reading the book, but what was the point? She had already perused the romance once; she knew what lay behind the black veil that was believed to cover a picture on the wall, and how Miss Milk-and-Water Emily and her faithful Valancourt were finally united. What was a point of reading a book when you already knew the ending? One of the new romances recently translated from the Lutécian, a bit spicier than this, would have been more to her taste; but doubtless Steinnland knew better than to allow his young wife to order such books from the capital. He wouldn't want her thoughts turning to pleasures he was too old to give her.

Erlend was not too old.

The murmur of voices from the terrace had ceased while she looked through the books, and now she heard two sets of footsteps in the hall. Shite! If he had finally gotten up his courage to make love to the girl, he would be bringing her back to his chamber, and she might never catch him alone.

But no; the steps stopped at the door before hers, and she heard young Lady Steinnland bidding Erlend goodnight exactly as coolly as she had done the same to Ailsa, uncounted hours ago.

As soon as the girl's steps retreated down the hall, Ailsa slipped out of her room and scratched lightly with one fingernail on Erlend's door.

The heavy wood and the shadowed hall seemed to muffle the slight noise. Well, so much for the courtly manners she had once been at such pains to acquire! She tapped with her knuckles, first lightly and then more loudly, and the door opened to display Erlend, already in his shirtsleeves.

"Mama?"

"Do be a pet and unlace me, my love," Ailsa requested. "I realized after retiring that I could not possibly manage this dress without help."

""I told you, Mama, you would need your maid," Erlend began as he followed her back to her chamber.

"Yes, yes, I should have brought Nicolette, and what a to-do that would have been!" Ailsa responded lightly, turning her back to Erlend that he might begin the complicated task of loosening her overdress and stays. "If you think me too much the city-dweller for this raw island, only imagine how Nicolette would have wailed and fussed!" Her maid thought Din Eidyn itself a wilderness, after Lutéce. It was impossible to imagine the woman here on Faarhafn. Besides, if... if matters went poorly... the fewer witnesses, the better.

Erlend chuckled, his fingers deftly freeing the knotted laces. "Yes, she'd have seen nucklaveen in every wave that lashed the ferry!"

Ailsa's shoulders stiffened and a chilly wave of gooseflesh prickled down her spine. "What do you know of Nucklavee?"

"Ah – only what Lady Steinnland was telling me just now on the terrace," Erlend responded. "You know Jenneret has interested me in his collection of folk tales of mischievous spirits, and this type is rather an amusing curiosity. Not only are they said to be of tremendous height and ugly beyond imagining, but they are thought to have an unparalleled range of powers, from raising storms to blighting crops and spreading deadly plagues. And what makes them truly a local curiosity is that they hate the smell of burning kelp."

He turned his back courteously while Ailsa stepped out of her loosened clothes and put on a loose wrapper of white crape trimmed with scallops of blonde, but kept on talking. "So if we encourage the kelp industry on the coast of Quoy, Mama, we must have a care of the nucklaveen, lest they come to torment us as they do these poor islanders!" He chuckled quietly. "Funny thing, y'know. Young Lady Steinnland spoke almost as she believed in them."

"Him," Ailsa murmured so softly that Erlend could not possibly hear her. Her studies had revealed just one such monster. A whole race of them was beyond credence – and anyway, more than she needed. One would be quite sufficient, and she would not even require that one if only Erlend would be reasonable. She fastened the wrapper about her waist and turned back to face her son. "That reminds me, Erlend. What do you think of this kelping business?"

"It seems a back-breaking and wearying matter," Erlend said, "from what I've been told. The peasants must carry the seaweed away from shore, by horse and cart if they can get 'em, in heavy baskets else; it must be spread out to dry and turned frequently, not that it helps much in this climate; and finally they must spend full days burning it in their stone kilns, constantly turning and raking the burning mass."

"Yes, yes, but all that is the peasants' concern," Ailsa dismissed his comments. "Only think of the income it would bring in to the estate!"

"Not so much, if they keep two parts out of three, and besides-"

"I have no intention of allowing them to keep so much," Ailsa interrupted sharply. "Steinnland is soft with his people. One part in ten is enough for the peasants; more wealth would only unsettle them."

"And besides," Erlend went on steadily as though his mother had not spoken, "the shores of Quoy are not so rich in seaweed as are these northern islands, and the lands are far more cultivable. The islanders can easily procure enough kelp to make their few fields fertile, and have plenty left over for burning. If we set up kelp kilns, what would the crofters put on their fields?"

Ailsa shrugged. "The dung from their beasts, I suppose."

"They dry that for fires."

"Then let them pick up sea-coal for fires! Am I supposed to solve all their problems? I suppose you would have me sit in each croft and feed the palsied old folk by hand, that the women might have more time for spinning!"

Erlend smiled. "You always try to provoke me by exaggerating, Mama. But you know as well as I do that for years we have been taking more than we put back into the land, and we must reverse that trend. My father bequeathed me, with the title to Quoy, the richest lands in Dalriada. I have no intention of leaving my own son an impoverished and overgrazed estate, cumbered with starving peasants."

Ailsa made an impatient gesture. "Time enough to think of that when you get sons. As Duke of Quoy you will be the most eligible gentleman in the realm. We can easily find you a wife rich enough to pay for all the farming experiments you wish – if you still care for such things when you are wed."

"As heir to Quoy," Erlend said quietly, "I should think shame to hang out for a rich wife, like some fortune-hunter. The estates can and should keep us in comfort; we need only retrench for a few years now while I make the necessary improvements."

Ailsa looked up at her tall son. The boy was well-made enough; he'd had the best tutors and had always lived in Din Eidyn, that he might have as a matter of course the town-polish Ailsa herself had had to acquire quickly and with great difficulty. What ailed his head, that he must always be dabbing his hands in dirt and worrying about the condition of the farms? No true gentleman concerned himself with such things.

"Are you then quite determined, my son," she asked, "to reverse all the care of the estate when you come of age in a few weeks, and to make us poor in order that our peasants may sleep on silk and eat from silver plates?"

"Exaggerating again, Mama?" Erlend laughed. He took her hands in his. "My pretty, tiny Mama. Don't look so worried, I do not mean to retrench so far that we shall be begging in the street. Nor do I blame you for the ruinous condition into which the estate has fallen. You pretty ladies are all alike, you never look at the source of your wealth as long as the gold pieces come quickly enough. And it's not a woman's job to manage an estate. I do mean to have some sharp words with our factor upon my coming-of-age, but that need not concern you. It is time I took this burden from you, that is all."

"There is no help for it, then," Ailsa said in a low voice, more to herself than to Erlend.

"And no need to look so downcast about it! How many times have I heard you complain about the boredom of looking over the accounts and hearing the factor's report? Now you can be free to amuse yourself as you will."

"As I can, you mean," Ailsa said sharply, "on whatever little income you allow me."

"I think you will find it adequate. Are not you tired of leading Din Eidyn society, of being kept up till dawn every night and having to find a new dress for every occasion? I think you see more hours of candlelight than daylight. It cannot be good for your health, Mama. I've thought you were looking a bit fagged lately. A little less entertaining, and a little more time spent in healthful pursuits, will do you a world of good."

Ailsa let her shoulders droop. "You tell me that I must decline into an old woman, my son."

"Hardly that! But you have been looking tired, Mama, and I think you have not been sleeping well. I wish to make your life easier, not harder."

"Well, well, you must do as you think best," Ailsa said, "men always do, anyway. But will you be guided by your old mother in one thing yet?" She picked up a silver cup that stood by her bedside. "This is a new remedy for that cough of yours. I wish you will try it before you sleep tonight."

Erlend took the cup and sniffed. "Phew! What's in this one – essence of rotting seaweed? I don't think I need it, Mama. I've hardly coughed once since we crossed the Strait. Sea air, and being out of the smoke of the city, is all I need."

"But you will drink it anyway," Ailsa coaxed, "to please me, will you not? Lady Steinnland gave me the ingredients," she lied, "She says it is a traditional island cure and never fails." As she expected, the boy was too enamoured of that little peasant slut to ask her just when Lady Steinnland had had a chance to mix this 'traditional island cure'; he drained the cup with scarcely a wince of distaste at the bitter herbs within.

CHAPTER SIX

What slight noise awakened Iveroth he could not have said. In this cliffside house where the timbers creaked in the sea breezes and the sound of the sea crashing against the rocks was always in one's ears, he would have sworn that, waking, he would never have noticed a light footfall outside the closed door of his bedchamber.

He had been sleeping lightly, like a soldier; and he woke like a soldier, into full alertness and a sense that something was out of place. He strained his ears and eyes. No one else was in this room; what had he heard? Was that a footstep in the hall, the rustle of a garment, a whisper? What was the hour? This close to Langsday the northern isles were never entirely dark, and tonight the full moon hung high in the sky, adding her own illumination to the scene. But there was no warmth of sunlight in the beams that entered his casement window; it could not be morning, and there was no reason for anyone in this house to be abroad in the small hours of the night.

No good reason.

He dressed as quickly and quietly as he could, all the while jeering at his own suspicions. Someone might be ill in the village and they had sent to the lord's house for aid. There could be a thousand other innocent explanations – what of it? The worst he risked was to look a fool. But there were two women in the house tonight, and he trusted neither of them; if some midnight mischief was afoot, he meant to follow and unmask the perpetrator.

There was no one still in the hall when he left his chamber. But a spatter of wax from a carelessly held taper marred the shining perfection of the stair-rails that had just been so carefully polished; and the wax was still warm. Iveroth peeled it from the polished wood and rolled the soft, warm wax into a ball between his fingers.

The great entrance door had been left unbarred.

Outside, Iveroth saw what he had both expected and feared to see; the tall slender form of Lady Steinnland, her long fair hair falling loose down her back. No trick of moonlight and shadows could make him confuse her form with that of the petite Duchess of Quoy.

Very well. He knew now what he had to deal with – and just after that instant of recognition, a cloud passed across the moon and the light changed from a clear cold white to a murky twilight in which he could no longer make out the form he had just recognized. The moonlight, returning, made a crazy puzzle of a landscape that had seemed serene and clear by day. In the strange chill light he had no sense of size or distance; the sweep of the sea on the horizon before him blended with the smooth sweep of the turf under his feet, the rock piles to his right that marked the way to the steps of the Vaardens looked like a tumble of building blocks thrown down by a giant child, and the light from a distant cottage seemed as close as –

Wait! There were no cottages in the direction of the Vaardens. The villagers, sensibly, built beside the sea that provided three quarters of their livelihood, not among a barren tumble of rocks.

The light was gone now. Iveroth stared at the blackness of the turf at his feet for a moment, to recover his night vision, and then looked back at the path leading to the Vaardens. He could just make out a white wisp against the blackness of the rocks – was it his imagination that interpreted it as a feminine figure in a trailing gown?

He felt as if he had been plunged into the midst of one of those Gothick romances that Lady Steinnland loved. A trail of still-warm candle wax, a moonlit night, a glance at something that might have been lady or ghost – at any moment he might expect to meet a mad monk, or be driven mad himself by strains of mysterious music from an undiscoverable source!

Iveroth drew a breath and let it out again. Very well, the setting befitted a romance, but he was still in the real world. Forget about ghosts and monks, mysteries and music: if he meant to follow what he had seen glimmering in the darkness, his worst foes were gravity and the sea-wet steps of the Vaardens. It was fortunate that he'd not had time to draw on his boots; at least he need not worry that his steps would be loud enough to alarm the woman he followed.

Several times in the next few minutes he had occasion to curse that particular piece of "good fortune." The Vaardens might be slippery and difficult to navigate in boots, but they were vicious to his soft house-slippers. Before he caught the trick of reading shadows and moonlight as rough and smooth stones, he had bruised his feet several times. And he could not even relieve his feelings by swearing – at least not out loud. A steady stream of imprecations and invective ran through his head as he made his cautious way down the rough and winding steps, always watching to make sure he did not accidentally catch up with Lady Steinnland. Remembering how abruptly the stacks of rock had opened onto the smooth sandy cove at the foot of the Vaardens, he paused each time he caught a glimpse of the sea.

At the last such pause, he was able to inch sidewise along a rock stack to get a view of the beach. He was still too high to make out any details in the moonlight, but one thing was clear. There were two people standing on the sands, beside one of the great cliffs that guarded the cove on either side. The pale ovals of their faces stood out against the darkness of the cliff, as did the foamy white wrapper of the woman and the full-sleeved white shirt of the man who bent over her.

Almost as sickened with his role as voyeur as with the confirmation of Lady Steinnland's unfaithfulness. Iveroth withdrew from his vantage point and returned silently by the way he had come. What was the good of continuing on down to confront Lady Steinnland with her lover? The man must have come to meet her by some secret way into the cove, some path known only to the locals. He could vanish by the same path long before Iveroth made his way down to the beach, and as for Lady Steinnland – he already knew, from their previous confrontation on the beach, that she could lie with a clear untroubled face and innocent eyes.

But this time, he also knew what he had seen.

And he wished with all his heart that he had not seen it.

**

There was no time to spare; the work must be done before sunrise, and her son and Lady Steinnland, that precious pair, had wasted nearly half the short summer night in talking. "Turn round, Erlend, and face the cliffs," she said. There was no need for him to see what followed; modesty did not trouble her overmuch, but any shock might startle Erlend out of the hazy dream into which her potion had sent him.

It was the work of a moment to shrug off the lacy wrapper, so fashionable for a lady appearing en négligée in her own home in the capital, such a useless and even dangerous costume for climbing down the rough-cut stairs of the Vaardens. She rejoiced in her freedom for half a breath before the cold wind struck like a thousand knives, covering her lovely skin with goose-pimples. What a barbarous place – even in midsummer it was not truly warm! And were there no stones to be found in this cove? She had counted on those, at least, being ready to hand; but here was nothing to be seen except smooth sand and the forbidding rock stacks that enclosed the cove on three sides. It seemed to take forever to gather a handful of pebbles, and she was not sure these would be big enough; the old wife who'd taught her the rite had said stones, not pebbles small enough to hold in one hand. Well, she must make do with what was available, just as she'd done all her life.

Fortunate that she'd had to sit out and admire the moonrise; she'd marked the points of the compass then, otherwise she'd have had no clue to directions now that the moon was high overhead. Still holding the pebbles, shivering in the cold wind, she turned around three times against the direction of the sun's path, then arranged the pebbles on the sand. Two where her feet would be, one where her head would lie, one for each hand. She laid herself down between the pebbles, flesh shrinking from the chill damp sand, and set one of the remaining pebbles between her breasts and the second just over her left breast, above her heart…that was where the heart was located, wasn't it? She pressed down, palm open, and felt the sharp pain of the pebble and, after a moment, the rapid pulsing of her heart, It was beating so fast, as if she were going into battle.

Well, and so she was, in a sense; a battle to keep what she'd won at such cost. She remembered her husband, the flabby middle-aged man, sweating and thrusting himself into her, then telling everybody he'd gotten her with child, so that they too could look at her and imagine the obscenity that was Donal of Quoy using the fair young wife he'd bought to warm his old age and give him an heir. She remembered her body swollen and disfigured by pregnancy; she remembered the astonishing pain of childbirth that had taken her so by surprise – she who was so healthy, who'd never known a day's illness, made to suffer so, and no escape! Oh, yes; she'd paid the price for her wealth and position, and she would keep it. Whatever the cost.

Fully certain now of her will to follow the only path left, she stretched out her arms, holding a pebble in each hand, and cried out the doggerel the old wife had finally told her after long and forceful persuasion.

"All between these stones is thine,

I give thee all that is mine,

Give me the power of the sea

Come and serve me, Nucklavee."

It seemed to her that the words were torn from her mouth by the surging winds, blown away without effect. And she was all icy from top to toe. If this Nucklavee did not appear, what a fool she'd look, going through the rite for nothing more than to half freeze herself, naked on the shore!

But there was one part of the rite yet to perform. She rose from the sand, and smiled to prove to herself that she still could move as lightly and easily as a young girl. Well, hadn't she already shown that, coming down those horrible rock stairs by moonlight with that trailing wrapper like to trip her up on every step? Oh, yes, she still had many years to enjoy the position she'd earned. Erlend could take his turn when she was too old to have fun any longer.

She cast one glance to reassure herself that he was still standing with his face to the cliffs, dazed and obedient to her slightest command. A pity one could not keep him so indefinitely; then she'd have no need to do this. But the ingredients of the potion were not easy to obtain, and she had been warned that repeated use of it could cause a strain upon the heart. She would not have him harmed – not as long as there was any other way to retain her position. It was for his sake, really, that she was going through this; he had forced her to it with his unreasonable insistence on taking over control of the estate upon reaching his majority.

The sea had risen since she came down to the cove; black waves lapped at her feet. She knew a moment of panic; was the entire beach covered at high tide? Well, what if it was? She could retreat to the steps of the Vaardens at any time, couldn't she?

One at a time she threw the pebbles into the black, surging waves, with each one calling on Nucklavee. There, it was almost done; the fifth pebble fell into the water, the sixth... She held the last pebble in her closed hand for a moment, shivering with cold. Suppose it did not work... or would it be worse if it did work?

She would not be a coward; she would not turn back so close to her goal. Had she not faced down the assembled nobles and gentry of Din Eidyn, ready to sneer at her for her lowly origins, and forced them to accept her? Had she not become a leader of the society that would have rejected her? This monster of the sea, however horrid his appearance, could not be as frightening as her first entry into Gilroy's Assembly Rooms, her first attack on Din Eidyn society.

She hurled the seventh stone as far as she could and called, "Nucklavee!"

The black waters seethed and boiled before her, rose in surging waves almost to her feet, fell back again with a sighing sound as fragments of sand and small broken shells were sucked back into the sea.

"Nucklavee!" she called, and again the waves rose, this time breaking about her ankles and chilling her feet until they ached. But once again the water fell back and left her standing cold and naked upon the sand, half frozen by the gusty winds that surged and howled through the cove.

"Nucklavee!" she shrieked a third time, desperate, into the winds that snatched her voice and called it away.

This time the roiling waters rose higher, and she took an involuntary step back. And this time, as they receded, one spot in the center of the wave did not fall back. It swelled and quivered and grew, a monstrous boil on the face of the sea; it rose dripping above the waves and took form as an enormous round head that wavered from side to side as if the neck were not strong enough to support it out of water. A single round, red eye in the center of the forehead burned like a coal. Ailsa took another step backwards. If that thing should touch her –

The moonlight was cruel, illuminating the details of the monster's appearance as it rose from the sea. From neck to waist it resembled a man newly flayed by the executioner, with tarry blood coursing through veins that stood out against the raw flesh. Below the waist the form was amorphous, bulky like the body of a horse, but with flippers instead of legs. Or did it have both? Ailsa found that she did not want to know any more details. She looked down at the sand before her and the edge where dark water met white sand.

The voice, when the monster spoke, reminded her of Quoy's iron mine where raw ore was crushed in a gigantic hopper: it was not so much a voice as a series of grating noises interspersed with strange gurgles and whoops. "What would you of me, Ailsa of Quoy? To kill yon fool, I suppose?" It raised one flipper-like raw arm and gestured towards Erlend.

"No – no, not that! I mean no harm to him," she said.

"No more harm than you have done already, you mean, Ailsa of Quoy."

"I have not harmed him!" she began, then stopped herself. She would not stoop to defend herself before the beast she had called from the deep to obey her commands.

"You folk of the sea sometimes take children, and replace the babe in the cradle with a changeling made in its image, do you not?"

"Babes, yes. Though I personally have little interest in the matter. It is the finfolk who cannot get enough children, and for some reason want more of the squalling brats around."

Ailsa drew a deep breath, and then wished she had not. The monster was so close to her that its stench overpowered the clean air of the sea. She breathed in rotting fish and slimy decaying seaweed, all that was foul about the salt sea, and gagged on the smell.

"This is no squalling brat," she gestured towards Erlend, "but a strong young man who can serve you well. Can you make a changeling in his form?"

Nucklavee's fiery eye swiveled to cast an unholy red glow on Erlend, still standing stiff and obedient with his face to the cliff. "Bid him turn about."

"Erlend," Ailsa called, "close your eyes and turn around."

Nucklavee's chuckle was worse than his speech; it squished and squelched its way out. "Do you think to protect him? He will have time in plenty to grow used to me after I take him under the sea – if I take him."

"I thought the bargain pleased you."

"Not yet." The eye was focused upon her again; its heat should have been welcome after the cold she had endured, but it made her feel sick and dizzy. "First, you must understand and agree that the changeling may be like this young man in face and form, but it will never be able to pass for a sensible man in your world. The beings that the finfolk create have neither speech nor sense. Such changelings may pass unnoticed a while as babes in the cradle, but not as human beings grown to an age of reason."

Excellent. "I agree," Ailsa said at once.

"Second, you put me to some trouble with this request. The young man I would take willingly, but I must ask the favor of my neighbors the finfolk to build the changeling – and the finfolk are not overfond of me. What will you give me in recompense?"

"I have already offered you my soul," Ailsa said.

That horrible burbling laugh again. "Ailsa of Quoy, your soul is damaged goods. With every small magic you practiced to lure the old Duke, to keep your beauty, to gain the ascendancy over the society of Din Eidyn, a bit of your soul was eaten away. What's left would give me no more than two good bites. You must offer me something else."

"What do you want? What can Nucklavee do with gold or silver?"

"Nothing," the monster agreed. "You must give me something I want." It paused. "Now shall we play a riddle-game until dawn, to see if you can guess what I desire? I think not. You bore me, Ailsa of Quoy, and you might never guess. All I want from you is a drop of your blood and a word from your lips."

"And what word might that be?"

"Give me the freedom of the shore." The great head fell forward, almost touching her. "Without mortal blood and mortal words, I cannot come on land beyond the highest mark of the tide."

"What would Nucklavee, lord of the ocean, want on the shore?" Ailsa fenced, playing for time.

"I want to stop those who offend me," the monster said. "The smoke of burning kelp disgusts me, and those who do it show their disrespect of the sea and its wealth. The bounty of the sea is not to be caged, and burnt, and shipped abroad as dry cakes for inland men to use in their manufactures. Give me the freedom of the shore, and I will strike the horses that draw the kelp carts with the mortasheen, and I will tear apart the kelp ovens, and I will kill those who persist in making that foul smoke."

Ailsa thought it over for a minute. There seemed nothing injurious to her in the proposal – as long as Nucklavee convined his activities to the islands and did not interfere with her own shore properties of Quoy. In fact, he might be doing her a favor; if the kelp industry of the isles was disrupted, she would be able to charge whatever price she liked for her own products.

"I will give you the freedom of this island," she offered.

"Agreed," said Nucklavee after a pause. "About here is my home. I care not what men do on the mainland. Now seal it in blood! Shall I bite thy finger?"

"No need," Ailsa said hastily. "There is a pin in my wrapper." She felt through the soft folds of fabric, found the pin by dint of accidentally pricking her finger, cried out in surprise, and showed the blood on the fabric to the monster.

"Blood must fall on land," Nucklavee insisted.

Ailsa pinched her finger till it was white and managed three drops of blood that fell in dark circles on the shining sand. "With this mortal blood I give Nucklavee the freedom to walk the island of Faarhafn as he will, in return for his keeping my son Erlend safe and well below the sea and making a changeling to show in Erlend's place until I am ready to exchange them back," she said in one hurried sentence, afraid that Nucklavee would somehow interrupt her before his part of the bargain was made.

"Nothing was said of keeping the young man safe and well," Nucklavee pointed out, "but let that pass. If I have a desire to taste of man-flesh, I shall choose from the kelp-burners, who deserve it. By this mortal blood and the freedom of the isle, I promise to keep the son of Ailsa of Quoy safe beneath the sea and to send her a changeling to show in his place." On the last words the sea-monster moved and thrashed horribly closer to shore, towards Erlend. "Send him to me," it commanded, "I would not be at the trouble of changing form only to walk three paces on the sand."

"And the changeling?" Ailsa demanded.

"I shall need the man as a model," Nucklavee pointed out, as reasonably as any earthly craftsman. "Send him to me, and as for you…" There was that burbling, squelching laugh again. "You may as well put on your clothes, Ailsa of Quoy. You will have some cold hours to wait, and there was no point in your stripping off; there is nothing under your clothes of interest to me. If there were, we might well have struck a different bargain."

CHAPTER SEVEN

As we watched the rise of the full moon after dinner, I felt the power that moves the sea rising and calling in my own blood, drawing me back to the water. At this time of the month I always returned to my people, no matter how recently I had visited; it was not a matter of courtesy but of need to swim free under the moon.

For politeness' sake I resisted the call while young Lord Gairloch was minded to sit out on the terrace and talk – and how the boy talked! He was filled with enthusiasm for the new farming practices introduced in Anglia by such gentlemen as Mr. Coke of Norfolk and Mr. Ellis of Gaddesden, and eager to apply them to his own large and sadly neglected estate as soon as he came of age this fall. I feigned an interest I could not feel in affairs of the land, which meant little enough to me now and would mean nothing at all after Steinnland died and I returned to my own people. It was not difficult; all Gairloch wanted was someone to nod occasionally and make approving noises instead of complaining as his mother did over the loss of immediate income. I did wish that Iveroth had remained with us; he seemed to like talking about land matters, and with him to entertain Gairloch, I could with civility have retired much earlier.

Finally, when the moon sailed high above the waves that battered at the red rocks of Faarhafn, I pretended to suppress a yawn. Gairloch instantly took the hint and proclaimed himself tired by the journey – as if anything ever tired out a boy of seventeen! – and ready to retire. He was really a very amiable young man, though something of a bore. In courtesy I had to light him to his chamber; but then, at last, my duties as a hostess were at an end.

Steinnland was long asleep; not that he would have objected to my nocturnal excursion in any case. He knew that dearly as I loved our quiet life together among his books, there were times when the sea called so strongly that I needed to return to my old home.

I left my embroidered slippers and my overdress in the room adjoining his where I slept, as a sign that I was gone down to the shore; whenever possible I was careful of the fine things he gave me, that they might not be spoiled by sand and salt water. With only my petticoat to cover me, I hastened down the winding stairs on bare feet, unbinding my tight braids as I went. A whole evening of playing hostess to land-folk had left an aching band of tension about my brow, and my feet were tired of shoes. I looked forward to a peaceful night disporting myself among my own sort, with nothing to conceal, no need to pretend interest, nothing but green floating peace among the colored coral towers of Finfolkaheem.

I should have known better.

The call in my blood was now so strong, stronger than I had felt it at any other moon, that I never looked behind or about me after I was free of the house. At the time I thought the sense of urgency was only because I had been forced to delay so long. At least, at this late hour I need not fear being observed by any passing land-folk; the fishers of Faarhafn and their families were all within doors and asleep. I could take the shortest and easiest path to the shore instead of climbing down the Vaardens.

It was sheer joy to let my petticoat free to fall into its natural folds behind me, to run unhampered in the moonlight, with my blood urging me towards the salt water. My bare feet seemed hardly to touch the turf that was green by sunlight, but now black in the moonlight. The winds sang in my ears and the sea rose upon the sands as if eager to meet me. I ran on into the shallow water and cast myself down upon a wave.

The shock of the cold water, the taste of salt in my mouth, the moment of change; I always forgot those, they were always an unwelcome surprise that lasted but a breath. Then I was moving freely beneath the water, my petticoat fully unfurled into the graceful tail that fanned back and forth to propel me faster than landfolk, with only their feet, could ever move. In the shallows I was skimming over the sand, my toes even grazed the bottom at intervals; then the land fell away and I was free in my own element, free of the bonds of gravity that pulled so hard on land, free of pretense and politeness, free to sport with the great whales and to skim through schools of silvery fish that wheeled and played delightfully around me.

I see that it is necessary to address certain misconceptions caused by landfolks' poor understanding of our kind. As soon as I mentioned my tail, you will have begun imagining one of those poor creatures of myth, half woman and half fish, unable to live or even to move out of the water. We finfolk are not so constructed; we have legs and feet like landfolk, but we also have our marvelous tails, that spring from our backs at waist height and spread out gloriously in the salt water, alive and strong and capable of propelling us, as I have said, faster than any landfolk could possibly run or swim. On land, a finwife wears her tail wrapped about her like a petticoat; in the freedom of the ocean, such constraint is not necessary. So, you see, it is entirely wrong to picture me as a being half crippled and confined to one element. We are more, not less, than landfolk, and we would not have it otherwise.

Usually the moment of changing and entering the water satisfied the full moon's call to my blood, but this time, to my disquiet, the urgent pull was still there. I had visited my family only recently, yet something drew me on towards Finfolkaheem. A herd of kelpies swam past and I longed to invite myself for a ride on one of them as I had done so often in childhood, but the call of Finfolkaheem was stronger still. Well, I could enjoy the bright coral edifices and pearl-lined passages of the city without necessarily staying to talk with anybody, could I not? I moved my tail more strongly and propelled myself towards the great deeps, enjoying the freedom of movement so much that I managed not to think about the problems that I was perfectly well aware of. The chances that I could swim through the winding passages of Finfolkaheem without encountering someone I knew were poor; for some reason there are fewer of us now than in the great centuries when the city was being grown from imported corals, and we all know one another well. The chances that those of my acquaintances whom I encountered would all be friends of mine, and not gossips of one of my aunts, were very small. In short, there was no possibility of my visiting Finfolkaheem without my family hearing of it, and if I did not stop at home I would have my ears well blistered by Aunt Maarit next time she caught up with me.

I knew all this and yet chose to ignore it, pretending I was as free as I felt, until I caught sight of the first lights of Finfolkaheem glimmering in the deeps.

You must understand that we do not build as land-folk do, with towers yearning ever upwards, as though in height were our security. If you have read tales of Finfolkaheem that describe it like a land castle of high towers and turrets, only made of coral instead of grey stone, then you know the teller was never really there. Why should we make towers upwards towards the surface of the sea, to catch fishers' nets and be broken again? Our building is all downwards and inwards, to capture the heat that rises from broken places at the bottom of the sea and nurture the bright corals we have brought from southern climes to be our architects.

If a land-man were brought to Finfolkaheem (and many claim to have been brought so, though all I ever met were lying) he would never recognize it from outside as a city; he would see only a shapeless mass of colors, with waving fans of living coral and schools of silvery fish distracting his eye from the entrances. His eyes would not be adapted to see the lights that shone so bright to me, and if he saw the great gate of the city he would think it a narrow, dark cave that he would not enter for fear of being trapped.

I was in luck, or so I thought; a little fingirl who was actually not one of my nieces sat in a sheltered cove by the nearest entrance, watching the school of young codfish that was her charge to herd.

"The Sea Mother be with you, Tahti," I said as I passed her.

"Sabira! Aren't you a landwife now?" The child looked shocked to see me, and not all that happy about it.

"I'm wed to a land-man, but see! My tail hasn't fallen off," I said, "and I hope I have not grown quite ugly overnight. Or are you trying to tell me I had best avoid mirrors from now on?"

She dropped her eyes and stammered that I was the most beautiful finwoman in the sea, or some such nonsense; some of the children make quite a romance out of my running away to marry Steinnland. My aunts Eliina and Seija are the beauties of the family; I'm just the awkward one.

Beyond the opening in the corals the seascape of Finfolkaheem spread out before me, lovely and beloved as no landscape could ever be. Our city had been many hundreds of years in the building; the memory keepers spoke of a time when it had been only a cold, dark refuge in the deeps of the northern sea, but even the oldest finfolk could not remember their oldest grandparents knowing anything but the warm and glowing city that opened out its branches to me. The minuscule organisms that bloomed on the corals and filled the seascape with pearly light had been brought here and cultivated in times long past; the magics that captured the warmth rising from vents at the bottom of the sea had been set in place when Din Eidyn was only a collection of stone huts where the river met the ocean. Centuries upon centuries we had cultivated the garden of Finfolkaheem, coaxing the corals to grow in shapes that would make homes and paths and meeting places for us. Now bright colors and fantastic forms lined paths that were themselves sprinkled with pearl dust; a turquoise helix surrounded by waving coral sea fans, a compound of gold and green sponge corals for a large family, the open spaces of the public squares bounded with gems and silver that we had won from the landmen in generations past.

But the homes were quiet, the passages strangely empty. And the calling in my blood was still strong, assuaged neither by salt sea water nor by homecoming; there was something else required of me. I wound my way downwards along a spiraling passage lined with the bright irregular coral walls of private homes and opening to the glowing deeps of the center, wondering what had happened to the normal bustle of the city. The only folk I passed were a finwife watching two unhappy finmen grinding pearls in querns, a punishment they'd doubtless earned for being drunk and unruly the night before; they looked as though they still had sore heads from their frolic. The finwife overseeing them knew me, though I could not put a name to her at first.

"On your way to the palace, Sabira? And not before time. You'd best make haste, not to annoy them further."

"I did not know anyone waited upon my coming."

"Ah, you've been on land too long." She inspected my tail suspiciously, as though expecting to see tatters in the fine web that spread out between the long muscles.

"I've done nothing that would change me," I said. I had not even had congress with Steinnland – nor had he ever suggested it – and I was certainly not carrying some landman's seed in my belly, to poison my blood and turn me into a landwoman.

"No, but you forget how to listen," she said. I remembered her name now: Dyrfinna. All the older finwives seemed to take the same disapproving tone when they spoke to me, as though I had betrayed the finfolk just because I liked to read Steinnland's books, but Dyrfinna was the most censorious of all. "You were summoned to the queen's presence at moonrise; have you become such a landwife that you can no longer hear her summons?"

At moonrise I had been seated on the balcony outside Steinnland's house, my long filmy tail wrapped about me like a gauzy, iridescent silken petticoat. Over that I had been covered with the layers of stuff landfolk like to put between themselves and the air, making polite conversation with the Duchess of Quoy and imagining that it was her presence that made me so eager to be away. I dropped my eyes. "You are right, Dyrfinna. I was too much caught up in business of the landfolk; I was not listening properly."

My admission of fault seemed to soften her. "Well, then, away with you, lass, and make your apologies when you reach the palace. She'll excuse much in you, seeing what you're to bring us."

This reminder of what the finfolk expected of me did nothing to ease my growing apprehension as I approached the palace. I had but seldom been in this part of Finfolkaheem, where the highest-born finfolk transacted the business of the realm. As a child I was never allowed to play so far from our home in the corals on the eastern side, and when I grew older I preferred the seashore and the dangerous, exciting business of spying on the landfolk to exploring my own city.

The vast open space around the palace, that had so overawed me when I glimpsed it as a child, seemed smaller now that I saw it as an adult. Or perhaps it seemed small only because it was so packed with finfolk. No wonder the outer parts of the city had been empty! It seemed to my astonished gaze that every finman and finwife in the realm had gathered here – and they were all looking at me.

I was not a child, to cry in terror and run away from their accusing glances. Moreover, I had done nothing wrong. I lifted my chin and waited. After a moment, the crowd parted and left a space of clear water, narrow but just wide enough for me to swim towards the gleaming golden palace.

As I swam down towards the palace, I realized that I had been wrong in assuming the entire population of Finfolkaheem was assembled outside the palace to greet me. The high nobles of the realm were nowhere to be seen; they must be within the palace.

As would Queen Loviisa, whom I had kept waiting.

At the moment, that troubled me less than the fact that my mother and her sisters were also not to be seen among the crowd outside the palace. Whatever the queen had to say to me, she would be courtly about it; I had far rather face an audience with her than be flayed by Aunt Maarit's cutting tongue.

As it turned out, I had the pleasure of experiencing both.

The palace gates were guarded by young, noble finmen whose seahorses were all but covered with their harness of woven silver studded with pearls and polished coral. The finmen themselves were equally overdecorated – and overproud. They acknowledged my humble presence only with lifted heads and a motion indicating that I might continue inside.

Landfolk, who have only the sun and candles for light, are accustomed to entering darkness when they cross the threshold of any building. My people, on the other hand, are as well able to cultivate the phosphorescent algae that light our world within doors as out; the interior of the palace glowed with the same silvery light that suffused all of Finfolkaheem. The only differences between inside and outside were subtle; the overarching roof of entwined corals, far above my head, that sheltered Queen Loviisa's court against the deepest storms; the fact that the sponge and tube corals had been persuaded to grow in patterns that supported soft cushions for the courtiers to rest upon; the network of fine silver chains that kept her favorite seahorses dancing in the water overhead, adding the sparkle of their jeweled harness to the gentle silver light.

My mother and her sisters reclined on cushions immediately to the right; the left side of the audience room was filled with nobles known to me only by sight. The queen on her throne of specially cultivated and polished mother-of-pearl was at the far end of the hall, placed where those on the cushions must look up to her. My father, lucky man, was probably peacefully working a puzzle somewhere, or even watching my nieces at their play. Even Maarit had long since given up trying to make him take a part in public affairs.

My mother leaned forward and would, I think, have spoken, but the queen hushed her. "You may speak of family matters later, Norin," she said. "Sabira is brought here to answer to me alone."

My mother and my aunt Eliina looked unhappy; Maarit looked grimly excited, as though expecting fireworks of an unpleasant sort.

I swam past them and upwards through the gently moving water until I was facing Loviisa on her throne. My loosened hair swirled about me on the slight currents caused by all these people and their moving and breathing, and I felt slightly distracted by the possibility that it would become entangled in the chained and jeweled seahorses kept captive just above us. But it would have been a mistake to drop lower in the water; it would have seemed like a gesture of submission.

In my head, as soon as this thought formed, I could hear Maarit's voice: a little submissiveness would not come amiss from you of all people! But she was not summoned before the queen; I was, and I would bear myself as I saw fit.

"My lady queen." I made the full sweeping *grande révérence* of our people, lowering my head until I made a full circle in the water and rose upright again, my tail spread humbly behind me; I wished to show decent self-respect, not impertinence. "You summoned me?"

"I did," said Loviisa coldly, "at the rising of the moon which now sails full in the sky."

I repeated the apology I had made to Dyrfinna, and she seemed slightly softened by them.

"Well, and it is no great matter, I suppose, since you do still come and do still acknowledge my authority."

"My queen," I said, "I have never acknowledged any other, and never will."

"Some say you feel greater loyalty to the landfolk than to our own people," Loviisa said in accusing tones.

"Some don't know what they are talking about." I turned my head slightly to give Aunt Maarit an accusing stare. "If I have chosen to make my habitation on land for a time, for reasons of my own, that does not mean I have turned my back on my own people."

"But you neglect our reasons and our needs, which should be as dear to you as your own," the queen said. "When will Steinnland say the words that return our summer home to us?"

"When he has settled his people elsewhere," I told her. "He too has responsibilities. He will not see the fishermen and the other landfolk who look to him drowned when we take Faarhafn back into our care."

"And how long will that take?" demanded a bejeweled young finman who lounged on cushions set just below the queen's thrown, toying with the pearls bound into his long plaits of dark hair. I recognized him now; the royal prince Heiki, rumored to be wild and unkind of nature. "We have waited overlong already."

"Hush, Heiki," the queen said in an indulgent tone. "You are here to listen and learn, not yet to speak in council." She looked at me again, piercing me with her pearl-bright eyes. "Yet my son speaks truth. Sabira, we need our summer home again. Though we are people of the sea, we are also earth's children, and both landfolk and finfolk are born under the same sun. Without our island refuge to visit in summer, our race will eventually sicken and die. Already there are few of us compared to my great-grandmother's time. Have you not seen the empty habitations in Finfolkaheem? Do you not wonder why we are so proud of your mother's family, with seven sisters from one marriage? And yet all seven have as yet given us but five children. Without the summer sun we grow ill, we do not make enough children, our race slowly dies."

"My lady, I – I was not aware that our need was so great," I stammered in surprise. "I knew that Faarhafn had been ours in the distant past, but not that any great matter hung upon its return."

"I too am surprised," she said, now looking past me at my mother and aunts, "that no member of your immediate family saw fit to inform you of these facts."

"Sabira was taught all that a pure, innocent fingirl needs to know," Maarit said angrily. "Is it proper to speak to her of breeding and childbearing?"

"She's a married woman now, by the laws of the landmen," Loviisa pointed out.

"And still as pure as the day she was born! Look at her tail!" Maarit darted forward and lifted my tail by the tips of the fins, spreading it out as wide as her arms could reach and turning it from side to side for all to see. "It is as fair and bright as ever, and perfectly firmly attached!" She proved the last point by a vicious yank I had not been expecting, and I cried out before I could stop myself. Young Heiki dropped his pearl-bound plaits and laughed loudly and most rudely at my discomfiture.

"Maarit, Sabira, stop your clowning and settle down," Loviisa said, most unfairly; _I_ had done nothing. "We are not here to evaluate Sabira's purity; that is her family's concern and not something to be discussed in public. Though I am glad to see, my girl," she added with a regal nod to me, "that you have not succumbed to the blandishments of the landmen so far as to lose your fin-nature."

She had, of course, never met Steinnland. "Blandishment" was not a word one associated with the March-Lord of Steinnland and the Isles.

"The March-Lord grows old," said a counselor whose name I could not recall.

"By the laws of the landfolk, upon his death our holy isle and all his other lands will pass to the possession of his next male relative," said another dour-visaged, richly decorated finman standing just behind the queen.

"Who will that be, Sabira?" Loviisa demanded.

"I – am not exactly certain," I stammered. "There are no near relatives. I believe there is a cousin living abroad, in Venezia – no, in the Borghesan service."

Loviisa leaned forward on her throne. Her long, heavy plaits swung forward to frame her face. They had been so wrapped about with pearls and jewels that her golden hair was hardly visible; they might have been extensions of her bejeweled crown. "Sabira, this cousin, whoever he may be, must not inherit our island. You must see to it that Steinnland says the words of renunciation before he dies."

"My lord is hardly on his death-bed," I said, "and he has a care for his people of the land, just as you care for our folk of the sea. He will see them settled on his mainland estates first; he has just received papers from Mr. Tulloch, his advocat in Din Eidyn, that will enable him to arrange all as it should be before we can take possession of our island." I was not being quite truthful here, for Steinnland had not discussed the parcel brought him by Iveroth. We had not had time before the household was turned upside down to prepare for the Duchess' arrival. But I knew that the papers were from Steinnland's man of affairs in Din Eidyn, and I knew his plans to resettle the Faarhafn tenants elsewhere with good compensation, and what else could the parcel have concerned?

Loviisa pushed the heavy plaits back from her face. It was a mistake; without the jeweled frame, one saw the narrowness of the face and the sharpness of the jaw. I thought of those great fish of prey that glide silently through the waters, looking for what unsuspecting creatures they may snap up and devour. "Laws, advocats, papers - this is all nonsense!" she declared. "What do finfolk care for such matters? Faarhafn is ours by right, and you talk of laws and inheritance among the landfolk!" She glanced from one to another of the counselors who had brought up the matter. I was glad those sharp eyes and pointed jaw were not aimed solely at me.

"My lady, landsmen's laws have governed the possession of Faarhafn these four hundred years, ever since Steinnland's ancestor tricked Queen Sanelma in their game of riddles," the dour-faced finman said.

"And it is time they paid for their cheating ways!" Queen Loviisa announced. "All that is needed – all that has been needed this long while since Sabira caught Steinnland's fancy – is for her to trick him into saying the words of renunciation, as his ancestor tricked Sanelma of cursed memory! Cause him to say the words, child, and Faarhafn will be ours again, to sink into the sea when we will and to rise under the summer sun again when we will have it so."

"And Steinnland will drown," I said in a small voice that could hardly be heard under the acclaiming shouts of those all around me.

Loviisa heard me, though. "And you place this landman's life above that of a whole people?"

I could not answer that. Instead I said, "And all the landfolk living on the island will drown."

"They have no right to be there in the first place."

"And anyone who just happens to be innocently visiting at the time will drown." But it was not Ailsa and Gairloch I thought of; it was the dark-browed face of that annoying man, Iveroth, silenced forever, his mouth bubbling out useless air under the salt sea.

"It would seem," said the queen, ominously calm now, "that Sabira places the lives of a few landfolk above the welfare of her own people. What are you now, Sabira? Finwife or landwife? Your family made great claims for your purity of body, but it seems that your mind has already been infected by the land. You have dallied long enough; it's time and past time for you to choose. Your people or theirs – which has your loyalty?"

It was an unnecessary, stupid demand she made on me. I tried once more to explain. "My queen, Steinnland's desires are reasonable. He wishes to see his tenants live, not drown, and he is even now making arrangements to have them resettled on his mainland estates. He wishes to spend his last years in the house that he and his ancestors built on Faarhafn, on the island that he loves as much as we do, and he has promised me that when his health fails we will take the last ferry for the mainland and on departure he will say the words that restore Faarhafn to our people."

"We have waited long enough!" growled young Heiki. "Make him restore our island now!"

"Now! Now!" repeated the throng about the throne. My aunt Maarit's voice was as shrill as any; but I saw Norin, my mother, biting her lips. She alone, of them all, understood the cleft stick in which I had been placed.

"Steinnland chooses a manner of reparation in which people will live. You choose one in which they will die unnecessarily."

"Only landfolk," said Heiki. "Since when does that matter?"

"I have studied Natural Philosophy," I said, "and it teaches that all men, finfolk and landfolk alike, have an equal right to life." Actually Mr. Douleur had not mentioned finfolk, being no doubt unaware of our existence, but I am sure he would have said this had he known about us. "I am not on the side of finfolk or of landfolk, but of Reason and the Rights of Man. I will not trick Steinnland, even if I could. We will have Faarhafn back soon enough without causing unnecessary death and suffering."

"Unnecessary!" Loviisa repeated, her lips curled. "So you weigh the slow death of our people, the babes unborn for want of summer light, the barren families, as nothing against the drowning of a few peasants of the land?"

The throng of nobles roared.

"Both matter," I tried to say against the shouts that all but overwhelmed me. And had they only explained this problem to me earlier, some of those finbabes might have been born alive and healthy. Steinnland could easily have divided the isle and set apart some of the uncultivable land for our people to visit when they felt the need of the sun. It was their ridiculous prudery in not speaking of such matters to an unwed girl – well, essentially unwed – that was to blame for the delay.

Little chance had I to explain this or anything else requiring more than a single shouted word. The anger of the nobles raised a boiling turbulence all around them that spilled out of the throne room in racing currents. I was swept out in one of those currents, unable to do more than use my tail to steer myself through passages and out of the way of coral outcroppings, and even so I collected several bruises and scrapes on my way out of Finfolkaheem. Nor did the water cease buffeting me even then. The queen in her wrath must have called upon Teran to raise a summer storm; I was flung this way and that at the will of the current, quite unable to make my way back to the island, until a twisting funnel of waters hurled me into the midst of the kelpie herd I had seen playing near the shore.

"Hold onto my mane, daughter of the sea," snorted the kelpie I had just thumped into, "and we'll soon have you out of this." I mounted him thankfully, grasping his sides with my legs and arms while my tail streamed out behind. His great finned legs, so much stronger than my tail, struck out and freed us from the walls of the undersea whirlpool. One wave after another buffeted us as we moved towards the shore, but my friend was strong enough to override them all. Finally his fins retracted as he felt the sand of the cove under his hooves. He stepped delicately through the angry surf until only a few inches of water covered his hooves. I slid off and touched his long head with my fingers.

"Do not I know you of old?" The kelpies, being shape-changers, are difficult to recognize, but something in the feel of this one under me reminded me of my childhood games with the wild horses of the sea. "Are you not my old friend Meldun?"

"So you have not forgotten us entirely," said the kelpie. "You are in my debt now, Norin's daughter." He took two more steps up the slanting beach, so that his hooves were entirely out of the water, and changed form. I looked away; the prohibitions of the landfolk had had some effect upon my habits.

"Then, Meldun, I will be doubly indebted to you if you will return to your water-form. Any landfolk who saw us just now would think me to be conversing with a naked man, and that would be a shocking thing in their world."

"But a naked horse — or kelpie - is no great matter?" inquired Meldun, returning to water-horse form and shaking his webbed mane so as to spatter me with sea spray. "I will never understand these landfolk."

"Nor I," I acknowledged, refraining from adding that right now I felt even less understanding of my own people. "But you had best return to the deeps in any case, Meldun, before the storm rises out of all control."

Even as I spoke, the waves breaking on the shore had risen higher and were falling on the sand with an angry roar.

"And you to the high cliffs, land-fin-lady," Meldun said, "unless you will trust yourself with me to ride out the storm."

"I have duties on land," I said with some regret, wrapping my tail about me like a petticoat again. When I was a child, nothing had pleased me more than to beg a ride on the back of a kelpie during one of Teran's great storms, to feel the strength of the kelpie's wide-finned legs and muscular body braced against the currents or, suddenly, diving into one and letting it carry us again at fantastic speed over the coral castles and sand bars below. Now, though, I knew something of the devastation these storms could wreak on land. As Lady Steinnland I would have to be on hand in the morning to repair whatever damage my enraged kinfolk had wrought.

CHAPTER EIGHT

Breakfast the following morning was one of the few occasions on which I regretted that we did not follow the fashionable custom mentioned in several of my favorite novels, in which each member of the household took a cup of chocolate and a few morsels (such as one of Antoine's excellent croissants) in his or her bedchamber, *en negligée*, and put off facing the world until some later hour. Of course, it appeared that in this fashionable world breakfast was not served until some time after noon, and I would have been starving by then, so perhaps it was not such a desirable custom in general.

On this particular morning, however, I felt as though I could easily have slept until noon, and I could certainly have dispensed with Iveroth's blackavised countenance glowering at me over the chocolate and croissants (Antoine's contribution) and oat porridge (prepared at Steinnland's insistence; only his loyalty to Steinnland sustained Antoine through the daily ordeal of preparing such a barbarous food.)

Steinnland and I were in the comfortable habit of bringing a book apiece to the breakfast table and reading and sipping chocolate until we felt equal to acknowledging the fact that another morning was actually in progress. Naturally courtesy towards our guests prevented our continuing this custom. There might have been some hope that Iveroth would select a breakfast book, but none at all that the Duchess of Quoy would follow suit.

It seemed, however, that the Duchess and her son had not chosen to put in an appearance this morning. Assuming – or rather, hoping – that she kept city customs even in the country, I requested that Antoine take a tray of chocolate and croissants to her room, and something more substantial – porridge, perhaps, and a rasher of bacon – to Gairloch's.

After a few minutes of nibbling on a croissant and throwing out conversational openings to which Iveroth responded only with a black-browed glower and as short an answer as was consistent with the demands of minimal courtesy, I began actually to regret the Duchess' absence; she at least could have been counted on to fill the air with a stream of self-centered chatter. My lord was even more abstracted than he usually was in the mornings, so the burden of maintaining polite conversation fell upon Iveroth and me. I was still tired and distraught from the previous night's scene and the demands of my people, and Iveroth, whatever his excuse might be, was certainly not keeping up his share of the conversation. I was positively grateful for a clattering on the outside stairs which turned out to be Inga's Androw of Neip, one of the crofters, requesting help of Steinnland.

It seemed that my people had accidentally done the landfolk of Faarhafn a favor; the storm their fury had raised the previous night had cast an unprecedented quantity of kelp upon the shore, and fishing and all other work was at a halt while both men and women struggled to get this bounty above the high-tide mark before the turn of the tide. They were accustomed to carry the kelp in creels that one strong young woman could lift and carry on her back, but so much had been deposited by the storm that there was no hope of saving it all by these methods. The two or three farms nearest the shore had supplied carts, and Androw hoped that Steinnland could contribute more carts to the project.

"Sabira, can we help?" my lord asked plaintively. He was not in the habit of paying attention to such practical details. Neither was I, to be honest, but clearly someone had to. My lord's factor Hendrie was on the mainland as usual. Fortunately the recent exercise of scouring the entire house in preparation for the Duchess' visit had left me aware of exactly how much rubbish was piled into unused rooms and store-rooms.

"There are several carts stored in the undercroft," I said, "not in very good condition, but you should be able to patch them up to serve your purpose,

Androw. And...." I hesitated, fearing this might be a sore subject, but then concluded Steinnland had no reason to be embarrassed over the follies of his forbears. "There is always the Coach of State."

"That gilded monstrosity! Why have we not broken it up for firewood long since?" Steinnland asked with a cheerful laugh that reassured me. I was not sure which of his ancestors had been so optimistic as to cause an entire coach to be taken apart, brought over the Strait in pieces, and reassembled on the island. Whichever March-Lord it had been, his attention span had not been equal to the task of building roads suitable for his coach – even such short roads as were possible on Faarhafn - and so the thing had sat gathering dust and salt in an outbuilding for who knows how many generations.

"No longer gilded, but perfectly serviceable for the purpose, "I said, "if you do not mind having it filled with wet seaweed, my lord. The upholstery – "

"- has probably rotted away long since," Steinnland interrupted me. "If there's a practical use for the thing, by all means let Androw take it away. As for horses... that may be more difficult."

I could think of a solution to this problem, but it was one I was reluctant to discuss before Iveroth. Fortunately, the appearance of the Duchess at that moment distracted all the men present from their practical difficulties.

She was dressed and painted as carefully as ever, her impractical shoes clicked on the polished wooden floor with the same brisk assurance, but her hair showed the effects of a night in a strange bed and a morning without the ministrations of a maid; and she looked older under the paint, almost haggard with weariness or – could it be worry?

"Give you good morning, Steinnland, Iveroth," she said, and then after a pause almost too slight to notice, "Lady Steinnland." She inclined her head fully a quarter of an inch in my direction before turning her blue eyes back to the genetlemen. "Steinnland, I must crave your pardon for so unceremonious a departure. My dear Erlend is ill and I must take him back to Din Eidyn at once."

"Ill? How? What troubles him?" Steinnland asked.

"If he is ill," I said reluctantly, "ought he to be moved?" It would be perfectly all right with me if Ailsa of Quoy returned to Din Eidyn this morning, but not if the price was dragging a sick boy across the De'il's Strait and down the rough coaching road south. But then, Lord Gairloch had been perfectly well last night; how sick could he really be now? What kind of illness came on so suddenly and without warning?

Her Grace made a dismissive gesture that seemed to erase me and my question from the breakfast table. "I wish him to be seen by our own physician in Din Eidyn as soon as possible. He knows Erlend's constitution and how best to treat him."

"I fear that may not be possible until the turn of the tide," Steinnland said with regret, and explained to her that all the island's able-bodied men, women and horses would be occupied in dragging kelp up the beach to take advantage of the coincidence of a low tide and a midnight storm that had covered the shores with seaweed from the deep. He offered to take a look at the boy himself, but Ailsa refused the offer.

"He has taken these turns before," she said. "What he needs is absolute rest and quiet, and skilled care from Dr. Rangage, who understands his case."

"At least let Lady Steinnland see if anything can be done to make him – and you – more comfortable while you wait."

"Not for my life!" the Duchess snapped, and then relented to make a sort of explanation. "When he is in this sad condition, the company of women – apart from myself, of course – is most distressing to him. With your permission, my lord, I will remain quietly in his room and care for him myself until you are able to arrange carriers for my chair and a boat for the mainland. I do hope it will not take long." And she was gone again, with a click of red shoes and a swish of petticoats, leaving the three of us temporarily united in staring at the doorway where she had appeared.

"And just how much of that do we believe?" Iveroth eventually asked, in a low-pitched voice that could not have reached beyond the breakfast room.

"It seems strange," Steinnland agreed. "He was well enough last night. Now he requires absolute solitude and quiet – unless I can persuade two of the crofters to carry Ailsa's chair to the harbor, in which case I presume she will declare him well enough to walk behind. Or do you think she means to put him in the chair and walk herself?"

"That seems most unlikely," Iveroth agreed.

"Reluctant as I am to disregard a guest's expressed wishes," Steinnland said slowly, "Gairloch also is my guest, and if he has fallen ill while visiting Faarhafn, I should visit him and see what I can do. Also, if he is truly too ill to travel, we will have to make sure that no carriers are available to Ailsa until the boy is stronger. Sabira, could you...." He paused. "No. Iveroth, you have the best chance of distracting her Grace; could you draw her away from the boy's room for a time, while I see what's what? Sabira, my dear, I fear I must ask you to show Androw the carts we have available, and to do what you can about allocating the island's few horses equitably. Iveroth will come and help you as soon as he can."

Until that moment, I think we had all three forgotten that Androw was still in the room, shifting from one foot to the other and twisting his hands while he waited for the gentry to finish discussing their affairs and turn to solving his problems.

"If you ask me," Androw said as he followed me to the undercroft where the old carts were stored, "he's a changeling."

"Who?"

"That there boy of the old Duchess's. Seen him a-looking out of window as I come up, all yearning for the sea, and his face that twisted I'd hardly have known him. Could be that something snuck in under cover of the storm last night and took the real one to live under the sea, leaving some poor sick-looking imitation in his place. But you'd know more about that than I would, my lady, begging your pardon."

"I know no more about Lord Gairloch's illness than you do," I said with perfect truth. I didn't know anything but what the Duchess had said just now. Well, I knew that most of the fin court had been too occupied with scolding me to bother with making changelings, at least for the first part of the night; and I knew that they would hardly have wanted a grown man who could not adapt to our life when there were healthy babes on the island; but neither of these facts was something I wished to discuss with Androw. "And we have other problems to solve just now." The old carts were indeed a sorry sight, all of them missing planks and one of them lacking an entire wheel.

"And even do we get them in working order, where are we to get extra horses to pull them?" Androw said as if to himself while we walked around the undercroft. There was certainly no spare wheel hidden anywhere in the barren stone cellar.

"Does not Effie Scrabster's man do some carpentry in the winters?"

"Yes, but—"

"There is no point in worrying about anything else until we have made the coach and carts usable," I cut him off. "Do you go down to the shore and tell Scrabster he must come up and mend the carts, and I will concern myself with the other problems." I gave one last doubtful look at the rickety piles of lumber. "At the very least, he should be able to take the worst cart apart and use its pieces to patch the others. Go on now, there's no time to waste before the tide turns!"

***

Distracting Ailsa of Quoy from her son's illness was easier than Iveroth had expected; easier, he thought, than it should have been if the boy was really so ill as to require urgent removal to Din Eidyn. A tap on the door; she slipped through without properly opening it, and whispered that Gairloch was asleep and not to be disturbed. A suspicious corner of Iveroth's mind whispered that he had not actually seen Lord Gairloch since the previous night. But that suspicion made no sense. Even if Ailsa were selfish enough to kill her own son, doing so would not be in her interests; the property would pass in the male line to the old Duke's younger brother Laxfurd. Gairloch was probably fond enough of his mama to make her a generous allowance once he came to control his inheritance; Laxfurd, who still referred to Ailsa as "the goose-girl," would allow her as little as propriety required. No, it was in Ailsa's interest to keep Gairloch alive, and her concern for his health was probably not assumed.

This line of reasoning helped him to feel sorry for the haggard woman in the crumpled, once-stylish dress who stood outside her son's chamber. Much as he might dislike her personally, right now she was a woman in distress, and all Iveroth's inclinations and training went to alleviate that distress in whatever small ways he could manage. He persuaded her to take a turn on the terraces with him, pointing out that Gairloch would not be helped by her allowing herself to fall ill in the close air of a sickroom. Indeed, someone from the village—

But this suggestion Ailsa refused at once. No one but herself must nurse Erlend, she insisted. She did not know the villagers; they seemed a sly lot to her, and ignorant besides; she could not bear the thought of leaving him in the care of some stranger.

Steinnland was neither sly, nor ignorant, nor a stranger; still, Iveroth judged it would be tactless to mention that their host meant to examine Lord Gairloch himself while they walked on the terrace.

The steps from one section of terrace to the next were rough and uneven, part of the endless patching and building-on that Steinnland's rambling house had endured for generations; Iveroth offered his arm and Ailsa took it, and this enabled him to guide her gently halfway around the house before he found his store of light chatter about the social life of the capital running out. Surely Steinnland had had enough time by now to slip in and determine what ailed young Gairloch? Perhaps another few minutes….

Iveroth praised the view over the village and the sloping shore. Ailsa said pettishly that she had had enough grand views on the previous evening to last her a lifetime, but then she cheered up as the changing colors of the strand made her think of a new way to use the current fashion of a skirt cut high and drawn back to show the underlying petticoats. She would begin with a sea green overskirt in *soie de Londres*, then a sandy beige just lightly overdyed with green, then fine white lace *alla Borghese* worked to imitate the rounded shapes of the pebbles. Would not such a costume be vastly becoming?

Years in Din Eidyn society had equipped Iveroth with the ability to praise a woman's dress – or even her imaginary dress – in flattering detail while his brain was occupied with other matters. He did so now, commenting on how the sea-green would set off the whiteness of her skin – "the true mark of the patrician, if I dare say so, that perfect, ivory skin," he said, outrageously, but knowing Ailsa would always be pleased by a line of conversation that pretended her birth was superior to that of the common people. He followed with other ready-made compliments while his eyes followed quite a different story; the knot of people and horses at the edge of the village, the men attempting to harness the horses, and finally the confusion as one wild, sleek black beast reared up and shook off all restraint except for a slim girl with gold braids who kept hold of its mane.

"Madness, to send a girl to such a task!" he exclaimed involuntarily. "Your Grace, will you excuse me? My help is needed down there." And he left the Duchess pouting on the lowest terrace while he ran to Lady Steinnland's aid.

By the time he got there, the momentary confusion had subsided; he put his hand to the head of the restless horse only to hear Lady Steinnland say crossly, "I have everything quite under control, thank you very much."

"It did not look like it from the house," Iveroth said.

She turned her head to give him a cool glance from those cold green eyes, one hand still mechanically caressing the horse's neck. "Many things, my lord, look different from a distance." Then her attention was back among the villagers. "Scrabster, I told you, the black ones are only to be harnessed by me. They are not accustomed to be used as cart-horses, but they will cooperate if used rightly. And that does not include putting a bit and bridle on any one of them!"

The black, sleek horses moved to group themselves behind Lady Steinnland, staring at the villagers and their cart-horses as if looking at an alien species.

"I had not realized there were so many horses on the island," Iveroth said.

"I... asked some of my... our... friends for help," said Lady Steinnland, which did not quite answer his implied question. She looked at the flustered villagers, then back at Iveroth. "If you will just keep these people from interfering, I shall have Steinnland's carts harnessed in no time at all." Assuming his consent, she moved among the black horses, whispering in their ears and passing soothing hands down their flanks, until they moved into positions that allowed her to harness them to the carts. As she had insisted, no bits or bridles were used.

"How do you plan to direct them?" Iveroth asked.

"They are.... used to voice commands."

But not, evidently, to the short words the villagers shouted out to get their own horses moving. Lady Steinnland spoke to the black horses herself, in a language that sounded like water splashing over stone. When the heavy coach settled into a rut and refused to move, her urgings sounded more like the waves crashing against land, and from somewhere the six black horses harnessed to the coach found the strength to haul it out of the rut and on down onto the shingle beach.

As the horses moved, a woman hurried towards them from one of the fishing huts, a youngish wife with black curls bouncing under her kerchief and bright black eyes that spared a measuring look at Iveroth even in her obvious distress. "My lady, would you look at our Sinnie? She's too poorly to get up this morning. I reckon she needs one of your charms."

Lady Steinnland seemed to suppress a sigh. "One moment, Bessie. I must speak to the horses first." She moved among the black horses, placing a caressing hand on the neck of one and stroking the nose of another, murmuring in their ears and pointing at Iveroth; almost as if she were telling them to take him for their master.

"They will do your will now – I think," she said, rejoining him, "but you must explain politely what is wanted, and not shout at them as the villagers do to their carthorses. Can you manage that, do you think?"

"I have," said Iveroth, "had some little experience with horses before."

The corners of Lady Steinnland's mouth lifted slightly. "But not, I think, with this particular breed."

CHAPTER NINE

Strange it was indeed, to be creeping about his own home like a thief in the night, and it broad daylight, thought Steinnland as he waited in the shadows for Iveroth to coax Ailsa out of her watch over Gairloch. He was surprised how quickly Iveroth managed it; Ailsa had been so nearly plausible at the breakfast table, and so pale and hagged beneath her expertly applied paint, that he had almost believed her really concerned for the boy, whatever other parts of her scrambled tale were lies. And strange it was again to feel like an intruder when, after the tap of Ailsa's heels had died away, he knocked lightly and then more strongly upon the door of Gairloch's guest chamber.

No answer came from within, and Steinnland felt worse than ever as he quietly opened the door. It would serve him right if he startled a sleeping, feverish boy into worse illness, and exposed himself – Kosta Greenmark, March-Lord of Steinnland and the Isles – as a sneaking intruder on his own guests.

The mental recitation of his title reminded him of the arrangements he had made for Sabira's sake, and the papers Iveroth had brought from Tulloch in Din Eidyn, now signed and witnessed, sealed and safe in their leather case; papers that would keep Sabira safe in case of any unforeseen accident to him. At least that one thing had been done right, long and costly though the task had been. Remembering it gave him strength to go on and break the laws of hospitality.

At first he thought the door swung open on an empty room. Gairloch's bed was smooth as it had been when Sabira saw it made up for him the day before; no one slept there, nor had since the Duchess' arrival. He saw nothing at all except a tumble of leather bags and cast-off clothing in the corner below the one narrow window that overlooked the sea.

Then the pile of clothes stirred, and Kosta looked into a face out of the nightmare visions of his scrying-glass: the features of his old friend Donal of Quoy – or of his son Erlend, Lord Gairloch – in a face that seemed melted and run like the wax of a burnt-out candle, a face and form that shaped themselves as he entered and rose from their huddle beneath the window, babbling like an idiot.

"Gairloch?" But it was not, could not be the strong young man who had dined with him last night.

"What are you, and whence come you?" Kosta demanded, while his head whirled. He knew the answer already, knew it from Sabira's artless chatter in their long evenings together, knew it from the island tales that were older than his ancestors, knew it from the rising sickness in his blood and the smell of salt and seaweed in the close chamber. "*Far du fae?*" he demanded in the island dialect.

"Sa-sa-sa-sa," babbled the idiot thing, waving at the window. "Sa-sa-sa-sa?" it pleaded.

It touched Kosta's hand, its fingers clinging like wet kelp flung up by the tide, and it would have drawn him to the window; but the March-Lord was incapable of movement. The horror of that touch sent the whirling darkness in his head into a frenzy that drummed in his ears and darkened his eyes.

When he fell to the floor, he was beyond knowing the fall or feeling the bruises.

***

It seemed to Iveroth that the sun stood still that morning, as though Nature had decided to help the fisherfolk of Faarhafn in their struggle to collect as much as possible of the bounty that she had thrown in their way. Cartload after cartload of seaweed creaked up the shingle to be sorted by the women and children into ware and tangle and stored safely beyond the reach of high tide. Once satisfied that the black horses Lady Steinnland had left in his care knew their business and would wait for him to load a cart before they set off on their patient weary way uphill, Iveroth took his part in the kelping. He'd seen enough of how the men worked in the surf to think it an easy task requiring more muscle than brain.

"Can you lend me a rake?" he called out. The nearest man stared at him as if he'd spoken in some foreign tongue.

"The gentleman is meaning a pick, Wullie," said his neighbor patiently. "Lend him thy wife's, and let the auld woman go to the sorting."

"Not too auld to enjoy working next to a fine gentleman," the woman working beside Wullie said, "better let Wullie go to the sorting, for he's no hand wi' the pick at all, and I'll drag kelp beside the gentleman!" She hoisted her skirts, already kilted up, to give Iveroth a flash of white legs that were still firm and shapely in contrast to her weather-beaten face, then winked at him and handed over her man's rake.

It was exhilarating at first to charge into the foaming surf, trying to catch the seaweed before the waves could wash it away. And Iveroth quickly discovered that it was not as simple as it seemed. At first his rake came back from the surf almost as empty as it had gone in. He glanced at his neighbors, all of whom seemed to be holding their faces very still and pointedly not laughing at him; watched young Androw dash into the surf and give a curious twist to his rake that brought it back loaded with kelp; saw, with brief glances to left and right, that nearly every man had some dexterous way of handling his tools that improved the chances of filling a rake with seaweed. He imitated them as best he could and by the time the carts were brought round for their second loading, fancied that he was doing at least as well as the women among them.

But it was a welcome break in routine to guide the horses lent by Lady Steinnland's mysterious 'friend' back up the shore, to tilt the carts and dump out their loads, to exchange a laughing word with the women who were already busy sorting the weed and to take the offered sip of their bitter, island-brewed ale.

And then the carts had to be filled for a third time, and men took off their shirts because the work kept them more than warm enough under the midsummer sun; a fourth trip with the carts, and Iveroth became more aware of aching muscles and blistered hands than of the slow creep of the tide. The shout to leave off took him by surprise; he stood, unconsciously rubbing the small of his back, and saw that the pebble beach on which he had been working was all but covered by the water.

"High tide," Androw said unnecessarily. "There'll be no more kelping the day." He surveyed Iveroth's shirtless, sweating form and the dark breeches that were now molded to his person by sea water and sweat. "Not bad work, for a mainlander," he conceded. "When the women do klokk the tangles, there'll be a kossel or two of thy crooking. Will that be lord's share, then?"

"Divide it among yourselves," said a cool clear voice behind Iveroth. He started and looked for his shirt, but it was no longer on the coach where he had thrown it.

"My woman took it for washing," said Wullie, divining his search. "Have it back to you tomorrow, dry an' all."

"Ah – convey my thanks to your wife," Iveroth said, "and I must make my apologies to you, Lady Steinnland, for appearing before you in such a condition."

The cool green eyes surveyed him with about as much interest as if he had been a man-high pile of ware or tangle. "If I could not bear the sight of shirtless men, I would not come to the shore at kelping time," she said, and turned away from him, starting back to the house on the cliffs.

It was evidently time for a general rest and celebration of the morning's work; the fisherfolk were gathering in groups of two and three families around the heaped seaweed, enjoying bread and cheese and the pale bitter ale of the islands. Iveroth looked for the horses that had been hitched to Steinnland's carts, blinked, rubbed his eyes, and looked again.

The harness trailed on the ground; the horses had vanished as if they had never been there.

He hurried to catch up with Lady Steinnland on the path. "How did you do that?"

"Do what?"

He waved back towards the carts. "The horses – the carts – "

Lady Steinnland looked backwards. "Oh. I suppose my friend has taken the horses back where they belong."

"Very quiet and stealthy, this 'friend' of yours," Iveroth said.

"Or else you were too busy looking up Wullie's Elisetter's skirts to notice what was happening," Lady Steinnland suggested with a smile. "She was doing her best to give you a good look, every time you stopped for ale."

"And as a gentleman, I could scarcely be so uncivil as to pretend it was not worth the looking," Iveroth said. This was dangerous ground. He searched for safer, and found it. "How is the child?"

A faint frown marked two lines between Lady Steinnland's brows. "I think there is nothing wrong with her but having eaten something that did not agree with her," she said. "The trouble is that Bessie's Sinnie will eat nothing that comes from the sea; no fish, no lobster, not even dulse broth."

"Surely that's not enough to make her ill?"

"It makes her weak and sickly," Lady Steinnland said. "The food grown on this island is not enough, in itself, to nourish the children of men. Those who eat fish – which is most of them, I'm glad to say – do reasonably well, but occasionally there is one like Sinnie. I must ask my lord to have some bread and fruit from one of the other islands brought over for her."

It sounded quite mad to Iveroth. The turf on this island was as green, the crops as healthy, as one could expect so far north. But if the islanders had such a superstition, could the belief in itself make them ill? Or was it another convenient explanation, like the folk-tales of changelings, to explain the occasional child born without normal health and strength?

"Bessie keeps her kitchen and milk room as foul as any I've seen," Lady Steinnland went on, "so there is no great matter for surprise when one of the children has an upset stomach. I gave her – Bessie, I mean - a charm to cure her wranged milk."

"And will it work?"

Lady Steinnland's teeth flashed in a brief smile. "If she follows the instructions precisely as I gave them her, and cleans and boils all her utensils three times between saying the words, I daresay it will. I have noticed that milk does not sour so fast in a clean kitchen, and it's easier to churn butter, too, though I don't know exactly why."

"An acquaintance of mine in the Philosophical Society would claim that it is due to the presence of animals too tiny to see – he calls them 'animalcules' – which flourish in dirt and are killed by boiling water."

"And Bessie believes it is due to someone ill-wishing her and sending tiny, invisible demons to infest her churn and kettle – which demons will be killed by boiling water and certain words which I have given her to say. Difficult to choose, then between the theories, since in either case we cannot see our enemies."

"Ah, but we can – now," said Iveroth. "Have you heard of the improvements to the Majuloscope? There is a version now with corrected lenses – I do not pretend to understand the theory – but it is now possible to use two lenses to double the magnifying power without creating distracting rainbows of color."

"Achromatic lenses," Lady Steinnland said thoughtfully. "There was some mention of them in one of my lord's journals, but the optical theory is somewhat difficult to follow."

Thank God for that, thought Iveroth. He had no wish to be embarrassed by a peasant girl explaining something he himself had found extremely confusing. "Well, that does not matter – the point is that now anyone can see far more than even the best trained natural philosophers could make out before. Put a droplet of milk from Bessie's kitchen on a piece of glass, and look at it through the compound Majuloscope, and you shall see those very animalcules that my friend claims are the source of all disease and illness. Then look at a drop of boiled water, and you will see no animalcules."

"Oh, how I should like to try the experiment!" Lady Steinnland exclaimed with longing and delight. Then she frowned again. "But, you know, these 'animalcules' could be little demons, so nothing is proved thereby."

"If they are driven out by something as simple as boiling water, with none of your charms, then I would be inclined to think of them as something that is part of nature, rather than supernatural beings." Iveroth took a deep breath of the cool sea air and noticed, not for the first time, how curiously bright and clear all things seemed on Faarhafn. "Don't you see, this is how we make progress; one small step at a time, but using deduction and inference rather than old wives' tales and superstition."

"And do deduction and inference never lead you wrong, my lord?" Lady Steinnland enquired sweetly.

They were quite alone, midway between the village and Steinnland's rambling house; there would never be a better time to raise the matter of last night. Iveroth took a deep breath, then hesitated, half convinced that he was making the biggest mistake of his life. He could go away, he could tell himself that Steinnland's wandering wife was no business of his — but a man didn't stand by and see his friend betrayed and say nothing. "No," he said through a throat suddenly grown thick, "reason never leads us astray, but sometimes it does lead us to unpalatable conclusions."

"As when you decided, because I chose to spend some time alone at Hamarrvoe, that I must be betraying my lord? That was not a leading, my lord, but a leap to a conclusion wholly unjustified."

Gods, but she was quick on the attack. Iveroth felt as though he had been forced into a corner by a fencer of unsuspected strength and agility. There was nothing for it but to counterattack with all his own strength.

"The second time I saw you there," he said, "you were with a man. Do you dare deny that?"

"Second time – Are you dreaming? I have not returned to Hamarrvoe since our unpleasant meeting there."

"Did you think you had escaped the house unseen last night?"

There was a long silence. She would be assessing her options, Iveroth thought harshly, trying what lie would best fit this discovery.

"So," she said at last. "Do I take it that you followed me from the house last night? Without making yourself known? Lord Iveroth, you know that I am ignorant of the ways of fashionable society. Tell me, is this customary behavior among the fine gentlemen of Din Eidyn?"

"I might have been concerned for your safety," parried Iveroth.

"Concerned for my safety?" she repeated, fair brows raised. "On my own island? And you speaking never the word as you crept along behind me? I think, my lord, you were in rather more danger than I."

Damn the girl, she'd managed to wrong-foot him and change the subject. "Never mind all that," Iveroth said, "the point is that I did follow you to your destination."

She should at least have blushed, instead of looking coolly amused. "I very much doubt that. You could not have followed where I went last night, my lord. Reason and inference therefore suggest to me that you lost sight of me."

"It was a cloudy night," Iveroth said, "I had to manage with what glimpses the moonlight gave me."

"And somehow, I know not how, you convinced yourself that I had returned to Hamarrvoe."

"Devil take it," Iveroth snapped, "I saw you leave the house, and in the next moment when the moon shone clear I saw a female form about to descend the Vaardens. Not much room for doubt there!"

"I think, my lord, your inference is riddled with gaps. You recognized my face, no doubt? From a distance, in the moonlight, while I was clambering down those slippery steps?"

"Who else could it have been?"

"A question you might well have asked yourself earlier." The cool words sounded like ice just barely containing a volcanic lake. "I assume you followed the woman you saw on the Vaardens?"

"I followed you, yes."

"That remains to be seen. If necessary, I could take you a little way towards my actual destination last night – not far, just enough to convince you that you had not the ability to follow me there."

A man could drown in the green of those eyes, could imagine the braided hair loose and wet and cold, wrapped around his neck like seaweed.

A man could certainly feel well out of his depth. But he had seen what he had seen, and no woman's tricks should persuade him otherwise.

"And when I was far enough down to see into the cove of Hamarrvoe," Iveroth said, "I saw you with a man bending over you. Do you have the audacity to deny that?

She seemed not near as shaken as she should have been by now. "You recognized both my face and his, did you? Who was it, I wonder?"

"The friend who lent you his horses, I should not be surprised."

Lady Steinnland's face shook. For a moment he was afraid she was going to start crying on his shoulder; then he realized that she was, unforgivably, trying to suppress a laugh. "So you saw no faces, or you would be more specific in your accusations. If all you saw was two figures in the cove, how do you even know that one of them was a man?"

"Because he was wearing shirt and breeches, and he overtopped the woman by two heads...."

"Ah," said Lady Steinnland, almost gaily. "At last your friends Reason and Inference return to your aid, my lord. You stand what, six feet in your stockings? And I can look level into your eyes. You need only find the giant on Faarhafn who is near to seven feet tall, and you will have unmasked this secret lover of mine whom you are so determined to find."

Iveroth swallowed in dismay. The fisherfolk of Faarhafn were a small race, probably stunted by malnutrition and a hard life. If Lady Steinnland had a lover so much taller than she was, he would be one of the wonders of the islands....

"Or you could consider another possibility," Lady Steinnland added after he'd had a moment to think it over. "Perhaps I was not the only woman abroad last night. Perhaps her Grace of Quoy looked so hagged this morning because she, too, had a midnight rendezvous. I think you would not have to look far to find a man who stands taller than she does. Even you, my lord, would fit the description – oh, but I forget. You were having no secret meetings last night, were you? You were *honorably* skulking about in the dark, trying to uncover something to some poor woman's discredit, never mind whose."

Iveroth felt as though he had been neatly sliced into paper-thin sections, preserved in alcohol, and placed on glass for inspection under the Majuloscope. Also, his throat was so dry that he would have welcomed even a glass of the bitter island ale.

"Perhaps," he said, and then his throat dried up and closed again. He tried again. "It seems I may have been in error. I should be... most grateful... if you would not repeat my stupid mistake to Steinnland."

"No fear of that," said Lady Steinnland grimly. "I have but one more thing to communicate to you, my lord, after which I hope that whatever sense of decency you retain inspires you to cut short your visit to Faarhafn and return to Din Eidyn."

He saw the blow coming – she had no more science at fighting than any other female – and made no move to avoid the open hand that cracked against his cheek. It was, he reckoned, the least he had deserved of her.

Only, as he followed meekly behind her up the steps to the house, one thought remained to tease his brain.

Lady Steinnland *had* slipped out of the house last night. She might not have been the woman he had seen at Hamarrvoe, but she had as good as admitted that she had – what were her words – 'a midnight rendezvous.'

She was keeping secrets of some sort. Whether or not they involved a lover he was no longer sure, but this he did feel sure of: loyalty to Steinnland would force him to prolong his stay until he determined whether Lady Steinnland's secrets were any danger to his old friend.

CHAPTER TEN

What was it about Iverroth that made me feel always unsettled and edgy, so that I kept quarreling with him? Well, it was certainly not my fault this time; he had insulted me in the foulest terms – oh, all right, not in actual words, but in implication and thought. How dare the man accuse me of such things? As if I would even consider having congress with a landman, with their gross hairy bodies and heavy bones and rippling muscles and sweaty skin and –

Just because Iverroth had been walking beside me in a state of undress no true gentleman would have considered was no reason to quarrel even more with him. But I felt that I could not bear another moment's proximity to him. Especiallly after slapping him like that. The very air between us seemed lowering and heavy, crackling with sparks like a summer storm about to burst, impossibly, out of the cloudless sky. I ran ahead of him and up the steps into the shelter of my lord's house, where ancient timbers and pillars carved from sea-soaked driftwood and green-tinted, wavering glass panes all welcomed me home. "My lord?" I called as I came in. "My lord, all's been done that can be done. It's high tide and we can all rest at last."

The silence of the house was somehow as close and oppressive as the air outside, though in a different way; cold and quiet as one of the stone tombs where the islanders thought ghosts guarded long-hidden dragon's treasure. "My lord?" I called again, and the shadows within seemed to swallow up my voice so that it was only a thin, fearful cry, soon silenced.

Iveroth came quietly up behind me – oh, very quietly and carefully, as well he might! But I could smell the thick human sweaty odor of him. It did not belong in this house of the sea, and neither did he, and the sooner he was gone, the sooner my lord and I could resume our peaceful life as though nothing had ever disturbed us.

It seems odd, now, that I did not wonder where the Duchess of Quoy and Lord Gairloch were; only my lord's failure to answer disturbed me.

"He will be in his reading room at the top of the house," I told Iveroth, and began mounting the stairs. It was the obvious explanation for why he had not heard me – except that whenever I left the house during the day, my lord was somewhere within call when I returned, happy to see me again. I had come to expect that, though there was really no reason why he should put himself to the trouble of waiting for me if he wanted to go and read upstairs. No reason at all – unless Iveroth had put his nasty suspicions into my lord's mind?

No. That was impossible. He knew me better than that; he would have shown Iveroth the door if any such thing had been said. Still, my heart would not be at ease until I found him and saw the smiling welcome in his eyes, unchanged as ever. I fairly flew up the first flight and started on the narrower spiral of stairs leading to the library . Iveroth followed more slowly, and called to me from the landing.

"Sabira!"

Something in his voice made me terribly afraid. I stopped and turned with as much slow dignity as I could pretend to in my haste.

"Lady Steinnland to you, sir."

"My lady," he said, "there's something – I think you should come back – no, don't," he contradicted himself, "just wait right there for me."

"What's wrong?" That cold, reasonless fear clutched at my heart again. "Is it…" Something about Gairloch, of course; hadn't the Duchess said he was ill? How could I have forgotten? "Is Lord Gairloch worse?"

"Not he," said Iveroth, but he was no longer on the landing; his voice came oddly muffled, as though he had gone back along the hall leading to the bedchambers.

I found him at the open door of Gairloch's chamber, kneeling over a long form that wore my lord's customary coat of dark brown velvet with silver buttons. "Steinnland!" he was saying urgently. "Steinnland, can you hear me?"

My lord's silver hair was all in disarray, and his body seemed lifeless, but his eyes were bright and alive. Kneeling beside Iveroth, I took his head in my lap and smoothed back the long silver hair that he wore unfashionably knotted in a black-ribboned queue, and wiped away the smear of saliva on his cheek with a corner of my skirt. How he must hate to be found thus, all helpless and untidy!

"What did you do to him?" I demanded of Iveroth.

"Nothing. He was lying thus when I found him, and the chamber stripped bare."

I saw, without much caring, that this was true; Gairloch and his belongings were gone. I supposed the pretty Duchess his mother was also departed. Sitting here upon the floor with the low light slanting across the room, I could see the fine prints in the dust: the prints of a high-heeled shoe with a fashionable scalloped toe. So much the better. I should have no time to take care of fine gentry from the city now.

"I suppose it was a kind of apoplectic seizure," Iveroth was saying. "Not uncommon among men of his age, you know, Sabira, though usually men so spare of flesh as Steinnland are not prone to these fits. It must have been a sudden shock of some sort."

"Oh, who cares about that?" I interrupted him. "My lord can tell us all about it when he recovers. Please find Antoine and – can the two of you get him to his bed? He is too heavy for me to lift alone." My people are stronger than landfolk, but even so I doubted I could move Steinnland without hurting him. *Oh, my lord, my lord, so tall and big-boned, for all your leanness I cannot even put you in a comfortable bed without help.*

His eyes were on my face all the time that Iveroth was busy about finding Antoine and removing a door to serve as a stretcher and padding it with blankets so that my lord should not be jarred unnecessarily while they removed him to his own chamber; and I could do nothing but stroke back his hair and promise him that he would be better soon and that I would not leave his side until he was well. Naturally the two men with their great clumping feet soon destroyed the traces I had seen of the Duchess' footsteps, but that seemed of no importance now. My lord's mouth worked once or twice as though he would speak, but no intelligible sounds issued from it; only the stream of saliva that I kept wiping away, knowing he would hate to be seen in such a condition.

Once abed, his lids fluttered shut and for a moment I felt the greatest fear; but he was only dozing.

"Exhausted," murmured Iveroth, "exhausted from the effort of holding onto life."

And I had been wasting my time, coaxing kelpies to work as cart-horses and persuading a sluttish fishwife to boil her milk vessels, while my lord lay cold on the floor!

Iveroth took my hand and drew me away from my stool beside the bed. He was uncommon strong for a landman; I could not escape his grip without an unseemly struggle. I would have struggled if he tried to make me leave the room, but fortunately he had better sense than that. We went only as far as the doorway.

"Is there such a thing as a surgeon on the island?" he murmured, his lips close to my ear that Steinnland might not hear. His breath was warm and not as foul as landmen's were said to be. My lord's breath also had never smelled foul. Perhaps my aunts had been wrong about that.

"No. No surgeon, no physician. The people are too poor to support one, and my lord can always – could always consult a man in Din Eidyn. But he was always strong and healthy."

"Well, it may be all for the best. A surgeon would insist on bleeding him, and I am not at all sure that would be well for Steinnland. For a fleshy man, yes, but for him – "

I followed his glance. My lord's spare form was starkly outlined by the blankets over him; his face was white as the linen he lay on, and it seemed to me that the bones beneath the skin stood out in sharp relief.

"For Steinnland," Iveroth continued, "I think the best treatment is warmth, and rest, and quiet – and some broth for nourishment, if we can get it down him."

I had no objection to the implied partnership. Whatever Iveroth's and my private disagreements, we shared the goal of caring for my lord.

"Perhaps you could direct Antoine to prepare the broth," he suggested.

"If I know Antoine, he is already at work," I said. "Perhaps you could see if it is ready yet."

When he had reluctantly departed for the kitchens, I took my seat beside the bed again, holding my lord's cold hand and trying to warm it in both of mine. When Iveroth returned, I should have to tell him to have Antoine heat a brick for the foot of the bed, and to light a fire, even if it was midsummer.

My lord's poor stiff lips twitched and a grunt forced its way up from his throat. "What is it? What can I get you? Water?"

His eyes closed as they would, briefly, whenever he despaired of making me understand the complexities of some bit of scientific news. "No, no, of course not water, how stupid of me," I said hastily. "Oh, if only you could tell me what you need!"

He looked past me, staring with curious intentness at a far corner of the room. At first I thought he was trying to see out of the window, but then I realized that his gaze was directed lower, towards the desk where he kept his estate papers.

"You want something from the desk?"

He rolled his eyes upwards. *At last she gets it!*

"All right, all right," I scolded him lightly, though I was delighted to see that he was still capable of teasing me. "Even without speech you can be sarcastic, can you? Very well, but you mustn't expect me to take your meaning instantly."

He stared at me.

"Oh. All right." I stood and moved to the desk. "Top drawer? Second? Third?"

His eyes did not move. "Well, really, my lord, what else is there?"

Another roll of the eyes. *Idiot girl!*

"Oh. *That* one." I pressed the carved scroll on the bottom right side of the top drawer and the little compartment at the back opened, revealing a cylindrical leather case. I opened it and drew out a tight scroll of papers wrapped about with linen and sealed in red wax with the hawks-head crest of the March-Lords. "You want these papers?"

A rapid fluttering of his eyelashes, a negation, and then he stared at me.

"You want me to have the papers?"

A single blink, and then the upwards roll of the eyes. Almost right.

"To take them somewhere?"

His eyes widened in agreement, and he struggled desperately, lips working now but without sound. I knelt on the footstool by the bed, so that my ears should be near to catch any sound he managed to make.

"In-eh-in." It was a thready whisper.

"Iveroth?"

A furious blinking. "*Din*-eh-in."

"Din Eidyn."

His eyes widened and he struggled to say something else. "U-ach."

Well, they had the look of legal papers, and had not Iveroth said something about bringing papers from…" Tulloch? You want me to take them to Advocat Tulloch in Din Eidyn?"

His whole body seemed to relax.

"Very well, my lord." I tucked the scroll into my sleeve. "I promise that I will take these papers to your advocat in Din Eidyn – as soon as I dare leave you." And my lord had best learn patience, because I had no intention of leaving him here and setting off to Din Eidyn while he lay helpless like this. But there was no need to upset him by arguing just now. His eyes crinkled at the corners as they used to do when he could smile at me, as though he felt he had made his point. And I could hear Iveroth tramping along the hall. I hoped he had not let the broth get cold, or spilt it; men are so clumsy around a sickroom.

***

I lay long awake that night, at first on a mattress that Iveroth had unhappily dragged into my lord's chamber for me. He had offered to stay with my lord while I rested, but I scarcely cared to be under so much obligation to him. The evening had been bad enough; moving a man the size of the March-Lord was beyond even my strength, so Antoine and Iveroth between them had been obliged to lift my lord's helpless body and perform the most intimate offices for him. What should I do on the morrow? Iveroth could hardly be expected to stay here indefinitely, neglecting his estates and his friends in the city to act the part of Steinnland's body-servant. He would have to go back to the mainland, I decided, and told myself it was quite irrational to feel bereft at the thought. He was a rude, crude man who had grossly insulted me – and he had been extremely rational and helpful since we found Steinnland ill – and it didn't matter what I felt about it, anyway; he was going to return to the mainland and send servants and a physician to attend my lord. Until they came, Antoine and I could make shift to manage. Some of the fisherfolk were not troubled by any superstitious fear of my kind. Inga's Androw was a good lad; he would probably agree to help out for a few days if I promised that he should be reimbursed for the loss of his income from the fishing.

Once that decision was made, I found it easier to rest. I had no intention of sleeping, of course; as soon as I had heard Iveroth making his way down the hall to his own bedchamber, I abandoned the mattress for a deep, straight chair that was uncomfortable enough to ensure I would not drop off accidentally. I would have begun so, save that I would not have put it past Iveroth, that ill-mannered man, to look into the room to make sure that I was lying down as I'd promised.

It was cold that night, unusually so for a night so close to midsummer. In the usual way of things my people do not feel the cold so much as landfolk; we have the skill of protecting our body heat against the ocean waters, and the summer air is nothing to that. With the fire burning, I should have felt rather overheated than cold. But that night I felt chilled to the bone, and when I touched my lord's hand, that too was cold; only the irregular beat of his pulse reassured me that he still lived. I borrowed the bedclothes from the mattress on the floor to wrap around me until both the chair and I were wrapped in a cocoon of linen sheets and wool blankets, and still the fog seemed to seep in through every crack and touch me with clammy tentacles. It was like a cold current twisting through the sea and slipping into Finfolkaheem, chilling and blighting our coral gardens. The brilliant reds and blues faded to gray and black, the living plants were stilled…

My head jerked and I realized I had actually fallen asleep, even perched in this stiff chair that was too deep for me. The fire was no more than a handful of coals smouldering in the ash, and the candles were almost out – I should get up and light new tapers… the dancing lights of Finfolkaheem were going out one by one… The dream dragged me back into a heavy trance of sleep, haunted by strange sounds and foul odors, until my head fell forward again and roused me.

I woke slowly, feeling like a swimmer struggling upwards against the pull of seaweed and worse things, with a confused sense that I had spent the brief hours of darkness in the thrall of evil dreams. At first I was not sure who I was, or where; I only felt an overwhelming gratitude to see the early dawn light of Langsday and to know that I was myself again and not one of the creatures of nightmare that had peopled my dreams. I was stiff as an old woman from sitting night-long in that chair; I wanted to spring to my lord's side, but it seemed to take forever to unwind the sheets and blankets that had somehow tangled themselves around me in the night. As I worked to free myself, my nose wrinkled. Something in the room did not smell right – and it was not just the smells of a sickroom; there was something worse, like kelp that has not been well spread out to dry after klokking and has rotted within the kossel.

There was decomposing kelp, dark and slimy, trailing across the floor from the open window.

And my lord was stiff and cold beyond any waking.

***

I am ashamed to say that I was almost useless for the next few days. I did wash my lord's body with fresh water from a silver bowl, did wind him in a linen sheet with seven folds and a sprig of a healing herb tucked within each fold. But once that task was completed, I was at a loss what to do next. I had no knowledge of how landmen of noble rank buried their dead. It would be right for the March-Lord of Steinnland to go to his grave with the dignity and funerary grandeur appropriate to his station; but what was that, and how was it to be managed with Faarhafn's scanty resources? The novels I had read were sadly lacking in details of such practical information, and in any case I could not force myself to concentrate on the problem. I would try to make plans and would find myself, instead, mounting the steps to the reading room where he and I had spent so many companionable hours, where now I sat staring out at the sea and turning the scroll he had entrusted to me over and over in my hands.

Downstairs, I knew, Antoine and Iveroth were making some sort of arrangements for the burying. It seemed well enough to me, when I thought about it, that it should be so. They would certainly know more of the proper customs than I would; all I was good for, now, was to stare at the sea to which I would soon return, where I was no longer entirely at home.

Once or twice it came to me that I should look in Steinnland's scrying bowl to try and see what truth, if any, was in my visions of Finfolkaheem turning dead and black and dark. But this was a magic of the land, not of the sea, and it did not work for me; when I filled the silver bowl with clear water and waited till it stilled, I saw only the reflection of a thin-faced girl with dark circles round her eyes and wisps of fine hair coming loose from her braids. I might have seen true if the bowl had been filled with salt sea water instead of fresh, but it seemed too much trouble to make my way downstairs and out to the shore. Somebody might speak to me, if only to offer condolences. I did not think I could speak without shaming my lord's memory with unruly tears.

No doubt those images of decay had been only dreams, not true visions; if some blight had struck Finfolkaheem, my family would not be slow to tell me about it. Nor, when I brought them the news of Steinnland's death, would they be slow to berate me for letting this chance of retrieving Faarhafn slip through our fingers. Another reason for remaining here, safe among my lord's beloved books.

Downstairs, the funeral plans; outside, a village of landmen and women who had not loved me over well before their lord's death, and would have no cause to love me more now; and under the water, my family's recriminations. The tower room seemed very much my best choice. For the most part I was allowed to sit undisturbed. Sometimes Antoine brought up something on a tray, a plate of fresh flaky pastries, a dainty cup of chocolate made strong and spicy with sugar and pounded cloves. The smell of food nauseated me, but he went trustingly away, so there was no need to insult his cooking; the gulls were glad enough to have the morsels I tossed to them, and one old fellow with a pulled wing began coming to the window regularly in the hope of an easy meal.

Iveroth was not so trusting – or so considerate. He threw the door open, one foggy summer morning, slammed a plate of thick-cut bread and ham down on the gilt bookstand, pulled up one of the fragile chairs and sat astride it like a man who dearly wished to be riding somewhere on a horse instead of dealing with funerals and wayward widows. "Eat," he said.

"Thank you, maybe later. I'm not hungry right now." I looked past him, through the far window at the glinting, dancing line where sea met sky, and waited for him to go away. I imagined the sandwiches wheeling through the air, falling towards rocks they would never meet, for the gulls would snatch the food from the summer winds. My fat old Cripple-Wing would probably enjoy the ham, though I should have to pull it into small bits for him.

"Eat now," he said, "the funeral is in an hour, and I've been to enough trouble without having you fainting for lack of nourishment."

"Indeed, my lord, I cannot express my gratitude for all you have done."

"Yes, you can," Iveroth said. "Eat the bread and ham, and when you're done, smooth those braids and put on a clean, dark – oh, never mind." He slid a pot of ale across the bookstand. "Wash it down with this, while I act the lady's maid to make you decent."

Of course he would carry a comb in his pocket, a dandy like Iveroth; he probably rearranged his artfully cut black curls as often as he tied a fresh stock. I tensed as he went behind me and pulled out the bone pins that held my braids in place, anticipating a period of small, painful tugs and yanks such as had accompanied hair-combings when I was very young and handed over to one of my aunts to be made decent for a family occasion. But his hands were gentle and his fingers were soft and warm and very soothing on my scalp, and he kept up a reassuring flow of talk about nothing at all until I found that the stiff wire running through my backbone had quite melted away. "My little sister Charlotte had masses of fine hair like yours, and oh, how she used to scream when the nurse tried to comb it! I was the only one she trusted near her with a comb, so you see, I come by my expertise honestly. Take a bite of bread, there's a good girl. Antoine said to tell you he used only Scrabster butter on it, whatever that means."

"Effie Scrabster's a cleanly wife," I said indistinctly through the bread and butter. It was surprisingly good, but I had somewhat forgotten how to chew and swallow. "She boils her vessels and keeps her dairy clean, and never lets her cow get into the wild garlic. I would never let Antoine put any butter but Effie's upon... my lord's... table." A lump in my throat stopped the bread from going down; I gulped some of the bitter ale. That would make my head light if I did not keep eating. I took a morsel of ham and nibbled at it carefully.

"And I suppose you know the entire history of — watch out now, this is going to pull no matter what I do — of that ham, from its earliest incarnation as a squealing piglet?"

The mix of herbs used to season it gave me a clue. "Jonat Farchar cured the meat, but the Farchars don't raise their own pigs; it will have come from one of Goody Neip's Blossom's litters out of Old Tawny."

"Lord save us," Iveroth said in mock awe, "even the bacon here has a genealogy as long as my arm." He wrapped the repaired braids around my head and very gently inserted the long bone hairpins that held them in place. "Finish your ale, now, and tell me which of these dresses you will wear, and I'll help you lace it."

He had even brought up three simple, dark dresses from my press, that I might not have to go back through the chamber where my lord had died and into the small dressing-room opening off it where I was used to sleep and keep my things. Tears prickled behind my eyes at this further evidence of consideration where I had been used to meet only enmity and suspicion. "My lord, you are too kind."

"Not at all," Iveroth said in a drawling, sarcastic tone that was more like what I had come to expect from him. "I must appear with you at this affair, and it would ruin my credit entirely were anyone in Din Eidyn to hear that I had been seen in public with a weeping woman on my arm."

"I do not weep!" I said. "And you need not act the lady's maid to lace me, either, for these dresses are not cut so tight as to require it; how do you think I have managed until now? Get out and let me dress in privacy!"

"I shall be waiting outside," he said as he withdrew. "You will go down to the church on my arm."

"I had rather not, thank you, my lord."

"All the same, you will do so."

I had cause to thank his consideration when we came to the small church on the windy headland and I saw all those faces turned toward me. A few were sympathetic, but most looked wary or angry or both. More than a few hands surreptitiously moved in a sign against evil as I walked down the aisle to the front pew where Iveroth seated me before moving on to the lectern.

Faarhafn had never been able to keep a clergyman; one of my lord's ancestors had built this church and imported a man from the mainland to preach in it, but he left after only a few months, complaining that he could not sleep with the sound of the sea in his ears. Subsequent clergymen were more outspoken, talking of nightly dreams of drowning and of demons that threatened their slumbers, until finally the March-Lords gave up the experiment.

The island remembered its past; it was not friendly to the sons of men, nor to their gods.

Now the church was used mostly for meetings and festivities, but also at times of marrying and christening and burying. At such occasions it was customary for one of the islanders to take the part of clergyman and read some lines from their holy book. Iveroth took on that role now, and it was only as he read aloud that I understood they meant to bury my lord behind the church. I began an instinctive gesture of negation and then held my hands tightly together in my lap. This was the way of landmen with their dead, and I must accept it, even to hearing the clods of earth falling over my lord.

The villagers kept a decent silence – one might even say, a stony silence – during the reading. Afterwards, when the box containing my lord's body was lowered into the earth, all except the men who had offered to help with the task gathered outside the churchyard. I might have thought they were being kind, offering me this last moment of privacy with my lord, but I could sense the whispers and the uneasy movement of feeling that ran through them as they pressed close to one another.

When the earth began to fall upon the coffin, Iveroth took my arm to lead me away. The crowd outside the churchyard fell away hastily, as if each individual person dreaded my touch; and the whispers grew louder and bolder.

"Witch."

"Finwife."

"How was Steinnland drowned, and he high in his chamber on the dry land?"

"Who gave the old lord a winding-sheet of seaweed?"

Not I! I wanted to cry, but there could be no good end to such a confrontation at such a time. I held my head high and matched my steps to Iveroth's and told myself that it would be over soon, that it did not matter what these people thought about me; I could return to my home. Not that I would be over-popular there either, having failed to secure the island for my people.

Bessie Clipagarthe was one of the last we walked by, and she glared at me with open hostility; but I thought she would not speak against me, for caution, and for her child whom I had tried to help. I was wrong.

Just as I came past her, she darted forward with a clod of earth in her hand, spat on it, and threw the dirt against the skirts of my dress. "Tha's overlooked my Sinnie, fin-witch," she cried. "Let this charm take thy eye of evil off my child."

Iveroth would have responded if I had not gripped his arm so tightly that I thought my fingers must sink through the fine cloth of his coat. "Just let us go home," I whispered. What did it matter what a slut like Bessie said of me, or to me? I would not be here long enough for it to make a difference.

Behind us, I could hear Bessie whining to the crowd. "Our Sinnie's never known a happy or a healthy day since yon witchwife came to our cottage."

"Hold your tongue, you stupid old wife," Androw Neip said.

"Androw! Speak polite to your elders and betters," Goody Neip remonstrated, and it saddened me that she took Bessie's part.

"Well, and didn't she beg the lady's help to salve her Sinnie? Begging your pardon, Mam, but Sinnie was aye a sickly child, and it's none of my lady's doing."

We passed beyond earshot. I was grateful to Androw, not only for speaking up in my behalf, but for distracting the crowd. I had felt it would want very little encouragement for them all to follow Bessie's lead and come after us, throwing earth and foul words together, and there was a limit to how long I could hold on to Iveroth.

CHAPTER ELEVEN

Once we were safe at home – what had been home to me these three years, anyway – Iveroth called to Antoine for wine, then made apology to me for acting like the master of the house.

"It is of no consequence," I reassured him. "Neither of us rules here now. It will pass to…." I did not even know the name of my lord's heir; it was not a subject he had liked to discuss. Probably the man would sell out of the Borghesan army when he heard of his inheritance. My head and my feet were both aching; I could do nothing for the head-ache, but I longed to slip my feet out of the tight slippers I had put on for the funeral.

"We must talk," he said. "Where would it please you to sit?"

I felt most comfortable in the library at the top of the winding stair, the room with windows looking out onto the bay and deep shelves full of the books my lord and I had loved best. But when we had once made our way there, it seemed that Iveroth had nothing to say that I did not already know.

"You cannot stay here," he began, as soon as Antoine had left us alone with our cups of wine – or almost alone; I could tell, if Iveroth could not, that his steps had not receded down the staircase after the door closed. I had no objection to his listening at the door; after all, it was his future being discussed as well as my own.

"I do know that," I said. "You think me only an ignorant girl, my lord, but Steinnland was at pains to explain the laws of entail to me. This house and all else will now descend to his cousin in the Borghesan Army, unless the advocats can find some closer heir. In any case, I have no more right here."

"I was not thinking of that." Iveroth drained his cup, too fast for courtesy, and set it down – hard – on one of the book-stands before rising to pace about the room. "It will be weeks, more likely months, before Steinnland's heir is apprised of his inheritance and all the advocats' formalities are completed. No one would dispute his widow the right to remain here for a time while she considers her future plans. If it were at all suitable for you to remain in this house, I promise you, I should see to it that you were not turned out before you were ready. It is the temper of the villagers that concerns me. I have business in Din Eidyn and on my estates; I cannot stay here much longer, and I will not see you left alone here without protection."

It was on the tip of my tongue to assure him that protecting me was none of his concern, but I bit the words back. He meant well, and I daresay he could not help being overbearing.

I should have spoken; then he might not have laid his hands upon my shoulders. "Sabira – Lady Steinnland - you must understand. You are not safe here. How can I let you stay where so many dangers threaten?"

I removed his hands and stood to face him. I found it difficult to think clearly when he was towering over me like that, and holding me into the bargain. "My lord, I think you refine too much upon a few angry words from a bad-tempered village wife." But even as I said this, I remembered – and he did too, I make no doubt – the low hum of agreement that had followed Bessie's attack. I did have a few true friends among the landfolk of the island, but it would be a sad repayment for the trust of such as young Androw to let them wear themselves out and anger their fellows by defending me.

"It is not just the villagers," Iveroth said slowly. "The manner of Steinnland's death also troubles me."

I took two paces back, the limit the small room would allow me. "Then you, too, accuse me?" The words caught in my throat. I knew already that Iveroth was a nasty-minded, untrusting fellow who thought all women bent on intrigue and folly. Since he was also my lord's friend, I had been attempting to think of this in a charitable fashion, as an unfortunate defect in an otherwise admirable character. But I could feel no charity with one who thought me to have had a hand in my lord's death. And this hurt more than there was any reason it should, for what was Iveroth to me but a chance-met acquaintance, cast into my company only by the circumstance of his visit to my lord?

"Sabira, sit before you fall!" I had been scarcely aware of swaying, but Iveroth's arm was about my shoulders and I found myself shamefully grateful of his support as he lowered me into my chair. He thrust the untouched cup of wine at me. "Here, drink this, and put some color in your cheeks. Of course I don't suspect you of compassing Steinnland's death, I hope I am not such a fool as that."

I swallowed some of the wine. It burned in my throat. "Why not, since you have already accused me of every crime against him short of murder?" Perhaps he was at last going to admit he had been mistaken in his estimation of me.

"You do not profit from his death," Iveroth said, "quite the reverse."

"Oh! And otherwise, I suppose, you would have been out there throwing clods with Bessie?" I would have thrown the remains of my wine in his face, but he caught my wrist and bent it back with a casual strength that surprised me. Most landmen are rather weak compared with the folk of the sea.

"I did not think this the time for pretty speeches," he said, "but if you insist – I do believe that you truly loved Steinnland and did not seek to do him ill. Now are you satisfied, or like a town Miss, will you insist on my losing track of my argument amid a quarter-hour of pretty compliments to your silver hair and stormy eyes?'

I could not speak until he released my hand and in his turn retreated a pace, as though still afraid I should make to strike him.

"Thank you, my lord," I said, "my person is not in question here. I am quite satisfied with your improved opinion of my character." Silver hair? And stormy eyes? Was the man an amateur poet as well as everything else? My hair is extremely fair, but not so colorless as to be quite silver. And I had never stormed at him – well, anyway, I had done my best to remain calm in the face of intolerable provocations.

"But don't you see, Sabira – my lady - what a position it leaves us in? Men may die of an apoplexy, but I'll lay my fortune that Steinnland's was no natural death. Some evil came out of the sea and murdered him. I can scarcely leave you here, at the mercy of whatever attacked Steinnland, and with few or no friends among the villagers."

"And you with business in Din Eidyn and on your estates. Yes, my lord, I see your dilemma, but you have nothing to worry about. I shall leave on the morrow."

"To return to your family?"

"Yes – no!" In the grief and strain of the past days, I had all but forgotten those last, heartbreaking moments with my lord of Steinnland. "I have an errand to do first. I must take some papers of Steinnland's to his advocat in Din Eidyn."

"This is the first I have heard of such an errand."

"He told me only in his last moments. You were out of the room."

"He could not speak!"

"I thought you had broken the habit of insinuating that I am a liar. My lord and I communicated in many ways, my lord Iveroth. Perhaps if you are ever so fortunate as to form a similar connection, you will understand how unnecessary is speech between two who share a true sympathy of mind. Whether or not you believe me, the plain fact is that he directed me to the hidden compartment in his desk, and desired me to convey the papers therein to Advocat Tulloch in Din Eidyn by my own hand."

"Those, no doubt, will be the papers I brought him – the ones he signed with Antoine and myself as witnesses."

I shrugged. The papers were nothing to me, except the chance to do one last thing for my dead lord – and an excuse to go to Din Eidyn. I had certain unfinished business to discuss with Ailsa of Quoy. "It may be. They are sealed now. What do they concern?"

"I have no idea. Steinnland required me only to bear witness that he had signed them, not to peruse their contents. Since he thought it ineligible for you to be one of the witnesses, my guess is that he wished to leave you some bequest out of his unentailed fortune."

My guess was that he asked Iveroth to witness his signature because he was uncertain how much weight a finwife's signature might carry in a court of law, and did not wish to force me to continue my masquerade as a landwoman after his death. But there was no need to go into that with Iveroth. His habitual disbelief both of me and of all things not contained in the landmen's study of Natural Philosophy was such that, even should I loosen my petticoat and display the full glory of my tail before him, he would believe me to be a landwoman afflicted with an unfortunate deformity. If I threw myself into the sea before him, he would mourn me as one drowned – to the extent that he mourned at all – and would be mightily puzzled when I reappeared, since his Natural Philosophy also did not admit the existence of ghosts!

It was entirely possible that I had drunk too much wine; the thought of confounding Iveroth in this way tempted me more than it should.

"In any case," I said finally, "you need have no further care for me, my lord Iveroth. You are free to attend to your pressing duties elsewhere. I shall leave for Din Eidyn tomorrow."

"I shall escort you," he said immediately.

This, if I permitted it, would be disastrous to my plans. I had no wish to make the slow, uncomfortable journey to Din Eidyn overland; the city was also a port, and I could travel much more swiftly – and in more comfort – underwater.

Fortunately, I did not have to be that precise about my plans. "Thank you, but I intend traveling by water."

"That," said Iveroth instantly, "would be quite ineligible!"

At length, without even knowing my real intentions, he persuaded me to change them. He was quite forceful about the badness of the neighborhood surrounding the wharves and the poor impression that would be given by a young woman arriving alone and unescorted in a boat. Apparently there was no possibility that I could come to the wharves unobserved; Din Eidyn must be an extremely crowded place, to judge from the number of individuals Iveroth claimed would be thronging the streets, night and day. I could see that to rise dripping from the water, with no luggage, would make an even worse impression than coming by boat, and would also make it extremely difficult for me to visit Advocat Tulloch – not to mention completing my other business - as a landwoman. There was no help for it; I would have to travel by that gilded monstrosity, the Coach of State; and it would have to be repainted and repaired first, that observers might respect my quality; and Iveroth meant to stay and oversee the repairs, and then to ride beside the coach to protect me on the journey.

I expected to feel annoyed at having to put up with him so much longer than planned. For some reason the thought did not bother me as much as it should. Perhaps because he had given up accusing me of betraying Steinnland, and had even gone so far as to allow that he did not think I had murdered my husband? If he could get over a few more of these little quirks, the man might be reasonably pleasant company – for a landman. Of course that made no real difference in the long run, since I should certainly return to the sea as soon as I had finished my business with the Duchess of Quoy.

I finished my wine. It still had an unpleasant, burning taste, and it made my head swim. Perhaps Antoine had taken exception to Iveroth's tone, and had opened a bottle of an extremely inferior vintage – except that I could not believe my lord would have kept such bad stuff in his cellar at all. I asked Iveroth for an explanation, and found my tongue unaccountably thick in my head; in fact, I stumbled over the words.

"I told Antoine to lace the wine well with Steinnland's best brandy," Iveroth said, smiling down at me where I sat. "You have not rested in days, Sabira, and I wanted to make sure you slept after the funeral."

I should have given him the sharp edge of my tongue for taking such liberties with my name and my person, but it was too much work. I was tired, so tired, and the brandy, foul though it tasted, was making the funeral and the clod-throwing and all the unpleasant reality of the day seem like a distant dream. I smiled up at him stupidly and made no objection when he lifted me into his arms to carry me to my chamber. Only when he muttered that I should have a maidservant to loosen my clothing did I force myself to wake to full consciousness again. This was no time to be allowing some land-man to unwrap my petticoat and discover its peculiar construction and attachment; particularly not Iveroth, who would be quite incapable of believing what he saw.

"Let me go, my lord! I as-assure you, I dressed myself and I can manage to undress myself just as well. It is certainly not your task to do so!"

"Forgive me if I have overstepped the bounds of courtesy." He let me go so suddenly that I sat on the bed with a bounce of surprise, and stepped back to the doorway. His mouth was set tight; what did he have to be angry about? Perhaps he thought I imagined he was about to ravish me; he seemed to think a great deal about infidelities, and ravishment, and things like that.

"You have not offended, my lord, and I hope I have not done so either. But it is quite enough that you have already been pressed into service as steward, factor, clergyman and who knows what else, without adding acting as lady's maid to your chores!"

The slightest of smiles softened the tight line of his lips. "As to that, it would hardly be the most unpleasant of the tasks I have undertaken these last few days! But if you are certain that you can manage alone – "

"I have never required the services of a maid, my lord."

"Admirable woman! But you will find that things are quite different in Din Eidyn. Sleep well, then."

CHAPTER TWELVE

And so it came about that instead of making the quick water journey to Din Eidyn, I traveled in the clumsy overland style, in all the glory of the hastily refurbished and repainted coach that had lain neglected so long in the undercroft of Steinnland's house, and with far more company than I deemed either necessary or desirable. First there was Iveroth riding beside the coach and deciding where we should stop for each night and change horses. Within the coach I had with me Antoine, who had prevailed upon me to take him back to the city upon his solemn oath never again to visit a gaming-house and, more importantly, not to remove the beard and luxuriant mustache which materially changed his appearance from that of the young Lutécian who had been attacked by hired bravos some twelve years prevously. I had also young Breta Scrabster, one of Effie's daughters, supposedly acting as a lady's maid, since Iveroth assured me that my credit would be irreparably ruined in the capital if I arrived without one. Since she knew no more how to perform the duties of a maid than I knew how to require them, we traveled more as companions than as mistress and servant.

I must admit that I pressed up to the window as often as Breta did, staring at a countryside so unfamiliar to either of us. The northern reaches of the mainland, comprising Steinnland's estates, looked not unlike Faarhafen or one of the other isles, only larger; more acres of windswept grass under grey sky, more clusters of crofters' houses, more rocky crags breaking through the thin soil. The only difference was that the sea now lay not just beyond sight, but farther and ever farther behind us. We even passed a tall standing stone like the ones in the circle on Faarhafn, which caused Breta and me much confusion.

"What is amiss?" asked Iveroth when we stopped for a nuncheon and to rest the horses. "You two have seen standing stones a-plenty in the islands, have you not?"

Breta turned red and looked down, all confusion at being directly addressed by a gentleman, leaving me to answer for both of us.

"It is only that the sea seems so far away. Everyone knows that the great stones move but once a year, on Yule night, when they go down to the sea and take the drink that refreshes them for the entire year. That one we passed just now will have so far to travel!"

It was my turn to blush as Iveroth could no longer restrain his laughter. "Lady Steinnland, my learned lady, is it possible you can study Natural Philosophy and the courses of the stars, and yet believe such nonsense as that? Have you ever seen a stone lumbering down to the sea for its yearly drink?"

"Of course not. Everyone stays well indoors on Yule night. We don't want to be turned into stones ourselves for having watched what men are not supposed to see." Could something that both seafolk and landfolk believed be untrue? And yet, now that Iveroth raised the point, it troubled me that the fact of the stones' yearly pilgrimage had not been tested by direct experiment.

"In six months I shall come north," Iveroth asserted, "and watch through Yule night for myself, if nothing else will convince you."

I should not care to see Iveroth turned to stone. Fortunately, there was another flaw in his plan. Long before the next Yule night, Steinnland's cousin of Borghese would have claimed his inheritance, and I would, of course, have returned to my family. And I doubted that this cousin would take up residence in so isolated a spot as Faarhafn, so the house would remain closed up as we left it. I did not think Iveroth's whim would surmount these obstacles.

I, of course, would still be residing quite close to the standing stones of Faarhafn. And if my family had not quite driven me mad by harping on my failure to recover their summer home, I might employ some small tests of my own – a fine thread spun of seafoam and moonlight, perhaps, linking the stones in their circle so that when they moved the thread must break. Or would it be better to set something in their path that must be crushed on the way to the water? Considering various possible experiments, and also wondering whether I dared meddle with a magic so much older than that of my people, kept me quiet until we reached our first night's lodging; by which time Breta was heartily bored with my company and would have darted off to gossip with the inn servants, had not Iveroth reminded us both that her duty was to attend me at all times.

There was some little difficulty attached to the change of horses; we were to hire horses at this inn for the next stage, and apparently the custom was that travelers hiring horses left their previous mounts behind, so that the innkeeper was never without enough horses to draw another coach. Iveroth explained to him that our horses were borrowed from a friend in the north and would not be stabled, but would find their way home on their own; but as he did not entirely believe this explanation, which I had made to him, he made a poor fist of it and left the innkeeper half convinced that we had made our way this far using stolen horses. However, since the man did not wish to be taken up for keeping stolen horses, his belief served as well as the truth would have done, or even better. When we released the black horses from their harness, three of them cantered away without being told any more. The last one stood still in the innyard, nuzzling my shoulder, despite Iveroth's repeated slaps on the flank and orders to go home. "Lady Steinnland," he said at last in exasperation, "you borrowed these horses. Have you any idea how to persuade this one to go safely home? Or should we stable it and send word to your friend that he may recover his property here?"

Neither the innkeeper nor I cared for that plan; he because he feared to harbor stolen property, I because there was no messenger that I could send to the kelpies telling them that one of their kind had insisted upon remaining on land, far from the nearest sea. I led the horse back behind the inn to reason with him in private.

"Meldun," I said, "you cannot draw this coach all the way to Din Eidyn. It would exhaust you, and in any case I do not plan to explain at every posting-house between here and Din Eidyn why we require to change only three horses!"

Meldun shifted shape into his human form to answer me, and I hurriedly shoved him behind a clump of bushes. "Your family charged me to see you safe to Din Eidyn."

"Iveroth is already doing that," I said.

"And while you are there, and when you return, who will watch over you?"

"Don't you think I can take care of myself?"

"No," said Meldun.

"I assure you, I shall only be in Din Eidyn for the time it takes to deliver these papers" - and to do one other errand – "and I am well able to handle any problems that may arise. You forget, perhaps, that I have lived as a landwoman these three years past. I know how to deal with these people better than you do."

Meldun shook his head.

"For instance," I said, thoroughly exasperated, "my worst problem right now is that I appear to be conversing with a clump of shrubbery, and *you*, not the landfolk, created that problem!"

"You pushed me in here. I am perfectly willing to come out again." The leaves shuddered; I grasped Meldun's bare shoulder and shoved him back.

"No, no, that is even worse. I must absolutely not be seen conversing with a naked man. Landfolk get very excited about nudity, although I cannot think why," I muttered, distracted by memories of Iveroth's breeches and Ailsa's lowcut dress, "since their costume seems designed to attract attention to the very parts they affect to cover."

With a sigh and a snort, Meldun changed back to horse form. The shrubbery was not large enough to contain him in that form; small branches snapped and leaves fell as he trotted forward. "Look," I said, "you really cannot draw the coach all the way to Din Eidyn. And if you follow along behind us… oh, never mind, I have thought of an explanation. But you will have to put up with a bridle and a leading-rope."

Meldun gave a great slobbery snort expressive of his sentiments on that subject.

"It is a great deal better than pulling the coach," I pointed out, and went to tell Iveroth that I had "forgotten" that my friend had offered me the use of one of his horses in case I wished to ride in Din Eidyn, and that he was going to have to lead Meldun for the rest of the journey.

***

Acting on the assumption that Steinnland's heir would not begrudge me a few days' use of the townhouse, I desired Iveroth to direct us through the narrow streets of Din Eidyn to that lodging.

"No need," said Antoine, who had been looking less like a drooping weed and more like a freshly watered lily ever since the clatter and smells of the city reached out to surround us. "I know the way well enough. But you may come with us, of course, my lord," he said quite kindly to Iveroth, "should you be desirous of seeing that all is well with us there."

Dilapidated without by twelve years' neglect and enshrouded within by holland dust-covers over the furnishings and chandeliers, Steinnland's tall, narrow townhouse had a distinctly unappealing air. But Antoine reported that the kitchen, at least, was clean and that the couple left to manage the place had food to offer us for the night, even if no better than bread and cheese and small beer.

Iveroth offered to take Meldun around to the stables for me. "Do whatever he wants," I hissed in Meldun's ear before he moved away. "And *stay there* until I can come to you." Management of a kelpie in the city was one problem I had not thought out in advance.

Before the question of hospitality came up, Iveroth announced that when in town, he usually put up at the Philosophers' Club, having no wish to go to the trouble and expense of opening the family house when his mother was not in residence.

Iveroth with a mother! The thought made him seem almost human. Did she criticize his starched white shirt-points and nag him to settle down with a nice girl? I could hardly picture that. Still, if he had a mother, it was possible he also had aunts; and I was certain they, at least, would tease him to the limits of his patience.

It probably wouldn't take much.

Fatigue claimed young Breta even while she was exclaiming (with a mouth full of bread and cheese) over the glories we had glimpsed on our evening entrance to Din Eidyn: streets lined by tall poles on which lights burned as if by magic, buildings several stories high, and people thronging everywhere, as if they had swarmed up out of the ground like ants. Privately, I thought the lights and buildings of Din Eidyn dull and grey compared to Finfolkaheem, but naturally I was not so impolite as to voice this opinion aloud. Besides, I feared that speaking too openly of my undersea life might make Breta nervous of me. She would not be a very useful "maid" if she went in fear of my casting an enchantment of the sea upon her.

How wrong I was in that estimation of her, I was soon to learn. This evening, however, I was very nearly as tired as Breta. After eating a few bites of bread and cheese and quietly conveying the rest to Meldun, who was heartily tired of grain, I was happy enough to let Breta be my bed-fellow for the night rather than wait for Mrs. Clydie, the housekeeper, to clear and find linen for another bed in a grander room.

"It's not proper, your ladyship," she protested.

"We shared a bed in the posting-houses. It will do for tonight." For several nights, at most. I did not expect to spend very long in Din Eidyn; as I had pointed out to Meldun when he complained about bread and cheese and longed for a nice draft of little live herring.

"The only herring you'll get here will be dead and salted," I told him, for I certainly had no intention of hiring men to bring barrels of live fish to the house for his delectation. That would draw attention and speculation from half of Din Eidyn; Iveroth, for example, would probably leap to some irrational conclusion and start getting excited about my affairs all over again. Although now that he had done his duty and seen us safely deposited at my lord's townhouse, I supposed Iveroth would have no more interest in my affairs.

The thought was a curiously lowering one.

I learned my mistake about Breta the next morning. It was an extremely busy morning, beginning earlier than I liked with the discovery that in my sleep my tail had unaccountably escaped its neat petticoat-like folds and had spread over the bed, all but burying Breta under the full width of the fine, silky folds between the ridges of cartilage and muscle. Why it should so misbehave now, after behaving perfectly in the post-houses where Breta and I had shared a bed on the way down, I could not explain; unless it were that the townhouse, for all its long neglect, still bore some air of Steinnland's long residence and made me feel unconsciously at home. The bookshelves lining passageways and staircases, even though they had been emptied of their contents, put me in mind of my lord and his stacks and shelves of books on Faarhafn.

At my first, cautious attempt to free my tail, Breta awoke and stared round-eyed at the mass of pale green, iridescent, feather-soft stuff that enswathed her. Her eyes went unerringly to the narrowing fins that led to my back. "Oh, miss," she breathed, "I mean, my lady. I knew you was a magic sea princess."

"Nothing of the sort," I said crossly, tugging to free myself. Breta slipped out of bed and helped by flinging back the sheets so that I could retract my tail and bring it about me like a petticoat again. "You have known about the finfolk all your life, Breta. We all look like this." Well, some – my aunts Eliina and Seija, for instance – look significantly more beautiful than the rest of us, but I assumed it was the tail that had impressed her; she'd been looking at my face for three long days without blethering about magic and princesses. "I am just – I am a perfectly natural phenomenon, just as you are."

She blinked back tears. "I am not!"

It was my fault, I supposed, for snapping at her; but I couldn't divine the exact cause of her grief. "Not what?"

"What you said. A fin-nomy-whatever. I'm a landwoman, I am!"

What with clearing up that little misunderstanding, finding a decent suit of men's clothes for Meldun to wear when he chose to take his human shape, cutting back Mrs. Clydie's hopeful menus to a more modest list of dishes, preventing Antoine and Mrs. Clydie from coming to blows over the question of salt versus fresh beef in the ragout á la mode de Lutéce, and hauling Breta bodily back from the balconies of the front windows when she grew dangerously involved in the street scene, I was already tired and had not yet had time to learn the location of Advocat Tulloch's office when Iveroth called to escort me there. And he apologized for coming so unfashionably early!

***

Advocat Tulloch was a round little man with a prodigiously starched shirt front, half-moon spectacles precariously perched on a nose almost too small to support them, and a formal manner which his person was definitely not adequate to support. He made half a dozen bows to me when I entered his rooms, and another dozen to Iveroth, and with each bow his spectacles tried to slide off. It wasn't until he was induced to sit down and actually consider the documents I had brought him that he got his spectacles under control. Hooking the ear-wires firmly behind his ears, he unrolled and scanned the documents, saying, "Hm! Hm! Hm!" several times and clearing his throat fiercely each time he began a new page.

I saw no reason why Iveroth and I should wait for his perusal of the documents; whatever business Advocat Tulloch had with the house of Steinnland would surely be for the new heir to consider. And if this hour was indeed, as Iveroth claimed, "early" in the fashionable day, I might be able to complete the rest of my business in Din Eidyn today and take my own road home tonight. I cleared my own throat gently to get his attention. "My lord desired that these papers be delivered to you," I said, "but I myself have no further business here. With your permission, Advocat Tulloch, Lord Iveroth and I will leave without further disturbing your day."

"By no means, Lady Steinnland – by no means! These documents concern you most nearly."

"In what fashion?"

"Just let me finish looking this over," he said fussily, "and I shall explain all in good time. But I really must insist –" A phrase on the page before him caught his attention and he ejaculated, "Hm! Hm! Hm!" again, and then, "Most unwise! I warned his lordship – oh, unwise indeed!"

If Iveroth had not taken a hand, we might have spent another hour or more listening to Tulloch's hmms and ejaculations. Now he stepped forward,

125

looming over the little man at his desk. "Steinnland told me that you yourself had drawn up these papers for him to sign," he said.

"Hm? Well, yes, but – I told him, but most unreasonable – "

"In which case, I take it that you are tolerably familiar with the contents?"

"Oh, aye. The form is not unknown, you understand. Unusual, especially in these days – but not altogether unknown. Though Lord Steinnland was fortunate, if I do say so myself, in finding an advocat with enough knowledge of past legal formats to draw up such papers at all. It is not usually done, you know – not usual at all."

"Since you yourself wrote the papers," Iveroth persisted, "you can presumably explain to Lady Steinnland for what reason you dare demand her further attendance upon you. Without," he added, "reading your own work over and over again." He emphasized his intent by picking up a leatherbound book from the advocat's desk and setting it down flat on top of the papers we had delivered from Steinnland. Clouds of dust rose up when he slammed the book down, and the little advocat gasped and choked for a moment.

"But – I thought you knew!" he exclaimed when at last he could draw breath frequently. "Do you mean you had no part in this, Lady Steinnland?"

"No part in what?"

Tulloch looked from one to the other of us, first through, then over, his half-moon spectacles. "Why – the breaking of the entail. Since it was done primarily for your benefit, Lady Steinnland, I had supposed – "

"Just. Tell. Us. What. Has. Been. Done." Iveroth's voice was low but carried a force that seemed to push the advocat back against his chair with each word. "We did not come here to consult your opinions in the matter, but to discover Lady Steinnland's legal standing."

I started to say that he was quite wrong. I knew I had no "legal standing" in the courts of landfolk and my only business here was to fulfil my lord's dying command by delivering the papers with my own hand. But once Advocat Tulloch started speaking, I couldn't get a word in edgewise.

"March-Lord Steinnland – the late March-Lord," he corrected himself, "was a man of considerable substance apart from the houses and lands that were bound by entail to pass to his successor. The spice-trade with the Corians alone – not that I mean to say he was in trade, but owning the vessels – and then of course there was that affair in the late war with Lutéce, prize-money and such, before your time, that would have been, Lady Steinnland – "

"Get. To. The. Point." Iveroth suggested, gently but firmly.

It seemed that my lord had expended much of his personal wealth in breaking the entail with respect to certain of his lands and compensating his heir for the loss. Paying off his heir's debts had been a major part of the expenses. He had begun the project three years earlier – about the time he married me – and the final legal proceedings were only now complete, in these documents which Iveroth had brought north for his signature. Major Adrian Greenmark of the Borghesan Army would, when he claimed his inheritance, be master of all the broad acres we had passed in the first day's coach journey, with the exception of a strip of fertile shoreland which had been reserved to me with a note that it was intended as the future home of the current residents of Faarhafn. The island of Faarhafn itself, the winding house which generations of Greenmarks had constructed there, and the Din Eidyn town house which I had thought to have borrowed last night were all mine in law. So was what Advocat Tulloch referred to as Lord Steinnland's 'greatly reduced' personal fortune. The money had apparently been cleansed from the taint of trade or war-prize by investment in some things called Consols which somehow created a quarterly income for me just by lying in the bank.

And landsmen accuse us of working mysteries and magics!

Advocat Tulloch seemed very apologetic when he named the sum which was to be my income, though it appeared great beyond my comprehension. But then, on Faarhafn we spoke in terms of skillengs and pence, not to mention that most of the tenants paid their rent in kind. Effie Scrabster's man, who had earned sixty skillengs – or three korona, as Din Eidyn reckoned it – last year by the kelp burning, was a rich man on Faarhafn. My quarterly income was to be so many korona that I could hardly reckon it in skillengs.

I left the advocat's rooms dazed with numbers and legal terms. The one thing he had made clear was that none of this was to happen immediately. There would be some weeks of presentations to the court, and attestations and findings and other matters, before Steinnland's will was settled; and it would be desirable, if not necessary, for me to remain in Din Eidyn until all this was completed. In the meantime, Tulloch had said – with a great many more words than I am using now – that there could be no objection to my remaining in the town house which would, after all, be my property when the proving of the will was done. And he had advanced me what he called "a small part" of my quarterly income – a purse so heavy with korona that I felt weighted down by it – for my expenses during this time of waiting.

Just outside the advocat's rooms, five cobbled streets came together in a star-like point that had been turned into a small park, with a circle of grass edged by tall stones, two stone benches, and a miniature fountain playing in the center of the circle. Without thinking, I turned instinctively to the water. It was not salt, but it was still something of home. I dropped down on one of the stone benches and Iveroth sat beside me.

I lifted the purse Tulloch had given me. It jingled. "So, Lord Iveroth. On Faarhafn this would make me a rich woman. The little advocat seems to think Steinnland reduced himself almost to beggary in clearing the entail. What does this purse really represent?"

"Steinnland was extremely wealthy," Iveroth said. "He had his prize-money, I suppose, from the Lutécian war – though that was before my time – and he invested in ships trading with the Corians and even farther east, and increased his fortune to an almost indecent level. That was one reason he left public life. Folk said that he did not need to speak in support of or against any measure proposed by the Council of Regents, because he could buy and sell any of the regents. That…annoyed him. And society became no pleasure to him, because there were so many women angling to get his attention and a share of his wealth, either as mistresses or…."

"As his wife," I finished the sentence that Iveroth had abandoned. "I recall that you assumed I had trapped him for his fortune."

Iveroth cleared his throat. "I made many unfortunate assumptions when – before I knew you. I beg you will forget them."

It would be unmannerly to tease him further, when he had been so helpful about the journey to Din Eidyn and in shaking information out of the advocat. "Consider them forgotten," I said – which was not exactly the same thing. "I wish you will advise me now. Am I rich? Shall I buy four horses and ride about town in the Coach of State, throwing largesse to the population? Or will this purse full of korona only permit me to clean and inhabit one or two rooms in my lord's town house, and live on mussels and kelp soup while I wait for the legal business to be resolved?"

"You are well enough off," Iveroth said absently, "you might even be considered an heiress by some of Din Eidyn's fortune-hunters. You can certainly live in comfort in the town house, with enough servants to do you credit, and set up your own stable if you wish – although you would be better advised to let me be your agent in finding a less weighty carriage and appropriate horses, and to take a chair in the meantime. If that is what you want?"

"For the present," I said, "it seems I have no choice but to remain in Din Eidyn, if only to sign things and swear before justices and all that Advocat Tulloch described." If the law always moved as leisurely as Tulloch did, the proving of the will would leave me with ample time to discharge my other errand in the city. "But I see no reason to fill up the town house with servants. Breta and I will do very well with Master and Mistress Clydie."

"No, you cannot do that," Iveroth said absently.

"Why not?"

"It is – it is just not done. A young girl, living in a house with only her maid and an old caretaker couple? There would be talk. Even if you had a full staff of servants it would still be quite ineligible."

"A full staff! How many servants can one woman require?"

"At a minimum, you must have housemaids, kitchen staff, a footman to accompany you when you walk out. Oh, and a groom for that black horse you brought with you."

I suspected Meldun would not react well to being groomed by anybody but me. And as for the other stable tasks, he could change shape and fork out his own stall and put out his own food and water. Oh, and once I acquired a livery for him, he could be a footman as well. As for the other servants Iveroth imagined I needed, well, I should be returning to Faarhafn soon. Doubtless I could put off actually hiring anybody until then.

"If you propose to open the town house and live here," Iveroth added, "you will need far more servants than that."

"Well, I don't. I shall return to Faarhafn as soon as my business here is done."

"We can discuss that later," said Iveroth, just as if he thought he had any say in my plans. "In the meantime, you *must* have a chaperone at once, whatever we decide to do about other servants."

"I do not at all see the necessity for a chaperone. I am a respectable widow."

"Well, you will not be respectable for long, once the town bloods get a look at that hair and those eyes, and find out that you are an heiress living alone, and that I brought you down from the north with no better chaperone than your maid!"

"Lord Iveroth! Are you saying that you are bad for my reputation? And what does that say about yours?" After all his wild notions of my having a secret lover, it would serve Iveroth right if I discovered that he was keeping a mistress in town.

That potential turning of tables should have delighted me. For some reason I felt reluctant to dwell on it.

"Never mind my reputation," he said, "just understand that it'll do you no good to be introduced to Society by me. You must have a chaperone. No, more than just a chaperone – someone to show you how to go on, an older lady with connections and impeccable breeding." He rose. "I know just the person. I'll send her to you directly."

On the way home I explained to Iveroth several times that I had no need of a chaperone and did not intend to have any involvement with what Din Eidyn called "Society." He paid no attention.

CHAPTER THIRTEEN

By good fortune, Richert Dalkey was at home when Iveroth called directly after seeing Sabira to her door. His business was properly with Dalkey's mother, but he looked forward to some simple, straightforward masculine company in between dealing with Sabira and her whims, and Lady Dalkey and her whims.

"I've come to make you a happy man, Dalkey," he said as soon as he was announced.

Dalkey glanced about the room with somewhat the look of a hunted fox; a look which red hair worn *en brosse* and slanting amber eyes only enhanced. "If you've another well-bred miss to recommend as a marriage prospect, I wish you will talk to my Mama about it – or rather, I wish you won't."

"Hounding you about getting an heir, are they?" Iveroth drew up a delicate gilt chair with a green velvet cushion and seated himself astride the chair, resting his arms on the carved and gilded back.

"I thought she'd wait until the middle of July, when everyone brings their girls to town," Dalkey said, "so I made plans to be away by then. After all," he said with an air of conscious virtue, "since Lutéce has been at war with either us or Borghese for most of my life, I've never had the chance to complete my education as a gentleman should."

"A *petite amie* in Lutéce," Iveroth said, "and a tour of the classical monuments in Borghese and the Elladic Islands? With a tutor in tow to explain the history and literature of the countries? Give it up, Dalkey. One

131

does that at seventeen, not at twenty-eight."

"You went abroad," Dalkey pointed out. "You were what, twenty-five?"

"Seven years ago, in that brief pause between the wars," Iveroth agreed, "and it was not the brightest thing I've ever done."

"No? I don't recall any juicy scandals around that trip of yours. Of course, I was still at university then. What went wrong?"

"Among other things, I made the mistake of taking a letter of introduction from Steinnland to his heir."

"And what was the problem with that? Don't tell me the heir is a dashed commoner!"

"No, not bad *ton*," Iveroth said absently, "but the man's military-mad, can talk of nothing but enfilades and flanking movements – Damn it, Dalkey, you are distracting me from my point again. How do you do it?"

"Years of practice," Dalkey said gloomily, "evading Mama and her Very Nice Girls. And if you have found me another one, I don't want to hear about it."

"Calm yourself, my boy. I come not to increase your burdens, but to take one away."

"What, you want one of 'em? Lady Cecilia Lauder? Plays the harp and sings, but you could break her of the habit; I think she only does it because her mama insists she have some accomplishments. Or there's Sophy Westlin. Bran-faced, but her Accomplishment is watercolor painting, which is nice and quiet. Your house is large enough, you could find some dark corner to hang the things. Or Dorothea Turvoll, who don't have any accomplishments and don't need 'em, because she comes with the Turvoll fortune – yes, yes, I know, smells of the shop, but your name is good enough to cleanse it."

"Dalkey, you are beginning to sound like your mother. I don't want a nice young girl. I want an unattached lady of a certain age, with impeccable social connections and marked respectability."

"Come now!" Dalkey expostulated. "And you with your pick of the prettiest faces in town?"

"I don't want a woman for marriage," Iveroth said, "I want – "

"Well, a respectable female ain't going to settle for anything less."

"Will you stop interrupting long enough to let me tell you the facts of the case? Lord Steinnland has died."

"When?"

"A week past. His widow has come to town and must stay some weeks to see to the settlement of his estates."

"What? I thought everything was entailed upon Major Greenmark."

"Apparently the major had run up impressive debts by borrowing upon his expectations, and was already being dunned. Steinnland persuaded him to break the entail by offering to pay those debts, as well as – well, never mind that now. The point is that Lady Steinnland wishes to stay in the family town house while she is here, and it is my responsibility to see that she has a chaperone of the utmost respectability."

"Oh, a companion for the old lady?"

"She's not old," Iveroth said, "that's the problem. She's young. Not above twenty, at a guess. You did not hear about Steinnland's December-May marriage?"

"Forgot," said Dalkey apologetically. "He wasn't a particular friend of mine, y'know. Oh – my condolences. You held him in great esteem, did you not? I suppose that's why he saddled you with looking after the widow. Knew you'd take on the charge. You are afraid the girl will kick up her heels, now she is loose in town?"

"That or worse," Iveroth said, "Major Greenmark – Lord Steinnland, I should say, now - still inherits the bulk of the land. With time, and if he has the sense to sell out of the army and manage the estate himself, the rent-rolls should be sufficient to allow him a comfortable living. Lady Steinnland has only the town house, the island of Faarhafn, and what remains of Steinnland's personal fortune after what he spent on breaking the entail. Unfortunately, that is quite enough to attract the wrong sort of followers. She's a child who knows no more of Society than what she has read in romances, and I want someone who can introduce her properly and tell her how to go on. I thought to ask your mother if she could spare Lady Askerton."

"Iveroth," said Dalkey earnestly, "if you can remove Lady A. from this household I will be indebted to you for life. But ain't you afraid she'll bore Steinnland's relict to death?"

"You seem to have survived."

"Oh, I sink into a coma after about five minutes of Lady A.," Dalkey said, "but Mama will bless your name nightly. M'father might even spend the occasional night at home again if she were gone. Being Mama's only relative, the old bat assumed we would give her a home after Askerton gambled away everything he owned and blew his brains out. Well, of course we had to take her in, but Mama didn't reckon on her trying to be a Friend and Confidant and Spreading Joy About the House and all that sort of thing. I tell you," Dalkey said, "I've actually considered marriage as a way to get away from her – excuse to set up my own establishment and all that – but it's too damned risky. How can you tell that one of these Cecelias, or Dorotheas, or whatever, won't turn into the same kind of bore?"

Iverton thought of Sabira and smiled. "I feel tolerably certain that young Lady Steinnland will never become a talkative bore. She says very little, and what she does say usually means something – more than is apparent at first, in fact."

"I suppose she married Steinnland for his money?"

"I was with her when she spoke to the advocat. The inheritance was a complete surprise to her."

"Then why – oh well, who can tell why females do anything? I suppose the real question is why Steinnland married her. If ever there was a confirmed bachelor, I should have thought he'd be the one, with his books at the breakfast-table, and never going into society, and retiring to live at the ends of the earth."

"Steinnland was… a collector," Iveroth said slowly. "He always had his curiosities; a bit of ironstone that fell from the sky, a narwhal's tooth, a piece of Iceland spar that broke the light passing through it into separate rays… I believe that, although she did not know it, he looked on Sabira as the last and greatest addition to his collection of natural curiosities."

"She's that beautiful?"

"No," said Iveroth slowly, calling Sabira's features to his memory, "she is well enough, but she'll not pass for a beauty here in Din Eidyn – especially as she does nothing to show off her best features. She keeps that torrent of silver-gilt hair well bound in plaits round her head, and her eyes...I don't think she knows how to use those amazing green eyes as our town beauties do."

"Damme, Iveroth, I think you're in love with her yourself! I never heard you speak of a female in such detail before."

"Not I! She is also the most irritating, annoying, difficult female – well, let me just say that I think it will serve her right to have to put up with Lady Askerton. Indeed, it should be the perfect match; Sabira – Lady Steinnland – hardly speaks at all, and Lady Askerton never stops talking."

"You are in love," Dalkey persisted. "Otherwise you'd walk away. I've never known you waste time with a bird-witted female, let alone one who's not even a beauty."

"She's not bird-witted," Iveroth said, "quite the reverse. Reads Douleur on the Rights of Man, and Galois on mathematics, when she's not buried in three-volume romances."

"An intellectual female," said Dalkey, "is a violation of the natural order of things. And not, I should think, in your style."

"Definitely not in my style," Iveroth agreed, "and as for the natural order of things... Dalkey, did you know of Steinnland's interest in alchemy and magic?"

"No, how should I?"

"Well, somehow he managed to combine a scientific, rational mind with a belief in all sorts of nonsense that modern society is finally discarding. He thought he could see the future in a bowl of water; he thought the standing stones of the islands went down to the sea on Yule night for their yearly drink of water; he believed that there really were folk who lived in the sea and who sometimes stole human babies and put changelings in the crib. And Sabira – Lady Steinnland – is extremely vague about her home and her life before marriage, and extremely fond of the sea, and I have actually seen her do some very strange things..."

"Iveroth, I think staying up at the ends of the earth with Steinnland has turned your brain! Do you really believe this girl is a mermaid whom Steinnland added to his collection of curiosities? How could the creature walk?"

"The islanders call them finwives," Iveroth said absently, "finwives and finmen… and they are said to have legs like humans as well as a tail… and no, of course I don't believe in such nonsense! But I think Steinnland believed her to be a finwife, and the crofters on Faarhafn definitely thought she could work magic."

"If a peasant girl enthralled Steinnland into marrying her," Dalkey said, "she certainly worked some sort of magic. And creating an aura of mystery about herself, and letting people believe she came out of the sea, is an excellent way to disguise her peasant origins – or would be, if anybody still gave credence to those hoary tales."

"Oh, there are fools enough in Din Eidyn who will believe anything," Iveroth said. "Look at Jenneret and his set. Their so-called Mythic Society is nothing but a cover for filthy-minded little games; rites for raising spirits and such, usually involving a naked girl or the torture of a stray cat – "

"And just how do you know what goes on in the Mythic Society meetings?" Dalkey teased.

"I make it my business to keep informed," Iveroth said repressively. "At present they are a harmless group, but should they ally with someone interested in political power, they could be a serious danger to Din Eidyn."

"Do you go to the Fiendish Masque tonight, then?"

"One of Jenneret's little affairs?"

"Not exactly. I suspect, though, that he hopes to recruit members for his society. It's been bruited abroad as a particularly select affair. None of your common public masquerades at the Rotunda or in the Water Gardens – Vivienne de Larue is hostess, and there's nothing so vulgar as a ticket of invitation required to get in; instead they have a delightful system of password and counter-password."

"Which you, of course, know."

Dalkey grinned. "I, too, keep informed. I'd no particular fancy to go – but if you wish to, as it were, broaden your circle of information, why do not we procure a pair of dominos and go together? You will get a look at Jenneret's potential converts – and we might manage to disrupt the assembly somehow. Do you still have the collection of lights and mirrors you were using to study refraction? Combined with a bit of smoking powder, we could conjure up an apparition that would terrify them all into running. It would be a famous jape!"

"Yes, let's go," said Iveroth, "but forget the smoke and mirrors. You might set them running into Jenneret's arms, converted to a belief in real devils. But first we must get Lady Askerton settled at Steinnland's house. You will understand that I do not particularly wish my old friend's widow to become involved in such a set. Lady Askerton will make certain that her acquaintances are all of the utmost respectability."

"And too old to get into trouble," Dalkey added. "You should see the dried-up old prunes she brings here! Your widow will die of boredom."

"She don't plan to remain in Din Eidyn long enough to need any real acquaintance in Society," Iveroth said. "As soon as the will is proved, she plans to return to the north – and what she does in Faarhafn is none of my responsibility!"

***

At first I thought it rude in Iveroth to take his leave as soon as he had introduced Lady Askerton and seen to the unloading of her bags. After five minutes of the lady's company, I understood perfectly. He had taken her up in his curricle and conveyed her across town. Enduring any more of her conversation was a sacrifice not to be expected of him; gentlemen have a very low tolerance for boredom.

Fortunately, having practiced since childhood how to ignore six aunts, I was able to treat Lady Askerton's conversation as no more than a mildly irritating background noise, save when a response was required.

"....and Iveroth gave me to understand that you have no acquaintance at all in Society," she was saying now. "How clever of him to ask me to introduce you! All my acquaintances are of the first order of respectability and ton; nothing can give you a better position than to be brought out as Lady Askerton's protegée. The dear Duke of Balcladich quite adores me; when I visited his country house, nothing was too good for me. He ordered his cook to create only those dishes which my delicate digestion could tolerate – you understand, what I eat is of no importance to me personally, I could dine quite happily on a few wafers and a glass of ratafia, but the Duke insisted I sit at his table – "grace his table" was the phrase he used – and saw to it that I was offered no mutton or turnips, which are foods very upsetting to the system. And when I was ready to return to Town - in fact, a few days before I had actually planned to return, for he was always beforehand with his services, a delicate attention characteristic of the highest society – he made his own coach available to me, that I might not risk taking a chill by riding in an open curricle; and he rode beside the coach for the first league, to make sure the coachman did not mistake the road, although to be sure I have no idea how he could do such a thing, because..."

"I have no desire to be brought out in Society," I interrupted her. I felt badly about the rudeness of the interruption, but by this time I had deduced that somehow she had mastered the art of talking continuously without pausing to draw breath. Later in our acquaintance I became inured to the necessity of breaking in on Lady Askerton's constant flow of speech whenever something actually had to be said.

"But how else will you meet a convenable *parti*? To be sure, Iverton is most eligible, but having remained a bachelor until the age of two-and-thirty, he must have no interest in marriage. Then there is his friend Dalkey – he must get an heir soon, and I happen to know that dear Lady Dalkey is making a push to introduce him to some eligible girls, but that insipid Cecelia Lauder with her incessant plucking at the harp, and that freckled little Sophie Westlin, and so forth, will be no competition for you, my love, once your hair has been dressed and you have appropriate clothing. Naturally you cannot go out in those garments. Not only are they totally out of the mode, but it will be expected that you wear black or at least grey in mourning for Steinnland. Where is your footman?"

Meldun appeared as if he had been standing in a shadowed corner of the room all this time – which he might indeed have been doing. He was capable of being extremely inconspicuous if he chose. I silently thanked the Sea Mother that he had at least chosen to wear the shirt and breeches Antoine had procured for him. The appearance of a naked man might have silenced Lady

Askerton briefly, but I felt the resultant hubbub would hardly be worth it.

"Well," she said, looking him up and down disdainfully, "he will, of course, have to have an appropriate livery, but I suppose he can go abroad like that, as long as no one knows he is associated with you. Have him go at once to Madame Olympe; tell her to come to the Steinnland house to measure Lady Steinnland for a complete set of mourning costumes in the latest mode. Oh, and tell her to bring samples of fabric for us to –"

"No!" I said without even worrying about the interruption.

"But we must see and feel the fabrics. All dressmakers are cheats; Olympe is the most fashionable now, but I would not put it past her to charge for true Lutécian crepe and deliver only a cheap imitation."

"Never mind the fabrics. I will not be measured!"

Lady Askerton threw up her hands. "To enter Society you must be properly dressed, and to be properly dressed you must have clothes made to your measurements. Are you shy? We can tell Olympe to send only female servants-"

"Male, female, or spirit, it makes no difference. I will not have somebody reaching and touching all over my body. I will not tolerate it!" I dared not tolerate it; whoever took the measurements would discover my tail. A small show of temper seemed in order here; I stamped my foot and began shouting and waving my hands until Lady Askerton quailed.

"But how are we to dress you?"

Breta had been attracted to the drawing-room by all the noise, and it was she, bless her, who came up with a solution.

"Send one of my lady's dresses to Madame Olympe, and tell her to create a simple black walking dress following those measurements. No, two. One for my lady to wear, and one for us to send back with alterations so that she shall know the precise fit. I am clever with my needle, my lady; if the walking dresses are not perfect, I can alter them so that Madame Olympe will know precisely what is wanted hereafter. And my lady can wear one of the dresses to visit Madame Olympe's establishment herself and select the fabrics and styles she wishes for everything else. Wait – I will bring a dress now for Meldun to take to Madame Olympe."

Lady Askerton held up my second-best day dress as though it had been picked from a rag pile. "You wish to take measurements from this?" She looked from the dress to me. "It will be far too loose when you have your stays laced."

"My lady does not wear stays," Breta interposed while I was still wincing at the thought of having a contraption of whalebone and elastic strapped around my body, bruising the delicate veins and cartilage where my tail emerged above my hips.

So the dress matter was settled, if not to Lady Askerton's satisfaction, at least to mine. I had, of course, no intention of wasting Steinnland's money on such a complete set of mourning dress as she suggested – walking dresses, sacques for receiving morning visitors, evening dresses, riding habits, gloves, hats, veils, and who knew what other fripperies? But if a black dress in the current mode was absolutely required before I could call on the Duchess of Quoy and ask her certain questions concerning my lord's illness and death, then I supposed I could wait until it was made. Lady Askerton assured me that for such an important customer as she thought me to be, this Madame Olympe would have the dress ready by tomorrow – "even if her seamstresses are required to sit up all night."

I was not prepared to oppress other girls just to speed my visit. After all, even if I received satisfaction from the Duchess of Quoy, I would still be required to remain in town until the will was proved.

"That will not be necessary," I told her and Meldun. "I have no objection to waiting a day or so for the dress. After all, it's not as if I have anywhere to go."

Lady Askerton fretted; she was the one in a hurry, not I. Until my full costume of day and evening dresses was completed, she could not take me to the Assembly Rooms or anywhere else where I might catch the eye of eligible gentlemen.

It seemed impossible to convince her that I had no intention of remarrying and no desire to enter Society. She fretted about the clothes until Breta began combing out the braids I had pulled out and tangled during my temper tantrum; this redirected her attention to my hair. The braids, she declared, were impossible; they made me look like a governess or a companion. Wearing my hair loose was equally impossible – "My dear child, it is indeed quite lovely, like a silver cloak about you, but only girls not old enough to be out wear their hair loose like that. When your footman returns, we must send him for Patrice-Henri to cut your hair and curl it á la mode. I assure you, Patrice-Henri is the only man I would entrust with the task. I recommended him to my dear Lady Ormsgil for her daughter Eugenia– a plain little squab of a girl, by the way – and she said to me, she said, 'Your hairdresser has worked a miracle,' those were her very words. And Eugenia married Sir Flodin Hultstrom, which was indeed a miracle, him being just turned forty and having evaded all marriage-lures successfully for twenty years, while his fortune allows Eugenia to keep her own carriage in town and he never even objects to her losses at loo-parties, so you see – "

"I'm not having my hair cut." I was too tired to fake another tantrum.

"But, my dear child, you cannot go abroad looking like a governess! Not that I have anything to say against governesses, for I believe they are mostly very virtuous and learned persons, although I never knew one myself, since my dear Papa disapproved of education for women, and I am sure he was right, because nothing, my dear, can be more fatal for a female in society than to appear learned, or to be argumentative with the gentlemen upon trivial points of fact, and…."

Patrice-Henri, when he arrived, resolved the dispute first by taking me up to my dressing-room – with Breta for chaperone, but without Lady Askerton, because he said he had to Concentrate on his Art – and then by talking to me like a reasonable human being instead of a doll to be dressed and shown off to strangers. His real name turned out to be plain Patric and he came from the north, like me, but he said that changing to a Lutécian-sounding name was a compromise he had had to make in order to be accepted as a fashionable hairdresser in Din Eidyn society – and that perhaps I might wish to make some compromises as well? Not cutting off my long fall of hair – that, he decreed, would be barbaric – but perhaps trimming a few locks to frame the face with becoming curls, and looping up the rest on top of my head in what he called a Lutécian Pouffe, which he claimed Breta could easily learn to do for me. He had her practice with his ribands and clips until she had mastered the pouffe, and we were both so engrossed in the project that I scarcely noticed his sharp scissors working around the edges.

When he held up a glass, I saw a stranger. A fashionable, beautiful stranger, with a soft pile of pale silvery hair held up by a riband and spilling over the sides of the band, and a fringe of short, silver-gilt curls framing her face.

Beauty was something I had never attempted; not with my aunts Seija and Eliina to demonstrate what could be done with true perfection of features and body. But Seija and Eliina were in Finfolkaheem, and I was in Din Eidyn and so bemused that I actually allowed Patric to paint my face – not heavily, for he said it would be sacrilege to cover so perfect a complexion, but he produced little pots full of color to tint my lips and bring color to my cheeks. "As for the eyes," he said, "we shall do nothing, for they are quite large enough and brilliant enough already. How fortunate that your lashes are dark, we need not even paint them!"

Fortunate indeed. I did not think myself a coward, but I quailed at the notion of allowing a stranger with a brush so close to my eyes. How did ladies of fashion bear it?

While Patric worked, he chattered – oh, nearly as much as Lady Askerton, but more to the point! As hairdresser to half the fashionable ladies of Din Eidyn, Patric knew all that was happening in town, and he advised me that it would be of no use trying to call on her Grace of Quoy.

"They say her only son has gone mad, just weeks before his majority, and she is distracted with grief and calling all the physicians in town to witness his condition. She receives no one. But," Patric added with a catlike, mincing malice, "she does go out. She's not one to shut herself up in a house of illness, not her Grace! You won't find her at the Opera this season, or at the public dances in the Rotunda, but she enjoys many a private party. In fact, this morning I myself dressed her hair *á la Meduse* for a masquerade at the house of Vivienne de Larue."

"A masquerade? Does that mean that all the guests come in disguise?"

"Indeed it does, my blossom, and for this particular one – "

"Then how is it kept private? Could not anyone in a mask enter?" I had, obviously, a particular reason for asking this question.

"Some ladies send out tickets of invitation," Patric said, "but that's too common for my lady de Larue. She vows she will not have her guests showing pasteboard cards at the door, as if they had bought admission to a public place. Instead she has given a password and counter-password to all she chose to invite. A mistake, as I could have told her. Passwords can be given to anybody who is willing to pay the price."

"I do not believe I have paid you yet for your services," I said. "Would four korona constitute adequate reimbursement?" Lady Askerton had whispered to me not to give him more than two korona.

Patric smiled and whispered a few words into my ear. I felt a blush rise to my cheeks. The language of fashionable society was somewhat grosser, it seemed, than what I had been used to in discoursing with my lord. Patric smiled again at my blushes and said that the lady Vivienne's house was no place for me, and he recommended I not use the password; he did not think I would find the masquerade amusing.

I did not, of course, explain to him my particular reason for wishing to attend the dance.

CHAPTER FOURTEEN

All I can say in defense of my decision to visit the Lady Vivienne's masquerade is that it seemed a good idea at the time. I might not yet have day dresses suitable for society, but the long jeweled tunic of my Finfolkaheem court dress, supported by the glory of my tail wrapped once around and then spread out behind me, should pass as a masquerade costume. Breta was all for the idea, and happily ran out to the shops during Lady Askerton's afternoon rest to procure a green and silver mask that perfectly matched my "costume." Meldun took a fit of the sulks and would not help, even after I pointed out to him that in *Modern Manners* Ermina had gone masked to a public dance in search of her beloved Alfonso. If that was allowable, my visiting a private dance in search of a lady must be even more respectable. In any case Meldun could not have been much help; with my tail unfurled, I should have to call a chair to carry me in any case – and that took care of the last difficulty, for the chairmen would surely know the way to Lady Vivienne's. To be sure, there was some risk of embarrassment should I be unmasked as an uninvited guest; but I hoped my late lord Steinnland's credit would be good enough to carry off my visit as a harmless frolic. And when should I have a better chance to find Ailsa of Quoy alone, unprotected by her house and servants, with no escape from my questions?

Well – not at the house of Vivienne de Larue; that became clear to me within five minutes of my joining in the masquerade. After exchanging the password and counter-password that brought a blush to my cheeks, I was admitted not to the quiet social entertainment I had envisioned, but to something more closely resembling a Hel-ish orgy. The room was so tight packed with costumed masqueraders that I was fain to retire into a corner to protect my tail from being trodden upon. From this corner, tall though I was, I could hardly see past the array of fantastic heads and hats that passed and repassed before me, their masked bearers conversing as easily and pleasantly as though they had but met in a coffee house or an assembly room – though hardly as politely. Of such scraps of conversation that I could hear in that throng of satyrs, fiends, executioners, torturers, incubi, and dancing girls in transparent gauzes, scarcely a word passed that did not send me blushing more fiercely than before; all their talk, like their costumes, seemed directed toward unnatural acts and the infliction of pain.

As for locating the petite Duchess of Quoy in such a crowd, my hopes were immediately dashed. I had thought the clue Patric gave me, in mentioning that he had dressed her hair *á la Meduse*, would allow me to recognize her in costume. But within minutes of my entrance, two lines formed for a dance in which I saw at least three women, all somewhat below the common height, dressed in scanty and diaphanous draperies parodying the modest dress of the ancient Elladians and with their hair dressed like a tangle of snakes. It seemed that Medusa was a popular character among the lady Vivienne's intimates.

One elderly woman more decently dressed than most, although in the mode of the previous century, found no partner for the dance and turned away with an expression of frustrated anger which she satisfied by quite staring me out of countenance. "Very pretty, child," she drawled, "a charming little costume, but hardly suitable for this gathering. I don't ask your worldly name, for that is forbidden by the laws of our little society, but do tell me the name of the character you represent!"

"Why, madame, this is a costume-ball, is it not? And obviously I am come in the character of a mermaid," I replied, for so Steinnland had informed me that the landfolk of Din Eidyn refer to all the people of the sea: finwives, selkiewomen, and female nucklaveen are all mermaids to them.

"Little innocent!" She tapped me on the shoulder with her fan. "And what gallant brought you here on the pretense that this was a common masquerade? Depend upon it, my dear, he means you no good, and you had best get your nurse to take you home to bed before your gallant ruins you – if indeed you are not already ruined? No, your eyes could not look so innocent if that were the case. Know, then, that we who gather here are a select group within the larger society of Din Eidyn. We believe in freedom and in obeying our own will in all things."

"So much I had gathered from the password 'Fais ce que voudray,'" I responded. The counter-password, indicating what things might be the will of the speaker, was too rude for me to repeat it willingly. "But does this freedom not extend to selecting whatever costume pleases you for the masquerade?"

"By all means," she said, "so long as it is suitable to our style and purpose. Look about you, child; you will see many a Nero, but no Caesars; any number of witches, but no good fairies; Medusas in plenty, but no virtuous Lucrece. Now do you comprehend your error?"

I was quite happy to converse with this woman on the subject of the superfluity of Medusas; perhaps she might identify the Duchess to me. "Not perfectly, madame," said I, "for there was in classical history but one Medusa, and here I see at least three. Pray, who are the ladies who thought fit to assume so horrid a character?"

"Ah-ah-ah!" said my interlocutor, smiling playfully while with her fan she delivered a second blow to my shoulder that was anything but playful. "Have not I already told you that it is strictly forbidden to inquire for the identity behind the mask? Those who wish to know or to be known can identify themselves to their friends by certain signs; the others must be allowed the freedom of anonymity."

While we talked, the formal contra-dance had disintegrated into a general groping and clutching in which more than one lady was exposed beyond the general dictates of landfolks' propriety by the disarrangement of her costume, while several pairs and at least one trio appeared to be proceeding even further into intimacy right upon the dance floor.

"If this behavior is freedom," I said, fixing my eyes upon my interlocutor's face rather than upon the unseemly goings-on about us, "I can well understand why it must be coupled with anonymity. But not everyone is dressed as an evil spirit or a villain of antiquity. Your own costume, though outmoded – "

"Ignorant child! I am here in the character of Madeline d'Aubrey, Marquise de Brinvilliers. Have you never heard of her? One who suffered all for love, she poisoned her father and brothers in order to secure the family fortune to herself and to support her adulterous lover."

It seemed to me that it was the family of the Marquise, not she herself, who had suffered for her love.

"And over there," she said, pointing at a stooped figure concealed under a heavy cloak, "is my confederate, La Voisin, who disposed of many an unwanted baby, saved many a fine lady embarrassment, and made candles of the baby-fat to burn at her Black Masses. An exemplary figure who performed real services to society before the narrow-minded judges of the time had her burned at the stake!"

At this point the "Marquise de Brinvilliers" was interrupted by a horrid cackling cry of "Mine, mine, another one of mine!" which presaged the leap of a black-clad gentleman between us.

I say "gentleman" because Patric had given me to understand that only the upper orders of society were welcome at private masquerades, but in truth there was little gentle or civilised about his appearance. His suit of fine black velvet was partially obscured by a demi-cape of black embroidered with pentagrams, letters of ancient alphabets, and suchlike symbols; his face was covered from forehead to chin with a black mask embroidered with more cabalistic symbols, and in one black-gloved hand he held a fat black wand with a five-pointed star adorning the end.

"Begone, my servant of Brinvilliers!" he cried, flourishing his cape and waving his hands in her face, so that she lost countenance and retreated back among the general throng. "Go and plot with your dear neighbor, and let me have more poisonings, more infanticides, more hangings, more burnings, and more general joy throughout the realm! Leave this child to me. I'll entertain her with my sorcerous charms!"

"I see your wand is already well raised for her entertainment, Baron!"

called a man on the dance floor, with a high-pitched giggle that underscored the double-entendre he thought so amusing.

"Indeed, sir," I said, half rising from my chair, "I was just this instant…"

"Going home? And abandoning the lucky dog who escorted you hither? Then his ill fortune shall be my joy, for I'll take his place rather than see so fair a flower draggled through the mire of the streets."

I sank down upon my chair again, wishing most bitterly that I had heeded Lady Askerton's strictures upon the impropriety of going abroad unchaperoned. If only Meldun were here now, how little I should mind his disapproval, his capricious ways, and the certainty that he would report all my behaviour to my family! Solitude held no terrors for me, but the inability to repel "admirers" such as this Sorceror with his fantastical dress and behavior was a problem which had never presented itself on Faarhafn. Even the two gentlemen whom I observed at the entrance to the hall, soberly costumed in half-masks and dominoes, would be preferable to the company of this capering ape – or would they? Who knew what hideous costumes their dominoes concealed?

"Well, then, stay awhile, and we shall entertain one another," declared the Sorceror Baron upon seeing me still seated. He dragged a chair away from the wall and placed it between me and the company, then bestrode the seat and crossed his arms on the back of the chair. "What is it you claim to be? A mermaid? Nay, do not tease me! Did you think you were talking to one who cannot tell a selkie from a nucklavee? Oh no, my pretty, I know your sort and know it well. You – are – a FINWIFE!" He roared out the last word and pointed most rudely at me. I felt the color leave my cheeks.

"And now you shall tell me, if you please, how you contrived to imitate the traditional costume of the finfolk so exactly, for I had thought myself the only person in Din Eidyn possessing a copy of Kuylenstierna's *Engravings Anatomical and Descriptive of the Supernatural Inhabitants of Din Eidyn and the Surrounding Seas.*"

As it happened, I was famliar with this work, for there had been a copy in Steinnland's library, and many times we had laughed together over the inaccuracies in Kuylenstierna's depictions of the seafolk.

"That book is not, perhaps, so good a reference as you believe," I said, happy to turn the conversation to matters I knew somewhat of. "There are several errors, particularly regarding the nucklaveen—"

"You have read Kuylenstierna? Aha!" exclaimed my interlocutor. "Then I know who you are, for the only other copy of that book was in old Kosta Greenmark's private library, and he refused to sell it to me at any price, the dog. Perhaps you will be more accommodating, *Lady Steinnland!*"

He pronounced my name so loudly that it seemed to me half the people in the hall must have heard him. Certainly the two gentlemen in dominos turned towards us.

"I believe it is not the custom to use real names here," I reproved him.

"Oh, between intimates all is permitted," the Sorceror said, "and we shall be intimates, for I could never allow so lovely a creature to escape me again. You must know, my dear, that I am the most celebrated student of esoterica and folklore in Din Eidyn, and that is sufficient to identify me. As for you, I know more about you than you imagine, beautiful finwife."

I tensed, then relaxed as he went on to explain to me certain matters that I knew well enough already. "For instance, since you have dressed as a finwife, you must tell people that you come from Finfolkaheem, your lovely home of coral towers and high arched bridges beneath the sea."

People who have not been there always make the mistake of envisioning Finfolkaheem as a sort of underwater Din Eidyn, only more brightly colored.

"And your summer home, of course, is Faarhafn, a corruption of Finnalhafn, that is to say, the haven of the finfolk. But you know all this already, do you not, Lady Steinnland? From the accuracy of your costume –"

"Etymology is of all studies the most interesting to me," I said. "Pray continue explaining the origins of these names."

"No, no, I have done with polite gibble-gabble!" roared the Sorceror, springing up from his chair and waving his arms so wildly as to discommode the two domino-clad gentlemen who were approaching us at last. "I must and will know how you have attached that tail so cleverly, and since you do not dance, I will discover your stratagem by direct examination!"

He overleaped the chair – knocking it over as he did so – and caught my wrist in a grip that pulled me upright before I twisted and freed myself.

"She has the strength of a finwife as well as the costume!" he exclaimed. "Now just let me feel, divine creature – "

I believe he would actually have slipped his hand up under my jeweled tunic, had not the first of the men in dominos interposed first an arm and then his entire person between us.

"You grow overexcited," drawled a voice all too familiar to me. "I am sure you did not mean to offer an insult to a lady under my protection." Iveroth's steely arm – for it was he – held the Sorceror's gloved hand and forced it back against his own shoulder.

"What, have you already laid claim to the Steinnland fortune? I cry unfair play, Iveroth. You have no need of an heiress to settle your debts."

"And you had best find another way of settling yours. You are not to annoy this lady again."

"They who dance at Vivienne's masques must pay the piper," retorted the Sorceror sulkily. "What business had she coming here, and sitting alone, if she meant to cry out with missish propriety at the first gentleman who offers her attentions?"

"Being a newcomer to Din Eidyn," said a lighter voice belonging to Iveroth's masked companion, "perhaps she made the natural mistake of thinking that at a party in a private house she would indeed meet only gentlemen, rather than libertines who pursue where their advances are clearly unwelcome."

"I could call you out for that, Dalkey!"

"Oh… please, do." The man called Dalkey seemed to purr like a cat at the prospect.

"Save that, of course, no one takes offense at anything here," said the Sorceror Baron quickly. "I must abide by our motto and password."

"Oh, well," Dalkey sighed, "another time, perhaps." He turned and offered me his arm with courtly grace. "May we have the honor of escorting you home, my lady?"

Iveroth let go the Sorceror's arm with a contemptuous shove and positioned himself on my other side. Together, they made a clear path to the door which enabled me to escape the masquerade with the delicate outer folds of my tail draped safely over one arm.

Once outside, Iveroth found me a chair simply by nodding at someone in the throng of men waiting to collect their masters and mistresses. "Rautenberg will not object if I borrow your services," he told the bearers. "He will not wish to leave for some hours yet."

I hastily drew the folds of my tail close about me. He handed me into the chair with cold courtesy and I sighed with relief that the humiliating confrontation was over. If I had been happy to see him when the masked Sorceror was tormenting me, that happiness was entirely overpowered by the lowering reflection that he must despise me for having attended such an affair in the first place. At least tonight I need not suffer his reproaches; I could go home and salve my bruised tail and compose myself for whatever he said tomorrow – and I had no doubt that he would have more than enough to say.

I was correct in that, but wrong to feel relief so soon. Instead of simply giving the bearers their direction and returning to his amusements, Iveroth announced his intention of walking with me to Steinnland's house. His friend fell into place on the other side of the chair, and Iveroth hired a link-boy to light our way through the murky streets.

We had scarce passed beyond the lights cast by the Lady Vivienne's torches when he began.

"This sort of adventure was precisely what I feared you would get up to, and is what I placed Lady Askerton with you to prevent. Pray, what possessed her to allow you to go to such a place by yourself?"

"I did not ask her opinion," I said in a small voice. "She retires early."

"In the future I wish you will be guided by her," Iveroth said, "instead of acting like a wayward child who is too young to understand the dangers of the world! Perhaps in those foolish romances you read it is customary for the ingenuous heroine to attend a Fiendish Masque unescorted, but perhaps now you understand that there is some reason for Society's restrictions! I do not like to think what might have transpired had Dalkey and I not seen you."

Neither did I, but his tone was intolerable. "I collect, my lord, it is perfectly in order for you to attend a masquerade at Lady Vivienne's private house, but not for me?"

"Do not begin with me," Iveroth warned. "I am in no humor to listen to a defence of the Rights of Woman. If you intend reforming society, could you not find some more savory place to start than affirming your right to attend a Fiendish Masque? What ever possessed you to go to such an affair in the first place?"

"I particularly wished to speak to the Duchess of Quoy."

"Hmph! Well, it is certainly her style of entertainment, but how did you come to hear that she might be there?"

"Patric – I mean, Patrice-Henri – told me that he had dressed her hair *à la Meduse* for the occasion. I thought I would be easily able to pick her out by that. I had not realized that Medusa would be such a popular figure. And," I added to get it all over with at once, "I bribed him to tell me the password."

"God give me patience! If you wish to speak with Ailsa of Quoy, why not call upon her in the usual way? Or is that too tame for you?"

"Patrice-Henri said she was not receiving callers."

Iveroth heaved an exasperated sigh. "And, of course, you choose to get your information about society, and your ideas of proper behavior for a very young widow, from your hairdresser rather than accepting my direction. If you wish to call on her Grace, I shall escort you myself."

"My hairdresser is at least civil, and treats me like an adult! All you do is shout, and say I must do this, and I must not do that, without giving the least reason!"

"If you had any sense, you would accept my guidance and be grateful for it. At least I have been enough years on the town to know what's what! I have no need to explain myself to a chit of twenty who has never been off her native isle!"

"And I, my lord, have no need to obey your orders! I did not come to Din Eidyn to please you – "

"That is quite clear," Iveroth interjected, "because you must know that it does not please me at all to see Steinnland's widow making a public show of herself and dragging his name in the gutter."

Oh, my lord, my dear lord. Had I done that to him? I had only come here on his wish; I had only gone to the masquerade to find out more about what caused his death.

"Is it so bad as that?"

"We can only hope that you were not recognized," said Iveroth.

"Not much chance of that," put in his friend, who had been silent up till then. "Not with that fool shouting out her name."

"I had forgot that! Very well; I shall put it about that you were imposed upon, that some mischief-maker invited you to Lady Vivienne's masque and gave you the impression it was a small private gathering of the first respectability. And in the future, Sabira, you will please consult me before flying off on mad capers like this!"

"Why? Obviously you do not care what happens to me, you are just trying to protect my lord Steinnland's name from the gossip that's bound to attach to a bold and licentious creature like myself!"

"I had hoped," said Iveroth in freezing accents, "that you might have cared somewhat yourself for Steinnland's name."

***

After they had seen Sabira to her door and Iveroth had paid off the link-boy and chairmen, the two friends walked together back to Dalkey's house.

"I had always supposed you to be a gentleman of singular address," Dalkey said after a while. "Why has it deserted you now?"

Iveroth snorted. "What, should I have petted and caressed the silly chit for making a fool of herself?"

"She said you didn't care what happened to her."

"Well, obviously I do, or I would not have troubled myself to get her out of that!"

"Women like to hear you say these things, y'know. If all you ever do is criticize their actions without saying anything kind, she just might think you don't care for her."

"I am much obliged to you," Iveroth said, "for applying your vast experience with women to point out my errors in dealing with this one. Would there be anything else?"

"Well, yes," Dalkey said apologetically. "One of us really should have mentioned her costume. Very pretty dress – very striking. Thought so at the time, but I'm not acquainted with her – not my place to say so."

"And you conceive it is my job to compliment her on her dress?"

"That is the usual thing," Dalkey said, "when courting."

"I'm not courting the jade, just trying to keep her out of trouble!"

"Really?" Dalkey raised one russet eyebrow. "I've not seen you put yourself out so much for any other female. You could have fooled me."

"If you weren't such a damned good shot," said Iveroth between his teeth, "I'd call you out for that, Dalkey!"

"Ah. But I am such a damned good shot," said Dalkey comfortably. "Pity Baron Jenneret backed down, ain't it?"

"A great pity."

CHAPTER FIFTEEN

Starting the kiln required some skill, and raking out the burned cakes was work for a strong man, but the day-long task of watching the fire and piling on fresh ware and tangle as needed could be left to anyone, even a responsible child. Grete Farchar watched in the early morning while her mam laid down smouldering peats in the bottom of the earthen pit, then covered them with the driest tangle from the piles that had been spread and turned to dry above the tide line. Jonat held a ragged sack first at one side of the kiln, then at the other, as the wind shifted, until the tangle was burning well.

"Mind well now how I stack it on," she told her daughter, "and we'll see if you can build the fire next time."

Nobody else under twelve had been trusted with laying a kiln without supervision. Grete watched closely, muttering under her breath to make sure she remembered exactly how her mam did it: ware laid round about the outer edge of the burning circle, then the longer strands of tangle placed crosswise over the fire "to give it air to breathe," Jonat explained. "Fire's a living thing, and 'twill die just like a Christian if it canna get air."

Grete put an experimental palm over her own lips and pinched her nose with the other hand. After a moment the stones of the kiln danced before her eyes, the air seemed dark with smoke and the aching to breathe was too much for her. She dropped her hands and took great gulping gasps of air just as Jonat noticed what she was doing and slapped her for it.

"No fooling! I told you to pay attention, not to play bairns' games like holding your breath till you're too dizzy to tend the fire."

Grete blinked back the tears that had come to her eyes – Mam had a strong hand – and concentrated on keeping her breathing quiet and even until the pounding in her head had subsided. Mam was unfair; it wasn't that hard to start a kiln. You just went round and round and across and across, over and over again, starting with the driest ware and tangles and moving on to the damp stuff.

"Now mind well, and no more games," Mam said when she'd layered the seaweed until the center of the mound rose well above the two-foot circle of stones surrounding the pit. "If you let the fire burn through, it'll burst into flames and turn all to useless ash. If you pile on too much wet stuff, you'll smother it. Watch it well, and every time the ware sinks this much below the walls – "she held out one broad hand turned sideways – you put on tangles and ware as I showed you, round and cross, until it's all a hand's height above the stones again. And always finish with ware, mind, so that we don't leave any stems of tangle unburned. Can you do that for me?"

"Mam, I've been doing it these three summers past."

"Aye, but with me to check on you. With the new babe so sickly, I'll need to stay at home all day." Jonat stared hard at Grete. "I must trust you now, d'you see? Don't let all your father's hard work go up in flames!"

After Mam left, Grete stared at the mound of kelp until her eyes watered from squinting into the clouds of pale blue smoke. Finally the burning mass had sunk and it was time to put on more tangle and ware – or was it? She measured the width of her hand against the top of the stones. The mass had sunk more than a thumb's width below that – but it was all right, Mam's hand was broader than hers. She warmed herself by running circles around the kiln, dropping in the ware and pretending that she had slept and almost let the smoldering fire burst into flames. It was an emergency, she had to run faster, faster, and now she had to lay the stalks of tangle crosswise over the middle….

She dropped onto thin grass still wet with dew, panting with exhaustion, but that lasted only a few minutes. Then it was back to the long boring wait until the next layer had to be put down. She rocked a handful of tangle in her lap and sang it a lullaby; she let her eyes go out of focus so that the wisps of pale blue smoke seemed to take the shapes of kings and castles out of ancient ballads; she caught her eyes closing and pinched herself, hard, on the soft flesh inside her arm, to make sure she did not drop off to sleep. Then it was time for the next layer, and the next... What would she do if she burned up all the kelp they had laid ready before her da came to do the raking-off? She became a miser with the next few layers, so that she had barely spread out one before it was time to renew the mound. Her back ached and she scarcely noticed the clouds that had covered the sun, the mist blotting out the view of the sea; the work was keeping her warm enough. The piles of unburnt ware and tangle were hardly lower; it wasn't necessary to be so careful. She made the next layer a good heavy one that would take time to burn, that would give her time to sit back away from the smoke that stung her eyes and enjoy her nooning of bread and cheese.

Even then she worried; had she laid it down too heavy? Was the fire going out? No, the writhing shapes of blue smoke rising into the sky were as strong as ever, perhaps even stronger, or maybe it was just that the white mist coming up from the sea made them look darker by contrast. White mist parting and swirling over the darkness of the sea, white and dark forms dancing behind the blue smoke...Strange, how when you could not actually see the water, the slap of waves upon stone sounded so much closer...almost like something coming to get you. Grete shivered involuntarily and told herself not to be a silly bairn. When you lived on an island, the sea was food and fuel and life, not something to be afraid of. *And sometimes it takes its own back*

No, that was foolishness. Of course sometimes men drowned at the fishing, but that was no reason to be frightened like a bairn when you were sitting on dry land and warmed by a good hot kiln burning ware and tangle.

Was that a step, or a slither, or what, on the far side of the fire – the seaward side? It sounded like the movement of a wet, heavy body.

There were creatures in the sea, but they weren't the dark monsters of the Yule-night stories. That finwife Lord Steinnland married in his old age had been good and sweet and pretty and she had given Mam extra pennies for darning the sheets, and Mam had called Bessie Clipagarthe a fool for saying that the lady had overlooked her Sinnie. Mam said that if you treated all God's creatures with courtesy and without fear, they would treat you the same way.

The finfolk were said to be capricious, but the selkiefolk were only gentle and sweet. Maybe it was a selkie come to shed its sealskin and dance on land.

Slap-slop-thud. Heavy and clumsy it sounded... not like a thing that wanted to dance. And there was a foul, acrid smell that made the blue smoke of the burning kelp seem like sweet air by comparison.

Show courtesy, and no fear, Mam had said when Grete was first nervous of the old lord's finwife.

She sat quite still, her face upturned, smiling, until the thing out of the sea lumbered over the kiln, squelching and moaning and putting the fire quite out with its great wet body. And then she would have screamed, but there was only salt water and seaweed choking her, and no air to breathe anywhere.

***

After that exceedingly unpleasant scene with Iveroth, I remained quietly at home for several days, finding sufficient occupation in setting the town house to rights and in listening to Lady Askerton's words of guidance on the proper conduct for a young widow in Din Eidyn.

Oh, all right, that is not precisely true, but it was my intention. At least, it is true that I stayed within doors, but Iveroth and Antoine between them had procured what seemed to me a small army of servants who did first, and (truth to tell) usually better, whatever I thought of to do in the way of removing holland covers from furniture, polishing chandeliers, dusting, and whatever else one is supposed to do to take care of a house. As for Lady Askerton's words of guidance, they were plentiful enough, but they would have driven me quite mad if I had actually listened. She was not ill-natured, though, merely something of a snob and quite foolish. For the most part I was able to think of her words as a mere soothing background noise, like the roar of the ocean on Faarhafn, while I embroidered decorative motifs on table linens.

I am an extremely bad seamstress.

On the third day of my immurement Advocat Tulloch called with some papers for me to sign, and rescued the current victim of my embroidery attempts from the snarls and bloodstains which were spoiling a perfectly good napkin.

"If ye'll permit me to say so, lassie, it does not seem to me that either you or the linen are enjoying this experiment."

"I'm certainly not," I confessed. "I have no talent for needlework. I can knit, but I left my knitting needles behind in Faarhafn – that is – I lost them." I felt the heat rise to my cheeks at the memory of that scene, in which Iveroth had been even ruder than after the masque, and with less excuse. "Anyway, Lady Askerton says that knitting is common and embroidering upon linen is an Appropriate Occupation for Young Ladies, and it's better than trying to play the harp."

"Not musical either?"

"I used to like to sing," I said, "but only country songs. I haven't the voice for Borghesan opera airs. So it's either the harp, and make everybody suffer, or embroidery, in which case only the linens and I suffer. And Lady Askerton won't let the linen-maid give me any more tablecloths to practice on, only napkins."

"You'll be wearying to go out in society, nae doubt."

I felt my face color unbecomingly; I don't look good with pink cheeks like a landwoman's. "Not really. That is, I – I have no objection to waiting until I can be dressed appropriately. Mourning and all that," I added, in case he thought I meant my "costume" for the masque. Surely he hadn't heard about that disastrous venture? Iveroth had promised to hush it up, hadn't he? I stole a look under my lashes. He did not have the look of a man bent on tormenting me; he was just a little round advocat, a kindly man who had no more idea than I had how I was to amuse myself in Din Eidyn.

"Well, until the mourning clothes come, perhaps you could send to Fountbell's for some books – oh, no, I forgot; it's closed."

"Fountbell's is closed?" To my knowledge, it was the only bookshop in Din Eidyn; certainly the only one my lord dealt with. It had not occurred to me until Mr. Tulloch mentioned it that I could send for books to be delivered to Steinnland's town house just as we had sent for them from Faarhafn, and now I felt as though a promised pleasure had been snatched away just as I glimpsed it.

"Oh, not permanently," Mr. Tulloch hastened to reassure me, "but Fountbell always goes south for a few weeks to rest before the summer crush begins. Din Eidyn is so cold and rainy in the spring that it is very thin of company; things will be much more cheerful after the second week in July, when the Lords' Council convenes and the social round begins in earnest."

By the second week in July I expected to be back on Faarhafn for good.

"But in the meantime," Mr. Tulloch added casually, "you may wish to have Lady Askerton put your name down for Cromertie's Circulating Library, where you may borrow one book at a time."

I sat up, dropping my scissors and my case of embroidery silks. "Tell me more about this Circulating Library, if you please, Mr. Tulloch." How foolish of me! My lord had never objected to my sending for any books I wanted from Fountbell's when we lived on Faarhafn, and I felt sure he would have considered it a reasonable expense now if only the bookstore had been open. But the Circulating Library, as Mr. Tulloch explained it, seemed like an even better plan. On payment of a small deposit you could borrow any book in their stock, and when you returned that book you could have another one, and so forth, as Mr. Tulloch put it, "ad infinitum."

"As many books as I want to read? For just one fee?"

"Annual fee. Three korona. And you'll understand, there is quite a wait for the newest romances."

"I am accustomed to waiting," I said. The mails between Din Eidyn and Faarhafn were erratic, to say the least. "And I am certain they have many older books which I have not read. I shall subscribe today – that is, I shall desire Lady Askerton to do so in my name. Oh, thank you, Mr. Tulloch!"

The one problem with the Circulating Library was that, unlike Fountbell's, there was no printed circular listing their books. The disadvantage of this did not fully strike me until I had sent Lady Askerton, with Meldun in attendance, to put down my name at the library and to bring me back something to read.

She brought back a book of improving sermons. And I could not exchange it for something else until the next day.

On the morrow I sent Meldun by himself. Where he had learned to read I do not know, but he chose a volume entitled, "On the Proper Management of the Horse," and sat in the servants' hall all evening reading it and snorting to himself in a manner that quite alarmed the Din Eidyn servants. I was obliged to request him not to sound quite so much like a neighing horse when he read.

"But it's so ridiculous!" he protested. "The author says – "

"I have not the least interest in what the author has to say," I cut him off, "and I must say, you need not have been quite so selfish in your choice of book. I hope you've enjoyed it, for I'm returning it tomorrow!"

On the third day I sent Breta Scrabster, thinking that since she could not read, at least she would not choose something appropriate to her particular taste rather than to mine. This was correct, but I cannot say that I found much amusement in Volume 42 of the County Annals of Kinlochbervie.

By late that afternoon I was near to defying the edicts of Society (as interpreted to me by Iveroth and Lady Askerton) and committing the solecism of appearing in public not only out of mourning, but in one of my drab old country dresses, just for the privilege of choosing my own library book. Then Lady Askerton's endless chatter set my thoughts to quite a different direction. I was obliged to ask her to repeat herself, for I had not been attending to what she said. I will say for her that she was never ill-tempered about such a request. Doubtless few of her acquaintance ever cared enough about what she said to make the request in the first place!

"Why, my dear, I was just commenting on the Countess of Torquhan's receipt for the cleansing of the complexion and purifying of the blood, which is certainly nothing you need, child, with your fair clear skin, but you must know that all three of her daughters are sadly spotty, poor things, and she was at her wit's end how to clear the oldest one's skin before it is time to introduce her to society, but I saw Lizzie Tornstrom just the other day and she was quite in looks, and her mama – the dear Countess, you know, we were the best of friends at school – is hoping now to hold a ball in her honor before the end of the summer season. We shall of course receive cards, and I feel it would be permissible for you to attend, but not to dance; not until you are out of black stockings, as the saying is, though why stockings in particular I shall never know—"

"Never mind about the dancing," I cut in upon her flow of speech, "tell me the Countess's receipt again."

"Why, child, 'tis nothing you need; your complexion is flawless!" She stroked my cheek with one wrinkled finger. "Like a white flower in the dew of morning. A young man said that to me once – yes, hard to credit now, is it not? But I was young once, and renowned for the purity of my complexion."

She could scarcely have been renowned for any other feature, having, poor lady, small squinting eyes, a large beak of a nose, sloping shoulders and a generally flat and angular body. But she sighed now, like one remembering long-ago days of nosegays and serenades, and I was loath to break in on her daydream of times past.

On the other hand, this might be my only chance; by the next time she stopped talking, she might have completely forgotten what she was saying about the Countess of Torquhan's beauty secrets. Or I might have gone mad.

"The receipt," I prompted her. "You said she uses cucumbers and sea salt?"

"Yes, cucumbers on the face, and sea salt instead of table salt on all your food, as much as you can stand, but only the best sea salt, mind you. Any spicer will sell you something he claims is sea salt, but nine times out of ten it is just common table salt mixed with ink, or something, to make it look gray and damp and coarse. She says you cannot trust any but Gairdie's in the Langmarket to purvey the right kind of salt, properly evaporated from the water of the northern seas and with all sorts of magical minerals in it. Of course Gairdie's prices are outrageous, but for a miracle such as his salt seems to have worked on poor Lizzie Tornstrom, I suppose it means nothing to the Countess, although I vow I do not know how she supports her son's habit of deep play at all the worst houses in Din Eidyn – she must be depending on Lizzie or one of the other girls to make a good marriage to restore their fortunes—"

"Gairdie's," I repeated, committing the name to memory, "in the Langmarket. I could send my girl there to buy some?"

"Yes, but whyever would you trouble? Your skin is perfect as it is!"

"But my maid's is not," I said, trusting that Lady Askerton would not admit to the short sight which made her squint and made it most unlikely that she had subjected Breta's features to any close inspection.

"You'd not wish to waste so much money on curing a serving girl's muddy complexion!"

"I am minded to make the experiment," I told her, "for the sake of abstract scientific knowledge."

"As it happens," Lady Askerton said, "the dear Countess pressed some of her receipt upon me, though I told her you had no need of any such thing. But now let me get it – oh, no, I insist, my dear! Only think, when I tell her that you used it after all – for your maidservant!" She tittered behind her hand, and I gathered that somehow my using the Countess's beauty receipt for a servant would give Lady Askerton some points to score in the complicated game of ups and downs which, to judge from her recital, all the women of Din Eidyn played continually against one another.

All the ladies, anyway.

I had a fine time getting rid of Lady Askerton after she brought me the pinch of salt wrapped up in brown paper that the Countess had given her; she wanted to begin immediately by applying cucumber slices to Breta's cheeks, and I needs must go along with her for fear of revealing my true interest in the salt. Breta, bless her, put up with the application of cucumbers and lay for an hour, eyes closed, while Lady Askerton rambled on. But at last I was rid of both of them, and late that night I sat alone in my room with a pinch of sea salt – all that the Countess had given Lady Askerton – and a bowl of clear water.

If salt could be taken from the sea, then logic dictated that restoring it to clear water would give me a bowl of sea water, with which I should be able to work at least a small salt magic. I stirred the pinch of salt into the bowl and lifted my dripping hands slowly from the surface, drawing up the last drops of salty water into a thin sheet that hung suspended between my fingers and the bowl like a fine membrane, a liquid mirror, a curved and distorting window into – what did I most wish to see?

My family: the wish formed in my mind before I could think of anything more useful, like the whereabouts of the Duchess of Quoy. The membrane of water trembled, clouded, and cleared, and it was as if I looked through stormy water at my home beneath the waves. Two of my nieces were teasing an eel through their hoops, my mother mended my father's cloak, and my aunts Eliina and Seija were trying a new way of looping up their hair with strings of polished corals.

"I miss Sabira," my mother said. "How long has she been away now?"

Before I could hear the answer, the membrane of water fell in plinking drops across the bowl. There had only been salt enough for a very small magic. And my eyes were full of foolish tears. What was there to weep for? I did not need to hear the answer; I knew exactly how long I had been gone.

The next day I sent Breta to Gairdie's with a korona and instructions to buy as much sea salt as she could. I had no chance to try the stuff immediately, though, for before she returned the first of my new garments were delivered, and even as I was trying them on another caller was announced.

"Iveroth!" I dropped the hand-mirror with which I was trying to see the mass of veiling at the back of my neck, but Breta caught the glass before it fell. "What does he want?"

Lady Askerton fluttered and assured me that it was quite proper for gentlemen to pay morning calls, now that I could receive them decently. I had not been concerned with propriety. I had half expected Iveroth to call on the day after the masque so that he could continue scolding me for my folly. Now I wished he had done so; while I was still angry with him, I could have stood up to his censure better. Three days had been quite long enough for me to realize what damage I could have done to my lord's name with such reckless conduct. I had been hearing the voices of Society in my head: *a girl from nowhere, my dear, and the old lord had not been in his grave a week before she had installed herself in his town house and was making merry with the worst elements of society; but what can you expect? These mésalliances never work out well. Look at Ailsa of Quoy. No moral sense whatever, but at least she is clever enough to disguise her amours. The March-Lord's young widow must be stupid as well as underbred.*

I tucked Breta's packet of sea salt into the new black reticule which had come with all the rest – the walking dresses and evening dresses, the black gloves and stockings and veils – more clothes than I had owned in all my life, nor ever thought to need. I could think of no circumstance in which the salt would enable me to avoid Iveroth's just criticism of my conduct, but at least it made me feel that I had something of my own with me in this new life.

I had to pause and take a deep breath – oh, all right, several breaths – before entering my own drawing room. I reminded myself that he had no right to come to my own house and lecture me, and marched into the room before I could forget this.

His face changed perceptibly when he saw me, but I could not read his expression; his wide mouth was set at the corners and his brows drew together slightly, but otherwise he was quite still.

"Lady Steinnland," he said with a slight bow, "I must tell you – "

"If you mean to continue lecturing me about the other night, my lord, you need tell me nothing. I am quite conscious of my duty to March-Lord Steinnland's name and do not need to be lessoned on the subject! Besides," I said, feeling more and more like a sulky nymphet who had been caught riding wild kelpies instead of minding the hatcheries, "it is none of your business."

"I was only going to remark that you look well in black," Iveroth said mildly – throwing me completely off-balance.

"Oh! I – well, that is – thank you," I said, aware that I sounded as ungracious as the unruly nymphet I had been some ten years earlier.

"And to invite you to come for a drive with me. My curricle is outside."

"Oh! You are – very kind."

"You need not sound so surprised," said Iveroth with a faint smile. "Have I been so unkind before?"

I looked down and pleated the fine crepe of my skirt with one hand.

"I see you think so, in any event. Well, perhaps I may redeem myself by taking you to some place you have been wishing to visit."

"Cromertie's Circulating Library!" I cried in delight.

Iveroth looked surprised. "I had not thought that would be your first choice."

"If you had been stuck in this house for three days with nothing to read except a book of sermons, a study on the management of horses, and an odd volume of the County Annals of Kinlochbervie, you too would be desperate to get to Cromertie's," I said.

"Dear me! Did Steinnland take all his books to Faarhafn when he retired there?"

"It seems so, yes."

"Well, then, my poor girl, our second stop shall certainly be Cromertie's Circulating Library. But first I mean to fulfil a promise that I made to you on – on a certain night which we need not discuss further."

I must have looked as blank as I felt.

"I told you," he said patiently, "that if you wished to speak with the Duchess of Quoy, I would escort you to call on her. I could not keep my promise until your new clothes were delivered, but you will allow that I have been tolerably prompt within that restriction."

He bowed again, this time in farewell to Lady Askerton, and offered me his arm.

CHAPTER SIXTEEN

At the first sight of Sabira in her mourning clothes Iveroth felt breath and speech driven from him. He had expected that all that black would somehow darken and diminish her; that in the layers of petticoats and bodices and overdresses and stockings and veils demanded by society, she would look more – oh, more normal, more biddable, as a young girl ignorant of Din Eidyn ought to be. And less disturbing.

He had been wrong on all counts. Why had he been fool enough to imagine that costumes cut by the best dressmaker in Din Eidyn would detract from the impact of her appearance? In the loose, much-worn country dresses she wore on Faarhafn, she had been striking; now she was breathtaking. These so-called "mourning clothes" somehow emphasized the sweet curves of bosom and hip, drew the eye to a neat waist encircled by a belt of crushed silk with silver buckles. And the concoction of black silk and black lace veiling that passed for a hat was the perfect backdrop to silver-gilt hair piled up in artful loops, a pearly complexion and eyes as green as the sea.

Iveroth had never considered himself a town-gallant, but he did wish he could have thought of something cleverer to say than "You look well in black." Richert Dalkey, no doubt, would have turned a pretty phrase that would have cleared the stormy look from Sabira's eyes.

All he could do was offer his services in taking her to call on the Duchess of Quoy. And even that was not a totally disinterested offer. Iveroth felt there must be some connection between Ailsa's sudden visit to Faarhafn, her even more sudden departure, and the apoplexy that had felled Steinnland. But he did not know what to ask the Duchess, nor how to account for the mystery of Steinnland's subsequent death, drowned in his own bed with strings of rotting seaweed besliming the linens and the bed-curtains. If Sabira knew what questions to ask, he wanted very much to hear them – and the answers.

She was awkward as any girl would have been on her first time being handed up into a high curricle and hobbled by a fashionably narrow skirt. That restored Iveroth's confidence somewhat. His man jumped on behind, with a heavier thump than usual; were the servants, too, dazzled by Lady Steinnland's fair beauty framed in black lace and silk? Iveroth could hardly blame them if they were. To give himself time to think, he did not drive directly to the Quoy mansion, but turned aside into the long, narrow park that stretched the length of downtown Din Eidyn, softening the grey stone houses and towers of the city with trees that were now covered with a shower of June blossom.

Sabira drew in her breath and reached out from the curricle as if she thought she could touch the flowering trees, then looked about her at the plots of carefully tended blooms surrounded by no less carefully tended grass. "But this is beautiful!" she exclaimed. "You have everything in Din Eidyn – trees, and gardens, and libraries!"

She fell suddenly silent, and Iveroth supposed she was remembering the masque with renewed embarrassment. "But we do not have the sea," he said.

"What, is it not a harbor city? That much, I learned from my lord's books on geography."

"Yes, but –" Iveroth had been about to explain that the area around the docks was no place for a lady, when to his annoyance he was greeted by Richert Dalkey, riding with two friends who blocked the drive so that he was forced to pull up the curricle.

"A fine day for a drive, Iveroth!" Dalkey greeted him. "Will you not introduce me to your friend?"

Of course. The night of the masque had never happened; therefore Sabira had not met Dalkey. Iveroth made the introductions with as good a grace as he could manage, and then was in politeness forced to introduce Dalkey's friends as well. "Ranald Westlin," he said. "Gavin Farquhar. Lady Steinnland, relict of the late March-Lord of Steinnland and the Isles."

"Here, Iveroth," cried Farquhar, "this will never do for an introduction. You have failed to tell the lady all of our good qualities."

"If I could think of a single one," Iveroth countered, "be sure I should mention it. Now, if you gentlemen will excuse us—"

"Oh! Not so fast!" Gavin Farquhar somehow moved his horse so that it stood broadside across the narrow drive, completely blocking the way. He swept off his hat and bowed to Sabira – a courtier's bow, a rake's bow, with much flourishing of his hat and his white, ringed hands. Iveroth was forced against his will to admire a man who could give such an impression of making a graceful leg while simultaneously mastering a spirited mount. "You must know, Lady Steinnland, that I am the leader of such society as exists in Din Eidyn. In Lutécc I should be nobody at all, but here I have the honor to be the best-dressed gentleman in the city, and the one most able to bring you into fashion. Shall we see you at the Assembly Rooms tonight?"

"As you must know," Iveroth said between his teeth, "Lady Steinnland is very recently widowed."

"Yes, but she ain't required to immolate herself on the grave, like a Corian Islander, is she?"

"Here now, what about my good qualities?" interrupted Ranald Westlin.

Gavin regarded him in mock dismay. "If you yourself cannot think of any, what do you expect me to do, my dear Westlin? Lady Steinnland, this gentleman is a sad rake and it will do you no good at all to stand up with him at the Assembly Rooms. I, on the other hand – "

"Never mind," Iveroth interrupted. "I have thought of one good quality for which I may praise you, Westlin. Lady Steinnland, of all Westlin's acquaintance, you are the one person whom he will not lead into gambling."

"Why d'you say that? There must be half a dozen young men in town whom I haven't yet invited –"

"Yet," Iveroth interrupted again, "being the operative word. Lady Steinnland, on the other hand, is completely safe from being introduced by you to the pleasures of bassett and faro, since ladies ain't admitted to the hells you patronize."

"I say, Iveroth! You will give her a completely false idea of my character!" Westlin protested, but to no avail.

"And now," Iveroth said, "we really must be getting on." With a twitch of the reins he guided his horses around Farquhar's mount, onto the very edge of the grassy verge and back to the path.

"If we had gone one inch farther to the right," Sabira said, rather breathlessly, "would not your wheel have fallen into the ditch?"

"Doubtless. That," Iveroth said, "is why I did not drive one inch farther to the right."

They were accosted two more times on their way through the park, once by a party of military gentlemen including two of Iveroth's friends, and once by Iveroth's old friend Elspet Rattray, riding doucely with her brother beside the carriage in which their mother was taking the air. On the whole the meetings did nothing to sweeten Iveroth's temper, but at least the second one gave him the opportunity to tease Elspet about her sedate mount.

"She is only as demure as I wish her to be, Brandubh!" Elspet retorted, and demonstrated her control by shifting her seat slightly and clicking to the mare, who instantly broke into a canter, then into a full gallop across the grass. Elspet guided the mare at top speed in a figure-eight course around two circular flower beds before rejoining them, slightly flushed and with a few tendrils of curly auburn hair clinging to her neck. "Well?" she demanded.

"You gave me ample time to admire your riding, Elspet, if not your manners."

Sabira gave a choked gurgle of laughter and both of them turned to look at her. "My apologies," she said, as decorous as the mare before Elspet kicked her into action, "but it is a relief to know that Lord Iveroth is as uncivil to everyone else as he is to me!"

"Oh, there's no training Brandubh," Elspet said carelessly, "but we all forgive him for – for – let me see, Iveroth; why is it we forgive you for being so ill-mannered?" She gave Sabira a conspiratorial smile. "There must be some reason. Perhaps it is because he used to cut whistles for me when I was in the nursery. Lady Steinnland, will you ride out with me some day?"

"Oh, yes, do, Lady Steinnland," Elspet's brother Tammas urged just as

Iveroth said repressively that Lady Steinnland was very recently widowed.

"There can surely be nothing ineligible in her taking fresh air and exercise with a small party of friends!" said Elspet. "If you do not permit at least that much, Brandubh, we will all think that you are trying to keep the heiress of Steinnland to yourself." She reached out a gloved hand to Sabira, with a winning smile. "And if Sabira and I do not ride together, everybody else will think that I fear to be seen in the company of the fairest beauty in Din Eidyn. And you must know, Lady Steinnland, that would be intolerable, for I have based my entire reputation on fearing nothing. Besides, we will make such a striking pair, one fair and one carrot-topped, that all the beaux of the city will be at our feet. Do say you will come! Tomorrow morning? It will be most amusing!"

"I'll come too," volunteered her brother, who then wilted under a look from Elspet.

"I do not recall inviting you," she said. "This is to be a ladies' riding party only."

"Until all the beaux of the city are at your feet," Tammas countered.

"Ah, but you are merely a brother, not a beau, and so you don't count!"

"Well, someone must restrain your wild starts, Elspet," said Iveroth. "I shall escort Lady Steinnland."

Elspet gave him a slanting look under her lashes. "Indeed? We'll see about that! May I call on you this afternoon, Lady Steinnland? Do say I may! We ladies must stick together, you know, or the gentlemen will have things all their own way without ever consulting us!"

"So I have already observed," Sabira said. "I should be happy to see you this afternoon, Miss Rattray, for there is much I must learn about how to go on in Din Eidyn, and I feel you will be a more congenial instructress than Lady Askerton."

Elspet hooted with laughter. "What, have Iveroth and Dalkey conspired to foist her off upon you? I see you are definitely in need of rescue. Please, though, do call me Elspet."

"And I am Sabira."

Iveroth felt like taking off his cravat and mopping his brow when that encounter was past and they were back on the city streets. He had been mad to drive Sabira through the park in an open curricle! But then, he had expected her to look like a widow, not like – like an enchanted mermaid, all pearly skin and flashing green eyes framed in black tulle and crepe. Now, instead of thinking out their approach to the Duchess of Quoy, he was spending all his time fending off suitors and would-be suitors. Who knew what idiotic tricks Sabira would get up to, exposed to all these dashing young people? Especially since she appeared to have no sense of propriety herself and no willingness to take instruction from those who knew how to go on.

"What are you worried about?" Sabira asked after they had traveled some way in silence.

How to keep you out of trouble. No, that would not be the thing to say. He was not as ill-mannered as Elspet Rattray made him out to be… was he? Not when Sabira wasn't around, in any event. "Ah – why exactly do you want to see the Duchess?" Perhaps it was only something innocuous, like asking if her husband had spoken any last words. At the moment Iveroth was so exhausted that he felt he could very well settle for innocuous.

"You did not see the morning's dust on the floor of Gairloch's chamber," said Sabira.

Had she gone mad?

"The day we – found my lord there," she prompted, as if he might have forgotten.

"I was there with you," Iveroth reminded her. "I saw exactly what you saw."

"No, for you were not looking at the right angle," Sabira insisted. "I was on the floor, with…" she swallowed hard, "with my lord's head in my lap, and the sunlight slanting just so, and I could see the prints of the Duchess' high heeled shoes."

"So?"

"So," said Sabira, suddenly all icy fire, "the Duchess of Quoy stepped right over my lord's body in her haste to leave Faarhafn. And I should like to know what kind of monster would so abandon a stricken man – and what was said or done before he fell – and how she bound a nucklavee to her service."

172

"A what?"

"Never mind. Something you do not believe in. But do not you wonder why my lord died that night? And what left the rotting kelp trailing across his body and his chamber?"

"It is a question to which I could find no rational answer," said Iveroth, "and therefore I have tried not to think about it."

"Meaning, I suppose, that you – like the rest of Faarhafn – think I had some hand in his death!"

"Meaning exactly what I said!" Iveroth snapped back. "Remember what Elspet said about my manners. If I wanted to accuse you, I would do it straight out without hinting around."

"True enough," Sabira admitted. "I do recall that such is your habit."

"Do you have a rational theory to account for the kelp?"

"I have a theory," said Sabira, "but you do not wish to hear it. You do not believe in nucklaveen, or selkies, or finfolk."

"Or witches flying through the night sky, or fairies dancing in circles and taking folk under the hill for hundreds of years, or standing stones that walk on Yule night, or any of the other superstitions that have riddled our society and set our country so far behind others in science and invention! If we are ever to make progress, we must put such old wives' tales behind us and study only what we see, what we can measure and study and demonstrate in the light of reason!"

"Oh," said Sabira, much too innocently, "then you did not see the kelp in my lord's chamber."

"I saw it, I saw it," Iveroth said. "I just have not discovered the reason yet. That does not mean there is no rational explanation, only that we do not know what it is."

He was relieved to leave the Park and re-enter the city streets, where the crush of drays and carriages, young gentlemen riding horses too spirited for them and ladies in bulky sedan chairs and servants delivering packages demanded that even he give full attention to his driving for the few short blocks until they reached the gates of Quoy's opulent city house. This was laid out more like a country house than like the tall, narrow gray town houses typical of Din Eidyn's sloping streets; the grounds alone, bordered with high gray stone walls, occupied the equivalent of four city blocks in the highly desirable – and highly expensive – flat center of town. The tall, elaborately scrolled iron gates in the center of the front wall revealed a foreyard of knot-gardens bordered with low gray stone walls, through which the drive ran straight to an edifice of golden stone so embellished with turrets, bow-windows, balconies and glazed tile-work that it seemed at once to glow and sparkle in the pallid sunlight of early summer. Sabira drew in her breath. "It is like an enchanted castle!"

The iron gates were closed, but as soon as the gatekeeper recognized Iveroth's curricle he ran to draw them open. They proceeded at a walking pace down the drive. Sabira's eyes were fixed on the house; Iveroth had leisure to observe the knot-gardens. Having visited the house only for evening parties, and then as seldom as possible, he had never before observed the curious mixture of plants that filled the Duchess' gardens. He would have expected Ailsa's taste to run towards bright, gaudy flowers, preferably imported from the South at tremendous expense, like the honey-colored stone of which the house was built. Instead the tiny plots of earth inside their encircling and intertwining walls reminded him of the old-fashioned herb gardens used by his ancestors for decoration, and of which a remnant still remained in the kitchen gardens of old estates like his own country house.

"Strange," he said, "I would have expected Ailsa to be in the forefront of fashion with her flowers as with everything else. But these knot-gardens might as well have been planted in the back of the house for the kitchen servants to use."

Sabira glanced down. "Nightshade?" she said. "Thistles? Pennyroyal, monkshood, thornapple, yarrow, mullein. Nettles. And a hedge of hemlock. I do not think this garden is for the use of the kitchen, Iveroth."

"Well, they all look like weeds or kitchen herbs to me," said Iveroth, "and a damned dull garden it makes, too."

"Not if you have studied Arnelius' *De Propriae Herbarum*," Sabira said with a smile. "I believe our conversation with the Duchess will be very interesting indeed."

In the event, their call on the Duchess was damned dull. Warned by the servant at the door that the Duchess was distraught with concern over the illness of her son and was receiving only medical gentlemen, Iveroth requested that his card be sent in to her anyway. There followed a long period of waiting in the Yellow Salon, where Iveroth amused himself by inspecting the paintings that decorated the walls and Sabira studied the floral arrangements disposed in vases here and there about the room.

"She's been redecorating again," said Iveroth. "There was used to be a Gainsborough landscape on this wall, and some family portraits here, and a charming Boucher of court ladies dressed as shepherdesses above this table – what are you doing, Sabira?"

In his peregrinations about the room, he had failed to observe that Sabira was quietly rearranging the Duchess' flowers, distributing the contents of one vase among the others until there was nothing left except some greenish water.

"I shouldn't worry," she said in an undertone, "doubtless the servants do the flowers, and if they do not care for my arrangements they can easily put everything back as it was, you know. I am sure the Duchess does not trouble herself with such minor matters at a time of family illness. Do go on telling me about the pictures."

It was less discomposing to turn back to the study of the Duchess' tastes in art than to watch his companion behaving as if she had taken leave of her senses. Iveroth had never before been at a loss in a social situation, but now he wondered what was best to do. Pretend he didn't notice how oddly Sabira was behaving? Take her away immediately? What if she didn't want to go? She was not noticeably cooperative. His imagination shuddered at the idea of bodily carrying a kicking and protesting girl out the front door of the finest mansion in Din Eidyn.

"I can't tell you much about the new paintings," he said. He couldn't resist keeping a covert watch on Sabira out of the corner of one eye. "They're all confounded dark and gloomy things, and I can scarcely make out what's supposed to be going on in them."

Actually he could make out quite a bit, once his eyes became accustomed to the artist's use of darkness and shadow, and what he saw was nothing for a young girl like Sabira to be looking at – widow be damned, he had a strong suspicion Steinnland had never laid a finger on her! It would be quite improper for her to be looking at the tangle of naked limbs and discarded drapery that slowly emerged from one dark canvas, or at the glowing fire and the torturer's instruments laid ready to use in the next. Far better to leave her dabbling in the water of the vase that she had deprived of its blossoms. He rather thought she had taken something from her reticule and dropped it into the water, but the motion had been so quick and – well – furtive, that he was not entirely sure. Except for the furtiveness. That was not something he'd seen in her before, and it worried him.

Now she was dabbling her fingers in the water again, swirling it around in the vase, and raising her dripping hands with a disappointed expression on her face. After she'd done this three times, Iveroth found that his ability to pretend ignorance was at an end.

"Here," he said, offering her his handkerchief, "dry your hands and stop playing about in the water, will you! It would never do to greet the Duchess with your hands dripping water and – ah – green gunk."

"I may as well," said Sabira sadly, accepting the proffered square of linen, "for this did not work. And I do not believe the Duchess means to receive us, do you?"

CHAPTER SEVENTEEN

The Duchess eventually sent a footman with the message that she was too distracted with anxiety over her son to receive visitors. I had expected nothing better, but Iveroth's brow darkened; evidently he was not accustomed to being refused entrance at this house – or, most likely, at any other that he favored with his attention. I was disappointed, but not totally cast down, since I had not believed we would be received so easily; and I could not help reflecting that a little frustration would doubtless be good for Iveroth's character. In any event, since the failure of my salt magic, I had pressing business elsewhere.

Iveroth was even more vexed when we left the house and he found that the groom whom he had charged with walking the horses was nowhere to be seen.

"They will take a chill from standing so long!" he exclaimed angrily.

"I hope not," I ventured to say. "It seems they are walking of their own accord." Indeed the horses were dutifully pacing the circular drive immediately in front of the Quoy mansion, heads down as though they could look at nothing but the path immediately in front of them. I had no concern for the horses, but I had a very good idea who could have entranced them into this slow circular pacing, and I wanted him with me. Meldun would have been the ideal companion on my new and pressing errand, and it appeared that now he had disappeared on his own business.

Furthermore, I had no idea what he had done with Iveroth's groom or where the man might reappear. If Meldun had assumed kelpie-form and carried him off into the sea, I had murder on my conscience – Meldun having nothing resembling a conscience to trouble him. If, as I devoutly hoped, he had merely lured the groom into my stables and trapped him there, how was I to explain the man's reappearance to Iveroth?

We had waited so long on the Duchess of Quoy's pleasure that Cromertie's was already closed for mid-day. It would re-open in late afternoon, but I could hardly expect Iveroth to wait so long. We would certainly quarrel again, given so much time.

We made our way back to Steinnland's town house – I still could not really think of it as mine – in silence. Iveroth chose to take the city streets the entire way, either to avoid more social encounters in the park, or to have an excuse to avoid conversing with me after the humiliation of his refusal at the Duchess' house. Silence was quite agreeable to me; in particular, I had no wish to discuss the mysterious disappearance of Iveroth's groom. I was quite pleased when he drew up outside the house and apologized for not coming in, since without a groom he could not leave the horses.

I was unable to perform my errand immediately; I had forgotten various minor social problems. Lady Askerton desired me to partake of a small nuncheon with her, and insisted that it would not be at all the thing for me to walk out this afternoon in the same dress I had worn for riding in Iverton's curricle. The differences between the styles seemed unimportant to me, but to avoid a greater fuss I submitted to her desires; and by the time I had changed all the pieces of clothing with which city landfolk cluttered their bodies, Elspet Rattray had fulfilled her promise of coming to call on me that afternoon.

Had I not been concerned about my errand, Elspet would have made a most charming companion; she rattled on about the social life of Din Eidyn in an amusing way that made me see that world in a new and much pleasanter light. In Elspet's world there were no dragons of chaperones, patronesses, and disapproving great ladies; only inconvenient rules to which one paid lip-service while evading them in polite ways. From her I learned a great deal about the art of getting one's own way without putting up Society's collective back; I made mental notes while she chattered, and then realized somewhat sadly that I should have no occasion to use such stratagems and evasions as she recounted. All I needed to do in Din Eidyn was to sign a few more legal papers and obtain an interview with the Duchess of Quoy; then I would return to the north, resettle Steinnland's tenants of Faarhafn, restore the island to my people, and return to my mother's house.

Although my body was beginning to miss the sea, the rest of me found the prospect unaccountably... well, dull. Even my quiet life with Steinnland began to seem dull compared to Din Eidyn, with its flowers and circulating libraries and friendly people and even its scandals; attending the lady Vivienne's Fiendish Masque had definitely been ill-advised, but I could not deny that it had been interesting.

By the time Elspet left, Lady Askerton declared that it was far too late for a gently bred female to go out walking.

"Are the shops closed?" I asked.

"No, but you may send a servant for anything you require."

"I have not had the best results by sending other people to do my errands," I interrupted her, "and I feel the need for some exercise. At this time of year you need not worry that it will be dark before I return – and," I added, not only to mollify Lady Askerton but because I had just remembered that she would be much more useful than Meldun on this particular errand, "I will take Breta with me." Breta knew the way to Gairdie's. Meldun, even if he did know the way, might mislead me out of a love of mischief. You cannot trust kelpies; they have neither conscience nor common sense. Well, there was no use worrying about that; I had an interview with a cheating shopkeeper to get through first.

We reached Gairdie's well before the closing hour; two ladies were trying the merits of different perfumes at the shop counter, and I was content to let them finish their business and leave before I brought up my own concerns. When they had at last settled on the scent each of them preferred, I stepped forward to the counter, Breta hovering behind me.

"I am Lady Steinnland," I told the young man waiting behind the counter, "and I wish to speak with the owner of this business."

It was clear that he recognized Breta, for he looked first surprised and then alarmed, and would not meet my eyes. "My apologies, my lady, but the owner is not available at the moment."

"Then you will make him available," I said in my sweetest voice. "Or do you think he would prefer to have it generally known that Gairdie's sells false merchandise and that Lady Steinnland refuses to shop there?"

A not unbecoming flush suffused his pale, city-dweller's face. "I beg of you, my lady," he said, looking almost ready to weep, "My father is in poor health and has been directed by his physician to rest in the afternoons. I would not disturb him for the world. Cannot I satisfy your complaint?"

"If you are the owner's son," I said, thinking it over, "then I suppose the reputation of this shop is as dear to you as to him."

"Indeed it is!" he asserted quickly. "If mistakes have been made, pray allow me to repair them!"

"You have indeed made a very serious mistake. Yesterday I sent my woman to purchase some of your famous sea salt. You took the money and fobbed her off with a packet of common table salt, tinted to look like true salt from the sea. Do not defend yourself!" I said as he attempted to speak. "I have tested the mixture you gave her and know that I was cheated. You will now, if you please, replace it with the genuine article."

"I – I – She said," the young man stammered, "the girl, that is, her there, she said that she wanted sea salt just like what I gave the Countess of Torquhan."

"You gave the Countess of Torquhan true sea salt," I pointed out, "and fobbed my woman off with an imitation."

"My father sold some of our sea salt to the Countess," he said sullenly, "and a great waste it was, for all she did with it was feed it to her daughter to cure the girl's complexion. There's nothing about sea salt that makes it fit for such a purpose. So I thought…"

"You thought," I interrupted, "that when the business was yours to run you would cheat any customers who knew no better, and that you might as well begin now. No wonder your father is unwell; if he knows what kind of son he has raised, I would expect him to be sick unto death at the prospect of your taking over the business. No more excuses. The sea salt, if you please, and quickly!"

He disappeared into the back of the shop and came back with two bags of salt, each easily twice as much as the packet Breta had brought home yesterday.

"That is more than you gave my maidservant," I pointed out. "Is that the proper amount for what she paid, or did you cheat her on quantity as well as quality?"

"My lady, our price for sea salt is 5 skillengs the gram, or 5 grams for a korona. I gave your servant five full grams of salt for her korona. I would never –"

"You knew that short weights could be detected, so you would never risk that?"

He was now red to the tips of his ears.

"That looks like at least twenty grams of salt," I said.

"Pray accept it in apology for my error."

"Weigh it out, if you please," I told him. "I prefer round dealing. If this is genuine sea salt, I shall pay you a fair price for it – minus, of course, the korona my woman gave you yesterday. And bring me a bowl of water!" I added as he turned to bring out the scales.

"What for, my lady? If you would like something to drink, we have excellent tea and several flavored syrups…"

"Try not to be even more cork-brained than you have already shown yourself! I wish to test the salt, of course."

As soon as he had weighed out and set aside the first 5-gram portion of salt, I took a generous pinch of it and dropped it into the bowl, stirring it well with my fingers. Now what? I could not command any sea creatures to make themselves visible, for there were none in the bowl; I could not knit lace, for the water was still and not foaming; I did not wish to open a scrying veil before strangers, for my command of the veil was not as complete as I could wish. I would have to make a very simple test. A small fountain seemed reasonable; I closed my fingers, drew up a column of water a hand-span's height above the bowl, and commanded the water to continue rising and falling back upon itself.

The shopkeeper's face turned from red to an ashy pallor. "Oh, my lady!" he whispered. "I did not know – did not realize you were one of *those*. But this is all true sea salt, all the best stuff, I promise you!" He was all but gibbering in his fear. The poor creature had doubtless been raised on landfolk's confused tales, which mix together selkies and finfolk and nucklaveen and make us all out to be terrible monsters.

Breta smirked. "Guess I forgot to tell you my lady was magic!"

"It is all true stuff," he repeated himself. "I – I beg you will not test any more? I would not…"

"No," I said, "of course you would not sell false sea salt to someone who can detect the substitution, would you? Any more than you would give short measure to someone who might own his own scales." I smiled as sweetly as I could to take some of the sting out of my words. "Let me advise you, young man, to follow your father's excellent practice and sell true stuff at true weights to all your customers, that Gairdie's may continue to prosper. And if you do not take that advice, at least take this." There were four 5-gram packets of salt before me now; I dropped three korona on the counter and beckoned him to lean forward a little. "Look well on my servant's face, and remember it; and if I send her back to this shop, be sure to give her exactly what she requests."

I handed the packets to Breta and made to leave the shop.

"M-my lady?" the shopkeeper stammered.

"Yes?"

"What shall I do about that?" He pointed at the bowl where the miniature fountain was still merrily bubbling away.

"You need not be concerned about that," I reassured him. "The magic will gradually exhaust the power of the sea salt and it will die down of its own accord."

"But in the meantime - My customers – "

Clearly he was afraid even to move the bowl. "Your customers will be vastly impressed by your cleverness, and will put it about that Gairdie's is a most amusing place to shop. You need not thank me for the favor." And I swept out of the shop, trying to restrain my amusement. I hoped the fountain would bubble long enough to make a firm impression on that young man's mind; it would be a great nuisance to be obliged to go to Gairdie's in person every time I needed supplies.

Then I remembered that I was unlikely to make a return visit to the shop. Within the week, Mr. Tulloch had assured me, all the legal business connected with Steinnland's will would be concluded. During that week, if I exerted myself, I felt sure that I should manage somehow to have speech with the Duchess of Quoy; and then, my business in Din Eidyn over, I would have no need to remain on land, nor to put up with Iveroth's annoying, overbearing ways.

It was a depressing thought on which to walk home – and I am not particularly fond of walking; it is such a slow and clumsy way of getting about, compared to the pleasure of propelling oneself through the water with a flick of one's tail.

To alleviate the boredom, I proposed to Breta that we take a different street home, if she thought she could find the way.

"Oh, yes, my lady," she said happily, "just the next street over is the Circulatory Liberry, and you sent me there too, remember?"

I did indeed remember. What a pity that I had not brought Volume 42 of the County Annals of Kinlochbervie with me, to return in favor of something more readable! However, that mistake could probably be rectified. I introduced myself to the owner as Lady Steinnland, and he immediately said, "Oh, yes. The County Annals, Volume 42. Was you wishful of replacing that with some other book, my lady?"

"I forgot to bring it with me today," I told him, "but I shall make my selection now and ask my woman to bring the other book back when we return home."

Unfortunately, the proprietor of Cromertie's Circulating Library had a little more starch in his backbone than the young cheat at Gairdie's. He permitted me to set aside Volume One of *The Travails of Amanda*, but refused to allow the book out of the library until he had those damnable County Annals back – and since it was near to the closing hour, it was unlikely I should be able to complete the exchange that day. Well, there are ways around everything, and my lord had certainly left me well enough provided for to find a way around this one.

"My maid, Breta Scrabster, also wishes to subscribe to the library," I told him. "So does my companion, Lady Askerton, and my footman Meldun…. um…" Meldun was certainly a nuisance. First he had to be equipped with human clothing, and now he required a last name. "Meldun Faarhafn," I said, and laid out nine more korona for the new subscriptions.

By this ruse I was able to take home not only the first two volumes of *The Travails of Amanda* but also an exceedingly interesting pamphlet on the improved workings of the modern Majuloscope, while the third volume of *Amanda* was laid by to be called for when I should return that tiresome County Annals book. It did seem a pity to be paying for so many subscriptions when I should only have the use of the library for another week. But it seemed that I was rich in korona, if in little else.

It seemed even more of a pity that a week would scarcely enable me to get through the books I had, when I had seen many more volumes there that I wished to peruse. Well, I read fast, and since I had no acquaintances in Din Eidyn other than Iveroth and Elspet Rattray, I would not have to waste much time in socializing.

Or so I thought then.

I could not, without overt rudeness, refuse to dine with Lady Askerton and to pass at least the first part of the evening with her. She offered to teach me how to net a filagree reticule, but after my recent failures with embroidery I was not inclined to attempt anything new in the line of needlework. If we had to sit in the same room for politeness' sake, I at least would have been quite happy to sit and read my newly acquired books, but that would have left her with nothing to do. Perhaps it had been a mistake to return the volume of improving sermons.

At last we settled on playing a few hands of picquet. She thought this a great joke and rather daring, for it seemed picquet was a game played mostly by gentlemen and often for high stakes.

"Excepting, of course, Travelling Picquet," she said, "which we children was often permitted to play in the coach when Mama and Papa took us to the seaside, but of course that is nothing at all like gambling. One looks out of the coach window, you know, and counts points for various sights; a flock of sheep is worth twenty points, and a flock of geese ten — or is it geese that count twenty and sheep ten? For to be sure geese are much more commonly seen along the river road that we was used to take than sheep, although I suppose the case may be different, dear Lady Steinnland, on the road you traveled from the far north. And then a parson on a white horse wins the game – or is it a tinker with a bay mare? No, that would not be right, the parson is much more dignified and so by rights he, or the person seeing him I should say, must win the hand. Dear me, I said game before, did I not? Well, I suppose it makes no difference, hand or game...."

After this preamble I was not surprised to find that she played very poorly and had no memory whatever for the cards that had been laid down. I myself performed little better, being now required to restrict myself to the standard rules of the game rather than the baroque elaborations which had given Steinnland and myself so much amusement and had even enabled us to accommodate a third player in what was essentially a two-handed game. I blinked away the embarrassing moisture in my eyes at the memory of that last game of Liars' Picquet. We had been so happy that night, and I had not even known it; I had been incensed with Iveroth for disturbing the peace of our life, when he was only a harbinger of the true destroyer.

Lady Askerton noticed my sadness and inquired about the cause. When I told her that I was remembering how often my lord and I had amused ourselves with this very game, she exclaimed at her stupidity for suggesting it and accounted for my eccentric play by supposing me to be quite overset with grief for Steinnland. Normally I should have pointed out first that it was I, not she, who had suggested the game, and second, that I was not in the habit of allowing my sensibilities to become so refined that I wept over every memory of happier times. However, since I was thoroughly weary of her company, I allowed her imagination free rein. She insisted that I retire to my room immediately and I was more than happy to do so, though less happy that she conceived it her duty to accompany me. On the way up the stairs she convinced herself that I suffered the *migraine* and must lie down immediately in a darkened room, had told me about her second cousin twice removed who was used to burn a mixture of feathers and spermaceti oil as an infallible remedy for any kind of headache and had cured all her servants of the complaint by this method, and had called upon Breta to fix my pillow, lay a shawl over my feet, and loosen my stays.

"I do not wear stays," I reminded her.

"Well, and see what comes of it! When females suffer from any malady the first thing to do is to loosen their stays, and now what are we to do with you? Breta, bring me a clean handkerchief and my eau de cologne immediately; we will dab it on her temples, for my dear friend the Marchioness of Ingafells finds that to be an infallible remedy, but first do blow out some of the candles, for nothing is worse for *la migraine* than light of any kind, and try if you can find some feathers and send to the chemist for a bottle of spermaceti oil—"

"Breta," I managed to break in, "you need do no such thing. Lady Askerton, I shall be perfectly well if I simply rest a little while in quiet."

"And the chemists are closed by now," Breta pointed out.

"Do stop chattering, you tiresome girl," Lady Askerton said, "don't you see that your mistress is quite overset by grief and in no mood to have people jabbering at her? And why have you not brought my eau de cologne? Really, my dear Lady Steinnland, you should train your servants better. That footman of yours, Melon or whatever his name is, is never around when one wants him, and this girl dawdles so that you will be quite worn to the bone by her gossiping before ever she brings the cologne to dab on your temples."

Meldun's whereabouts were another of my worries, but I had by now put it out of my power to slip out to the stables and see if he had returned and was spending the night there in horse-form; Lady Askerton could hardly fail to notice if I departed my chamber immediately after she had left me there with only one branch of candles to light the room, a shawl over my feet and a cologne-dampened handkerchief over my forehead. That was, assuming she ever did leave me. At the moment I was beginning to suspect that she intended to keep talking and fussing until sheer irritation gave me the sick-headache she had diagnosed. And when I remembered that Iveroth had been responsible for foisting her upon me, my nostalgia for that night on Faarhafn was replaced by a very healthy anger. The man was indeed intolerable!

Somehow I passed from contemplating Iveroth's generally insufferable manner to remembering our curricle ride through the park that morning, and from that memory into a dream in which we rode together along an avenue of flowering trees with no interruptions, no strangers demanding introductions, just the two of us....

I woke at dawn, feeling cross and crumpled from having slept in my clothes and from dreams that could not possibly have anything to do with the real state of affairs. The sooner I settled my score with the Duchess and returned to Faarhafn, the better off I should be. That was the rational thing to do, and I have always been the rational one of my family, the one who did not allow herself to become overwrought by the constant small crises stirred up by a mother and six aunts all uncommonly gifted with magical power and the accompanying delicate sensibilities.

At least, at this hour, I could be tolerably sure of working without interruption.

Social interruption, that is. After putting off my crumpled clothes and washing myself at the basin, I was interrupted by the little girl whose task it was to light the fire in my bedchamber. She must have scurried to wake Breta, for the next thing I knew, Breta was there with a can of hot water for me to wash in.

"I have already washed," I said somewhat shappishly, "you know we were not accustomed to such luxuries on Faarhafn. You can take that away – no! Leave it, and leave me alone."

"You will need help to dress," she pointed out, with some truth. The intricacies of fashionable dress were far beyond the simple landwoman's garb I had adopted while living with my lord – and far beyond my ingenuity in their multitude of hooks, buttons, tapes and other fastenings, many of which seemed to have been designed especially to make it impossible for a female with only two arms to dress herself. And I was already shivering in my chemise from the impact of the icy water in which I had washed.

I must be growing soft in the city. That water was no colder than the sea in which I had spent the first seventeen winters of my life. Nor did a finwife's garb of a jeweled tunic, with some pearls twisted into the hair, require the services of a maid to adjust. It was high time I returned to the life I was born into. Doubtless I would not suffer from low spirits once I got used to it again.

Despite these reflections, I found a surprising pleasure in the layers of fine cambric and shimmering taffeta which Breta arranged upon me. The fall of lace that terminated each sleeve of this particular black dress was particularly graceful, almost as fine as the seafoam lace which I was used to knit at home. I began to think that I could easily grow used to some of the strange customs of the city; hot water to wash in, complicated and delicate costumes, curricle rides –

"All nonsense!" I said aloud, startling Breta, and then had to reassure her that my exclamation did not mean any dissatisfaction with her services. "In fact," I told her, "I believe you are learning to be a lady's maid far faster than I am learning to be a lady."

"It is less complicated," she said between the hairpins clenched between her teeth as she coaxed my long hair into the style created by Patrice-Henri. "I do not have to meet and talk to people all day long like you do."

"Well, that was only yesterday, and it is over now," I told her. "I daresay we shall be left quite at peace now – until I find some way of reaching the Duchess, anyway. And now you had better leave, Breta. I must do some things that you will not wish to witness. Pray tell Lady Askerton and anybody else that I do not wish to be disturbed this morning."

"What about breakfast?"

"To Teran's Seven Frozen Seas with breakfast! I shall eat when I am through with my work."

Breta scurried out, not quite slamming the door behind her, and I reflected ruefully that I was indeed acquiring the habits of a fine lady of Din Eidyn – including the detestable one of snapping at the servants.

The trouble with working water magic in the early morning was that no one in Din Eidyn was awake then. I raised the veil and was able to spy on the Duchess – asleep in her bed. And not alone! I quickly let the water fall back into the basin before I could identify her companion. There was some spying I would not stoop to. Perhaps Gairloch was awake?

An attempt to glimpse young Lord Gairloch was even more difficult. I kept getting windows into the seas around Faarhafn instead of the rooms of the Duchess' house. Twice I saw the queen's obnoxious son Heiki, laughing with a circle of his cronies. I had no wish to spy on his doings; nor did I wish to shift the scene to visit my own family, for that would only make me sad again.

I was sitting undecided before the basin, wringing the water from those trailing lace cuffs I had thought so attractive and rapidly losing my taste for Din Eidyn fashions, when the door opened without so much as a preliminary tap.

"Breta, I told you—" I exclaimed, and then saw that it was not Breta who had entered, but Meldun, looking very correct in the same livery that Lady Askerton had chosen for the other manservants hired by Iveroth.

"Where have you been?" I demanded. "And what did you do with Iveroth's groom? And where did you get those garments?"

Kelpie-like, he chose to answer the least important question first. "They are part of my shape. I do not know why I did not think of it before. This is much easier than putting on shirt and breeches." As if to demonstrate, he shifted into the shape of a naked man, then into a costume very like the one I had first acquired for him, then back into his livery.

"The groom?"

"He is unharmed." Meldun appeared to consider for a moment. "He may have a slight headache. Nothing worse."

I sighed with relief. "I was afraid you had enticed him to ride you into the sea."

"Oh, I would not do that," Meldun assured me. "The sea at this place is dirty with landmen's trash."

The discovery of his clothes-mimicking skill had given me an idea. "Meldun, since you are creating the livery as part of your shape, do you have any need of the clothes I got for you?"

"No."

"Then may I borrow them?"

"Why?"

"The Duchess of Quoy will not receive me," I explained, "but she receives physicians to care for Gairloch. I thought I might dress in shirt and breeches and try to gain entrance to her house as one of the physician's assistants."

189

"That will not work," Meldun said with calm assurance.

"How do you know? And anyway, do you have a better idea?"

This time he chose to answer both questions - after a fashion. "It will not work because you cannot fit your tail into a pair of breeches. And I do have a better idea."

"Well, what is it?"

"Something that I am doing. You do not need to worry about it."

"Well, I do worry," I said, "for you have absolutely no common sense." No conscience, either. Not that I should particularly object if some horrible fate befell the Duchess, but I did want to talk to her first. "What exactly are you doing?"

"The Duchess is going to the Water Gardens tonight," Meldun said, "to watch the Borghesan acrobats dancing on ropes."

"So much for all her worry about her poor sick son! She leaves Gairloch in the house while she goes out merry-making!"

"She does not leave Lord Gairloch in the house," Meldun said.

In retrospect, I see that I should have investigated that statement further, but I was too excited about the chance of catching Ailsa at the Water Gardens – whatever they might be – to remember the maddening way kelpies have of telling the truth in as misleading a fashion as possible. I simply assumed that Gairloch was sufficiently recovered to go out in society with his mother, which was what I wanted to hear.

"Meldun, you must escort me to the Water Gardens tonight. We can corner her there!"

"I cannot do that."

"Whyever not?"

"I am otherwise engaged."

"Break your engagements!"

"Finwife, I wear your livery, but I am not your servant."

I sighed in exasperation. Kelpies are also very stubborn. And Meldun was correct; the finfolk had no right of command over the kelpies, any more than we commanded the selkies or those disgusting nucklaveen. Alliances were made and broken, but we owed natural allegiance only to our own kind.

"Well, perhaps Iveroth will take me. Will you take a note from me to him, and wait for an answer?"

At that moment Breta tapped on the door to announce that I had a caller downstairs.

"Oh, never mind," I said, "I can very well ask him myself." I flew down the stairs, all eagerness to put my new plan to Iveroth, only to find the drawing-room occupied by two of the young men we had met in the park the day before.

"Oh... Breta said I had a caller," I said, stupid with disappointment.

"I was first to knock on the door," said Mr. Rattray, Elspet's brother.

"But I was first into the drawing-room," countered the other, whose name I could not recall, though I remembered him for his long fair moustachios and shaggy hair.

"Only because you shouldered me out of the way, rude soldier that you are!"

"Tactics, tactics, my infant," said the soldier. He bowed to me. "We met in the park yesterday, my lady."

"Yes, but – I am afraid – that is, I do not perfectly recall your name, I fear." I still felt a sick emptiness inside from the discovery that it was not Iveroth who had called, and it was making me dull and thick-tongued. The sensation was, however, perfectly rational. I felt that I could request Iveroth to escort me to the Water Gardens; Lady Askerton had drummed into me that it would not be at all the thing to ask a strange gentleman to take me anywhere at all. One was supposed to hint, and flirt, and wait for the gentleman to do the asking. It all seemed very odd to me, but after the Fiendish Masque I was resolved to amend my behaviour and to abide by the rules governing landfolk in Din Eidyn.

The military gentleman turned out to be a Major Maddox; he handed me his card and I apologized for having been somewhat lost in all the new faces and introductions of the day before.

"Iveroth mentioned that you were new-come to town," Major Maddox said, "and I wondered if I might make so bold as to escort you to view some of the notable sights of Din Eidyn. There is recently built a new carriage way to Artor's Seat, the mountain rising behind the town, from which you may have a fine overview of the entire city."

Lady Askerton interrupted, telling the major that it would not be at all proper for me to ride out alone with him.

"What, in an open carriage?" Major Maddox gave her his sweetest smile. "Surely you cannot think that I would be such a fool as to misbehave myself in full view of any passer-by."

"There are few enough passers-by at the top of Artor's Seat," Lady Askerton said, "and quite enough misbehaviour goes on up there – or so I hear," she said rapidly, with a blush that bloomed somewhat lower than the two circles of red carefully painted on her cheeks.

"I've heard tales of a beautiful young lady who visited the area more than once," said the major with another engaging smile, "before Lord Askerton swooped down and snatched her away from all the hopeful young beaux of the town."

Lady Askerton blushed still more, tossed her head like a young horse unaccustomed to the bridle, and smoothed down her overskirt with excessive care.

"Those tales were long before your time, Major," she said, "and you are a saucy fellow to repeat them!"

"Oh, but I've only hinted so far," said the major, "if you wish me to repeat them, that is quite another thing!"

"Indeed I do not!" Lady Askerton said sharply, and before he could continue teasing her, "Stay, I have a thought. How if you make up a party with Mr. Rattray and his sister? There could be nothing unexceptional in a picnic excursion for four, in broad daylight."

The Major's crestfallen expression hinted, even to me, that he had been thinking more of an evening drive for two, and I wondered uneasily if the tale of my visit to the Fiendish Masque had been spread about town so quickly. Tammas Rattray, too, was not well pleased by the suggestion, muttering that it was poor sport to drive one's own sister on a picnic.

And all of this went by so fast, even to the day and time being fixed between Lady Askerton and Major Maddox, that I had no chance to hint at my preference for visiting the Water Gardens. But then, the proposed excursion was some days distant. Perhaps the Major could make himself useful before that.

"I have heard so much of Din Eidyn's famed Water Gardens," I said with a languishing air, "I vow, I am all eagerness to see them for myself."

"During the day, there could be no objection to your visiting the gardens," said Lady Askerton, "with a suitable escort."

Before I could voice my preference for an evening visit – and an immediate one – several more callers arrived on the doorstep; Ranald Westlin, Gavin Farquhar, two more gentlemen in military dress whom I assumed to be friends of Major Maddox's, and Elspet Rattray.

"When I saw all these foolish men jostling on the doorstep," Elspet said, "I felt it only my duty to come in and help you deal with them. We do not want all these callers at once, do we, Sabira?"

I hesitated fatally, afraid that it would be unforgivably rude to say indeed not, and one of the new visitors stepped in.

"Indeed we do not," he said, "so if all you other gentlemen would kindly clear out—"

A loud chorus of objection was raised to this suggestion, and in the banter that followed I began to associate names with faces. One of the military men was a Lieutenant Cairdie; the other was not a soldier at all, but only someone called Lord Jenneret, a baron who affected a coat decked with so much gold braid and button that I felt I might well be excused for imagining him to be some kind of an officer. In any event, his voice and his manner of carrying himself were familiar to me, so he must be one of the men to whom Ivcroth had introduced me in the park; after all, I knew no one else in Din Eidyn.

"All these callers, and one of them Beau Farquhar!" Lady Askerton murmured to me while the gentlemen found their places and hastily summoned servants brought trays of refreshments. "Mind your manners with the Beau, now; he can bring you into fashion with a word if he chooses."

I felt that with all these lively young men crowding the room, I was already perhaps more in fashion than I would choose to be. However, surely one of them could be persuaded to escort me to the Water Gardens tonight? And once that was settled, I would find some way to be rid of them. I repeated my desire to visit the Water Gardens, adding that I had heard the illuminations at night were among the great wonders of Din Eidyn.

An embarrassing silence ensued.

"Very fine lights, to be sure," said Mr. Westlin, "but, if you forgive me saying so, perhaps too rough a crowd for a gently bred young lady. Now, in the afternoon a visit would be quite unexceptionable."

"I will go at night, or not at all!" I said pettishly, and was immediately surrounded with a sea of alternative offers. What about the Royal Menagerie? The Botanical Gardens? The Museum of Antiquities?

"La, you will bore the poor child to death," Lady Askerton exclaimed, "what female wishes to waste her time examining dusty old statues?"

"The exhibition of paintings at Thurvaston House is particularly fine this year," said Mr. Rattray.

"Out of the way, Rattray, you're going with the party to Artor's seat, you lucky dog," cried Lieutenant Cairdie. "Now, I am particularly well fitted to escort the lady to view the Thurvaston House gallery, for weren't two of my ancestors in the portrait-painting line themselves? Or anywhere else you would like to go, my dear lady."

It seemed that the Water Gardens were a lost cause, so I might as well take what enjoyment was available.

"I am sure Thurvaston House is all you say of it," I told Lieutenant Cairdie, "but my interests are more in the sciences than in the arts. I should dearly like to visit the Philosophical Society and view this Majuloscope."

Another general murmur of embarrassment, in which I distinguished the words, "-only every second Tuesday," and "never had a female within the doors," and "Damme, Cairdie, you can't explain the Majuloscope to a female, and neither can anybody else."

"Explanations," I said, "will not be necessary. I have been reading a pamphlet on the fabrication of achromatic lenses and the consequent improvements in the Majuloscope. It seems to be a straightforward application of known optical principles; the superior magnifying power of a compound-lens device has been known for long enough, but these new lenses apparently remove the chromatic aberrations which made it so difficult to interpret the results. I should simply like to see the images it displays for myself, rather than relying on these poorly printed reproductions."

"Damme, Lady Steinnland, I can't understand a word you're saying, but I like your style!" exclaimed Mr. Westlin. "I'll take you myself to the next meeting, Tuesday week, and if anybody objects to a female visiting the society, they'll have me to deal with."

"Better take our regiment with you, in that case," advised Major Maddox, "unless you can improve on the cross-and-jostle work you showed just now on the doorstep."

The gentlemen began laughing and throwing mock punches at one another, while Lady Askerton and the servants whisked trays of refreshments and breakable ornaments out of danger's way, and Elspet threw back her head and laughed. And during all this commotion, Lord Jenneret slithered behind my chair and leaned over me. "If you wish to visit the Water Gardens tonight," he said, "it happens that I have made up a party of gentlemen and ladies of the first respectability to view the Borghesan acrobats there. I should be honored if you would join us there."

I did not care for the Baron's insinuating manner, or for the way he held his lips so close to my cheek while speaking; but after all, he would not wish to be heard making a suggestion that Lady Askerton would probably veto, and he was – wasn't he? one of the men Iveroth had introduced me to in the park. I felt quite confident that Iveroth would not encourage my acquaintance with anybody the least bit disreputable; what harm could there be in accepting the Baron's invitation?

It seemed quite likely, too, that the Duchess of Quoy would make one of Lord Jenneret's party, and so I should be able to speak to her without the least difficulty in the world. I felt quite sure, from the embarrassed response to my first mention of the Water Gardens, that the place was full of private little nooks and niches, designed perhaps for lovers, but equally useful for confronting a murderess. It would be quite cowardly of me to shrink from the task, and surely no one could impugn my behavior when my motives were of the highest. Aemilia in *Love's Revenge* had gone into much more improper places, such as the Hareem of an eastern potentate, in order to discover the tragic secret of her lover's birth.

CHAPTER EIGHTEEN

Androw Neip kept a wary eye about him as he turned the burning stacks of seaweed in the family kiln. He was tired after watching the blue smoke rise and replenishing the kelp all day, but not so tired as to forget that three people had been found dead near their extinguished kilns, their lungs full of salt water and their bodies slimed with rotting weed. Little Grete Farchar had been the first, then the Ketsby twin sisters, of whom when they were alive folk said they shared but one brain between them. Some Faarhafners had given up on burning their kelp for this year's shipping, preferring to let it rot rather than risk the chance of another death. Androw, with a mother and two young sisters to keep, could not afford to lose the money that came from selling the burnt cakes to Southron glass manufacturers for the chemicals concentrated within them. But neither would he let a woman of his family tend the fire, not after what had been happening. Some folk said it was a monster from the sea; but Androw remembered the strange wild girl who had married old Lord Steinnland and had tucked up her tail like a petticoat, to live among landfolk as one of them. She had been no monster, and Androw could not believe that one of her kind would range abroad in this kind of senseless killing. It was as easy to believe that one of the Faarhafners had lost his mind and had taken to killing girls and women when they were alone in the fields.

Not that his theory was any consolation. To be trapped on an island with a madman or a monster, what odds did it make what race the killer came from? Something was abroad that killed for pleasure, and while it roamed the island, Androw would not have his womenfolk venture farther than their own garden plot. He could give up a day's fishing to tend the kiln. Indeed, it was no loss to stay on land today, for a rare summer storm had churned the waters around Faarhafn until only a fool would take his boat out.

And whatever monster had come to the island had apparently had no taste for attacking strong young men, for Androw had watched through the haze of smoke all day without being approached by anything worse than poor Wullie Keilo, slouching around in the fog and begging a mug of tea by the kiln rather than go home to his scold of a wife.

Wullie... was it possible that being henpecked at home and openly despised in public had turned his brain, so that he killed little girls and half-witted young women in place of the wife who was too much for him to handle? Androw shook his head. He could imagine Wullie some day, in a moment's rage, thrashing his woman with the business end of a scythe and then stumbling away, wailing, from the bloody mess he had made. He could not imagine him patiently, cruelly, holding little Grete Farchar under the sea until she drowned, and then laying out her body beside the kiln.

He could not imagine any of his fellow islanders doing that.

And yet it had happened. Three times now; four if you counted the old March-Lord, though he had not been burning kelp when the monster took his breath away.

Androw shrugged and turned back to tending his kiln. The long slow day was nearly over, the kelp turned to glowing ash. It was a relief to give up speculation and throw himself into the hard physical labor of turning the burnt kelp, which now looked like great clods of blue-gray earth shot through with flame. Raking and lifting the masses on his long pronged blade, he saw the colors of the dying fire like veins of living jewels running through the kelp, changing colors like the lights that danced in the midwinter sky. He did not think of it as beautiful, for he was not accustomed to think in those terms; he only knew that this part of the work, the raking and leveling of the burnt mass, was richly satisfying to him. Even the strain on his shoulders, the hard breath that panted out as he did the work of two men by running from one side to the other, the sweat that soaked his shirt – all these were almost pleasureable after a long dull day of watching the fire. His physical strength was something that he took for granted and used without thinking, unlike the painfully learned shapes that he had learned to scratch under the finwife's tuition until he could write his name and much more. That was work; this was just daily life.

He took such delight in the shooting flames and changing colors that came with the 'rinnin-oot' that he forgot to scan the brow of the hill as he had been doing all day, until a foul smell came through the smoke and he heard a burbling, squishing noise that belonged nowhere in his memory.

Then he straightened and looked across the fire, and his mother's tales sounded in his ears, and he knew what it was he saw: this thing with a single fiery eye, with ropy veins standing out against flesh as raw as if it had been flayed. And he remembered that Sabira's finfolk were not the only beings said to live in the sea.

But Androw was a strong young man, not a child or a half-wit, and he was holding a long wooden pole that ended in a row of prongs red-hot from the fire. He drew his rake out of the kelp masses and thrust upward and forward, straight at the nucklavee's single eye, and heard flesh sizzle and heard the monster give a keening cry.

And then he ran as he had never run before, away from the kiln and to the safest place he knew, the huddle of huts around the harbor, where other men who had not dared to fish the troubled seas might help him to hold this thing at bay.

***

Making my escape from Lady Askerton was easier than I had expected; when I told her that I had been invited to see the acrobatic exhibition at the Water Gardens that night, she leapt to the assumption that it was Iveroth who had issued the invitation.

"The Water Gardens? At night? Dear me, not at all the thing for a young girl – but then," she reminded herself, "you are a widow, and if Iveroth is to escort you I suppose there can be no harm in a very short visit to watch the acrobats. I had no notion that he had invited you! Though to be sure it is no surprise that I missed his card, among all the notes and cards that have been delivered today. Dear me! I must go back through all the correspondence and make sure that we have not overlooked anything of consequence. It would never do to offend the Countess of Torquhan, or Lady Dalkey, by failing to reply to an invitation, not that it will happen in those two cases, for I have already responded to them, but what if I missed someone of equal importance? Lady Dalkey has only one son, you know – quite an eligible connection, the Dalkeys! As for the Countess of Torquhan, although I should not wish to see you form a connection with her younger son, and the older one is unfortunately married these five years, dear Lillias Tornstrom knows everyone and it would not do to refuse her. I had better take everything to my room and go through it quietly, for you have no notion which invitations one ought to answer, which one should refuse and which one should ignore altogether. Only be sure and send to tell me when Iveroth calls for you, for I wish to be quite sure that he understands the delicacy of your position and the need to be quite discreet at such a place as the Water Gardens, where any nobody with ten skillengs can get entrance."

This settled both our evenings admirably. Lady Askerton would be happy arranging the invitations that had been sent us and the cards our visitors had left and enjoying the reflected glow of so many titled persons of consequence – and I would be free to take a chair to the Water Gardens, where I was to meet Lord Jenneret and his friends.

There could, I assured myself, be no impropriety in visiting the gardens with a party made up by someone to whom Iveroth himself had introduced me in the park the day before – at least, I was almost certain that the Baron had been one of the gentlemen we met on our way to the Duchess' house. His name was unfamiliar, to be sure, but there had been so many names! And everything else – his figure, his carriage, his voice – were familiar to me, so much so that during the short ride to the Water Gardens I teased myself with trying to remember exactly which group of friends the Baron had been with when we met. Not with Richert Dalkey, nor with the military gentlemen…but there had been others, had there not?

All the same, I decided to wear the green and silver mask that Breta had procured for my previous adventure, and when the chairmen stopped at the elaborate wrought-iron gates of the Water Gardens, I was glad of the decision. The crowd lounging before the gates was definitely not composed of citizens of the first respectability; there was a preponderance of rude 'prentice boys mixed with languid young gentlemen who quizzed the ladies entering the Gardens through their glasses.

And, I saw with relief, Lord Jenneret was waiting for me. As soon as I exited the chair he came up and greeted me with a polite bow and some nonsense about how the green and silver mask could not hide the glow of my beauty.

"Oh, never mind all that," I said, "let us join the rest of your party." I still hoped that I might be lucky enough to find the Duchess of Quoy among the Baron's guests. And if she were not with them, but with some other party, then I needed to wander the gardens until I found her.

"Oh, they are all gone ahead," the Baron said carelessly.

"How very strange." I felt a quiver of doubt. To be entering the gardens with only Lord Jenneret, rather than in a group, was – well, I felt sure that Lady Askerton would say it was Not At All The Thing.

"I requested them to do so," said the Baron, "that they might reserve good seats for us to view the Borghesan acrobats. There will be quite a crowd, as this is the last night of their performance, and I wished to make sure that you sat where you could see everything. Just come with me, and we will join them as soon as we have passed the gates."

I told myself that Lady Askerton had been quite complacent about the idea of my visiting the Gardens alone with Iveroth, so why should it be improper to do so with some other gentleman? Anyway, we should be in a group of friends soon enough. All the same, I kept my mask on while Lord Jenneret paid our admission fees and offered me his arm to walk down the shaded pathway that led to the famed falling pools of the Water Gardens.

So many people entered just before and after us that I was actually glad of the Baron's arm; I was so jostled that I feared my tail might loose itself and spread out behind me. Most of the crowd went to the left, down a wide paved path, and I was happy to move aside into the narrower path to the right for the moment. Still, it seemed odd that we should not be going the same way as most of the others.

"Is not that the path to the performance area?" I asked as we turned the other way.

"For the common sort it is," agreed Lord Jenneret, "those who only pay their entrance once or twice a year for some extraordinary show, and never trouble to explore the subtler beauties of the place. There are many winding and intersecting paths here, and since our seats are reserved we need not hurry along with the common crowd to reach them. I felt that you in particular would appreciate the views of the falling pools and other beauties of the gardens."

I felt that it would be difficult indeed to appreciate any views at all along such a dark path, but Lord Jenneret assured me that the falling pools and other special attractions were always well lit by torches. "See?" he said, pointing ahead to where I could just see the gleam of torchlight reflected off the leaves of the hedge. His steps quickened, as though he were eager to leave this shady pathway for the sight of the Falling Pools. I too would be happy to quit the path; smothered giggles and other sounds indicated that some visitors were using the secluded niches that opened at intervals to create their own form of entertainment.

"You are very kind to take so much trouble for my sake," I said, "but I had rather join your friends. It seems impolite to enter the Gardens and make no effort to find your party."

"Oh, never trouble yourself about them," the Baron said. "We are here to enjoy ourselves, are we not? And you must be longing to see the water by now, after so long shut up in the stone houses of the city."

"Why do you suppose that?"

Lord Jenneret laughed. "Oh, it is too late to come the shy maiden with me! You were very clever at Vivienne's masquerade, my lady, but you gave yourself away with that fountain at Gairdie's shop. I know what you are."

And I knew, now that it was too late, why his form and voice, but not his face and name, were familiar to me. Lord Jenneret had been the Sorceror who tried to molest me at the Fiendish Masque!

***

201

After an early engagement to dine with the eccentric Lord Kilburn, who kept country hours even in fashionable Din Eidyn and who also knew more than any other living men about the natural science of salt water fishes and other beings, Iveroth had no particular thought but to make an early night of it at his club while he digested his friend's radical theories. Kilburn was hardly the first man to look to ancient folklore as a key to modern science, but he carried his notions farther than Iveroth had ever expected to hear from a rational man. What Iveroth had always scoffed at as old wives' tales was held up by Kilburn as a perfectly rational, albeit unproven, possibility.

"How do you know that intelligent life does not exist beneath the sea?" Kilburn had asked. "Or, for that matter, beneath the crust of the earth itself? Have we so thoroughly explored every inch of the globe?"

"I know it the same way that I know the stars are not carried about by angels," Iveroth retorted. "Oghem's Razor applies: the simplest explanation is the best."

"Not," said Kilburn, "if one arrives at simplicity by denying inconvenient evidence. What is this story I hear about your ward's setting an endless fountain to bubbling in the middle of Gairdie's Chymical Shop?"

"Lady Steinnland is not my ward," Iveroth said stiffly. "I have no connection with her save that her husband was my good friend, and I feel an obligation to see that she comes to no harm in Din Eidyn."

"Quite so," Kilburn agreed smoothly.

"And it wasn't an endless fountain," Iveroth added. "It died down of its own accord after some hours."

"Ah, yes, people do exaggerate so," Kilburn said. "Naturally, a fountain that bubbles without apparent cause for several hours is much less likely to be of magical origin than one which goes on and on without ceasing." He held up one wrinkled hand. "Now, don't try to quarrel with me, Iveroth! I am much too old for you to take offense – and besides, I haven't even said anything offensive yet. I am merely suggesting that as men of science, we are obligated to pay attention to all the evidence – not just to those parts of it we find convenient."

"Men of science," said Iveroth, "do not talk about magical origins!"

"Cannot you accept the word as a way to describe those events for which natural philosophy has not yet found the explanation?" Kilburn smiled gently and launched into a quotation from one of his favorite poets.

"All Nature is but Art unknown to thee;

All chance direction, which thou canst not see."

The lines echoed in Iveroth's head as he made his way home from Kilburn's. "All chance direction which thou canst not see – and I did not even see this fountain that has set the whole town chattering about Sabira – Lady Steinnland. If I had done, no doubt I should easily have discovered the mechanism she used. But why the devil should she play such a childish trick? And why did not Gairdie himself uncover the mechanism?"

The answer to that was easy enough. A clever mechanical fountain, small enough to fit in a hand-basin, would draw the attention of the world to Gairdie's shop for a day or two. But a magical fountain, created by a beautiful and mysterious young woman who came from the northern isles with all their lore of sea castles and sea creatures, would attract far more, and longer lasting, attention.

All the same, Iveroth decided that on the way home he would call on Lady Steinnland – just to inquire after her health, and perhaps to drop a hint that it was not wise to draw attention to herself in such a fashion.

And perhaps to discover just how she had created the fountain – if she had – if it was not all some clever trick of Gairdie's to call attention to his shop by associating a fancied act of magic with a young and lovely heiress new-come to Din Eidyn. Yes, that was by far the most reasonable explanation. On the morrow he would speak to Gairdie himself, find out how the trick had been worked and suggest – politely, of course – that a mere shopkeeper had best not borrow the respected name of Steinnland to garner publicity for his business.

Still, as long as his steps had happened to bring him to Rannach Square, he might as well drop in on Lady Steinland anyway.

CHAPTER NINETEEN

"My dear sir," I said, endeavoring to withdraw my arm from his, "I have not the least idea what you are talking about, but your manner is offensive in the extreme. Pray conduct me to your party now; I have no wish to linger here."

The Baron clasped my hand so tight that I could not extricate myself without unseemly struggle. "Oh, you will be happy enough, my lovely lady, when you hear what I have to offer. On the one hand, my silence; on the other, the fulfilment of your dearest wish."

"I do not at all understand you," I said, and it was half true, for how could the Baron fulfill my dearest wish when I myself was not sure of my heart?

"Come now! As Lady Steinnland, relict of the late March-Lord, you have the chance of establishing yourself in Din Eidyn with an enviable position in Society. If you were discovered to be a finwife, the same society that now embraces you would utterly reject you in their anger at how finely you have fooled them—"

"Are you mad? Nobody in Din Eidyn even believes in the finfolk!"

"They have forgotten the old stories," the Baron agreed, "but the old laws still exist. By the ancient statutes of Din Eidyn, I may demand that you show your body before three noble ladies of my own choosing, to prove yourself human and without that lovely tail which we both know you possess, hidden under these flowing skirts." His free hand wandered down my back and came to rest on the slight swell where my tail emerged. "They may declare you a finwife who should be burned, or they may refuse to acknowledge the old lore and simply consider you a monster who should be exhibited at a fairground. In either case, you will hardly be received again in polite society. Nor will Iveroth, who will be held responsible for foisting you upon them." His large white teeth gleamed in the darkness. "How shall you like to strip down before Ailsa of Quoy, my fine lady? Would you not do better to accept my offer?"

"Please," I murmured, "do not hold me so close. I cannot breathe, I feel faint…"

Jenneret released me from his embrace, but held my hand firmly tucked beneath his arm.

"Let us walk a little," I requested. "I need air, and time to consider…" What exactly I was supposed to be considering I knew not; I merely hoped to come upon some other company at one of the torchlit pools, and there to escape Jenneret without an unseemly struggle. He was wrong to imagine I cared about being 'exposed' as a finwife, but could he really ruin Iveroth's credit as well as my own?

"There is really nothing to consider," Jenneret said, but to my relief he walked along with me instead of insisting that we remain in that lonely part of the path. "I have no desire to expose you – instead I mean to solve your problem, pretty child. I shall marry you and make you human."

"What?"

"I have not studied the old lore of our land to no effect," Jenneret said with a smirk. "I know all about you finwives, your one object is to marry a human man and to become human yourselves. Doubtless you thought to achieve this object when you married old Steinnland, but in your ignorance you made a sad mistake. It is not the form of marriage that makes you human, but the reception of the man's seed. You need a lusty man who can get you with child; only then will your tail drop off and your face and body stay beautiful. Otherwise you will grow uglier every day, until by your thirtieth birthday you have a hairy face and a snout like a walrus.'

I laughed; I could not help it, when I thought of my mother and my six aunts, all far more beautiful than I could ever hope to be. "You are mad!" There was a group of torches just ahead; I quickened my steps in the hope of finding other people, so that I could get away from Jenneret in the crowd, but was disappointed to find the poolside as deserted as had been the path. In truth, if this was one of the famous falling pools of the Water Gardens, I thought it a paltry affair; an arrangement of three rock-lined pools like stairsteps, with apertures allowing the water to fall a few feet from one to the next. Doubtless the mechanical device that drove the water back from the bottom pool to the uppermost one was a marvel of human ingenuity – but that is not saying much, for landfolk have very little natural understanding of how to manage water.

"Never fear," Jenneret assured me as though I had agreed already, "I mean to give you my hand as well as my seed. As my wife you will retain your social position, and only we two will know your secret. It's true, your fortune is smaller than I could wish, but I shall consider myself amply recompensed in the opportunity to study your kind at first hand. I shall record precisely the stages by which your tail deteriorates until at last you shed it, so that we may discover exactly how many couplings are required to make you truly human." His eyes gleamed with excitement. "There will have to be drawings, measurements— all must be recorded. Come now, give me your lips to seal our bargain. Our engagement can be announced tomorrow, we shall be wed as soon as possible, and I will take you away to my country estate until I have made you human." He put his arm about my waist again and swung me around to face him, his back to the falling pools. His other hand pressed upon the back of my neck as he tried to force my face against his, laughing at my resistance. In revulsion I put both hands upon his chest and pushed him away with all my force.

He was strong for a landman, and if he had not expected me to be as weak as a landwoman I would never have got away from him. But my people are much stronger than most landfolk. The force of my push forced him to let me go and to take a step backward to regain his balance; that step brought his heel down on the rocks at the verge of the lowermost pool; I pushed him again and he fell backwards into the water.

"You damnable hagwife!' he swore, floundering to regain his balance. "I'll – when I get hold of you I'll—"

He knew my strength now; he would not again make the mistake of underestimating me in that particular fashion. If I ran, he might catch me up before I found the lighted ways and the crowd of people – and even if I found them, could I trust landfolk to be of any help?

Since my visit to Gairdie's I had kept a packet of sea salt in my reticule. I fumbled for it now and broke the paper in my haste so that the salt poured out into my reticule. There was no time to sift it out; the Baron was on his feet, wading out of the pool with fury and revenge writ large across his face. I threw my reticule at his face; he dodged back into the water, the silk purse fell in with a splash, and I commanded the fountains to keep and hold him.

A spout of water glowing with light formed about Jenneret's form and slowly lifted him up towards the sky, higher and higher until he was spinning at the level of the treetops on a silvery column of water that sprayed salty drops and shed a shimmering blue-green light all around the pool.

"Look!"

"It's an exhibition!"

Cries of astonishment rang out through the gardens, and people started running towards the pool to get a better view of this amazing sight. The narrow path that had seemed so empty was now crowded with disheveled men and women, closely followed by more decorously clad observers who must have come from the main path.

"Now, Phyllis, if you'd just have waited a moment," complained one gallant who seemed not to notice that his breeches buttons were all undone.

"Eh, dearie, us can do *that* any ol' time," screeched his inamorata, "but did you ever see the like o' this? 'Ow d'you think 'e keeps goin' round an' round like that?"

"Oh, dear," I murmured, "I must have put in too much salt." Not to mention a silk reticule, one korona, five skillengs, an oystershell comb, and a kerchief of finest seasilk embroidered by my Aunt Eliina. I did not think there was much hope of retrieving my property while all these onlookers crowded around the pool; it was much more important to get away before the power of the salt was exhausted and the Baron was free to pursue me. But what should I do then? Lady Askerton had warned me that a lady walking alone at night was subject to all manner of insults, not that anyone could have insulted me worse than the Baron had just done, but I had no desire for more such experiences. Could I hire a chair to take me home if I promised the men should be paid upon my safe arrival?

Just then I caught sight of a glossy dark head at the back of the crowd and felt a most irrational sense of safety and wellbeing. Iveroth was here!

He extricated me from the crowd with his customary efficiency. "May I ask what is the meaning of this, Sa – Lady Steinnland? Lady Askerton thought you had gone to the Water Gardens with me! She was most surprised when I chanced to call tonight."

"I can explain everything," I said, "only pray, let us be away from here! I do not know how long the power of the salt will last, and I fear that he will be very angry when he gets out of the fountain."

Iveroth looked up at the spinning form in the center of the watery column. "An unfortunate admirer of yours, I collect? And somehow you pushed him into the center of this new attraction? It is a very clever device, I must own. I wonder how the proprietors keep so tall a column of water in constant motion."

"So will they," I said, "if they come upon it before the salt is exhausted. Please, take me home, Iveroth!" I tugged on his coat-sleeve.

"I should like to know how – "

"Very well, I will tell you all about it, but not here and now! Can you please find me a chair? Only all my money is in the fountain, you see, so I am afraid you will have to pay the men."

"By no means!" said Iveroth. "I shall escort you home in my curricle, which I brought out for precisely that purpose. I realized last time that hiring a chair was a mistake; it was hardly possible for me to tell you exactly how improper your behavior was with two sturdy bearers listening and grinning at every word. This time let us have no witnesses!"

He said no more until we had left the Water Gardens for the privacy of his curricle. As he whipped up the horses, I glanced fearfully over my shoulder. The coruscating fountain still lit up the night sky; I could see its blue-green glow through the leaves of the trees.

"Now," Iveroth said as the curricle carried us along the dark streets, "you said, I believe, that you could explain everything? I shall be most interested to learn how you defend a decision to lie to Lady Askerton and steal out of the house for an assignation."

"It wasn't like that! He – I thought he must be a friend of yours, and he invited me to visit the Water Gardens with a party that he was making up, only when I hired a chair and came to meet them, he said they were all gone ahead, and then he lured me down this dark winding path and, and – "

"I collect he then 'insulted' you," Iveroth said. "What else did you expect? And which of my friends do you accuse?"

"His voice and figure seemed familiar, and I thought when he called that he must be one of the gentlemen you introduced me to in the park, for there were so many that I could not remember all their names, but it turned out to be no such thing, for he was the Sorceror from the Fiendish Masque."

"Good heavens! You took a chair, unescorted, to meet Jenneret? How could you be such an idiot?"

"I told you. I thought he was a friend of yours, and anyway he said it was to be a party to see the Borghesan acrobats, and I particularly wished to go to the Water Gardens tonight because the Duchess of Quoy meant to be there. And however angry you may be," I added, "you need not bother to fly up into the boughs now, for I know perfectly well it was foolish in me, and in any case you can hardly insult me as badly as Lord Jenneret did, so you may as well save your breath!"

Iveroth drew the reins in and his horses stopped in the street. "Oh, can I not!" he said with surprising fierceness, and in the next moment his arm was about my shoulders and his mouth was pressed against mine, hot and warm and human, and he must have been employing some landfolk magic of his own, for I had neither the strength nor the will to push him away as I had done to Jenneret.

We were both somewhat breathless when at last he released me. "You see, my girl," he said, "I can be quite as insulting as the Bad Baron."

"Oh, no, you can't," I said. I felt giddy still from whatever magic he had used upon me, and elated as though the salt fountain I had raised were now bubbling through my own veins. "You have no idea how rude that man was!

He actually accused me of wanting to lie with a landman so that I might take human form – as if I would have any interest in such an odiously warm, hairy, air-breathing shape – and thought I should wish to lose my beautiful tail and become like you poor limited creatures – oh, I am sorry!" I interrupted myself as Iveroth made a strangled sound. "Now I am being rude. I am sure you landfolk are quite as satisfied with your form as we finfolk are with ours, only you see, I have no desire to change. Indeed, all my aunts were very worried that simply by marrying Lord Steinnland I might lose my tail and all my beauty, although there was nothing like *that* in our marriage. And Baron Jenneret thought that all finwives, unless made human by intercourse with a landman, must become ugly and hairy as walruses by their thirtieth year, so that he was doing a very generous thing in inviting me to lie with him."

Iveroth pulled up the horses and buried his head in his hands. "Lady Steinnland – damme, it's too much to expect a man to be formal when you insist on behaving like an enchanting child - Sabira, can you possibly try to tell me what happened tonight without mixing it up with fairy tales and phantasies? Or is that the only way you can bear to say it? My dear, did Jenneret force you to – to anything you might not like? Did I not come soon enough?"

"He, force me? Ha! I pushed him into the fountain when he only tried to kiss me, and trapped him in the waters."

Iveroth took up the reins again and clucked to his horses, who seemed to be quite bewildered with all these starts and stops. He muttered under his breath all the way to Steinnland's house in Rannach Square. As best I could make out, he was saying, "Either she's going mad, or I am."

His resistance to rational argument was truly amazing. I resolved that as soon as possible, I should have to make him understand my true nature, for it was not fair to let him ruin his credit with society by sponsoring a woman who, according to Jenneret, would be regarded as a demon or a monster.

Exactly how to make him understand, though, was a mystery to me, and one I had not solved by the time he set me down in Rannach Square. Time after time he had disbelieved the evidence of his own eyes. I thought that if he saw only the flowing fins at the end of my tail, he would take them to be some clever costume. And I could hardly show him how the tail sprung naturally from the base of my spine without disrobing before him – something that seemed to bother landfolk a great deal.

***

On the day following my misadventure at the Water Gardens I was resolved to remain quietly at home, doing nothing that should upset anyone's notions of propriety. The fact was that I was temporarily at a loss for ways in which to approach the Duchess of Quoy, so I felt I might as well stay at home and finish the second volume of *The Travails of Amanda*. The last few days in Din Eidyn had not given me nearly as much time for reading as I had expected, and it would be excessively annoying to have to return to Faarhafn without finishing at least this one novel.

For the first time in my life, though, I found it impossible to lose myself in the pages of a book. When Amanda's beloved Triunfione threw himself at her feet and implored her to plunge a dagger into his breast rather than keep him in that misery of suspense which oppressed his heart, I could not help but think him a poor-spirited creature compared to Iveroth; when Amanda fled, blushing and spilling behind her a spray of the meadow flowers which she had been gathering, I wondered just how I should greet Iveroth when next we met. Amanda, or any other heroine, would have been too nice-minded to make any reference at all to his shocking behavior. But then, Iveroth never minded referring to any behavior of mine that he considered shocking, so why should he not be subject to the same treatment?

Amanda's flight from Triunfione led her straight into the arms of the evil Count Vallombroso, whose coach had been waiting in the lane to carry her away. I had never questioned such occurrences before; now I wondered just how Vallombroso had known to place his coach there, and whether his horses had not caught cold by standing for so long, for no gentleman that I had met in Din Eidyn would be willing to let his horses stand so. Of course the climate was doubtless warmer in – well, wherever this story was set, which was not precisely clear to me. Like most romances, it seemed to take place in a country that boasted the most varied possible scenery, with snow-covered mountains giving way in half a day's ride to verdant hills and valleys sprinkled with the fruits and flowers of tropical climes. When I had had no knowledge of the world, such an arrangement had seemed in no way improbable to me. Now that I had endured the three days' coach ride from Faarhafn to Din Eidyn, watching the extremely gradual change of scene from the bleak headlands of the northern coast to the slightly less bleak hills around Din Eidyn, I suspected that the writers of romances had been guilty of improving on Nature's design in favor of their own picturesque imaginings.

"And another thing!" I exclaimed with some indignation. Lady Askerton woke with a start from the needlework she had been dozing over.

"What is that, my dear? Are you going to read aloud for a while? To be sure I should be vastly pleased if you have something of an improving nature to read. We are quite dull today, are we not? But then, with this rain we can hardly expect many callers!"

"I have only a trashy, stupid, unrealistic novel," I said. What had aroused my especial indignation was the realization that when the heroines of novels were carried away by villains, or rudely addressed by coarse banditti, or in any other difficult situation whatsoever, nobody ever told them it was their own silly fault for running into a shadowy lane in unknown territory, or for not screaming loud enough, or for behaving so improperly as to go off into a meadow with a young man in the first place. Whereas Iveroth always seemed to blame me – not, I admitted, without some reason; but I felt that the authors of these romances were themselves somewhat to blame, in having misled me about the real rules of society among landfolk. No one in novels ever worried a scrap about propriety, and no one in Din Eidyn ever seemed to worry about anything else.

"Oh, well," Lady Askerton said, "novels are not necessarily improper, unless of course they are translated from the Lutécian. If this is a good Anglian or Dalriadan work it is likely perfectly unexceptionable."

"Written," I read from the title page, "by Miss J_____, the daughter of a clergyman and the authoress of Little Moral Tales for Children."

"Ah, well, then I am sure there can be nothing harmful in it," said Lady Askerton comfortably. "You may begin reading whenever you please, my dear, for I am sure nothing will brighten our spirits so much as an improving work of literature."

"Unfortunately, this is Volume Two," I told her. "You would hardly enjoy it without having read the beginning of the story." Which was quite true; the untruth, if any, lay in failing to inform her that I had the first volume upstairs in my room. But I was quite out of patience with Miss J_____'s Amanda at this time, and I was not sure I could read Triunfone's protestations of love without grinding my teeth in a most unladylike fashion.

Lady Askerton appeared convinced that I was bored and required amusement, and as the scheme of reading aloud seemed to have failed, she suggested that she might teach me how to draw in perspective.

"We have neither drawing-paper nor watercolors," I said, "and only think how distressing if I should prove as unapt a student of drawing as I am of needlework! Dear Lady Askerton, I pray you will not concern yourself with amusing me. I believe I shall walk down to the Circulating Library and change these two volumes for something more worthwhile."

"But it is raining!"

"I do not mind the water – and Breta may take an umbrella to protect herself and the books."

"At least take the footman!" But I was of no mind to wait until Meldun chose to appear. At that moment rain seemed rather an attraction than otherwise; I should have gloried in even more water, in a positive thunderstorm, a flood in which I could cast off these restrictive garments and swim freely over a drowned Din Eidyn as I had disported myself in the waters about Finfolkaheem. And at least, on such a dismal day as this, no one would be walking or driving or riding about Din Eidyn for pleasure. I could probably manage the trip to Cromertie's Library and back without encountering anyone I knew.

In fact, the rain was not as strong as it had seemed from within doors; occasional gusts of fresh, cool air blew a spattering of water droplets across my face, but the streets and sidewalks were clear enough, with neither mud nor puddles to deter a lady's passage. For all that, I saw no ladies except myself; only servants and tradesmen went about their business on the damp streets.

On Faarhafn I should have been obliged to speak to anyone I encountered; in Din Eidyn, the rules of class and propriety gave me solitude in the midst of a city crowd. And solitude, I told myself, was what I craved after the upsetting experiences of last night; solitude and fresh air to clear my head so that I could think what to do next.

As soon as I had decided this, we turned the corner from Rannoch Square towards the library and my resolution was upset by the sight of a tall and all too familiar figure.

"Lady Steinnland," Iveroth said with a formal bow. "I was just proposing to do myself the honor of calling on you."

"What a pity, my lord," I said, "but as you can see, I am not at home."

"I shall walk with you, then," he said. "I see you are bound for Cromertie's." He relieved Breta of her basket of books. "I shall carry these and escort your mistress, Breta; you need not stay out in the rain."

Breta took my agreement for granted and scurried back to the house before I had a chance to say aye, nay, or maybe.

"I did not give you permission to dismiss my maid, Lord Iveroth," I said.

"But I particularly desired to talk privately with you," he said.

"And, naturally, my first object must be to meet your desires!"

"You are too kind."

I had to laugh in spite of myself. "And you are too ridiculous! Now pray will you call Breta back, and let me go on my way to the library? I have no desire for you to give me another such a scolding as you did last night."

"That was not my intention." Instead of doing as I requested, he offered me his arm. "We can talk on the way to the library. I see you have completed Volumes One and Two of *The Travails of Amanda*; are you going to exchange them for the third volume?"

"By no means! I found it a very silly book. I shall exchange it for some work of natural philosophy. I am quite out of patience with romances; they are nothing at all like real life."

"Your experience of real life is, of course, so broad."

"Considerably broader than it was a week ago."

"Yes," he said thoughtfully. "You have had some difficulties in adjusting to the life of the city, have you not?"

I kept my gaze firmly fixed on the pavement before us. "I thought you did not intend to scold me again."

"I do not," he said promptly. "Indeed, it had not been in my mind to have spoken with you on this subject at all – or at least, not until a decent interval had passed – but you destroy all my resolutions, Sabira. It is clear that you cannot live alone in the city and that Lady Askerton is not nearly competent to guide you. I did not – that is, I had never planned to – in short, when I came to Faarhafn, marriage was the last thing on my mind!"

"And so it might well have been," I said, "for there was not anyone on Faarhafn you would have considered eligible for the position of Lady Iveroth."

"Then, that may have been true; now, circumstances are quite altered. You are unprotected and too ignorant of the city to care for yourself; although to marry a lady widowed less than a month must violate every dictate of propriety, I feel it my duty to see that you are – to make sure – that is, madame, will you do me the honor of accepting my hand?"

I stopped where I stood and looked up at him. His dark-browed face was set in lines of firm control; he looked more angry than anxious.

I did not really wish him to throw himself at my feet and implore me to plunge a dagger into his breast rather than keep him in suspense, like Amanda's Triunfone; but surely there could be some medium between that melodrama and Iveroth's exceedingly unloverlike bearing? He could not really wish to marry me, or he would not have discovered his intention so stiffly and with such evident regret. It must be one of those things which he conceived to be the duty of a gentleman.

I would be no man's duty; especially not that of a man who did not even have the sense to recognize what I really was!

"My lord, I think there is some mistake. You neither like nor trust me; how can you wish to marry me?"

"Once, indeed, I misjudged you," he answered soberly, "but I had hoped I might have been forgiven for that error."

I bit my lip, considering my resolution of the night before. If Iveroth had taken such liberties with my person now as he did then, all common sense and reason might have been swept away. But a damp gray day in the gray city of Din Eidyn was no setting in which to sweep anyone away with passion. I was fully sensible of all the social disadvantages which Iveroth would incur in marrying me – a young woman with, as far as the world was concerned, no family and no history before her marriage to the old March-Lord; a woman who had been widowed less than three weeks; a woman whose fortune, though more than adequate for my simple needs, was as nothing compared to the wealth and status of his family.

I had no need to point out these disadvantages, for he had shown himself, too, to be fully aware of them; but there was one overriding all others which I had never managed to communicate to him, and which I felt could hardly be discussed in such a public spot as this.

"My lord, there are… complications which I cannot explain to you here and now, but which would surely make you wish to retract your offer if they were made clear to you."

"Then do so! Although I am damned if I can see," Iveroth said, "how matters can be any more complicated than they already are."

"Accept my word that it is impossible," I said, "and furthermore, that I am resolved never to marry an – anyone in Din Eidyn." It was a weak ending to the sentence, but I had almost said never to marry another man of the landfolk, and he would hardly have understood that.

"You cannot leave it thus! You will – you must explain yourself!"

"Must I, my lord? I think you take your conception of duty too far!"

"Children, children, do not waste such a lovely day by quarreling!" cried a sprightly voice all too near for comfort. I looked behind me and discovered Elspet Rattray and Iveroth's friend Mr. Dalkey. Elspet was dressed for walking in a round dress of cambric muslin with a tight, short jacket of fern-green *soie de Londres*, ornamented with cords and satin folds of a slightly darker green. The color of the jacket set off her fair complexion and auburn curls to perfection, and the muslin dress was trimmed round the hem with an extravagant profusion of poufs and ruffles that made her seem to be gliding, rather than walking, as she came closer to us. Not that such details of dress are important to finfolk, but living in Din Eidyn and going through plates of fashion designs with Lady Askerton had made me aware of them and the importance that landfolk placed on being always dressed in the latest fashion.

My own walking dress was of dove-grey satin, quite plain, with a bonnet of black straw and black half-boots. I had not really noticed how boring its simplicity was until now.

The intermittent rain seemed to have stopped, and the clouds were drifting into feathery wisps that allowed the sun to shine down into the narrow gray streets of the city, giving some justice to Elspet's claim that it was a lovely day – meaning, in Din Eidyn terms, that it was not actually raining at the moment.

"I had just been to call on you, Sabira, but found myself too late, so I resolved to catch you up on the way to Cromertie's if I could do so," Elspet said cheerfully. "Am I not a famous walker? Of course, I have not burdened myself with a basket full of books; that is a great help. And Mr. Dalkey, whom I met upon your doorstep, is also a great walker; we have had our share of exercise in striving to come up with you two!"

Lady Askerton had warned me that to be thought bookish was fatal in Din Eidyn society. This had not really concerned me before, and there was no reason why it should worry me now, when I was on the verge of returning home; nonetheless, I felt both bookish and dowdy.

"Some day," Elspet continued, slipping her arm through mine "you must tell me the secret of how you persuade Cromertie to let you have so many books at one time. He will never let me have another until I have returned the first one, and then, you know, somebody else may have taken out the next volume, and it is dreadful to have to wait weeks in suspense before one finds out what happened next. I see you have the first two volumes of *Amanda* there. Are you returning them? I have been waiting this age to read that book, for everyone says it is horrid beyond description and that Count Vallombroso's castle in the Alps is even more terrifying than Udolpho. Is it really that good? May I have the first volume, since you are returning it? I think this is a much more comfortable way of walking, do not you? We do not need these men; let them follow behind and carry our books while we have a comfortable chat all to ourselves. How becoming that bonnet is! I suppose it is because of that fair hair of yours, which looks positively silver against the black. But the shape, too, is just right for your face. You know I am desperately envious, for I cannot wear any round headdress; it makes my cheeks look positively fat. I am forced to go to the extremes of fashion to avoid looking like a little round squab of a thing. What is it made of? Black straw? what a pity it cannot be re-dyed in colors when you are out of mourning! But then, if black became me so well as it does you, I should be in no hurry to dress in colors again."

It was impossible to feel dowdy, or bookish, or sullen, under the flow of Elspet's lighthearted chatter and ridiculous flattery. She had made me laugh before we went many steps farther, and forced me to admit that I had not finished the second volume of *Amanda* and had no notion of Count Vallombroso's Alpine castle. When we were some way ahead of the gentlemen she managed somehow, without seeming offensively prying, to ask what Iveroth and I had been quarreling about.

Actually, she asked what ill-mannered and unconsidered thing he had been saying now to upset me, which I thought was an excellent way of phrasing the question.

"Oh, only the usual," I said with as good an assumption of carelessness as I could manage. "He thinks I shall never learn how to go on in society, and should have a keeper set to watch over me."

"Like the Duke of Quoy?"

"What – I thought he was long dead!" I exclaimed in surprise.

"Oh, not the old Duke; Erlend. Although I am not quite sure whether he bears the title now, even after his majority. The latest on-dit is that he is gone quite mad, poor boy, and Doctor Rangage despairs of any cure; so his dear mama the Dowager Duchess is to continue to manage the estates, and Erlend is to be shut away in one of her country houses with a whole set of keepers to look after him."

"I am sorry to hear it," I said. "And surprised, too. Are you acquainted with him?"

"No, he is too young for me, and too sober and studious to frequent the sort of places my brother likes," said Elspet. "I have only seen him at a few of those grand formal parties where everybody in Din Eidyn squeezes into one large room to shout at one another, and you know, in that setting a madman might seem as sensible as anyone else, for you cannot hear what anybody is saying."

"He visited Faarhafn shortly before my lord's death," I said slowly. "He seemed to me to be a perfectly rational young man. He was extremely interested in improving his lands by some of the new agricultural systems used in the south."

Elspet gave a dramatic shudder. "How dull! I am surprised *you* were not driven mad, my dear, if he bored you with a discourse on agricultural reform. Well, he would have had his chance to make all the changes he wanted, if he had but held on to his sanity. Now I suppose all will go on as it has been, with Ailsa of Quoy squandering the rents on fashions and fripperies and repairing her income from the pockets of those who are foolish enough to game at her house." She paused for a moment. "Do you know, it is a very shocking thing to speak ill of anybody, but there is something I cannot quite like about that woman. And I am quite sure she would have opposed Gairloch's plans for improving his lands, for although I know nothing about raising neeps and barley, I do know that when gentlemen begin to improve their estates they begin by spending a great deal of money on the project and promise themselves all shall be repaid in twenty years' time." A slight frown marred the white, soft skin of her face. "It is very strange that Gairloch should go mad just before he was to take over his inheritance, is it not?"

"A number of strange things have been happening around the Duchess of Quoy," I said, "including my husband's death. She was the last person to see him before the apoplexy which carried him off, and I have been trying to visit her, to find what she can tell me of his last rational moments, but she receives no one on the plea of being so very concerned for Gairloch."

"She is not so concerned as to stay at home of nights," said Elspet. "She has been seen at all of the best, and some of the worst, places in Din Eidyn. I hear she actually visited the Water Gardens last night when that surprise illuminated display occurred. Did you hear about it? The lighted fountain that sprang up out of nowhere? I should not be surprised if that was her doing. She is a witch, you know."

Remembering the plants in her knot-garden, I could well believe it; but I did not particularly wish to pursue the subject of the lighted fountain. "I thought no one in Din Eidyn believed in witchcraft, or magic, or anything of that sort. Iveroth is forever telling me that the rational study of natural philosophy has gone beyond such superstitions."

"Oh, Iveroth!" Elspet laughed. "He does not choose that there should be anything in the world which he cannot explain or control, and so he refuses to see anything that his Natural Philosophy cannot rationalize. But everybody knows that Ailsa trapped the old Duke by witchcraft, and that she uses daemons to control the fall of the cards when she gives gambling parties. That," she added with another slight frown, "is why I particularly dislike to see Tammas drawn into Ranald Westlin's set. They think themselves very dashing and daring because they lose money at Quoy House, and go about with that rake Jenneret. Well, Mr. Westlin may have his fingers burnt if he wishes, but I do not choose to see my brother playing with the same fire! Our excursion to Artor's Seat tomorrow will be much more the thing for him. Oh, wait a moment, I have an idea! Only we must let the gentlemen catch up with us. Are Sabira's books so heavy, Iveroth," she called, "that you must dawdle behind us so?"

"By no means. Only I thought that you girls wished to whisper secrets, and so in common courtesy Dalkey and I lagged behind."

"Common vanity, you mean," teased Elspet, "for you assumed we wanted to talk about you! Gentlemen always believe themselves the sole subject of interest in any conversation."

"By no means," said Mr. Dalkey. "I, at least, fully understand the superior attraction to the feminine mind of peau de soie ruffles, new bonnets, and the horrid mysteries of Udolpho."

"He means to be severe upon us," said Elspet to me, "and to imply that we are altogether incapable of rational conversation. If we are not whispering about men, then we can only be talking of foolish things not worthy their attention. I daresay it would surprise you excessively, Mr. Dalkey, to know that we were in fact discussing agricultural reform as it applies to the estates north of Din Eidyn."

"And naturally," Dalkey said, "you wished to apply to Iveroth and me, as being possessed of a fuller store of information on that subject than anyone else of your acquaintance."

"Iveroth, perhaps, but not you," Elspet retorted. "There is no one I would sooner apply to if I wished information on the best bootmaker in town, or if I wanted some obnoxious person called out and shot, but for almost anything else I fear you would be at a loss."

"Now that is unnecessarily severe," Dalkey protested. "I gave full respect to your interests; you must allow the making of a well-turned boot, or the art of using a pistol, at least as much weight as the latest Lutécian fashions or the newest three-volume romance."

"Very well! I shall allow you to have a mind at least as well-informed as mine, but on one condition."

"I did not know that such matters were to be decided at a lady's whim, and upon conditions."

"Then you are not so well-informed as you claim, or you would know that in society gentlemen are always obliged to submit to the desires of the ladies. In any case my condition is not so onerous. I desire Iveroth to join our excursion to Artor's Seat tomorrow; you must persuade him, and I suppose you had better come too, so that he shall be assured of some rational conversation."

Dalkey agreed at once and without consulting Iveroth, whose black-browed stare gave no hint of whether he actually intended to join the proposed expedition. I could not even decide what to wish for. Which would be worse – to leave our discussion as it had been when Elspet interrupted us, or to attempt to continue it under all the disadvantages of a carriage expedition among lively company? On such an excursion I could scarcely reveal my true nature to him in any way that would convince him, so nothing would be resolved. Doubtless it would be better if he did not come – and yet I found myself hoping that he would.

CHAPTER TWENTY

The next day was sunny, an occurrence so unusual in Din Eidyn that Elspet claimed it for a sign that the gods were smiling upon our excursion to Artor's Seat. Certainly the weather could not have been more delightful, nor had I any objection to the company; my only reservation had to do with the arrangement of the company. After visiting Cromertie's library we had all adjourned to the Rattray house to take tea and discuss our plans. In deference to my inexperience at riding – at least in the style of landfolk – Elspet had first planned that she and young Mr. Rattray should take me up in his chaise, which seated three persons comfortably, while Major Maddox rode alongside; the addition of Iveroth and Mr. Dalkey to the party made this plan ineligible in her eyes. I should have thought that Iveroth and Mr. Dalkey could also have ridden horseback beside the chaise, but Elspet complained that in that case they would go off on their own and we should derive no benefit from their society.

I could see her point; having gone to such pains to inveigle Mr. Dalkey into the expedition without admitting her desire to be with him, it would be quite a waste from her point of view to let him ride ahead chatting with Iveroth and Major Maddox while she was trapped in the chaise; also, she appeared to best advantage on horseback – a matter of no moment when her companions were only myself and her brother and a middle-aged major, but quite otherwise now that Dalkey was to be of the party.

Iveroth volunteered the use of his curricle but suggested that Major

Maddox, who suffered from pain in one knee due to a wound gained in the recent difference of opinion with Lutéce, should drive it while he and the others rode. This left me paired with Major Maddox in the curricle. As an alternative I might have proposed riding Meldun, for I felt quite sure he would never permit me to fall, but this would have been impolite to the Major. Also, I was not entirely sure whether Meldun would permit the imposition of a saddle and reins – and I *was* sure that to ride him bareback would earn me another of Iveroth's punishing set-downs for unladylike behavior.

At first the other members of the party rode close by the curricle at a staid pace, but this did not last long; as soon as we left the confines of the city for the winding road towards the mountain, Elspet gave Iveroth a teasing glance over her shoulder. Saying, "Now you shall judge for yourself how sluggish my mare is, Brandubh!" she impelled the horse into a canter and then to a full gallop. No longer bounded by the small area of the city park, she seemed to fly up the gently sloping road until she disappeared from sight, hidden by a fold in the hills.

"She will break her neck!" Mr. Dalkey exclaimed.

"Not Elspet," replied Iveroth, "she is more likely to break that poor beast's wind. But if you are truly concerned, you had better go after her."

Mr. Dalkey required no more encouragement to whip up his horse and follow Elspet. As I watched him, too, disappear among the hills before us, I remembered Elspet's confidence of the previous day, when we had a moment alone at her house. She had told me that she meant to marry Mr. Dalkey, but that it would be fatal to display any interest in him when he was so annoyed by his mama's perpetual attempts at matchmaking; instead she meant to ignore him, and so to be the one female he felt comfortable with. "So if you see me flirting with Iveroth, my dear Sabira, you need feel no concern; it is only a show to persuade Dalkey that I am not setting my cap at him!"

"It is nothing to me with whom you flirt," I said. "In any case I shall not be here to see you. Advocat Tulloch promises that the formalities of proving my lord's will should be complete within a day or two, and then I plan to return to Faarhafn."

"Oh, la!" Elspet exclaimed. "Without confronting your murderous duchess, and without making sure of Iveroth? 'Twould be monstrous impolite in me to accuse you of telling untruths, Sabira, but you cannot expect me to believe that!"

I was not entirely sure that I believed it myself. But my attempts to meet with her Grace had failed; even if I did get speech with her, nothing would come of it, for she would deny any knowledge of Steinnland's apoplexy and defy me to prove otherwise; and as for Iveroth—

I looked gloomily at the neat figure before me, riding so gracefully that he seemed almost one with his horse, conversing with Mr. Rattray about sporting pursuits; close enough for me to overhear their talk, yet making no effort whatsoever to have any particular speech with me. Yesterday's scene on the rainwashed streets of Din Eidyn might never have occurred. No doubt by now he was regretting an offer made stiffly and only from a sense of duty, and would be only too grateful if I never referred to the matter again. His untroubled behavior today was of a man perfectly heart-whole. There was not the least necessity for me to discover my true nature to him.

Returning to Faarhafn was not only the sensible thing to do; it was the only thing to do.

My people do not weep; if we ever come under the scrutiny of a student of natural philosophy, he will doubtless explain the biological reasons that make it impractical for beings already living in salt water to express more such water through their eyes. It was therefore not difficult for me to remain dry-eyed. I even made shift to desire Major Maddox to explain the history of our destination to me, and to make appropriate exclamations of appreciation and surprise while he unfolded the bloody history of Din Eidyn and the numerous occasions, before the Kingdom of Dalriada united the tribes, when possession of the peak looming before us had been decisive in some fierce-fought engagement.

Things were no better when we arrived at out destination – a low, grassy depression at the very top of the hill that loomed over Din Eidyn. While Elspet directed Iveroth and Mr. Dalkey in spreading out the picnic cloth and opening the baskets of food and utensils, Mr. Rattray vied with Major

Maddox in pointing out to me the various sights of Din Eidyn visible from
this vantage point. We were looking down on the city from the east; when I
looked westward, I could just make out the glimmer of the sea among low-
lying clouds; the barren lands to the north were hidden among mist. My
island of Faarhafn was as invisible as if it had already been given back to the
people of the sea.

"You do not seem very interested in identifying the Opera House or the
Mint," said Iveroth, startling me; I had thought him occupied under Elspet's
direction, and happy to be so. "Are you looking for Faarhafn? It would not
be visible from this distance, even if the mists were to clear; the distance, and
the curvature of the earth would prevent of your viewing it."

"I am perfectly capable of making those calculations for myself," I said.

"No doubt you are," Iveroth agreed. "I apologize for intruding." And he
rejoined Elspet and Mr. Dalkey.

Strange, how a party of only six people can shift, and rearrange itself, and
shift again, and yet one can be as separated from another member of the party
as though in a great assembly! Elspet and her brother kept up a gay chatter
and provoked a great deal of laughter from the other gentlemen; we ate bread
and butter and smoked goose and glasshouse fruit and other delicacies that all
tasted of nothing to me; we formed our cavalcade again for the ride home,
and it seemed I was to have no more private speech with Iveroth than those
few words exchanged on the mountaintop. To be sure, I deserved no better,
having rebuffed him then. No doubt he was already grateful that I had not
accepted an offer that he did not truly desire to make.

Only on the last stages of the return home, when the horses were not so
fresh and Elspet had to cease her foolery, did Iveroth draw level with the
curricle for a moment. "It is impossible to speak sensibly in any party of which
Elspet makes one of the number," he said with a smile so gentle, so forgiving,
that I could almost imagine he had forgotten my rudeness. "May I hope to
find you at home, if I call tomorrow morning?"

"Why – if you wish it - Certainly, my lord," I stammered.

"And I shall hope," he said with a serious look that made my breast ache,
"*not* to find Lady Askerton at home."

Certainly that would be best, if I were to explain to him the real impediment to my accepting his offer – apart from the fact, I reminded myself, that he did not love me and was only offering out of an exaggerated sense of duty.

When he looked at me so, with his mouth set as though something hurt him, and his eyes seeking mine, it was hard for me to be sure of that fact, and harder to remember that he would certainly not want me if he knew all the truth. Perhaps – although I resented it at the time – perhaps it was fortunate that Mr. Dalkey overheard his last words, and interrupted us with some raillery about Iveroth's now paying the price for taking Lady Askerton off his hands and out of his mother's household.

I thought that for all the sun and fresh air, I should not sleep that night, and in this I was correct; but it was not the anticipation of Iveroth's call that kept me awake. I returned to the house in Rannoch Square to find such news awaiting me as drove all such thoughts completely out of my head.

"My love, I have had a positive torrent of invitations to answer on your behalf while you were gallivanting with Miss Rattray," Lady Askerton greeted me. "My poor eyes are all but exhausted, and I am sure I shall have cramp in my hand from answering them all, but I made sure you would not wish to deal with them yourself, not knowing, as you do not, which are from people of good ton and which from mere social climbers trying to raise themselves by clinging to your petticoats. Really, some of these people—! Imagine trying to persuade me that their invitations are to be considered, when they cannot ever spell or write like gentlefolk. Why, I found the superscripture on this one quite indecipherable! Heaven only knows how it came to be delivered properly, and I cannot conceive that the contents can be of any interest to us."

The letter she produced for my amusement consisted of a sheet torn from Kuylenstierna's *Engravings Anatomical and Descriptive of the Supernatural Inhabitants of Din Eidyn and the Surrounding Seas*, with a superscription half in capitals and half in small letters laboriously printed over the small printed text as if with a split and blunted quill:

"TO: Sabira, LAdy sTeinnLAnd
sTeinnLAnd hoUse
Din Eidyn"

"And whoever sent it had not even the decency to pay the postage, so I was obliged to pay the postman out of the household cash for the cost of overland mail all the way from Faarhafn," Lady Askerton went on while I peeled off the improvised seal – a splash of melted tallow – and perused the contents of the inner sheet with growing horror.

Most of the page was given over to a fanciful representation of a nucklavee; the artist had got the single eye and the appearance of red veins moving over a skinless black body correct, but the rendition of the monster's lower half left much to be desired. Below the picture was more printing over the text:

"Three more peopLe hAve died in The sAme mAnner since yoU LefT here, my LAdy. My LAdy, no one BLAmes yoU now for The oLd Lord's deATh. We know now ThAT iT is one of The nUckLAveen, for I seen iT myseLf when I were Tending kiLn. I Think mAyBe I BLinded This one wiTh my kiLn rAke for I do noT know how eLse I goT AwAy. No one BUrns keLp now, nor The fishermen do noT go oUT Upon seA for feAr of Being cATched There. My LAdy, pLeese To come BAck And rid Us of This monsTer fore we Be ALL sTArved or kiLT.

"IngA's Androw of Neip"

"I am prodigious glad you saved this to show me, Lady Askerton," I said when I could control my voice. "This is from one of my lord's – one of my tenants," I corrected myself, "on Faarhafn."

"And what business has he to be bothering you, not to mention letting you bear the charges for posting?" Lady Askerton sniffed. "Had Lord Steinnland no factor to keep these people in their place?"

"This is – something the factor could not be expected to deal with," I said, a wild bubble of laughter rising within me at the discrepancy between my calm words and the monstrous reality. "I shall have to – have to – return to Faarhafn at once. Tell Breta…" I paused. It would be the height of idiocy to pack my clothes and take the lumbering coach for three days across the hills that slowly gave way to the barren northern plains and then to the crags that guarded the harbor of Faarhafn, when I could be there within a few hours by sea. "No, never mind, but leave me a little while, if you please? I must – I must write some letters."

"Ladies do not handle business matters," Lady Askerton said. "You should send for Advocat Tulloch and instruct him."

"I do not think this problem falls within the Advocat's scope either," I said, "or that of any man in Din Eidyn! Now leave me in peace!"

Even after Lady Askerton withdrew, protesting and mumbling, I could not think properly; my thoughts were like great sluggish worms, tumbling blindly across one another so that none could pursue a path without being baulked by another. The sea – Meldun had said that the water near Din Eidyn was dirty and he would not go in it – but he must have ventured down to the wharves, to discover this much. He could take me that far, and if he would not enter the water with me, I should go alone, and he could take my discarded clothes back with him in his guise of footman – no – he would have to dispose of them somehow, so as not to alarm Lady Askerton – oh, what was the use? She was going to be alarmed in any case; she would probably have a fit of the vapors, or hysterics, or something equally useless. At least I should be spared listening to her strictures on this particular bit of behavior. I did not think I would be returning to Din Eidyn.

Iveroth. How angry he would be if he knew that I proposed to throw away a perfectly good walking-dress of dove-gray satin and swim through the northern seas to Faarhafn! Not to mention the black half-boots… A corner of my mind seized on the subject of Clothes and chattered away, listing all the garments so recently made to my measure and delivered here, which would go to waste now. It was better than thinking about the fact that I should never have another quarrel with Iveroth. He proposed to call here tomorrow. He would be very angry. The least I could do was to leave him some kind of a letter of explanation. So my excuse to Lady Askerton was not entirely an untruth!

I dipped my pen and watched the black drops fall back into the inkpot, one, two, three. Dipped again – one, two, three; there was something soothing in the slow measured falling. What could I say to Iveroth? He would dismiss the plain truth as fairytales and lies. Yet I must write something. After all the trouble I had already caused him, I would not for the world have him come here tomorrow and think that I had run away, like a naughty child, rather than face him.

"My lord Iveroth," I wrote, "I am sorry that I shall not be at home to receive your call tomorrow. I am leaving Din Eidyn tonight, and ...."

I shall never return.

That was almost certainly true, but I could not bring myself to write the words.

It would be foolish and pointless to return just because I had missed Iveroth's last visit. No doubt he would be vastly relieved to have the problem of Lord Steinnland's widow retreat to Faarhafn, and would assume I meant to live in decent seclusion there. Which was, actually, more or less true, depending on what you meant by "there."

Breta and Antoine had come south with me. Antoine would certainly find other employment very easily, and Din Eidyn was home to him. But what of Breta? I rather thought she too would like to stay in Din Eidyn. She had learned very quickly how to be a good lady's maid. If she did not wish to stay, someone would have to help her travel north again, as she could certainly not go by my path.

One could hardly write to a man whose proposal of marriage one had just refused, asking him to find employment for a lady's maid. Perhaps Elspet would look after Breta for me. I should have to write that letter after I finished this one to Iveroth.

Only, I still did not know what to say to him. And my pen was dry now. I dipped it again.

I was still dipping the pen and watching the ink slide off the quill and drop back into the bottle when Lady Askerton opened the door.

"I told you –"I began, turning round in my chair, before I saw who had come in with her.

"Here you are, my dear!" she said brightly before turning to her companion. "You see, Advocat Tulloch, Lady Steinnland was too shy to send for you herself, but I knew she would be delighted to have your help with this troublesome tenant of hers on Faarhafn, for surely it is gentlemen's work and nothing a lady should be worried over."

"If there is anything in which I can be of service –" Advocat Tulloch said.

"Oh, no! I mean – I am sorry that you were troubled – it is a small thing and nothing at all worth calling you for," I said in some confusion. Lady Askerton made noises about ringing for some refreshments to offer the advocat. Tulloch himself sat down comfortably on one of the straw-yellow padded chairs decorating the drawing-room and opened a bulging leather portfolio. "As it happens, Lady Steinnland, I had called to see you earlier today, but I gather you were off seeing the sights of our fine city. "

"I am sorry to have missed you," I said automatically. Now that my preparations for leaving – such as they were – had been interrupted, my mind was beginning to work properly again. And I did not at all like the conclusions it was urging on me.

"Dinna' fash yerself, lassie. It's glad I am to see you enjoying life again, and not torturing any more linen napkins with needlework. 'Twas just a wee matter of business."

"More papers to sign."

"Precisely. If we might use your writing-desk….?"

I swept my unfinished note to Iveroth off the desk. "No, don't trouble to pick it up, it's nothing, a mistake, I need to start that letter over again," I babbled, hardly aware of what I was saying as Advocat Tulloch laid out sheaf after sheaf of documents upon the polished surface of the desk. *Three more people have died in the same manner… no one blames you now for the old Lord's death… one of the nucklaveen…I seen it myself..* If I had not been stupid with grief, I should have recognized the manner of my lord's death; it had the stink of the nucklaveen all over it.

"Sign here, my lady, and here," the advocat pointed out.

The pen that had scratched so abominably when I tried to write to Iveroth now flowed smoothly across the papers. I signed my name over and over again, always in the style of the landfolk – Sabira Lady Steinnland, not Sabira

Norinsdattr – while my thoughts ran on. How should I have thought of the nucklaveen? All the islands and northern coast had long been warded against the creatures; folk-charms of twisted hay and herbs, signs scratched into piers and breakwaters, prevented their walking upon land or preying upon the landfolk. Without invitation from some landman, a nucklavee could not have trespassed upon the land of Faarhafn; and no one would be fool enough to invite one onto his own island...

But two people who did not belong to Faarhafn had been there just before my lord's death – young Lord Gairloch and his mother, her Grace of Quoy. Oh, and Iveroth, but I did not count him in this thought; he at least would never have done aught to harm my lord. Gairloch had seemed a straightforward, rather dull young man, but I really knew very little of him; could his madness have been caused by a meeting with a nucklavee?

On the night of the full moon, Iveroth had followed me out of the house...but then had followed another woman down the steep steps of the Vaardens.

Ailsa of Quoy was a witch; Elspet had spoken casually of her use of magic to win at the gaming tables, and the plants in her garden were not kitchen herbs, but the working materials of herb-witches.

The madness of Gairloch had come on quite suddenly, and at a monstrous convenient time for the Duchess, who would otherwise have been obliged to hand over control of the Quoy estates this very week.

Ailsa of Quoy was the kind of woman for whom no one else was quite real; she lived in a universe bounded on all sides by her own reflection. She would have thought nothing of giving a nucklavee the freedom of the shore in return for driving Gairloch mad.

"But why kill my lord?" I no longer doubted that it was she who had directed the nucklavee to Steinnland's chamber – but why? What had she to fear from a man stricken by an apoplexy, who could barely speak?

"I beg your pardon, my lady?"

"Oh! I – I am sorry, Advocat Tulloch; my mind was wandering. Is this the last of the papers that I must sign?"

"It is that, your ladyship, and with it there's an end of the wearisome business. The will is proved and copies have been registered in the King's Court and the Dower Court. You have unquestioned title to Faarhafn, to this house, and to the remains of Lord Steinnland's fortune."

After Advocat Tulloch took his leave I sank down again on the chair before the desk, propped my elbows on the desk in a most unladylike manner, and rested my face in my cupped hands.

The Duchess of Quoy had killed my lord. I had all along believed her indirectly guilty of his death, in that she had callously stepped over his prostrate form rather than take a moment to call for the immediate help that might have saved his life. Now I believed her guilt to be far more than that. It had doubtless been the sight of the nucklavee that drove Gairloch mad and caused my lord's apoplectic fit; his mysterious death, with the signs of salt water and rotting kelp about him, had been the work of a nucklavee that was now continuing to ravage Faarhafn – on the invitation of Ailsa of Quoy!

I no longer wanted simply to confront her and shame her for her neglect of a dying man; I wanted to kill her. More than that, I wanted to bring her to justice before the people who had lost loved ones to "her" nucklavee.

And I thought that I could do that – without significantly delaying my trip north – if Meldun would help me.

I found him in horse-form, in the stables. Horses got fed at the fifth hour after noon, human servants at the seventh. For all Meldun's complaints about the staleness of land food, I had for some time suspected him of changing form to benefit from both meals; kelpies are notoriously greedy. I explained to him what I needed and told him to attend me in the hall – in human form – as soon as he had finished eating. I needed at least that long to make my own preparations for confronting her Grace, and in any case he would not have passed up a meal on my account.

The last thing I had to do before leaving the house was to lie to Lady Askerton. Thanks to Elspet's tutelage, I had become quite good at that. I told her that Elspet had invited all of us who had been to Artor's Seat to an informal dinner at her home, and that I meant to walk there and that Meldun would escort me. Since it was not yet even close to dark – our days in the north are very long in summer, though Din Eidyn felt dark to me compared with Faarhafn – she could hardly complain about my walking, and it gave some excuse for my not changing into dinner dress.

"You might as well take a chair," Meldun said as soon as we were safe out of the house. "I know how you feel about walking."

"I'm in a hurry, and I walk faster than those men would." I glanced sidewise at him. "Or if you really want to save me time and effort, you could shift back into horse form and let me ride you."

"In front of all these people?"

"Oh, don't be so silly! The alleys between the main streets are quite private enough. Here we go." I ducked around a pedestal covered with baskets of flowering plants and led Meldun into High Rannoch Wynd, a noisome alley not more than two feet wide at this end. Some optimistic builder had paved it with bricks that sloped down to the center of the alley, presumably in the hope that rainwater and other less salubrious liquids would drain into the center and run off quickly. The scheme hadn't worked. My boots would be ruined by the time we got through the wynd. But it was certainly private enough.

"I am not," Meldun said, "going to change into horse form in an alley too narrow to hold me!"

"Just wait until you are a horse before you put your ears back and shy at shadows, will you? It is wider at the top end. And I should have wanted you to become a horse before we reached Quoy House in any case."

"Why?"

I explained, as briefly as I could, my deductions about Ailsa of Quoy's part in Steinnland's death. Meldun had never really known my lord, and could not be expected to grieve him as I did; but at the suggestion that the Duchess had loosed a nucklavee upon Faarhafn, his nostrils flared and his hoofs rang out on the cobblestones and –

"I was not expecting you to change so fast," I complained, examining my right foot as well as I could without taking off or actually touching my indescribably filthy boots. I did not think that anything was broken.

"Take me to this woman," Meldun interrupted. "If you are strong enough to throw her over my back, I shall give her such a wild ride as never she has known before. From here to Faarhafn she shall be scratched by brambles and scoured by salt winds, frighted by bogles and goblins and threatened with becoming a morsel of good eating for a troll-stane!"

"Well, yes," I said, "that was more or less what I had in mind. Please do not drown her before you reach Faarhafn. We may need her cooperation to ban the nucklavee again."

Meldun promised that he would bring Ailsa to me alive and in an extremely cooperative mood, and as soon as I scrambled upon his back his hooves clattered again upon the stones and he set off for Quoy House at full gallop. With neither saddle nor reins I had to pull up my skirts and ride him astride, and had to lean down along his neck and shout at him in the Old Language before he moderated his pace to a walk, not a block from Quoy House.

"We have to be subtle about this," I told him after I had slid down and straightened my petticoat. "We can't just walk in and demand to see her."

"I can." Like most kelpies, Meldun considered subtlety and tact to be unnecessary complications in social intercourse. Usually I felt this was a good thing; since kelpies have no conscience at all about lying, it helps that they don't bother to make their lies even remotely credible. In this case – well, I would just have to hope that Meldun would follow my lead.

"No, you can't; she would have the servants throw you out. You are going to take human form again, and I shall sprinkle us with a solution of sea salt and water, and we shall walk in invisibly and find her." I showed him the packet of sea salt in my reticule and the flask of water which I had asked Breta to find for me just before I left.

Without regard, this time, for who might be looking, Meldun's black horse-form shimmered and melted into the shape of a handsome young man dressed as befitted a lord, at least: form-fitting knitted brown breeches, boots glossy as a mirror, a blue coat over a white shirt and an intricately pleated and folded neck cloth. Fortunately, I think no one was looking; we were now at the residential end of Din Eidyn, so there were no shopkeepers or apprentices or shoppers about, and the hour was too early in the evening for the fashionable residents to go out looking for entertainment.

At any rate, I did not hear any screams, and that was good enough. It was not as though I expected to stay around here long enough to be troubled by any gossip about Meldun's careless shape-changing.

"Mix your potion, and let us be about our business!"

"Do not be in such a hurry," I cautioned him. "I do not know how long this will last, so I want to sprinkle it over us just before we go in. Then we need to hurry, to find Ailsa and take her before it wears off." As we walked the last block, I kept dropping pinches of salt into the water and shaking the flask to make it dissolve. I wanted the solution as strong as possible, but I knew that one could not keep dissolving salt in water forever; eventually the water has taken on too much of the nature of the salt and rejects any more. I got about half of the packet in my reticule dissolved in the water before we reached Quoy House, and that tasted about right; I folded up the packet again, not unhappy to have the rest in reserve for emergencies.

"Let the seen be unseen, the unseen seen," I murmured while flicking droplets of salt water alternately upon myself and Meldun. "Let day be night and darkness light, the plain unshown, the hidden known." It was a good general-purpose turnabout charm that could, if it would, give us true sight while turning the eyes and minds of other away from us for as long as our clothes remained damp with the salt water.

Probably.

It was also entirely possible that the power of the salt would be exhausted before the water dried. Before coming to Din Eidyn I had never thought to conduct any scientific experiments on this subject; but then, I had never thought to find myself more than a few steps from the salt sea.

CHAPTER TWENTY-ONE

I was relieved to see that the iron gates were open. A traveling coach with closed blinds stood before the house; servants were bringing out chests and trunks and shouting contradictory instructions and bumping into each other. They took absolutely no notice of us. Indeed, I had to skip and leap nimbly to keep out of their way.

It was typical of Meldun that he didn't bother to get out of the way, and typical of his luck that the man who ran into him blamed the accident on his neighbor, and that the two of them started quarreling. If I had the luck of a kelpie – oh, well. I had other things that were supposed to be as useful, if not better; salt water magic, and common sense, and a measure of tact.

The very doors of the house stood open to accommodate the people running to pack things into the coach; we had only to walk in to see the whole house open before us. Well, I suppose "see" is not quite the correct term. It was rather that I had a sense of the house and its inhabitants. I could feel the scurrying of servants around us and the distracted clamor in the kitchens; I could feel the Duchess of Quoy sitting somewhere over my head; I could feel the blind emptiness of the salons that would open on each side of the hall when the Duchess entertained. The yellow room, the one where Iveroth and I had waited in vain, was simply empty. In the blue salon, behind the closed doors to my right, something not quite human was playing absently with a pair of ivory dice; the small click-clack, click-clack, thump of the dice knocking against each other and then falling on the tablecloth sounded as loud as a drumbeat to my enhanced senses.

"She is upstairs," I told Meldun, as though he could not sense her presence as well as I could. He might not have heard me for all the attention he paid; first he cocked his head as if to listen to the ghostly clicking of dice, and then he leaned against the wall and folded his arms.

"Didn't you hear me? Let's go get her. I don't know how long this magic will last."

"You still have more than half your salt water left," Meldun pointed out.

"Fine, wonderful, we have enough to get in and get out, but not if you will not move."

"There is no point to getting in and out," said Meldun, "if you do not listen. Have you not heard what all these people are doing?"

"Packing up to go somewhere?" Meldun was right; I had not listened properly. Now I set my mind to the chatter of human voices, made faint by the same spell that increased my sense of other things, and understood what he meant. "They are going to take Erlend to some house in the country where he can be restrained without harming him. I suppose that means Dr. Rangage has indeed pronounced him incurably mad. Meldun, it is very sad, but I do not quite see…"

"Where's t'young lord?" a man called.

"In the Blue Salon. Shall us take him now, or does his lady mother wish to say her farewells!"

"Might as well go and ask her," a third servant volunteered.

"You're just putting it off. You don't want to take him."

"Do you?"

"Faith, no! Fair gives me the creepies to be touching it – I mean, him."

"The servants," Meldun said, "think Gairloch is in the room to our right."

And I knew – knew with all the straining power of my enhanced senses – that nothing human was in that room. I had supposed it to be a tame demon of Ailsa's that played with the dice.

While someone clattered upstairs to ask if the Duchess would come down to see her son depart, Meldun opened the door of the Blue Salon for me and we walked in – unnoticed, of course, though someone in the hall did complain of a plaguey draft. The turnabout spell would have done things the easiest way, simply making sure that they were all watching the woman running upstairs when Meldun opened and closed the door. At least, I hoped it was using the easiest way and conserving its power; I did not want to have to renew the water in the flask from one of Her Grace's flower vases. It would be much simpler if only….

Strange, how my brain went on chattering while my eyes were taking in a worse horror than I had imagined. The thing that played idly with dice at a table was not Gairloch, though it had his likeness stretched over it. It was a changeling, a thing of water and spirit bound by a charm, a thing with neither life nor self-awareness in it but only a deep longing to return to its natural state.

It looked up at us, and I thought that I saw that desire through the eyes that looked like Gairloch's.

"Sar - sar - sea," it stammered with a bubbly sound, as though gathering all itself together to fight the charm that bound it to this shape.

"Oh, yes!" Pity and loathing together bade me pour the contents of my flask over the changeling while I said three words that broke the charm.

And then there was nothing to be seen but Gairloch's clothes, slowly subsiding into the puddle of salt water on the floor.

"I – I suppose it will get back to the sea?" I said, horribly unsure as to whether I had done the right thing.

"All waters return to the sea, and rise from it as vapor, and fall, and return again," Meldun said. "It is more certain, now, of a safe return than you are. Your magic is fading."

"Oh, well. I need only dip some water from this vase, and – "

"What," demanded an imperious voice from the door, "are you doing here? And where is my son?"

I dropped the vase. No matter; it was ugly anyway, and there were more flowers here and there in the room.

"I think you know the answer to that question better than I, Ailsa of Quoy," I said, "for the poor creature in this room was never born of woman nor meant to walk the earth, and I am glad that I have set it free!"

She closed the door behind her, took two steps forward, and slapped my face so hard that I could feel her fingerprints marked my cheek. "You again! Always you! I've had enough of your meddling ways, you foolish girl."

I was about to tell her that was just too bad, when she moved her fingers with a curious twist, sprinkling me with dried herbs and speaking some words that sounded very ugly indeed. As their echo died away, I made to brush the smelly fragments of herbs off my dress.

My hands would not move.

Nor would my throat open to cry for help, nor my feet take me from the room, nor my head turn to look for Meldun. All I could do was breathe in and out like a clockwork toy.

"Be thankful I left you the freedom to breathe," she said, "for I could have frozen your body entire. But you may yet be of some use to me, so you may stay there – and breathe – while I send to someone who will be delighted to meet you again."

She had left me more than breath, though much good it did me; I could see only the closed doors directly in front of me, could hear only what was said just outside the doors: Ailsa crying to her servants to leave off packing, that the journey was postponed; then the tramping of feet under heavy loads, and the bumps as the servants set down their burdens. From this I could guess when the Duchess left the entry hall, for the servants stopped putting things down gently and began to drop them any old way.

I could not hear any sound from Meldun. Had he not been behind me when the Duchess cast her herb-charm? Had he been caught in the same trap?

If he had, there was not much I could do about it now, save to reflect that landsmen who sought to catch a kelpie generally regretted the experiment.

A particularly unfortunate *thump*! in the hallway was followed by the distinctive clash and tinkle of breaking glass, then by the shouts of some upper servant berating an underling, and then by the Duchess' sharp voice.

"Now what will you be at?" she railed. "Can I not sit for five minutes to write a letter, but you clumsy oafs – Ohhhh. I did not know *you* were come, my dear." Her voice sweetened on the last words; I thought of over-ripe strawberries drowned in sugar to disguise the rotten bits.

The voice that answered her was Meldun's!

How had he escaped her spell? Or – had he? He was talking to her now, sounding for all the world like a young man so desperately in love that he did not care what the servants overheard; and she answered him with sweet cooing nothings. Had she put a love-charm upon him? I thought not; she did not sound as confident of him as all that.

She sounded like an aging woman trying to make sure of her young lover.

And trying, also, to distract him from the closed doors between us. He asked if she meant to keep him standing in the hall; might they not sit down? She invited him into the yellow room, and he said that he would not intrude on her writing; he would just wait, if he might, in the other salon.

"On no account," she said sharply, "my poor son is in there, and I will not have him disturbed!"

Meldun begged her pardon. I imagined I could hear soft sounds of skin rubbing against skin, kisses given and exchanged. Then the Duchess broke away from the embrace – or what I guessed to be an embrace – with a soft, contented sigh. "Come and bear me company a moment, my dear, while I finish this tiresome letter! No, nothing of importance; I had promised the Lutécian ambassador a card of invitation to my next little gathering, that is all."

A few minutes later I heard her sending her lover – Meldun, I must not forget that it was Meldun, but had he forgotten me? – sending Meldun upstairs to wait in her boudoir. No sooner had his steps mounted the stairs than she called to a footman. "Take this to Baron Jenneret, in Daviot Crescent!"

The outer doors shut and I heard the footman running on his errand. A moment later the Duchess reentered the Blue Salon. She circled me, at first from some distance, and then amused herself by coming closer and giving playful little tweaks to my skirts and hair while I stood motionless and unable to defend myself.

"I think Jenneret will be very happy to have you," she told me. "And it should not be so very different from being married to old Steinnland – if anything, I am doing you a favor, for Jenneret is a lusty man fully capable of performing his marital duties. And I should know!"

That tinkling laugh of hers had no doubt been charming once, when she was younger and it had a less practised sound.

"You cannot have married Steinnland for love. Did you persuade yourself, though, that he loved you? You seem just the sort of romantic young fool who would imagine such a thing. Do not deceive yourself, my dear. I understood Steinnland better than you. He was always a collector of curiosities, and in you, I believe, he found his last and greatest curiosity. Or do you think that Nucklavee should be counted his last acquisition? Not that he managed to keep Nucklavee – it was more the other way around, do not you think?"

What I thought was that this would be a very good time for Meldun to come back downstairs and rescue me.

Now her hands were pulling at the back fastenings of my gown. I flinched in revulsion and then felt a small flame of hope. At least I could flinch. I tried to hold myself as rigidly still as before, that she might not guess her spell was wearing off. I do not think I could have done so if I had known what she was holding; I thought she was only teasing until I heard the scratching sound of a blade tearing through fabric, and felt a draft of air on the spot where my tail sprung out at the base of my spine.

"Ahhhh." The sigh of satisfaction was curiously like the sound she had made when breaking free of Meldun's passionate embrace. "Yes, Jenneret will be pleased to add you to his cabinet of curiosities, and willing enough to do me the favor of seeing that you do not return to Din Eidyn! I wonder where he will keep you? I understand his family house is in ruinous condition; I should not mind if you were imprisoned there, but Jenneret likes his comforts. Perhaps I should offer him the use of the estate where I meant to keep Erlend; thanks to you, I shall not need it now. Or – no, I have a famous idea!" Whirling around to stand in front of me again, she clapped her hands and gave me a kittenish smile. "Of course! He can take you to Faarhafn. After all, once you are married, it will be his." And she left me to contemplate this while the long summer twilight faded into darkness. I counted my breaths, and on every hundredth breath tried to move a few more muscles.

It seemed an age until Jenneret arrived – but not long enough; I could barely take a step, and my hands were still all but useless.

The Duchess had dismissed her servants, and was waiting for Jenneret herself. I could hear their voices clearly on the other side of the door. She was displeased with him.

"Why did you come on foot? I told you to bring your coach."

"Had to sell my horses," Jenneret said. "Temporary reverses – planning to rusticate until next quarter-day!"

Her Grace sighed. "I suppose I shall have to let you take mine."

"Here, now," Jenneret said, "I'm not going anywhere with that thing of yours."

"My poor mad son?"

"Your poor sea-changeling! Rangage may be too much of a modern fool to recognize the thing, but you never deceived me. I am," Jenneret said, "possibly – no, certainly – the greatest student of esoteric lore in all of Dalriada, nay, in all Europa, and I knew as soon as I saw it that you had put Gairloch's semblance on some thing without proper life or sentience. And as you put about the tale of his madness immediately on your return from Faarhafn, you must have used salt magic to make the thing. What did you do with the boy's body?"

"I did not kill my son!" Ailsa said sharply.

The Baron chuckled. "If you say so, my sweet, if you say so. You need not fear me. I didn't tell Rangage the thing was a changeling, did I?"

"He would not have believed you if you had!"

"Best not put it to the trial, though, don't you think?"

Ailsa sweetened her voice. "Come, Jenneret, let us not quarrel. Do you not wish to see what a gift I have for you?"

"You planning to buy back my horses? I'll need more money than just that," Jenneret said promptly. "Can't afford to stable them – let my valet go, too. I told you, I shall be forced to ruralize – unless you want to help me – out of gratitude, shall we say?"

"I think," said Ailsa, "you will wish to retire to the country with my little present."

The door swung open. She was holding a branch of candles; the blaze of light blinded me for a moment. I sensed Jenneret's presence coming closer through the glare, until his body blocked the light of the candles and he put one hand under my chin. I could have turned my head away – but I remained still, enduring his gloating look and stinking hot breath. It was not in my interest to let either of this precious pair know how much power of movement I had recovered – not that it was enough, yet, to save me from whatever they chose to do.

"She's a true finwife," Ailsa said. "Look here!"

She held the branch of candles behind me to expose the rent in my dress. The Baron ran his hand up and down the flaring base of my tail, his hot fingers lingering under the sensitive tissues where it sprung free of my back. It was the most intimate of touches; no finman had ever dared use me so. The little freedom of movement that I had won back did not allow me to escape the touch.

"Very nice," said the Baron in a conoisseur's voice. "Very nice – but not much use to me, in this condition. If I wanted a statue of a finwife I could have one carved to my order."

"The spell will wear off," Ailsa assured him. "But not, I thought, too quickly. She'll be easier to transport this way, unable to cry out or struggle."

"And when it wears off?"

"By then, Jenneret," Ailsa said, "you should be many leagues out of Din Eidyn, and I think you should be able to control her."

He laughed under his breath. "It will be a pleasure. She'll be plaguey awkward to load into a coach like this, though. Cannot you loose her enough to bend a bit?"

"Oh, you can move her limbs," said Ailsa, "it is just that she cannot do so herself."

"Well, well. That should make for an amusing journey. May I borrow your knife?"

I tensed, but Jenneret only cut the strings of my reticule and upended it on a table. "Three korona!" he said. "That won't pay the posting charges to my country house. You'll have to let me have your horses as well as your coach." He picked up the half-empty packet of sea salt and poured it out onto the floor. "I am surprised you were so careless, Ailsa. Don't you know better than to leave a finwife near sea water, or anything that can be made to resemble sea water?"

"So that's how she destroyed my changeling!" Her Grace's pretty face contorted for a moment. "Bitch!"

"Salted it down, did she?" Jenneret laughed. "And you with Rangage all ready to sign the thing into a madhouse. What will you do now?"

"I am deeply distressed," she said, "that my servants were so inexcusably careless as to leave this room unlocked, allowing my poor mad son to wander off who knows where. Naturally I shall institute a search immediately. In the meantime, until he is found or until he recovers his senses, it is my duty to look after his estates for him. Dr. Rangage will testify that he was in no condition to do so himself." She tweaked my nose with her sharp little fingers. "So you see, finwife, you did me no harm with your interfering. I shall go on very well without the need to keep the changeling confined. I should thank you for saving me the trouble!"

"And me," said Jenneret, "for removing the girl, who could make you a powerful lot more trouble once your spell wore off."

"You are well enough paid with her person," Ailsa said. "Now you have a finwife of your very own – just like that old fool Steinnland!"

"I shall need money and horses," Jenneret said. "Enough money to put my country place into tolerable condition, if I'm to stay there with her. Last time I ruralized there were bats in the great hall and the roof leaked in a dozen places, the curtains had the moth and –"

"You have a better place to stay than that if you play your cards right for a change. Take her to old Steinnland's house on Faarhafn! You can send my coach and horses back from there. You'll be three nights on the road. If you are still any kind of a man, by the time you get to the island, the chit will be happy enough to marry you – and then Faarhafn, and Steinnland's money, will be yours."

Jenneret's face lit up. "And his collections." His voice lingered lovingly over the last word. "The old lord had the finest library of occult lore in Dalriada. He bought the Grimoire de Uthman before I knew it was on the market, but he would never let me visit his library to read it. Probably afraid I might find naughty books hidden behind the scientific tomes."

"Whatever you find there, you are welcome to it," Ailsa said with indifference. "I am content with my own estates."

"You mean, your son's estates." The Baron leered. "Are you not afraid I'll find his body on Faarhafn? Or have the fishes eaten it by now?"

"I told you, I did not kill my son, and it will be the worse for you if you try to blackmail me with such accusations. I have a dozen witnesses, lawyers and physicians, who can swear that he came back from Faarhafn as witless as a newborn babe, and that I've spared no expense in searching for a cure for him. If you are wise, you will leave it at that, and content yourself with Steinnland's fortune. Now play with your new toy while I have the horses put to."

CHAPTER TWENTY-TWO

The road north was smooth and well kept as far as the first posting house outside Din Eidyn; after that, as Iveroth knew only too well, it deteriorated rapidly into little more than a cart track punctuated by deep ruts and pools of standing water. He disliked intensely the thought of taking his favorite chestnut down such a road at any speed greater than a walk. The only thing he disliked more was the fear that left a sour taste in his throat, the fear of coming too late.

That footman of Sabira's must have been one of her fellow islanders, for no Din Eidyn servant would have had the nerve to demand speech with Lord Iveroth or would have spoken so bluntly and disappeared so quickly. The man would have come south to Din Eidyn to make his fortune, perhaps, and on learning that the streets were not paved with silver skillengs, would have been happy to take service with the March-Lord's widow.

And he was speculating on the man's origins to take his mind off the message, which had been short enough to leave room for all the unpleasant implications Iveroth did not want to think of. "Sabira has been kidnapped by Baron Jenneret. He is taking her north by coach." No more than that, and the man was gone as if by magic, before Iveroth could stop him and question him farther.

Well, and it was enough. There was but one road leading northwards out of the city that a coach could possibly take; the Dalriadan Council took little account of the wild northlands, preferring to strengthen roads to the south to encourage trade with Anglia. And if he did not catch up with the Baron by the time the road deteriorated, he would surely do so soon after; a horseman might have to pick his way with care, but a coach would crawl, rock, tumble and try to shake itself to pieces. There were the torches of the posting inn ahead; Iveroth drew rein and turned into the yard, inexpressibly relieved at the sight of a coach drawn up in the inn yard.

A coach with the arms of Quoy and the old Duke's motto, *Vincere aut mori*, picked out in raised gilt on the doors.

Quoy? What had the Duchess to do with all this? Perhaps nothing – perhaps, after all, Jenneret was still ahead of him on the road – but something was amiss within the inn, for no one had come running out to take his horse, and he could hear raised voices inside; men expostulating, and a woman answering them. Her voice rang high and clear and pure against their angry shouts, like a thread of silver running through tattered woolen rags.

Sabira. Muscles Iveroth had not know he had relaxed, and in the release of tension he felt momentarily angry with her for causing him so much fear. He swung down from the saddle and looped his horse's reins over one of the posts planted in front of the inn.

The door stood ajar, and the disputants in the hall were too occupied to notice his entrance. He took in the scene with one glance: Sabira, pale and disheveled, backed into the corner of the stairwell; a burly man with a stained apron shouting alternately at her and at a scrawny lad whose manure-stained trews betrayed his occupation. The babble resolved into a trio for bass, tenor and soprano.

"All I want to know is," the burly man shouted, "who's to pay me? Eh? Who's to pay?"

"In't my fault," whined the stable lad. "*she* let the horse get out."

"A good horse, my best parlor, wine and supper for two, and who's to pay?"

"My good man," Sabira said, "I did not bespeak your parlor or your food."

"No, you just came with him as did – and then tried to get out the back on a horse as didn't belong to you! I could have the magistrates on you, my girl! Don't think I can't tell what sort you are, leaving the poor gentleman with a lump the size of an egg on his head and then stealing my horse!"

Iveroth began to smile. It appeared that Sabira had matters well in hand without his intervention.

"And I certainly do not have your horse."

"And who does? Letting him loose to run around countryside on his own! As good as stealing, I calls it."

"She was trying to steal 'im," the stable boy put in. "Trying to get on his back, she was, and that there clout round her waist spooked 'im. You knows as how Trouble can't abide nothing fluttering at him like that."

For the first time Iveroth observed that Sabira appeared to be wearing a much-darned linen tablecloth tied round her skirt like a tight apron.

"And that's another thing, stealing my best tablecloth!"

"My good fellow," drawled Iveroth, "if that greasy rag is indeed the best this hostelry can provide for table linens, I am not surprised that Lady Steinnland chose to leave rather than consume whatever poisonous dishes you served atop it."

"And who might you be… sir?" The burly man's voice quavered and dropped suddenly on the last word, as he took in Iveroth's appearance. Travelstained the gentleman might be, but anyone could tell as his boots were best quality, and his coat fitted as only a Din Eidyn tailor cut them for the gentry.

Iveroth put on his starchiest manner. "Viscount Iveroth, at your service. Send this lad to stable my horse, if you please." He nodded at the stable boy, who disappeared after a jerk of his master's head towards the open door. "I must apologize, my dear Lady Steinnland," he went on, stepping towards Sabira and sketching a bow over her hand, "for being so late in catching up with you, but I had – er – inadequate notice of your intention to depart."

"You knows 'er? Kept saying she was a lady, she did."

"Lady Steinnland," Iveroth said, "relict of the late March-Lord of Steinnland and the Isles. Your ignorance may be excusable; your impertinence is not." Now what tale could he make that would match with what Sabira had already said and done?

"I have been trying to explain to this man," Sabira said, "that you would be most unhappy were our journey to be delayed any further on account of the Baron's sudden illness."

"Illness!" the innkeeper snorted. "If you calls it illness to get knocked on the head with a pewter tankard —"

"How dare you accuse me of such vulgarity! I would not dirty my fingers with one of your filthy tankards." Sabira turned towards Iveroth. "We had to pause here because poor Lord Jenneret felt ill, and indeed he collapsed just after ordering dinner. I fear he may have suffered an apoplectic stroke. I was taking the air in the inn yard, Iveroth, while waiting for you, when I noticed an outcry in the stables. I think that boy may have accidentally let one of the horses loose."

"That makes everything admirably clear," said Iveroth, keeping a straight face with some difficulty. He brought out his purse. "Lady Steinnland can hardly be held responsible for the inadequacies of your stable lad, but you certainly deserve some recompense for the difficulties and upset you have suffered. I shall be happy to pay for the Baron's charges; make up an account and bring it to me in – did you say he had taken a private parlor?"

"My only one! And now he's usin' up the best bedchamber, and who's to pay if he dies in it?"

"He will not do that," Iveroth said. "I suggest you have him carried back to his – that is, to the coach that brought him here – and give the coachman this in consideration for returning him to Din Eidyn, where he may be attended by a surgeon." Gold korona clinked into the innkeeper's palm.

"I gather the parlor is free already. You may send up...." Iveroth considered carefully. "I do not wish to put you out by ordering a cooked dinner so late. Could your good lady find some bread and cheese, do you think? Ale for me, and for you, Lady Steinnland, perhaps a cup of tea? Very good." He had his hand on Sabira's elbow by then, gently steering her away from the innkeeper and towards the stairs.

"I do not want tea!" Sabira protested.

"We will discuss it in privacy," Iveroth said under his breath.

Sabira maintained an offended silence all the way up the stairs. Iveroth admired the slim, straight lines of her back and wondered why she had seen fit to disguise her excellent figure by wrapping the lower part of her body in a tablecloth over her dress. Ah well, no doubt she had a good reason which he would hear in due course. He only hoped it would be as amusing as what he'd already heard.

As soon as the doors of the private parlor were closed behind them, she turned to him. "I am sorry, but I have not time to eat. I must reach the sea at once."

"Why?"

"It is the quickest way to Faarhafn."

"Boats are even slower than horses," said Iveroth, and in any case, I'm not going anywhere until I have a meal, so you might as well join me rather than sulk in a corner and starve."

"You do not understand. I must be in Faarhafn as soon as possible!"

"Was that how Jenneret lulled you into going with him?"

"He did not lull me," Sabira flashed, "I hope I am not such a fool as to trust that man again! He forced me into his coach, my lord – I mean, the Duchess's coach – and meant to take me to Faarhafn."

"Well, that is where you want to go, it seems. I can well understand your disliking Jenneret, but was it really necessary to half kill him at the first stop?"

"He thought he would – make me willing to marry him," Sabira said, "by the time we had reached there."

"And he thought he could take an unwilling bride on a three-day coach trip and put up at the public posting houses along the way?" Iveroth marvelled. "The man is more of a fool than I had imagined possible. If you didn't hit him with the tankard, by the way, just how did you disable him?"

Sabira's lips twitched. "There was a nice heavy candlestick on the table."

"Ah. A much more genteel weapon, I perceive. After which, you borrowed the tablecloth – I suppose your clothes were torn in the struggle – and rather than discovering your name and quality to the innkeeper, slipped out the back way and tried to steal a horse you couldn't ride."

"I was in a hurry," Sabira explained, "and he had taken all my money. And you see, I had pretended complaisance when we came in here, for I did not want to make him realize – that is, I did not want to make him suspicious –

and I collect he has brought women of a certain sort here before, so it was not at all certain that the innkeeper would believe me. And in fact he didn't until you came, so—"

"Well, that was after the – er – incident with the horse," Iveroth pointed out apologetically, "so at that point your credibility had been somewhat damaged. One cannot help feeling some sympathy for the man. Still, I see there was a certain logic to your actions."

A tap on the door heralded the arrival of a maidservant carrying a heavily laden tray. The girl managed to make quite a business of setting the dishes on the table, swaying perilously and brushing against Iveroth more than once, while her eyes offered an open invitation.

"How dared that man imply that I was no better than I should be," Sabira burst out as soon as the maid was gone, "when he employs strumpets like that! And you sympathize with him!"

"Well, I shan't do so if it offends you," said Iveroth, "but I do plan to have some of this excellent – well, anyway, this perfectly edible bread and cheese. And since we aren't going anywhere until I have eaten and my horse has rested, you might as well eat something too, while you explain what takes you to Faarhafn in such haste."

"You wouldn't understand. It's – it is island business."

"Try me," Iveroth offered. "And while you're at it, try some of the cheese. The inner parts are quite edible. I fear I cannot recommend the bread; it seems to be more straw and stone-dust than flour."

Sabira took a deep breath. "I have deceived you, my lord!"

"In what way?"

"I am not what I seem!"

Iveroth shrugged. "I never imagined you were well-born enough to please my family, if that is what you mean."

"Worse than that," Sabira said. She paused, blinking; then straightened her shoulders and lifted her chin. "I cannot marry you because I am not a human woman, but a finwife."

"My dear, these fancies of yours—"

"*Will you listen?* This is no fancy, it is the plain truth!" Her eyes flashed with the green of lightning over a summer sea. "I was born in Finfolkaheem, beneath the sea, and I must return there after I have settled the problem in Faarhafn. Problems. First there is the matter of the nucklavee who's killing people – it began by murdering my husband – and then I must get Gairloch back. I understand now why I could never raise a clear vision of him; all I saw was the sea around Finfolkaheem. He is being kept there, you see, while the Duchess passes off a changeling as her son. Except she can no longer do that, for I gave the poor thing sea salt to reverse the spell that trapped it in human form, and now it's dissolved itself." She stopped and frowned. "I think I am not explaining this very well. You see, I did not understand it all myself until quite recently – today, in fact. And I had only just freed the changeling when her Grace cast the herb-charm on me that prevented me from moving, and then she gave me to Lord Jenneret and told him to take me out of town, so that problem rather occupied my mind at first."

"I can see how it might," Iveroth nodded. "You seem quite well able to move now, though."

"Herb magic wears off, just like salt magic, when the power in the herbs is exhausted," Sabira explained. "I think distance affects this one, too, for the farther we came from Din Eidyn, the less hold it had on me. But I did not want Jenneret to realize I could move quite freely, so I had to stay limp and still while he...." Her lips tightened. "It was most unpleasant," she said at last.

"That, at least, I can believe!" said Iveroth. "But it's over now. Should you like me to call him out when he recovers from the blow you gave him? It would be a pleasure." He set down his ale and came around the table to take Sabira's hands. "My dear girl, you are quite safe from Jenneret now. Do you not feel safe enough to tell me the truth?"

Sabira took a step backward. "You have not understood anything I said, have you?"

"I could not quite follow all the details, but it seemed a very creative and interesting story, quite as good as any of those romances you read. But as you know, I have no taste for romances. I should rather know the plain truth of the matter, if you can bear to tell it to me." He was beginning to feel concerned again, after the first relief of seeing that she was physically unharmed. Had Jenneret raped her? Had the shock turned her brain? But no, she had talked wildly like this before – that time at the Water Gardens, she had raged about how he misunderstood finwives and how the idea of making love to a human disgusted her. It seemed to be a fantasy into which she retreated whenever she was frightened or angry.

Sabira threw up her hands. "I had to fall in love with the one man in all Dalriada whose nurse never told him about the finfolk and the nucklaveen!"

"I know the folklore," Iveroth said. "I also know better than to treat it as scientific fact." *Fall in love?*

"Do you, my lord? Then it is time you added some evidence to your *scientific* study of the world!" Sabira tugged at the tablecloth around her waist, untied the knot and threw it down. Her dress seemed quite unharmed – until she turned around and he saw the slit cut down the back.

"Ailsa of Quoy cut my dress and shift open," Sabira said, "to satisfy herself that I was indeed a finwife. What do you make of this, my rational lord?" She drew the skirts tight around her body, so that the slit gaped open and disclosed a – a growth of some sort, emerging from the base of her spine. An iridescent green swelling that disappeared into the froth of skirts and lacy underthings below the slit.

"Deformity" was probably not a tactful word to use. "My dear, if that is why you would not marry me – it makes no difference to me, you must know that. We can consult the best surgeons in Din Eidyn to remove this little – "

"To *cut my tail off?*" She whirled and retreated from him into the corner of the room, and the horror on her face was unfeigned. "What kind of monster are you? Even Jenneret did not propose to mutilate me!" Something had come amiss in the fastenings of her garments; he heard a rustling sound and saw yards of iridescent gauzy stuff falling loose about her ankles.

"Your petticoat-"he began.

"My *tail!*" The shimmering gauze moved of itself, took form, became a flexible webbing fanning out between long muscular ropy structures. "Now do you see what I am? Or must I strip quite naked to prove it to you?"

Iveroth found that his legs were not quite up to the job of supporting him. The landlord's ale must be stronger than he had thought. He lowered himself carefully to the bench beside the table, and looked carefully again at Sabira. The branch of candles on the wall gave a flickering light that could make a man imagine things were moving –

"You are not imagining it," said Sabira, as though she could read his mind, "and you know your head is too strong to be turned by the ale at a country inn. It's real, Iveroth. I am real, and I am not a human woman, a landwoman – I am a finwife. You must believe me now. Once I thought that I could go away without telling you, but perhaps it is better this way. Now you see why I can never marry you."

Iveroth thought back until he reached the one thing that made sense, that he could cling to in this chaotic nightmare. "You said you loved me."

Sabira's tail switched back and forth, endangering two chairs. "Can you not keep to the point?"

"I rather think that is the point," said Iveroth, "the rest is… details. Sabira, I fell in love with you when I thought you were deceiving your husband. I wanted to marry you when I thought you were a peasant girl who was ashamed of her family. If you can return my regard, a little thing like a tail will hardly put me off."

This time, standing in the corner, she had nowhere to retreat to. He stepped carefully around the iridescent froth of her tail. When she looked down, he put a gentle hand under her chin and lifted her face until her eyes were level with his.

Her lips were everything he remembered; warm and cool at once, sparkling and intoxicating.

After a moment, she returned his kiss; somewhat later, she put her arms around him.

***

A ray from the rising sun pierced the worn curtains and narrow window of the inn's second-best bedchamber and lay, sadistically, across Iveroth's face. He mumbled a drowsy protest and rolled over, rising through dreams and memories like a swimmer coming to the surface through green seas full of wonders. Sabira's sweetness in his arms – that at least had been no dream -

and something about magic in the sea that upset all he thought he understood about the rational world, but that was unimportant; it was Sabira he wanted to recapture, and the sun was interfering.

"Busy old fool, unruly sun," he murmured, "why dost thou thus/ Through windows and through curtains call on us?/ Must to thy motions lovers' seasons run?" Had Sabira read Donne? He would read poetry to her. They would experiment, together, to understand this sea-world of magic and mystery by the laws of reason and natural philosophy. And at night they would make their own laws, as lovers had always done… He reached out for her and found only tumbled sheets.

"Sabira?"

Awake now, he stretched luxuriously and stood to look about the room. She must have dressed and gone down to breakfast or – something – she would not have gone far. He drew back the curtain and looked east into sunrise, savoring the view of green fields and the reflection of the rising sun off the waters of the Westray Firth where it cut deep into the land.

The sea.

Sabira had been desperate to reach the sea, had even tried to steal a horse – of course she had no idea how close it was at this point on the northern road.

She would have known if she had risen before him and looked out the window as he had just done.

Iveroth's valet would have wept to see the haste with which he crammed shirt in to breeches and breeches into boots, ran fingers through the unruly black mop of his hair and stuffed his cravat into a pocket before clattering downstairs to demand of the innkeeper whether Lady Steinnland was about, and if not, whether she had left a letter for him. He ripped off the blobs of candle wax sealing a folded sheet of coarse paper and scanned it, too intent on the words to pay attention – then – to the innkeeper's grinning insinuations to the effect that the young lady didn't seem to want to stay with any one man too long, that she didn't, but he couldn't say who she'd gone off with now, having been asleep like a decent man when she demanded paper and pen of his good wife.

"My very dear love, I have been thinking all night and I see that what the Baron said is true. I cannot marry you, for your position demands that you take a landwoman wife and beget a human heir; besides, you would be laughed at in Din Eidyn if it were known that you loved someone who was not quite human, and I cannot bear to think of your suffering on my account. My love, I must go to Faarhafn as quickly as possible, for there is a nucklavee killing the people. It was probably set free on the shore by the Duchess, but that is not important now. You know what I am, so now you will understand that the nucklavee is also real, and the human folk on Faarhafn are my responsibility now that my lord is dead. I could see the sea from the window of the chamber we shared last night. By the time you read this I shall be in the water, and so I can come to Faarhafn more quickly than any way that I could travel by land. After I have seen to matters there I will go back to my own home. You know now that you cannot follow me there, nor would you wish to after you have considered the matter rationally. I already know your views on mésalliances. My love, look at the sea some times and think of me, and I will look at the land and think of you."

"P.S. I have been obliged to leave Breta Scrabster in Din Eidyn. She likes the city; do you think that you could put her in the way of finding work as a lady's maid to some one of your acquaintance? I had meant to ask Elspet Rattray's help but had not time."

Iveroth crumpled the letter in his fist and shouted for his horse to be saddled.

He reached the south shore of the De'il's Strait in late afternoon, weary and travel-stained, his horse plodding in a dispirited walk. The summer sun still illuminated the cluster of fishing huts on this side of the Strait, the ferry rocking idle in its berth in the tiny harbor and the small group of men lounging by the sea wall.

Sabira was not there. Of course not. She had written that she was going to Faarhafn, and she would require no ferry to get there. Iveroth's brain understood that now, but his heart had not caught up; he had been, however irrationally, expecting to see her at the ferry landing place.

It cost him only two skillengs to get a promise from the ferryman's lad that he would see the chestnut groomed, fed and housed overnight, but he had to use a half korona and all the influence of an aristocratic voice and an air of command to get the ferry moving. The man said he'd been hard at work all day moving crofters and their goods from Faarhafn to the mainland, and expected more such work on the morrow, and why couldn't the lord wait until morning?

"The people are leaving Faarhafn? Where are they going?"

The ferryman pointed down the shore, and Iveroth realized that what he had taken for rubbish dumped by the tide was in fact an improvised camping place with blankets draped over bits of furniture for shelter. "Wait," he said. "I'll be back, and you will be ready to take me across then." He showed the gold piece again, then strode down the shingled beach to the miserable little encampment. As he came closer, he saw a woman crouched over a pallid fire, heating something in a pot suspended from branches. Behind the camp, in the pale salty grass of the dunes, hobbled cattle grazed.

"Bessie!" She was sadly changed from the bright-eyed slut who'd swayed her rounded hips at him; if it were not for the black eyes, he'd not have known her, so thin and worn down by sorrow, with the plaid dragged half over her head. "What's amiss? Why are you leaving Faarhafn? Where will you go?"

"Folk die on Faarhafn," she said, staring at the pot. "Die and starve, for we darena dig in the garden or fish in the sea or burn the kelp. The island doesna want us. Young Androw wrote to our lord's lady in Din Eidyn, but she didna come."

"She is coming now," Iveroth said, and hoped he spoke truth. "It took a long time for the letter to reach her. And – where will you go? What will you do?"

"Starve, most like. Or wander like the tinkers."

Iveroth remembered the provisions of Steinnland's will. "The March-Lord set aside a strip of his lands here on the mainland for you islanders to live on, but he did not think you would go there."

Bessie looked up with a little of her old spirit. "Go there? We'll go wherever we can get a bit of land and not be troubled by the nucklaveen. You mean it? There's land for us? Is it by the sea, where we can fish and gather the kelp?"

"It is," Iveroth said. If the land Steinnland had kept for them was not on the coast, he would settle them on his own estates, though he feared that would be too far south for their tastes. "Now I must go to the island. Is there anything I can do? Do you need anything?" All he had to offer was money.

Bessie accepted a skilleng and some pence "to buy milk for the bairns, for the nucklaveen ha' cursed our cattle too."

Iveroth felt guilty leaving her and the others in such a state, but there was little more he could do for them that night. And Sabira – surely Sabira would be on the other side of the strait. On Faarhafn, at Steinnland's house. He would find her there and talk sense into her – and if that didn't work, perhaps he would throw her over his saddle-bow and ride off with her, like the hero of an old ballad.

The heros of ballads never had to deal with minor problems like coercing an unwilling finwife to cross on a ferry, or waiting a few days until their horses were rested.

And as it turned out, neither did he, for Sabira was not on Faarhafn. Steinnland's house stood empty and shuttered as they had left it, and none of the remaining fisherfolk admitted to having seen her.

CHAPTER TWENTY-THREE

This time there was no calling in my blood, no court awaiting my arrival in Finfolkaheem. It was just as well. The hours of swimming through turbulent seas had done nothing to calm the turbulence within my breast; I still needed time to compose myself and adjust to the fact that I was free to return home.

Like an idiot, I thought that my mother's house of blue coral would be a safe place to rest.

Only three of my aunts were there. Three was more than enough – especially when one of them was Maarit.

"It's been long enough since we've seen you, girl," was her greeting. "Thought you preferred playing the heiress in Din Eidyn to being back with your own proper family."

I failed to understand the implications of that remark, being mostly concerned with hiding my own unruly feelings. This was my home – I ought to feel happy about returning – no doubt I would, in a day or so. Perhaps when all my business with landfolk and the land was finished, it would be easier to forget.

I explained to my mother and aunts that I had good reason to believe in two serious breaches of our laws, begun perhaps by a landwoman but aided by some of our own people. A nucklavee had been freed to ravage the people of Faarhafn, and I had reason to believe that some of our own finfolk had made a changeling in the shape of a young landman. The young man himself was probably being kept here by the same people who had made the changeling.

My mother's fair face was taut with worry before I finished. "I cannot believe any of us would do such a thing."

"Try not to be a bigger idiot than the Sea Mother made you, Norin," my aunt Maarit snapped. "This will be the young prince Heiki's doing. Haven't you heard him and his cronies saying that they had a plan to reclaim Faarhafn without Sabira's help?"

"No one took them seriously, though, because they've never said how they meant to do it," said my aunt Seija. She held up a mirror of polished silver behind my aunt Eliina's head, so that Eliina could see how she'd woven silver coils through her tresses and twisted them into a knot piled high on the back of her head.

"It appears," said Maarit, "that we should have taken them seriously. It's obvious now that they found some way to loose a nucklavee on Faarhafn; perhaps they erased the warding signs, or got some landperson to help by inviting the nucklavee in, it doesn't matter which. It is a breach of the natural order and if it is not stopped we will all pay dearly for it. As for the matter of the changeling, I'll wager they are involved in that too. Someone will have to send it back to the sea, and…"

"I've done that," I said, and explained what had happened at Quoy House and afterwards – well, most of it, anyway. My one night with Iveroth was a precious and private memory that I did not propose to share with my aunts. I merely said that I had escaped the Baron, and that I believed Ailsa of Quoy had desired the changeling for her own ends, and that she had repaid a nucklavee for providing the changeling by giving it the freedom of Faarhafn. Nucklaveen are far too stupid to work the complex magics of building a form of salt water, animating it, and casting the guise of a living person upon it, so I had suspected this one had been aided by one of the finfolk. I was relieved that Maarit had been able to name the one most probably responsible; if Heiki had built the changeling, then he was also probably keeping Gairloch.

"I must have an audience with Loviisa," I said. "If she commands Heiki to give up his new toy – "

"How will that help with the nucklavee?" Eliina interrupted. "That, yes, we need to put a stop to it, for when one begins killing landmen it will soon go on to slaying finfolk. But this matter of the changeling is no concern of ours."

"It is, however, some concern of the landman being kept prisoner here," I said.

Eliina shrugged. "They're not like finfolk, darling. They don't feel things the way we do."

"It's probably a treat for him to escape his deadly dull peasant hovel and see what a real city looks like," added Seija. "Eliina, don't turn your head so fast! I'm trying to get a few ringlets to dangle loose of the knot, to soften the effect."

Maarit gave an exasperated sigh and rolled her eyes. "Don't even try to explain to these two, Sabira. *I* have no desire for a war with the landfolk, even if they cannot understand the concept."

"I understand it perfectly," Eliina pouted. "What can the landfolk do to us?"

"If you'd been paying attention when Sabira was telling her story, you'd know that there is magic of the land as well as of the sea, and some at least of the landfolk know how to use it. I will speak to Loviisa myself, Sabira. You can come to the palace at the turn of the tide; by then she should be ready to hear you. You'd better comb your hair and do something about your face while you're waiting. You look as if you'd been dragged backwards through a sea fan colony." Maarit left on those biting words.

Seija and Eliina happily joined forces to make me respectable for an audience at court, and while they were playing with combs and pearl dust and small magics to put color in my face and make my eyes sparkle, my mother held my hands and chatted about little things that had happened at home while I was away: who was shamelessly flirting with whom at the quarter-moon dance, and who actually disappeared into a very large sponge coral and didn't come out until long after the dance was over, and which of the little fishherd girls was in trouble for stealing rides with a wild kelpie herd, and how many love notes Eliina had received from her latest suitor. It was all very soothing… and rather dull. Still, it was pleasant to get caught up on the gossip of the city, and I did have the chance to ask her and my aunts some questions about matters of more interest to me than feuds and flirtations. Aunt Maarit would probably have made impolite deductions – loudly – about my questions, but my mother was too courteous to do the same, and Eliina and Seija were too involved in the work of beauty to care what I asked them, or why.

Far too soon we felt the shift of currents as the tide changed far above, and I swam to the golden palace at the heart of Finfolkaheem. My mother and Seija and Eliina accompanied me, and on the way my aunts Inghean, Osla, and Raonaid joined us. When Maarit greeted us in the anteroom, she took her place between Seija and Raonaid, so that all seven sisters were lined up behind me in birth order; an impressive array of family solidarity and one for which I was most grateful. It is not every day that one has to ask a queen if her son and heir has been playing nasty little games with the landfolk.

Loviisa was waiting for us; with her was Heiki, looking sulky, and beside him – my heart gave a tiny, tiny leap of joy at recognizing Erlend of Quoy, pale with his long confinement. That relief was not much compared to the ache that had only got worse ever since I left Iveroth asleep at the inn, but like my mother's gentle gossip and Seija's combing out of my hair, it was something to hold onto.

"Sabira Norinsdattr," the queen said.

I spread out my tail and made the *grande révérence* after the manner of our people, a slow circular bow that ended with me standing upright again, with my tail floating up behind me and waving gently over my head.

"I had hoped that on our next meeting you would be able to tell me that Faarhafn had been restored to our people. Instead you come back with this – untidiness."

"Life is seldom as tidy as one might wish, Majesty."

"Indeed." She inclined her head towards Heiki. "It's not nice to play with the nucklaveen, Heiki. I want you to stop doing it."

"I was getting Faarhafn back," Heiki said. "Without that land-lover's help. The sons of earth are frightened of the nucklaveen; they are all leaving the place. By sunset tomorrow they will be gone."

"How delightful," said Loviisa. "Gone or not, they still own the island.

Can you set it free to glide over the waves or to sink into the waters? Can you call up a mist from the sea to hide what is not yours to protect?"

Heiki flushed. "If we cannot enjoy it, why should they?"

"Exactly what good does it do us," Loviisa inquired, "to hurt and frighten landfolk who never had any ownership in the island? And you could not even do it yourself, Heiki; you had to use a nucklavee. You've unbound it; do you have any idea how hard it will be to bind the thing again?"

I made another *grande révérence* to get the queen's attention. "Majesty, the nucklavee was unbound by the invitation of a woman of the land. And by the law of the land, Faarhafn is now mine. When I return it to the law of the sea, will not the nucklavee be bound again unless one of our people invites it into the island?"

Loviisa looked pleased. "So. You have accomplished something at last. Yes, that should settle the problem of the nucklavee, and very discreetly too; there will be no need for an open session of the council. I am pleased with you, Sabira."

I curtseyed once again, though all this turning over and over was making me dizzy. Maarit must have an exceptionally level head to be able to serve as one of the queen's council. "If you please, Majesty, there is still the problem of the changeling."

She looked puzzled. "I thought you had dissolved its form."

"I have, Majesty, but the original must be freed."

"I'm not giving it back," Heiki protested. "Mama, I did all this for you, and you don't even appreciate it. At least you could let me keep my pet."

Loviisa smiled – at least, the corners of her lips turned up; her eyes never changed expression. "Well, Sabira? Ask us for some other reward, and you shall have it. I may not be altogether pleased with my son's actions, but I do not intend to cause him public embarrassment. He is too old for me to take away his playthings as if he were a naughty child."

I felt too dizzy – and too angry – to make another formal *révérence*. It had never occurred to me that Loviisa would refuse to order Gairloch freed. Yet I should have thought of it, after hearing Seija and Eliina: *They're not like finfolk. They don't feel things the way we do.*

"How about Faarhafn, Majesty?"

"That is another matter."

"With respect, Majesty – no."

The queen's silence was as deafening as another woman's scream. I could only plunge onward into that silence, praying not to stammer or shake. "To return Faarhafn to the law of the sea requres the consent of the one who holds it by the law of the land. At this moment, I am that one. But if I return to the upper world and marry a landman, then Faarhafn will be his, not mine. Do what is right, Majesty. Let this boy go, and I will restore Faarhafn to the law of the sea."

"You dare ——!" The queen leaned forward, lips thinned, and I recoiled involuntarily.

She recovered her composure faster than I did, sat back and smiled. "Well, child, this has not been quite as amusing as I thought. I was only testing your loyalties. Do not fear for your beloved landman here; I shall be happy to let him go, upon your word that you will not marry him."

I almost laughed in her face. She thought Gairloch was the landman I spoke of? That nice, dull boy?

"Mama, that's not fair!" Heiki whined. "It's *my* pet."

"And Faarhafn is ours, or will be again, and that is far more important than your whims. In any case, Sabira has a substitute to offer you."

I stared. "I do?"

Loviisa nodded to Maarit. "Let the kelpie in now, if you please."

As Maarit moved to open the door to the anteroom, I realised for the first time how extremely private this audience was. Loviisa had even sent away the young pages who would normally have handled the door.

I also realized the significance of Maarit's greeting to me. How could she have known that I was an heiress in Din Eidyn, unless somebody had already come and told her of my doings?

"Meldun," I said as soon as the tip of his nose showed in the doorway, "you are a vile, thoughtless, untrustworthy, immoral – oh my. How did you do that?"

I forgot my grievances with Meldun when I saw what he carried on his glossy black back: Ailsa of Quoy, naked but for a very short and almost transparent silk shift, her mouth frozen in a silent scream.

"So that's why you did not come and help me get away from the Baron!" I exclaimed.

"I knew that Iveroth would come to your aid," Meldun said. "In fact, I arranged it. Also the Baron is not very intelligent. I thought you would work a salt magic on him after Ailsa's spell wore off."

"Actually," I told him, "I hit him with a candlestick."

"How pedestrian! I had thought better of you."

"I had no more salt... How did you get her to mount you? She of all people should have known better than to ride a kelpie."

Meldun's horse form did not allow for much subtlety of expression, but somehow his entire body looked smug. "I was not in this form when she straddled me."

"Oh!" That explained her clothing, or lack thereof. I felt myself blushing.

"And," he added thoughtfully, "I do not see how I can be accused of being immoral, for I did not have any morals to begin with."

"That," I said faintly, "is quite obvious. I apologize. I should have said amoral."

"And I am not thoughtless either. I *thought* about letting her drown, but I have not done it yet. I *thought* you might need her alive, and now I *think* I was right."

"You are," I agreed, "clearly one of the world's great thinkers. Heiki, what do you say? Will you take this woman of the land as a replacement for Gairloch?"

Heiki was more than happy with the exchange, and I felt it was an excellent solution for the problem of Ailsa. It would not be necessary to kill her, and she would not be free to work any more magic on Gairloch.

Faarhafn would belong to the finfolk again, Gairloch would be freed, the nucklavee would lose its power of ravaging Faarhafn. Everybody except Ailsa clearly thought this was a more than satisfactory solution.

And I? Well... I had accomplished what I set out to do. Ailsa would pay as dearly as I could ever have wished for setting the nucklavee to kill my lord, and Erlend would be free to manage his own estates in his own manner.

I should have been perfectly happy, and no doubt I would be. Eventually.

***

After a restless night in the deserted house that had been Steinnland's last home, Iveroth woke to find the last few families of Faarhafn loading their bits and pieces on the ferry. He thought he could alleviate some of their anxiety by explaining the terms of Steinnland's will to them. They were indeed pleased to hear him repeat his assurance that lands on the mainland had been set aside to replace their island crofts and shore rights, but when he added that Sabira had inherited the island itself they scrambled in a frantic haste to rescue everything anybody might have left behind, loading the ferry until its decks were washed with water from the taller waves.

"What's the matter with them?" Iveroth demanded of Androw.

"From the sea it came and to the sea it shall return," Androw said. "D'you see, at first folk were taking just what they could not be doing without, thinking they might return after they were settled and get any little things they might want. But now we know there'll be no returning."

"Oh, come now," Iveroth said. "You don't think Lady Steinnland holds a grudge against the islanders for those rumors about Steinnland's death, do you? She is not so petty as that. I am sure anyone who wishes to return will be welcome to do so."

Androw shook his head slowly. "It's not that. It's… Haud yer hand, you fool, there's mair than enow to carry a'ready!" he bellowed at a man who was trying to drag his cow down to the overloaded ferry.

"I'll no' leave our Lybsie tae droon!" the man shouted back.

Androw went leaping down the slope to argue the matter. One hand on the man's shoulder, he gestured at Iveroth with the other and they shouted back and forth in dialect so thick Iveroth could not understand the scattered words the wind blew to him. Eventually the rope around the cow's neck was made fast to a stone, the ropes that tethered the ferry were cast off and the ropes from the far shore drawn tight, and the flat-bottomed vessel began another unsteady journey to the sandy shore on the mainland.

Androw came bouncing up the slope again. "I promised the man the ferry would be making more trips," he said. "It's not as if this is his last chance to get Lybsie over the water. It'll be going forth and back again at least two more times, most like."

"It will?" Iveroth looked skeptically at the one family standing around their cow, the two chairs and the black bundles enclosing their portable goods.

"You'll be wanting to take the old lord's books off, surely?"

"Why would I do that? They belong to Lady Steinnland now."

Androw threw up his hands. "Well, if you want them to moulder at the bottom of the sea, fine, leave them in the house. But the old lord was that fond of his library, I'm thinking he'll not have wanted to leave it to sink with the island."

"What are you talking about? Why should the island sink?"

"It came from the finfolk in the first place," Androw explained. "It was called Finnarhafn, the home of the finfolk, then. Everybody knows that. And some say our man cheated and killed the finman for doing too well at the riddle-game, and some say the finman was the one who cheated and the man who became March-Lord Steinnland was in the right to kill him, and who's to say the truth of it after so long? I think it was the March-Lord of those times who cheated, for why else would he change its name, as if he were trying to forget who he had the island from? But it's always been said that in the end the island would belong to one of the finfolk again and then it would sail upon the waters as before, and hide itself in mists so that none of our sort could find it, and sink below the water to keep itself safe when the finfolk were not using it."

As little as a week earlier Iveroth would have dismissed Androw's explanation as superstitious rubbish. Now he remembered the night before last, and the feathery touch of a finwife's iridescent tail wrapped about his body. It just might be that the islanders of Faarhafn – Finnarhafn – knew more about some matters than the rational philosophers of Din Eidyn and Lutéce, who preferred to study things that would hold still and not talk back.

"In that case—" Iveroth remembered the stairs winding up to Steinnland's library, and sighed in premonition. "In that case, you had best stay here to pay the ferryman, and tell him to bring as many strong men from the other side as are not afraid to work a day for more skillengs than they see in a summer's fishing and kelping."

Androw's eyes widened.

"Books," Iveroth explained succinctly, "are heavy."

It was an understatement. Even when Androw had bribed and persuaded enough men to come back and make a chain up the winding stair, so that all Iveroth had to do was take a stack of books from a shelf and hand it to the waiting hands at the top of the stair, the work was slow and wearisome. After half an hour his arms and back ached abominably; after an hour he had settled into an eternity of dull mindless labor in which he no longer cared about trying to take the rarest and most valuable books first, but merely cleared shelves automatically, whether they contained three-volume romances or recent scientific treatises. And some time long after that, he stared at the empty shelf before him and felt annoyed because there were no more books on it, and he would have to think about what to move next.

"My lord?" It was Androw, looking a bit flushed with excitement, but far from exhausted. Iveroth dropped the hand that had been rubbing the small of his back. "My lord, that's all of them. We're done now. Will you pay the ferryman and the others?"

Iveroth handed his purse to Androw. "Give them what's right. I... will stay here for a little." In this empty room he imagined that he could still sense Sabira's presence; when he looked out of the window, he could pretend that she was curled on one of the divans behind him, immersed in some adventurous tale of virtuous damsels and haunted monasteries.

All too soon Androw came clattering up the stairs again. "My lord, the ferry is ready to cast off."

"Tell him to come back later for me." Sabira had said she would return to Faarhafn.

"He's going to cut the ropes after this trip. There'll be no coming back."

"Oh." Well. It was foolish to stay. If he believed in Androw's tale enough to spend half a day moving books, then surely he believed in it enough to get off the island while it was still above water? Still... "Are there any boats left on the shore?"

"Aye, that lazy Wullie wouldna tak' his dinghy, said he meant to stay safe on land from now on. So ye could maybe row yourself across later, if the water's calm enough, but that's not the only matter. There's a man come out of the sea, says he is a lord in the south, and wants the ferryman to take him across."

Iveroth blinked. "Out of the sea? Is he a finman?"

"Looks as human as you or me," Androw said, "only wetter. Put me in mind of that young lord who came to visit here just before Lord Steinnland died, only he looks older."

At the ferry landing, Iveroth took Erlend's hands in his. The boy was dressed in the same clothes he had been wearing at midsummer, but salt water had faded the colors and shrunken the cloth so that they sat ill upon him now. And Androw had been right; he looked older. It was not just the unnatural pallor of his skin, but something in his expression; he was no longer a boy with the world opening before him, but a young man who had seen and suffered too much. "How came you here from Din Eidyn?"

Erlend looked past Iveroth, at the endless horizon. "Din Eidyn?" His voice was rough with disuse. "Din Eidyn. My mother and I came here from Din Eidyn, that is true."

"And went back again the next day."

"Perhaps she did. I never left," Erlend said haltingly. "I have been… have been… I dare not tell you, Iveroth; you would think me mad."

"Is the fine gentlemens coming or staying?" bellowed the ferryman.

"Ailsa said you were mad. She said you were in Din Eidyn, and the best physicians had examined you and declared you mad. Did you run away from them?"

"Then she lied. She may have returned to Din Eidyn, but I never left this part of the world. I have been – let us say, I have been a prisoner. That much is true. If I said where, you would never believe me. And since it seems that I must prove my sanity, I shall not begin by giving you an unbelievable tale – although," he said, "I suppose I could beg Lady Steinnland to witness on my behalf."

"Sabira! You've seen her? Where is she?"

"Why, she freed me," Erlend said, "and brought me home. Such a long, cold, green, watery way as I have come! And they would have kept me, you know; they would have kept me forever, but she threatened to marry a landman and let the island stay in the keeping of landmen if they would not let me go."

"Where is she now?"

Erlend looked around uncertainly. "We came out of the waters into a little cove, and she told me to climb the steps… I thought she was behind me."

Hammarvoe, her favorite place. "Here," Iveroth said, feeling in his pockets, and then remembered. "Androw has my purse. Take the ferry across and wait for me on the farther shore. I have to… have to…"

Another journey down the black, slick, sharp rocks of the Vaardens, and this time the premonitory aching emptiness in his breast; she would not still be here, she would have gone back into the sea where he could neither follow nor find her…

She was seated on the pebbles, feet curled under her outspread tail, humming something that made the foaming waves dance in fantastic shapes as they struck the beach.

"The only problem with loving a finwife," Iveroth said to her bare back, "is that every time I climb up or down these steps, I destroy another pair of boots. My valet will not be fond of you."

"Tell him this will be the last pair you ruin in climbing after me," she said without turning around, "and perhaps, in time, he will forgive you."

"If it were true, perhaps. But I suspect you will lead me over worse roads than this before we're done."

"We have done," she said. Now that she had ceased to hum her charm, the waves merely struck the pebbles, foamed up briefly, and retreated. "You cannot marry a finwife."

"Who told you that?"

"Jenneret. He said there were laws that could have me burned if I could not prove myself human. And that even if I were not taken and burned, you would face social ruin if you married me, because there would always be rumors."

"I always thought you were an intelligent woman," Iveroth said sorrowfully over the top of her head. "Whatever possessed you to believe anything Jenneret said?"

She stood and turned to face him, curling her tail up and around her body as she moved until it formed a translucent, clinging dress around her. "It's not true?"

"Sweeting, there may have been such laws four hundred years ago, when the country was in the grip of superstitious fears, but now? When nobody believes that there are such beings as finfolk, why would we make laws against them? As for social ruin," Iveroth continued, "a little bit of eccentricity never ruined anybody with Din Eidyn society. The greatest danger I will face will come from all the young fools who want to call me out for marrying the beauty of the season." It was getting too hard to keep his eyes on her face. He peeled off his coat and handed it to her. "Be so kind as to put this on."

"Why?"

"Because I am in danger of forgetting I am a gentleman," Iveroth said between clenched teeth. How could he explain to her what he had thought out in the lonely hours of the previous night, if he had to keep looking at the curves so tantalizingly outlined by her clinging, almost transparent tail while he talked? "Sabira, that night at the Water Gardens – "

A tint of coral tinged the pearl of her cheeks. "I was an idiot, and I know that now. I talked a great deal of nonsense, and I wish you will forget it."

"Some of what you said to me was not nonsense, though I thought it so at the time." Iveroth swallowed. "I – this would be easier if you would button the coat."

Her fingers moved slowly, she fumbled with the buttons, and it was all Iveroth could do not to button the coat himself – or rip it open – one thing or the other, he could not stand these flashing glimpses of a body that he could never possess again.

Finally she was done.

"You told me then that your family's greatest fear was that you would become involved with a landman and lose your tail and grow ugly and be unable to visit them under the waters. And you explained to me how great was your revulsion at the thought of intimacy with – how did you put it? 'such an odiously warm, hairy, air-breathing shape'. I believe those were your exact words. "

"I was talking about Jenneret," she said. Her face was all sunset and coral now; no pearly coolness about it.

"But intimacy with any man would pose the same danger, would it not? I thought," Iveroth said, "I was thinking… well, it does not matter. I suppose you are only here to sing this island free, and once that is done you will be quite happy to return to your life under the sea."

"It is where I belong," Sabira said. "Although… I do regret leaving Din Eidyn so soon. I had not begun to read all the books in Cromertie's Circulating Library. Also, Mr. Westlin was going to take me to a meeting of the Philosophical Society to see the Majuloscope."

"To the devil with Westlin! I'll take you myself. And you shall have a Majuloscope of your very own, and…." Iveroth realized he was getting ahead of himself. "That is. If you wished to stay in Din Eidyn for a while. I thought you might. Marry me. On the same terms as your marriage to Steinnland. I would not expect you to do anything – repellent – or to endanger your fin-nature."

She was silent, white teeth nibbling at the fullness of her lower lip.

"I am afraid that will be the only way you can move comfortably in Din Eidyn society, now," Iveroth added. "After leaving with Jenneret, and coming back with me, and your maid not with you… You would probably have to face a number of unpleasant social situations if you did not marry me."

"You mean my reputation is ruined."

"Well…"

"And everybody I meet will think to treat me as Lord Jenneret did."

"Well, only the men," Iveroth said apologetically, "and only the worst of those. But it might be uncomfortable for you."

"And you would tie yourself to a marriage that is no marriage, to a woman who would never give you an heir, to spare me a little discomfort. I cannot let you make such a sacrifice."

"I – it would not be a sacrifice. For me. To be with you." Doubtless he would conquer his lower feelings in time, and then that would be entirely true.

"I spoke to my mother and some of my aunts last night," Sabira said.

Of all the irrelevancies! Couldn't she tell him yes or no without winding all round a labyrinth first?

"My mother said it was absolutely certain that if I forgot myself even once with a landman, my tail would fall off. And you know, my tail looks quite healthy," she said, flourishing it before him and then wrapping it around her lower body again like a petticoat of finely veined silk, "even though I seem to recall that we... forgot ourselves... more than once, that night in the inn."

"You didn't tell your mother that, I hope!"

"Umm... not in any great detail."

Wonderful. Iveroth wondered what happened when you had an entire finfamily enraged at you for dishonoring and endangering their beloved daughter. He would probably never dare go near the sea again.

"But I did ask her how she knows for certain, and whether it had ever actually happened to anybody, and she said that the mother of one of my aunt Seija's friends had a second cousin who fell in love with a kelper and went to live on land and her tail fell off. So I asked my aunt Seija, and she said that was certainly true, except it wasn't the mother of one of her friends, it was somebody my aunt Eliina went to school with who had a great-aunt who ran away from home with a lighthouse-keeper. And my aunt Eliina said that she didn't actually go to school with the girl, but my aunt Ingheann knew someone who knew someone whose cousin's mother disappeared and was seen years later on the shore with no tail. And – "

"How many aunts do you have?"

"The point is," Sabira said, flushing even more than before, "that nobody has actually seen it happen. It is always somebody who knows somebody who heard about it from somebody else. There is no scientific evidence that being intimate with a landman causes any physiological changes at all. And after night before last, I certainly have scientific evidence that it does not cause an immediate change. So I think – I think the matter should be more fully investigated." She held out her hands and Iveroth took them, but it wasn't enough; he wanted to hold all of her, every filmy and pearly and glistening bit, and kiss them all, and —

"I think," Sabira said when he gave her a chance to catch her breath, "it was very foolish of you to insist on my buttoning your coat, if you intend to tear half the buttons off immediately afterwards."

"Sacrifices in the cause of science," Iveroth murmured into her hair.

"Well, if we are going to be any more scientific than this, perhaps we could find some place softer than these pebbles."

A head emerged from the sea; the head of a beautiful woman, her black hair plaited in an intricate coronet of braids and pearls. "Sabira, your aunt Maarit wants to know whether you plan to sing the island down or marry this landman."

"And some place more private," Sabira added under her breath before calling out gaily, "I mean to do both, Seija! First the island, then the marriage."

Another head, equally lovely, and as fair as the first woman was dark, appeared beside Seija's. "But Sabira, if you sing the island into the sea, will not your landman drown?"

"Don't be silly, Eliina. Look how long Heiki kept Erlend under the sea. I can certainly keep a bubble of air about him until we reach the mainland."

"Eliina, don't be a fool," said a third woman whose red hair was piled high and wound about with golden chains.

"Aunt Maarit," Sabira said under her breath, adding a few words whose exact meaning escaped Iveroth, but whose import was clear enough. "Now we're in for it."

"Sabira, you always were a dreamer. Now stop dilly-dallying and restore Faarhafn. The queen is getting impatient. You've had time to sing the charm a hundred times over by now, and..."

'Aunt Maarit, Aunt Seija, Aunt Eliina," Sabira interrupted, "with respect, tell the queen that if she is not pleased with the way I do things, I will be perfectly happy to do it in the other order. I shall marry this landman first and then sing the charm. Of course, it will have no effect then, because he, not I, will be the owner of Faarhafn, but if that's the way she'd like me to do it..."

"Sabira, dear, stop being silly and teasing your aunts," said a fourth woman who looked like an older edition of Sabira herself.

"Mama! I would have been done by now," Sabira defended herself, "if they had not started in nagging and interrupting and... "

"Done, hah! You'd be with child by that landman if we hadn't interrupted the two of you!" snapped the red-headed harpy.

"Let the child alone, sisters. She'll do what's right, and she won't do it any faster for your nagging her." Sabira's mother inspected Iveroth up and down. "It is a pity he has no fins, but maybe you will be lucky in your children. Bring him to visit in a few months, dear, when everybody has calmed down. Your father really should meet him, you know."

After the women had disappeared beneath the water, Iveroth shook his head. "I see why you left home."

"And now I must give this home back to the water," Sabira said sadly. "Do you want to climb the Vaardens first and look for a boat, or will you trust me to keep you safe in the sea?"

"The water," Iveroth said, "don't trouble me, but do you promise to protect me from your aunts?"

Sabira's little gurgle of half-choked laughter was the most beautiful sound he had ever heard. "Dear love, I cannot even protect myself from my aunts. We had better run away to Din Eidyn."

After all that fuss, the charm was really very simple; just a few changes to an old song. The difference, Sabira explained, was in the one singing it. Her family had wanted her to trick Steinnland into saying the words of the charm, but she had refused. Now that the island was hers by the law of the land, though, it was she who had to say the words; no other voice could free it.

"Faarhafn fair, Faarhafn free,
Faarhafn floats in the middle of the sea.
With mists and fog on every side,
No man can say where the island hides."

The first time she sang the verse, the water rose up to the lowest step of the Vaardens, and Sabira held his hand while she sang another charm that kept him enclosed in a bubble of air that somehow did not grow stale with his breathing. Somewhere deep inside him, a tiny, very rational Iveroth was screaming *This is impossible! this is not happening!* Iveroth suggested to his scientific self that it might just shut up and observe the evidence.

The second time she sang the verse, the waters rose to the threshold of Steinnland's rambling old house, and the two of them floated together over the deserted homes and fields of the crofters and fishermen.

With the third singing, the halls and towers of Steinnland's house vanished into the red and purple glow of a summer sunset, and Iveroth realized that he had not been experiencing the rising of the waters, but the sinking of the island; the mainland was just where it had been all along, level with his eyes, while the island sank into the depths of the sea.

There was a slight catch in Sabira's voice the third time.

"Unhappy, my love?" He did not even have to swim to stay comfortably at the surface of the water; her magic had given him buoyancy as well as air.

"Only that it seems such a waste. All those books..." Her voice caressed the word with the longing of one looking back on a first love.

"Don't worry about it," Iveroth said. "I have a little surprise for you on the mainland, that might make up for the sinking of Steinnland's library."

"What is it? Tell me now!"

"Just like a woman," Iveroth said. "Finned or not, you are all the same."

Sabira locked her arm through his and propelled them towards the shore with quick, vigorous thrusts of her tail. "Tell me, or I'll..."

"Dear heart, you cannot threaten a man who has faced the worst and survived," Iveroth informed her. "I have already stood up to your mother and your three aunts. What do you think could frighten me after that?"

The shore was almost within reach when Sabira said thoughtfully, "Perhaps I ought to warn you. I do not exactly have three aunts."

"Then who were those ladies?"

"I mean," she elucidated, "I don't have just three aunts. I have six."

Sabira's air charm was not strong enough to protect a man who lets his jaw drop and his body stiffen as though he had been subjected to a galvanic shock. Fortunately, the shore was quite near indeed, and there was a gentle slope underfoot. Iveroth swallowed some water, felt pebbles underfoot, and walked out of the sea on his own power.

"I suppose," he said when he had spat out the salt water, "I shall have to marry you anyway. Your reputation being ruined, you know, and all that."

"I'm afraid you will," Sabira agreed. "I must have someone to lend me countenance in Din Eidyn, you know, at least until I have finished reading all the books at Cromertie's Circulating Library."

Also by Margaret Ball:

Applied Topology series:

A Pocketful of Stars
A quiet math major has to fight in the magical realm for her life and those of her friends after the CIA decides to make use of her paranormal abilities.

An Opening in the Air
When a rival mage attacks, Thalia needs wits as well as magic to save the Center for Applied Topology. And the defense may cost her the man she loves.

An Annoyance of Grackles
It's bad enough when a rival mage tries to destroy you. When he turns out to be a god, that's worse. And when the god teams up with the most notorious contract bomber in America? If Thalia can't outwit the duo, she may wind up scattered across the campus in tiny pieces.

A Tapestry of Fire
Saving her best friend from life as a fish is difficult. Rescuing the man she loves from a past era of fire and fury ought to be impossible, so it may take Thalia a little longer.

A Creature of Smokeless Flame
When CIA officers' children are kidnapped for revenge, Thalia and her colleagues follow the trail across the continents to an African terrorists' camp whose leader has the help of his own personal genie.

A Revolution of Rubies
When the CIA sends Thalia and her colleagues abroad, they should have realized the diplomatic consequences could be explosive. Can Thalia stop the revolutionaries in Central Asia before all of Taklanistan is under water?

Harmony series:

Insurgents

The colony world of Harmony established its own separate colony to which everybody who disagreed with the government was banished. Now they're surprised that the exiles want to run their own country.

Awakening

Being a good citizen was never easy. It got harder when Devra realized that it was incompatible with being a decent human being.

Survivors

The pampered life of a holostar is no preparation for surviving the collapse of a country.

Earlier books:

Disappearing Act
Duchess of Aquitaine
Mathemagics
Lost in Translation
No Earthly Sunne
Changeweaver
Flameweaver
The Shadow Gate

Made in the USA
Coppell, TX
05 July 2021

58575904R00166